The author is now retired after a life time's work and has turned to what she truly enjoys – writing mostly about the unlikely and sometimes impossible. She places great importance on observing everyday people. It is a fascinating hobby and is the basis for her work.

Please Enjoy

Joan B. Pritchard

This book is dedicated to family and friends, all of whom have helped and supported me throughout my life. Through sad, difficult but often happy times, they've always been there for me and this is my way of saying thank you.

Joan B. Pritchard

FACTS, FICTION, LEGENDS AND LIES

AUSTIN MACAULEY PUBLISHERS™

LONDON · CAMBRIDGE · NEW YORK · SHARJAH

A CIP catalogue record for this title is available from the British Library.

ISBN 9781528992657 (Paperback)
ISBN 9781528992664 (ePub e-book)

www.austinmacauley.com

First Published (2021)
Austin Macauley Publishers Ltd
25 Canada Square
Canary Wharf
London
E14 5LQ

Table of Contents

Now You See Them,
Now You Don't

Rachel climbed the stairs one by one. She leaned over the bannister and looked into the hall where the twinkling chandeliers burned brightly. She didn't look upwards, as she knew she was being watched. She knew someone would jump out at her – would it be Great Grandfather or Great Grandmother? It would be one of them for definite. They were both dead and had died many, many years ago. Mother wouldn't believe that the house was haunted, as she'd never seen the ghosts of the great grandparents. Johnny had though, and he was just as scared of them as she was. It wasn't that they were horrid, or anything like that, it was just that they were always so unexpected. Great Grandma was standing at the top of the stairs with an ivory fan in her hand. She was dressed in Edwardian black and wore black jet beads around her neck, a large cameo broach on her right shoulder. She was a very dignified figure but that actually added to the fear Rachel felt. She never smiled – mind you, what was there for her to smile about – she was dead after all. Both the great grandparents had only started appearing in the past few weeks, as though something had happened quite recently to disturb their rest. Great Grandpa always appeared in the downstairs study – it must have been his favourite place when he was alive. He too was dressed in a sombre Edwardian suit, with waistcoat and a large watch on a solid chain hanging from his waistcoat pocket. They were both very much of their time – both with severe expressions and no smiles. The face everyone had in those days to have their photographs taken. Of course, they were actually Victorians – born way before King Edward VII.

Rachel hurried past her great grandma and went into her own bedroom. She plonked herself on the bed and lay down on the blue eiderdown. How was she going to persuade her mother that there really were ghosts in the house? Having asked herself this question many times before, she knew there was no answer. If her mother could see nothing, then why should she believe Rachel? She went across the hall and knocked on Johnny's door.

"Are you there, Johnny? I want to talk to you."

He was exactly the same age as his sister – actually, he was three minutes old – as they were twins, but they didn't resemble each other in the slightest as they weren't identical. Their characters too, were quite different – Johnny was more placid than his sister, whose personality was more vibrant. She tended to lead and Johnny followed.

"What are we going to do? The house has become really uncomfortable with those two popping up when least expected. I've tried to talk to Mummy and Daddy, but to no point. They say it's my imagination – what do they say to you?" She made herself comfortable on Johnny's bed.

"I've only told Mummy so far as I know Dad would think I was mad." Her twin was building a warship with lots of glue and screws. "Look Rachel, I don't want to talk about them just now. Go away and leave me alone." He removed a turret which he'd placed upside down.

Ignoring him completely, Rachel went on, "We'll have to form a plan to try to find out what they want. They say ghosts only appear when they want something, maybe they want to tell us something. The fact that the parents can't see them, must mean that it's you or me who could help. Right Johnny, listen. When we get back from school tomorrow, we'll have to confront them and demand to know what they want. Is that a deal?" She stood up and made for the door.

Loud voices floated upstairs. The parents were arguing again. It was becoming so frequent of late. What would it be this time? Rachel said, "It'll be about the house again, I bet. We might have to sell it apparently as everything is too costly. I don't want that, do you? We've been here such a long time, haven't we?" She looked thoughtful. "Maybe it's that, that's causing them to haunt the house. They don't want us to sell it either. What do you think?" Rachel felt she had sussed out the problem.

Johnny stopped what he was doing. "That could be it, Sis – after all, it was they who built it originally – about 1910, I think – so this family has been here for about 50 years. It would be sad to leave it, wouldn't it? Perhaps, we should go and confront Great Grandma now – you say she's at the top of the stairs?" Johnny was suddenly ready for action.

However, when they went out into the hall, the ghost had gone. "Right Johnny, tomorrow we face the problem. Great Grandpa always appears in the study beside the fireplace. It obviously was his favourite place. Okay?" Johnny nodded and went back to his boat building.

Next day, the parents were out, doing some shopping and wouldn't be back for a while. The twins arrived home together and after milk and biscuits, they sat in the kitchen to make plans. "There's no sign of Great Grandma, but I bet Great Grandpa's in the study. Come on Sis, let's get to it." Johnny was trying to be braver than he actually was. Sitting in the armchair beside the fireplace, the elderly Edwardian gentleman sat, staring at the fireplace. Strewn around the floor, there were some papers that looked like maps. He was obviously getting more agitated as he'd not made a mess before – the children weren't moving fast enough for him and he suddenly raised his right hand and pointed towards the fire.

Johnny asked, "Great Granddad, do you want us to burn these old papers? They're in a bit of a mess. Anyway, we can't burn them in that grate, it's not been lit for years." The boy began to pick up the papers. "Why Rachel, they're old maps of South Africa. He and Great Grandma lived there for a number of years when they were young. That's true, isn't it?"

"Yes, they did and when they came back to this country, that's when they built this house. I'm getting strong vibes that it's all to do with the house." Rachel knelt in front of the old man. "What is it, what do you want?" But all he did was point again at the fireplace.

Their parents could be heard in the hall. Needless to say, they were shouting at each other again. That's all they seemed to do these days. Great Granddad disappeared and left them to explain why they'd thrown all the maps on the floor. Mother just tutted and began to pick them up.

She said, "Is this your doing, Johnny – why must you always make such a mess?" Johnny started to defend himself and tell them that Great Grandad had done it but Rachel put her finger to her lips and shook her head. "Would you and Dad like a cup of tea, Mummy?" she asked innocently.

In the sitting room, they were all sat around the room, when Daddy suddenly said, "You know we're going to have to sell the house and move away from here? It's not something we want to do but we can't afford to do anything else. Things are so expensive these days and I've just been told that my company is to close down in three months and I'll be without an income then. You do understand, don't you?" he appealed to them.

"Of course, we understand, Daddy, but we don't want it. We love this house and it's been in our family for so long now, it seems disloyal to think of leaving it." Rachel was genuinely upset and began to cry. There was a banging sound from the study and Johnny went in to see what had happened. All the South African maps were lying around the room again. He started to pick them up, but Mummy came into the room. "Really Johnny, what are you doing? We can't talk about our problem just now. I think you two should go to bed anyway. It's getting late. Have you got homework to do?" She was obviously upset too.

As the children climbed the stairs to bed, they spotted Great Grandma sitting in her usual chair on the landing. She looked as serious as usual but was moving one of her hands in a waving gesture. They clearly heard the words "Windrush Mine, Windrush Mine" floating in the air. "Do you hear that, Sis?" Johnny was scared. Neither of the ghosts had spoken to them before.

"Of course I hear it, you wally. I'm not deaf." She was just as scared as her brother and wished again that Mother and Father would believe the ghosts did exist. "We'll just have to search tomorrow for something relating to a Windrush Mine. Okay?" They agreed and went to bed to dream of mines, ghosts and old maps.

Next morning, they were having breakfast around the table, when Johnny blurted out.

"Daddy, do you remember your Grandma and Grandad? What were they like? There doesn't seem to be any pictures of them around the house."

"What's brought this on, Johnny? You're suddenly interested in the past, are you? You've never shown an interest before. I'm sure if I hunt around, I'll be able to come up with some photos for you." Daddy buttered some fresh toast. He looked thoughtful for a moment and then said, "I don't know if I'll find any photos of my Grandfather – you see, he died in France while fighting for his country. They never found his body – but his wife, my Grandma, got one of those God-awful telegrams. You know the sort the War Office sent out – 'Killed in action, presumed dead.' And that was that, all the information my grandma ever was to receive.

"She was pregnant at the time and had a girl, who was my mother, Elizabeth. And that's the story in a nutshell. You know that my mother and father were both killed together when their ship went down in the North Sea. I was still quite young then but aunts and uncles helped to bring me up and it wasn't all that bad really. Then there was me, and now, you and Rachel. All of these lives were spent in this house at one time or another – and now, it's been left in my less-than-capable hands. I'm going to lose it for the family."

Johnny could see he'd upset Dad. Talking about the past always seemed to do that to people. "Did your grandma ever marry again? She must have still been very young when your mother arrived?" Johnny was becoming more interested in his forebears. Rachel came into the room at that point and stole a piece of daddy's toast. "What are you two talking about?"

"We're talking about Daddy's mother and his grandma – he doesn't remember much about his great grandparents – too long ago." Johnny explained.

"Well, that's not strictly true, Son. I know a bit about them. I admit I never knew them, it was too long ago. They lived in South Africa for a number of years before coming back and building this house. His name was Thomas and she was called Margaret. I don't know when they died and I don't think I've ever seen any photos of them. In fact, they were actually my great grandparents, although, you obviously think of them as yours – but they're really your great-great-grandparents – wow, that's a mouthful."

"Oh, that's all right, Daddy. We know what they look like." He could have bitten his tongue. He hadn't meant to bring up the subject of the ghosts – well, not just yet anyhow.

"Oh, don't start on the ghosts again. Funny how Mother and I have never seen them, don't you think?"

"I don't think they want you to see them but they come regularly to Rachel and me. Maybe they prefer younger people." Johnny realised he was digging a bigger hole all the time. Daddy looked at him over the rim of his glasses. "Why should that be, pray tell?"

"Well, isn't there some belief that spirits prefer adolescents more than proper grown-ups?" Johnny was getting desperate now and Rachel had to intervene to help him. "Either way, it's us they keep coming to, Daddy. Why did they go to South Africa, do you know anything about that?"

Mother came into the kitchen at that point and heard the end of the conversation. She was carrying a basket of dirty laundry and plunked it on the table. "Ghosts – ghosts. That's all I ever hear about from you two. If you've nothing better to do, go into the study and tidy up those old maps you keep throwing all over the floor."

"It's not us, Mother. It must be one of the ghosts. Come on, Sis, let's pick up the maps." They went into the study and sure enough, there were several papers strewn across the floor. Down on their knees, they began to tidy them up. They heard the doorbell ring and a man's voice in the hall. Suddenly, Mother's voice was different when talking to him. She was all sweetness and light now. She took the Estate Agent into the sitting room and offered him coffee. "No, thank you, ma'am. If I could just see over the house?" He was very business-like. Daddy cleared out of the kitchen and came into the study. "Get them all picked up before Mummy brings the Estate Agent in here." And he knelt down beside them and picked up some of the papers.

He sat back on his heels with a single map in his hand. "Well, I never! This belonged to my great grandpa from when he was living and prospecting in South Africa. I'd forgotten that that's what he did when he was there. He must have made some money there because that's what he must have used to build this house." He put on his glasses and stared at the map. "That's it, I remember now, Windrush Mine is where he staked his claim, but I don't think he got much out of it." He changed the subject and asked the twins, "Where is your great grandpa now? Is he anywhere near us?" Rachel said that he wasn't there just now and he probably wouldn't appear until the stranger had left the house. "He seems to prefer for us to be alone with him, I think." They heard the front door bang as the Agent left. Mother came into the room. "Come on, Bob, I've made a pot of coffee." And she beckoned him the way she always did when she didn't want the children to hear.

As soon as he went, Great Granddad appeared on the chair by the fireplace. This time, he was clearly pointing towards the grate and upwards into the chimney. Johnny said, "I told you before, I'm not going to climb up the chimney – even for you." But the apparition just kept on pointing. "Sis, go out into the garage and bring me the crowbar that's behind the door." Rachel did as she was bid, but she couldn't see why he needed a crowbar.

Johnny poked up and down the chimney wall to the left of the fireplace and then did the same to the right. He reached up as far as he could and suddenly his bar got caught on something. "It's probably just a step in the chimney bricks but I'm going to give it a whack." And so he did! A huge bang resonated around the room and a heavy, dirty object fell crashing onto the hearth. Mummy and Daddy came running into the room.

"Johnny, what are you doing now?" Mother shouted. All four looked at the object lying on the hearth. It was covered in soot and had a large padlock on the side. No one moved forward but continued to stare at it. "It's an iron box," Johnny said, "and the padlock is almost as big as the box itself."

Daddy knew he had to step forward and be the man of the house. Tentatively, he touched the box. He looked at his hands which were covered in soot now and gently touched the padlock which was firmly attached to the box. It was an old iron box and must have been there for years. The old map which he was still holding flew out of his grasp and fell onto the floor. "It's okay," he said, "I just dropped it." But he knew it had been pulled from his hands by some force in the room.

Hours later, with the box cleaned, but still unopened, they agreed to take it to the local Ironmonger the next day and ask that it be opened. The weight was considerable and something moved about inside it. They all sat in the sitting room with the box on the coffee table. Everyone stared at it.

Johnny said, "Perhaps, it's hidden treasure." But Rachel told him not to be ridiculous. "It's probably full of old stones," she said.

"Well, we'll know tomorrow, won't we?" Mother was as usual the practical one. "Let's have some supper, shall we?" And she left the room to fetch the food. Daddy sat on, still thinking.

"Come on, Sis, let's go up to our rooms and chat?" Johnny invited his sister. She agreed but looked at him with surprise, as he never usually wanted to chat with her.

As they climbed the stairs, they saw Great Grandma sitting in her usual place by the big bookcase. She was nodding silently and looking down at the books on the bottom shelf – she raised her hand and pointed downwards. The children knelt down in front of the bookcase and looked along the bottom shelf. They took the big, heavy books out and realised they were very old. "Let's shake the pages, in case there's something hidden in them." And they began to do just that. Half way along the shelf, they pulled out a grey covered book and were surprised to see it was a book about South Africa. They shook open all the pages and an old, yellowish-coloured envelope fell out. It had something inside it and when they looked, it was a small iron key.

"My God, it's the key for the box, I bet." And the two of them grabbed the envelope and ran downstairs, right through Great Grandma, as it happened. The key fitted beautifully into the lock and daddy forced the heavy lid open. He looked inside and found a handwritten note in beautiful italic lettering. All it said was 'Don't be fooled by the colour, everything isn't as it looks'. Under the paper were several whitish, cloudy pebbles – some larger than the others and some quite small.

Rachel couldn't help feeling disappointed and said, "Why would anyone go to all that trouble to hide some old stones? What a disappointment!"

"Well, I think you two should be very interested in the 'pebbles' as, according to you, my great grandparents chose you to tell of their existence, and I think we owe it to them to continue to find out what sort of 'pebbles' they are, don't you?" Daddy seemed more interested than they did. "Look children, no one would go to all that trouble to hide something, if they didn't think it was worth hiding. Tell you what, let's have a family day out tomorrow and go up to London to show a stone specialist what we've found. I'll go myself if you don't want to come."

As he'd known they would, the rest of the family travelled with him on the train. They'd put the pebbles into a lighter container as they were heavy enough themselves without the old iron box. They took a taxi to an area called the Diamond Quarter and made an appointment to see a specialist there. They went for a cup of coffee whilst the jeweller took the pebbles for closer examination. On their return however, they were met with the statement.

"Well sir, your pebbles are not stones but rather diamonds. They're not of the best quality which is why they're so cloudy and opaque, but they are diamonds and would be worth quite a penny to the right person. They could be cut and polished to a much brighter colour and used as very beautiful stones in high value jewellery. Obviously, I'd be willing to help you to dispose of them – for the highest price possible of course – it might take a little time – but could be done, nonetheless."

Bob touched the jeweller on the shoulder and asked if he could have a private word with him. They moved to a corner of the shop and Bob came straight out with it. "Can you give me a ball park figure of what you think they'll be worth – and I mean a ball park figure – I know you couldn't be sure at this stage." The man thought for a while and then came up with a figure that seemed to please Bob quite a lot. The family left the 'pebbles' with the jeweller and went home on the train. Settled on the sooty seats, Johnny asked, "Did the man tell you how much they're worth, Dad?"

"Yes, Dad, I think we have a right to know because we did help find them," Rachel added.

"Let's just say it's enough so that we won't have to sell the house and should be able to clear all our debts." Mummy gasped and said, "Is that really possible, Bob?" He nodded and said, "Yes, Betty, if we get anywhere near the figure he quoted, I believe it's all possible. Let's get fish and chips on the way home, we've got something to celebrate after all." Everyone laughed and Johnny said, "I don't want fish. I'd rather have a black pudding. Can we afford that, Dad?"

"Yes, I think we can Johnny."

Next morning, Betty was tidying the study and mentioned the iron box to her husband. "Bob, can we keep this in the garage, instead of in the house? And this old envelope – do you want me to chuck it out – there's nothing else inside it."

Suddenly, there was a breeze in the room and the curtains fluttered against the window.

The couple looked at each other and Bob said, "What was that?" His wife looked shaken and turned the colour of ash. She said, "I feel there's someone else here with us, someone not of this world. Oh dear, I sound like the children now. What's that in the corner over there by the small settee." Sat there, were two sombre figures, dressed all in black, very elegant and certainly of the Edwardian, if not the Victorian period. They looked just like the descriptions Rachel and Johnny had given. It was Great Grandma and Great Grandad – he stood up and crossed the room – she stayed where she was. He stood beside the table where the envelope was lying and a gentle breeze took it up and carried it to Bob's feet. He bent and picked it up. Great Grandma and Great Grandad disappeared and the study was empty except for Bob and Betty. The couple were both shaking. "The children weren't making it all up, were they?" Betty sat down in the armchair and then, remembered it was the ghost's chair and jumped up again.

Bob reached for the envelope and admired the italic hand-writing. "Gosh, the stamp is dated 1910, that's when Edward VII died. This must have been one of the last stamps in his reign and it's clearly franked by the Post Office. It's been addressed to Great Grandad himself so perhaps he sent it to himself to get it franked – he must have been a pretty shrewd man – I'll just check in my stamp book in case it's a bit valuable."

"Don't be silly Bob. Haven't we had enough good luck recently, without hoping for more?"

"I'd have agreed with you before seeing the ghosts for ourselves – now, I think they're trying to tell us something else. Don't you? And don't you think we should listen?"

Two hours later, he again appeared in the kitchen, where his wife was working. The twins were still at school, and he reached over and actually kissed her on the cheek.

"Whatever's got into you Bob, that's not like you." She was quite dismissive of the smile on his face.

"Well, it's going to be like me in the future, my dear. I've been doing a bit of investigation and have come up with some more information for you to digest. The stamp is Edwardian and in itself, worth a few pounds. There's lots of them around, you see. What's strange about this one however is that it's yellow."

"Stop building it up so much, Bob and tell me what you found out." Even Betty was getting excited.

"There were no yellow, Edwardian postage stamps in this country. It's been coloured wrongly, must have happened in the printing room." The stamp man took a long time examining it and finally came out from the back of his premises.

"Sir, this stamp is probably worth a great deal of money – I'll have to do more investigation and checking but we could be talking about several thousands of pounds. I'm afraid you'll have to trust me and leave it with me – I'll give you a receipt of course – I have two other people to check with and then I'll give you an accurate figure. Is that okay?" The man was flabbergasted and kept licking his lips.

"What did you say? Did you let him keep it?" Betty had never been as trusting as her husband.

"I've got the receipt, my dear," and he patted his pocket. "In a few days, we've gone from rags to riches – and it's all thanks to my great grandparents – and to our dear children, of course. Wait till they hear they can both go to university now. They'll be over the moon." He kissed his wife again and told her to get the Sherry bottle from the cabinet.

By the time the children arrived home from school, their parents were rather merry but they forgave them when they heard what else had happened in the day.

"And all because of the good old Great Grandparents, it's amazing, that's what it is." Johnny was so happy, he almost kissed his sister, but of course, then decided against it.

Rachel just looked at the fireplace in the study and said, "Thank you, you wonderful relatives. I'll never forget you."

The room was suddenly full of those relatives, they were standing side by side and there was actually a hint of a smile on their faces. 'Goodbye,' echoed around the room and the Edwardian couple walked out of the house and down the garden path. At the gate, they stopped and looked around at the house, where the family were standing at the window, their faces pressed against the glass.

"Well, Thomas, that was a job well done. It was quite a struggle to get them to understand but we managed it." Margaret smiled at him and took his arm to steady herself.

"Very true, my dear. It was quite a struggle indeed but look on the bright side – at least, we didn't have to get the message across that they'd have to dig up the cellar to save the house." Thomas agreed with his wife.

"Do you think it's all still down there then?" she asked.

"I most certainly do but let's hope we don't have to get through to them again for a very long time! It was quite exhausting but our last descendants were pretty sharp, weren't they? Good for Rachel and Johnny." They smiled at each other again and Thomas patted her hand.

They both walked down the garden path, arm in arm, back to the 'Other Side' for some peace and contentment.

Where Have All the Children Gone

"Come for coffee," she'd said, "and bring the children."

"Love to," I'd replied, and here I was, thirsty and ready for a good old natter. It troubled me a little though, to see Maggie standing there, resplendent in an old, brown duffle coat and stout, green wellies. Her denim dungarees were very muddy (at least, I hope it was mud) and her sole companion was a vicious looking, bad tempered goat, who was fastened to her wrist by a tatty – and not very strong-looking – piece of string.

The cottage-cum-small-holding silhouetted this odd pair and looked very much in need of a lick of paint. The setting was right though, and my new friend was in, keeping with her surroundings. The once white rendering on the walls was badly cracked, and here and there, black lines criss-crossed, higgledy-piggledy like a road map. It reminded me of my last Christmas cake and how the icing had fallen to pieces when I put the knife in. Needless to say, I'm not a very good baker.

Yes, both Maggie and her home were down-at-heel and scruffy but at that moment, I would have given my right arm to be just like them.

As I gazed around, my admiration knew no bounds. This was how proper, country folk lived and my cosy, semi-detached house and my city accountant husband would somehow have to be changed in the near future. I loved every broken roof tile and crumbling window frame. I made up my mind then and there, to look and learn and maybe one day, I'd be part of this genteel poverty that cried out 'I'm top drawer'.

"Don't mind Tommy," Maggie said, smoothing the rough coat of the animal. "She's just an old darling, completely harmless." Her plummy voice was music to my ears and went so well with her green wellies. The goat's eyes glinted in the crisp, morning sunlight and suddenly my mouth felt quite dry. That goat didn't like me, I could tell.

"Perhaps, I should come back another time," I volunteered. "You're obviously very busy just now." I didn't want to upset this untidy but valuable friend on my first visit, after all she was going to be the model for the 'new me'. I grabbed hold of my daughter's gloved hand and made to leave the over-grown yard, with as much speed and dignity as I could muster.

"Don't be silly darling, the coffee's all ready," and she marched towards a rusty, iron post that looked most impressively rustic. I resolved to get a post just like it for my back garden. It was well known that new estates always lacked character. Maggie glared at me, her expression looked the same as the goat's.

She was quite obviously disappointed that I seemed unable to come to terms with the goat making a third for coffee. Having negotiated the string, and Thomasina (the beast's full name as I was later informed) tied onto the post, she beckoned us to follow her through the deep, oozing mud, which at one time may have been the front garden. Several geese ran across my path and one had a broken beak.

In my haste to oblige I managed to leave behind, stuck firmly in the mud, my two-year old's new, black wellies (Oh, why had I not bought green ones?), Tommy began to eat them and Maggie walked on, unconcernedly. I tucked Sarah under one arm and was glad that I'd thought to bring her red, noddy slippers.

"Do let the girls stay outdoors and play with my Billy and Claire," her plummy voice had a lovely drawl. She rubbed her hands on a wispy, grey cloth and managed to get most of the mud off.

"When they're cold enough, they'll soon come inside. More healthy for them out there anyway – that sort of temperature is enough to kill off any nasty, old bugs that might be floating around." She hung the sodden cloth over the sink. I thought of the two, rather blue children I'd seen earlier, lurking outside the barn. Claire and Billy must be tougher than they looked.

I was dragged inside and the wooden door banged shut, shaking the entire building, I was sure. I watched as the children of my womb disappeared in a hail of muddy splashes, created by six, large, noisy geese with very sharp, pointed beaks. I felt sad as I watched Sarah's noddy slippers turn brown and knew that John would never come around to the idea of a gaggle or two of geese for our own back garden.

"Have a look around the place, do!" Maggie waved her hand in the direction of an adjoining room. I followed her instructions and found myself in a sitting room of sorts – very untidy and cold and with no television. I really knew that John would draw a line at that – mind you, so would I. I didn't like the thought of sitting on that sofa and knew I'd have to keep standing. Then, I noticed something rather strange. On either side of the hearth, sat two individuals, a man and a woman. There was no fire in the grate and they must have been very cold. I smiled and nodded to them but they completely ignored me. I tried the language of niceties. "A very cold day, isn't it?" Still, they ignored me.

I went back into the kitchen and asked Maggie who they were.

"Oh, just ignore them. They're always there, watching my every move. I get sick of them, I really do."

"Yes, but who are they, Maggie?" I persisted rather bravely.

"Oh well, you'll have to know sooner or later, I suppose. That's Jeremiah and Jennifer. They used to live in this cottage many years ago and even when they died, they wouldn't leave it. They were a mad old couple who tempted children from the village to come here and get some tasty treats. The villagers tried to stop the children, but somehow they always managed to come. They kept several of the children and let them live in the barn out there." She pointed out of the window. "Some of the parents didn't care at all as it was one less mouth to feed, when they had so many other children."

Maggie filled an old-fashioned copper kettle from the deep sink. I didn't know what to say next and crossed my fingers in the hope that she wouldn't find me boring – too much of a 'Townie'. I pulled hard at my fashionable Courtelle sweater, trying to hide the obvious Marks & Spencers blouse underneath. I realised that changing my character all at once – to be gentrified like Maggie – would be rather expensive as it would involve my complete wardrobe. Soon though, I'd be as tatty as Maggie and a plummy voice inside my head, reminded me that one had to make sacrifices if one wanted to better oneself.

I spoke again about the odd couple in the sitting room. "Maggie, that's a terrible story. Don't you mind them sitting there, day after day? Doesn't it give you the creeps? I don't think I could put up with it."

"I they?" Maggie was scraping some vegetables as she prepared the coffee.

"But they're not living, are they?" I asked and settled back in my chair to watch her working. I'd met her only the day before and already knew all her theories on the necessity of organic soil and on the horrors of central heating. I knew of her preference for vegetables over all other foods. I agreed wholeheartedly with everything she said. It was, as she explained, a recipe for a long and healthy life – the means of cleansing the mind and purifying the body. Allegedly, a good feed of turnips could also re-vitalise the soul. If this was what the 'in-crowd' in the country believed, then I believed it too. Anyway, Maggie knew somebody, who knew somebody who knew a third cousin, twice removed of the Queen's lady-in-waiting.

I came out of my reverie and looked at my host. Funny, but she looked harsher today, than she had before. I reminded myself that she was a busy woman and couldn't spend all her time trying to make herself look nice. It was odd though, I hadn't noticed before, but she did seem to have the same pointed beak as the geese. Her features shouldn't make any difference to her character, I told myself.

As good as her word however, she had the coffee tray prepared and waiting. I moved over to sit beside the old, battered stove. I was cold. The stove was smoking heavily and the dense, acrid taste in my mouth, reminded me of wet leaves and rotting wood.

"It's the cheapest way to heat the house and cook the food, both at the same time (the house was heated?)," she explained, "but of course, one has to use whatever fuel one can get one's hands on – and sometimes it can be a bit smelly. Never killed anyone though," she concluded in hearty tones.

I smiled to show that I understood and approved and made a mental note to store some wet wood in the cupboard under the sink. John needn't know about it. He'd just get used to the new, healthy smell that emanated from the kitchen. The coffee looked lovely, positively golden and frothy. I helped myself to two spoonsful of sugar, then felt guilty because it left an empty bowl. An inner warning told me not to ask for more (I usually took three) as this would be frowned upon. Sure enough, I was right.

"My, my – that'll never do. You really should use honey if you need a sweetener." She took a big sip of the elixir of life. "I, for example, use neither."

(Which explained why there was no honey around.) She looked very smug and patronising. I took a large gulp of coffee as I didn't know how to answer her. The fiery inferno filled my bulging cheeks and I had to choose between swallowing it or sending it gushing from my nostrils – all over my new friend.

Oh God, take me away now. Make me disappear in a puff of smoke, I prayed. Don't make me have to take another sip of this muck.

"An unusual taste, this coffee, Maggie." I raised my eyebrows questioningly and gritted my teeth. My burnt cheeks were screaming aloud.

"That'll be the goat's milk. I'd just done the necessary to Tommy before you arrived. It's much better for you than all that fatty stuff we get from Daisy-moo-cows." (Oh God, she'd just done the necessary to Tommy – what did that mean? what did that mean?) Truth to tell, I like daisy-moo-cows and the fatty stuff they produce. My head was moving ahead and I wondered how I was going to live a life of self-sufficiency if I couldn't have sugar and fatty stuff in my coffee. Oh God, my delicious, coronary-provoking, full cream milk would have to be cancelled. Would John understand? Could he also switch to de-caffeinated? The devil whispered, "Would he ever know?"

Suddenly, there was a loud commotion outside the kitchen window. Screeching, shrieking and flying puddles of grime preceded the entrance of my Sarah. She adopted the indignant pose so easily used by toddlers and spluttered in her baby words, "Mummy, dat big bird bited Sarah." Dirty, great tears coursed down her fat little cheeks and dripped onto her strangely still-white anorak. I lifted her and cuddled her on my lap and hopefully offered her a sip of my coffee.

"To make it all better," I told myself. Unfortunately, she shook her head.

"The nice old dicky-bird doesn't want you for his dinner." I cooed in my best mummy voice.

Maggie said, "Yes, I'm afraid he might do," and she disappeared outside.

Dropping my sobbing child onto the stone floor, I raced across to the sink. I tipped the offending drink down the plug-hole and turned on the cold tap. The evidence quickly disappeared.

"Mummy not like her drink?" My observant child noticed everything. Her normal, baby-mumbling suddenly seemed concise and clear. She'd summed up the situation with childlike accuracy. I hugged her face to my chest and tried to muffle her voice. If she smothered, I was sure she wouldn't have been the first child to die in such circumstances. At least, I'd got rid of Maggie's disgusting grog. The goose had actually done me a favour in trying to consume my infant.

"Ready for another cup, Ruth?" Maggie asked on coming back into the kitchen. Clutching firmly in her right hand was a very big, white bird, the one who'd had a broken beak earlier. He now had a broken neck as well. "He won't be having another go at anyone else now." She calmly proceeded to make two other cups of poison, dumping the carcass on the kitchen table, where its staring eyes fixed themselves pointedly on my face. I turned in my chair but still felt them boring into the back of my head,

"Why did you kill him, Maggie?" I asked politely. I had to admit I was curious as well as shocked. I knew it wasn't any of my business so I tried to play it cool. I knew the life expectancy of her livestock was her business alone and after all, she was the trendy small-holder, not me.

"Oh, I've been meaning to do it for a long time – today was the day, that's all. He's always had a nasty temper, that one – he's had it coming for a long time."

I felt a great sadness for the loss of life and a great responsibility for my part in it. If the goose hadn't been hungry – and if my daughter hadn't been appetising – then what? If I hadn't wangled an invitation for coffee, hoping to become one of the 'in-crowd', there might have been more geese alive in the world today. God, I felt guilty.

"Maggie, may I use your toilet please?" I felt I had to get out of the room for a little while.

"Straight upstairs, first on your left," she said without turning around.

I went back into the sitting room, and there they were, still sitting by the fireplace. I rushed past them as I wasn't really sure if they were really there at all. I made to go upstairs and almost fell over a little girl sitting on the bottom stair. Above her was another child on the next stair and all the way to the top of the staircase, a different child sat, all looking at me. They were rather sad looking children, all dressed in ragged clothes and some with great sores on their skin.

"Hello," I said. "And where did you all come from?" But no one answered me. "Do you live here with Maggie?" I tried again and one in the middle of the line, actually looked up at me. "We don't live with her, we've always lived here. We all died here, you see and we've nowhere else to go. The old couple downstairs kept us here and wouldn't let us go home." Another child butted in, "They made us work for them but they wouldn't give us any food and I'm afraid we all died. One at a time and at different times, but we couldn't live with no food, could we?"

"Of course, not." I didn't know what to say to the little string of ghost children. It was beyond imagination. I knew I had to get away from here but I didn't know who to tell about it. I'd forgotten about the toilet and I clambered back down stairs and into the kitchen.

"You really must try one of these sugarless buns." Maggie brought me down to earth with a bump. "They're made with bran and wholemeal flour, sea salt, of course and just a smidgeon of vegetable oil. I love them, I'm afraid," and she patted her ironing-board stomach and tried to look guilty. She failed, I'm afraid.

I stared at the brown lumps on the chipped, earthenware plate, which was pushed across the red and grey tablecloth. Avoiding the accusing, wide eyes of the goose, I reached for a wholemeal globule. Unfortunately, so did Sarah. Her small, chubby fists grabbed at the food and rivulets of saliva ran down her chin. Surreptitiously, I wiped them away with my sleeve. The buns were even more disgusting than the coffee and Sarah actually spat her bun all over the tablecloth. I remonstrated with her and cleared up the mess. "It's horrible Mummy, you eat Sarah's." The child was impossible, no guile at all. Maggie was combing out some grey sheep's wool and sipping her coffee at the same time. I took this opportunity to ask about the children sitting on the stairs.

22

"Oh yes, they've been here for absolutely years. I'd forgotten all about them. They're the children I told you about – the ones that Jeremiah and Jennifer stole from the villagers and used as free labour. Unfortunately, they were quite unkind to the children and they died off one by one. Their parents didn't really care about them – they always had so many other mouths to feed – that's how it was in those days, I'm afraid."

"But they look so unhappy. Do you really want them to sit around your home like that? It would break my heart." I couldn't believe what I was hearing.

"Oh, they don't hurt anyone and I just ignore them, half the time, I don't even see them."

I envied her aloof attitude, she really was of the upper-class. She gave me the wool to work on and a big comb to tease it. She got on with baking a cake. The rug on the floor was very sticky and brown and I knew I'd have to get one just like it, if I wanted to be really gentrified. My peacock blue rug in the sitting room would have to go – shame, I really liked it. But it was a Townie's rug, I realised that. I was getting more confused. I wanted to be like Maggie but then I didn't. Seeing her at home had affected my opinion of her. Whilst I was dreaming and making a hash of the sheep's wool, Maggie was getting on with her cake.

One by one, the eggs were cracked into a brown earthenware bowl. The third one fell from the shell with a squelchy thud and turned out to be a lump of unidentifiable tissue. Maggie scooped it out of the bowl, without batting an eyelid. She opened the window and threw it at an old scraggy cat who was sleeping in a corner of the yard beside an old tree trunk, trying to shelter from the icy December wind.

Maggie tutted and said, "Another fertilised egg, stupid old hens, they just leave them around any place."

Yet one more life hit the desk before my eyes. Now I was beginning to understand that my dream of becoming a true, country person was not realistic. It came to me in a blinding flash that I really did prefer my food to come in nice, plastic covered packs, straight from the supermarket. The sort of packs that didn't leave me with a guilty conscience when I scooped out the meat, or whatever it was, to cook. If the food didn't come rabbit or duck shaped, then I just enjoyed it as the good God intended.

Maggie put another nail in her coffin. "Good mouser that cat, of course, we never feed him 'cause if we did, he'd never trouble to keep the vermin at bay." Thoughts of my own fat moggy came unbidden into my head. He was never known to move unless forced to. A bit like John, really. I thought lovingly of my predictable husband, of his slippers, his pipe and his fascination for tinkering under the bonnet of his car, or under anybody's car, for that matter. I thought of Rachel, my oldest who was due at the dentist next week, and she was only six. Not good enough I know, but she did so like Smarties and Maltesers.

"Time to get those potatoes dug up." Maggie reached for 'THE GREEN WELLIES'. "Have to check on the pigs as well – old Bessie's had a bit of trouble with the runt of the litter – it probably won't live anyhow." I had visions of a small pig being thrown out of the window towards the cat. Her voice was practical, no sympathy for either the mum or the runt.

Outside in the crisp, Christmassy air, I looked at her two children, standing in the cold weather. Obediently, they just stood there and my blue, oldest child stood alongside. Maggie loosened the goat's string and it watched me from a lowered head, sizing me up, I was sure. Her children looked as tired and colourless as the run-down cottage. Now the cracked walls and peeling paint looked exactly like what it was – sheer, utter neglect. The ground was muddy and empty of any shrubs or flowers. I reminded myself that Maggie wouldn't waste time on trivial things like blooms. I looked again at the children's faces and thought how a nice, calorie-filled tube of smarties would do them the world of good. Their chores however, came first, and there they stood waiting for their orders, a well-oiled household if ever I'd seen one. I gathered my two and wrapped their woollen scarves around their necks. It didn't matter that I hadn't knitted them myself with wool I'd gathered from the hedges and roadsides.

"Come again one morning." She smiled but the smile didn't quite reach her eyes.

"Thank you, I will." I smiled as well, knowing I'd not be back again. Warm, mittened hands grasped mine and I smiled at my two cherubs. We walked home together. The trees were bare now but the shiny leaves of the holly bushes reflected the Winter sunshine and the world was speckled with the twinkling lights of a frosty day. *Nature is wonderful,* I thought, *but so is central heating,* as a rush of hot air met my face when I turned the key in the lock. The three of us tumbled into the warm, modern 'box'. The fat, lazy, moggy ambled towards us and the girls fell on him crushing him with love. Within seconds of course, he screeched and ran away but Sarah still had a fascination for the long, black tail.

A nice cup of instant coffee, full of cream and three spoonsful of sugar, would go down very well. I turned on the radio in the kitchen. *'I'm Dreaming of a White Christmas'* drifted around the room and I felt wonderful. I knew now that I probably wasn't cut out to be a Maggie. I was a Townie and would never be able to become a self-sacrificing vegetarian and country lady. Mind you, I realised Maggie wasn't only sacrificing herself with her austerity in everything, she was also sacrificing her family and animals.

Two orange squashes, one saucer of milk and a cup of frothy coffee later, we all settled down to watch children's programmes on our 40-inch screen. The girls watched me with greedy, little eyes as I reached for my second, chocolate biscuit. I held out the plate, first to Rachel and then to Sarah. "Me first, Mummy," was Sarah's usual try. "I need another biscuit."

The girls were engrossed in the television when my eyes fell onto a magazine lying on the table. In bold letters, it said:

Let us show you the proper way to eat
the proper food for a balanced diet
the proper, but enjoyable food
Let us show you how to care for your loved ones
to make them lively and healthy

to teach them right from wrong.

Suddenly, everything fell into place. I didn't have to model myself on Maggie or on anyone. Food didn't have to taste horrible to be good for you. I made up my mind, I was going to be good from now on. Avidly, I read the whole article, good quality food was going to be my motto. Central heating was good for you just as was salt and vegetables. After all, a little of what you fancy does you good! I'd bring a healthy outlook into my comfortable home. Maggie was the one who'd got it wrong. I looked at my girls and vowed we'd all be happy and healthy. I made up my mind then and there not to store wet wood in my kitchen cupboard.

The moggy blinked one eye and yawned. He was obviously having a very tiring day. Sharp talons dug deeply into velvet cushions. His ritual dance began. Six circles later, he snuggled down in exactly the same place as he'd first found. Curled in a tight ball, he fell asleep, exhausted, with one eye slightly open. *What the hell,* I thought and reached for my third biscuit. Two pairs of chubby, little hands did the same and suddenly, the plate was empty.

"Rachel, Sarah." Solemnly I nodded my head. "We're all going to begin to eat things that are good for us." Both faces turned from the television to look at me.

"And we start tomorrow." I smiled and made myself more comfortable in my big, squishy armchair.

Next day, I was walking along the village High Street when I met a woman I knew. Sarah was with me and Rachel was at home with her dad. I don't know what drove me to ask her about Maggie and her small-holding at the top of the hill.

"Maggie? Maggie?" She pursed her lips obviously trying to remember someone. "Oh, you mean the woman who used to live in the cottage there. Why are you interested in her? What happened to her must be about five years ago now? In fact, now you mention her, I think it was five years ago just yesterday. They took her children away from her, didn't they? Good thing too, or they wouldn't have lived for much longer. Why are you asking about her?" She looked mystified.

"No, you must be thinking about someone else, I saw her only yesterday. She invited me for coffee." I began to feel uneasy. I reinforced my belief and said, "She was waiting at the bottom of the hill and stopped me walking past. Her name was Maggie and she had two children. Goats, geese and pigs as well – she was real, I tell you."

"No way, my dear. Her story was the talk of the village for some time. She was quite mad, I think. She was a bit of a Druid and only believed in everything natural. I think she worshipped The Green Man for some reason. They used to say the cottage she lived in was haunted – by several people – lots of children, it seemed. She kept the livestock you mention, but never fed them. She was an odd ball alright." She made to move off but I grabbed her arm in desperation.

"I did see her yesterday, I tell you. The house was like a hovel and the geese and pigs were there too. I even met the children." I was beginning to feel panicky.

"Couldn't have dear – they took her children away just over five years ago – and she went completely mad – burnt her house and barn to the ground with herself inside. She's been dead all this time, I'm afraid." She was looking at me quite oddly. I could hear the gossip in the village beginning about the woman in one of the new estate houses.

I could do nothing else but thank her and walk away. Sarah and I walked on to the turn-off at the bottom of the hill. We slowly walked to the top and were amazed by what was there. It was a burnt-out cottage with everything strewn around the yard. The front yard was overgrown and all the windows were smashed. The barn had been burnt as well and lying by the kitchen door was a lot of debris including a broken earthenware bowl, just like the one Maggie had used the day before to hold her cracked eggs.

"Oh Maggie," I whispered, "why was yesterday so special?" Then I remembered it was probably the anniversary of the fire five years before, when she'd died. She had made one last gesture to behave as if nothing was wrong and when she still had her kids. I was her attempt at normality, something she was most definitely not. She was obviously quite mad even when I met her but she did show me a lot. She showed me that being a newcomer to the village and a Townie to boot, wasn't a bad thing and I shouldn't try to model myself on others. Just be myself and value what I had.

Sarah suddenly lisped, "Mummy, where's the house and the lady, Maggie? And where's those old dicky birds dat liked me enough to eat me." She laughed and covered her mouth with a woollen mitten.

Life could be strange, I thought and we went back down the hill, swearing never to come back again. I went home to my accountant husband, fat cat and lovely daughter. They were in the sitting room, working on a puzzle and drinking milk.

"Shall we have a pizza tonight – or would you prefer cabbage and liver – full of iron and very good for you?"

"Pizza" was the combined response.

Take Notice of Your Stalker

It was dark, wet and windy but she could hear the clickety clack of a woman's shoes coming along behind her. There wasn't much street lighting so she quickened her step to see if she could shake off the sound and crossed the street to nearer the park. Looking at the blustery trees, she wondered if this was a good idea and then she heard the same clickety clack on the different surface of the middle of the road. Now, she began to feel she was being stalked and by a woman, although she supposed it could be a man with a strange taste in shoes. She smiled in spite of being just a bit afraid.

She saw a man in the distance, coming towards her and she made up her mind to talk to him and ask if he would see her to her door, which wasn't very far away. Still the woman followed her and when she reached the oncoming man, the shoes stopped too.

"Excuse me, I know this is very cheeky but I wondered if you'd do me a favour and walk with me to my front door, it's only a few minutes away?" she asked.

"Of course, that would be no trouble at all," and he tipped the hat he was wearing and offered her his arm. She took it gratefully and they started on their way. The clickety clack started again and she knew this time, that the woman really was following her. "Can you hear that noise?" she asked the man but he said he could hear nothing. They passed a few parked cars and she caught sight of herself in one of the wing mirrors, and she saw too, the woman walking behind. The woman was identical to herself, even dressed in the red coat and high heeled shoes that she wore. She was closing on them and came to a stop near the garden gate, where the man escorted her up to the door. Before she had the chance to get her key out, the man grabbed her by the shoulders and put both gloved hands around her neck. He squeezed and squeezed and she could see the mad stare of his eyes as she felt the life drain out of her. In her last moments, she realised the stalker's clickety clack heels were to warn her of some impending doom. She wasn't a stalker at all but a guardian angel who had been sent to help.

The man was the one she should have feared and yet, there he was, disappearing out of the garden gate as though he hadn't a care in the world. She lay in a crumpled heap on the path and the rain began to soak through her coat. He'd taken a pretty red scarf from her throat as a reminder of how well he'd done. She wasn't found until the next morning, when the postman called to deliver a letter. The police came and then an ambulance, which took the body away. As they lifted her, her shoes fell off and the younger man picked them up and said, "Looks like she was on a good night out, poor girl."

And it was over. She'd only been to the cinema with a girlfriend from work, nothing exceptional, and had taken the shortcut home because the weather was so bad. He had probably left the cinema at the same time as she had and followed her home, then running ahead and double-backing so he could be walking towards her rather than behind. Why had he wanted to murder her in particular? Did he know her or could she have been just anyone?

After investigation, the police decided it had been a random killing and they had little chance of finding the culprit. The random killings were the worst, there was nothing to go on. Of course, they spoke with all her colleagues at work but even her best friend who'd been with her at the cinema that night could shed no light on why it happened. Another miscellaneous murder went into the statistics, recording 'lack of evidence'. Of course, the case wasn't closed by the police, but there was less attention paid to it.

Two months later, the police were called to a local fairground where a young woman's body had been discovered in the bushes. She was a pretty girl with long blond hair and could only have been about 18. Her black tights had been removed and used to strangle her. The strangulation caused her swollen tongue to loll out of the side of her mouth and the fear she'd experienced could still be seen, reflected in her wide blue eyes. She'd been known as Betty and she'd come to the fair with her friends from college. They'd all had a good time, going on rides and making themselves sick with toffee apples and candy floss – the last ride was the large swinging boats that passed each other high in the air. Two could ride in one swing and Betty and Mary had joined forces. The swings were going full pelt after a few minutes, when Betty noticed the girl in the one opposite to hers.

It was amazing, but she actually saw someone, who could have been her twin, sitting in the boat. She didn't have anyone with her but still swung higher than the others. Betty smiled at her but her twin didn't smile back. It was odd, but she was dressed just like Betty, even the colours were the same. The girl was watching Betty and she shook her head from side to side and mouthed the words, "Don't go off on your own. Stay with your friends. Don't go off on your own through the bushes." Betty could almost hear the words and she knew that the girl meant them for her.

The swinging came to an end and everyone clambered off the ride. They were all giggling and a couple of them realised how late it had become – one of them Betty. She would get told off when she got home, she knew that, so she shouted goodnight to her friends and said she was going to take the shortcut home. She thought she just might get home on time.

As she left the fairground, she turned her steps towards the field just across from the estate where she lived. Pushing her way through some bushes, she remembered what the girl on the swing had been mouthing and she felt a bit panicky. A man was in the bushes already and he said, "Hello, Little Girl. Let me help you over the fence."

"No, it's all right," she said, "I can manage. But thank you anyway." She stumbled and caught her tights on the fence. "Do let me help you. You've torn your tights." The man spoke quietly and seemed so nice that Betty let him help her over the fence.

He placed his hands on her shoulders and pulled her roughly down onto the ground, ripping her tights even more as he did so. She tried to scream but the sound stuck in her throat and the man reached down and pulled her tights off her legs. He wrapped them around her neck and pulled hard, causing her tongue to loll out of her mouth and fall to one side. It took him hardly any time at all to squeeze the breath out of her body, and eyes bulging, she lay on the ground, arms and legs akimbo. He looked at her and thought, *She deserved that! She must have known it was dangerous to come this way on her own.* He turned and without a backward glance, went off but first taking a yellow ribbon from her hair. He liked to take a little reminder of how well he carried out his tasks.

The pictures the police took of Betty as she lay there, were not the nicest she'd ever had taken. They wouldn't be showing them to her parents – best they never saw them. Again investigations were undertaken and all her college friends questioned as to whether they'd seen a man hanging around them at the fair. However, no one had noticed anything and her parents told them that she'd been warned, time and time again, not to cut across the fields, especially at night, but also in the daytime. The forensic team could find nothing either and said the murderer had obviously been wearing gloves.

Now, the police realised they could have a serial killer on their hands and stepped up their enquiries but to no avail. It seemed he'd got off scot-free again. He enjoyed committing the act of murder, there was no doubt about that. He'd only killed once before but that was a long time ago and he'd enjoyed it. The police were completely stumped and he relished their incompetence. He wondered how many times he could do it, and the answer was 'as many as he liked', as long as he was careful and random in choosing his victims. Ah! A teacher's life was a happy one. He could even choose one of his pupils, if he wanted but he knew he had to be careful. Still, it wasn't beyond the realms of possibility.

He taught 6th form maths in a girls' school and the next day, he'd hung a notice on the information board that he was willing to give private tutorials to those who needed them. The pupils all chatted about it and two or three of them volunteered for the extra lessons. They were to be held late afternoons, after normal lessons, and so the extra tutorials began. They'd been going for a couple of weeks when two of the girls stayed even later as they had a particular maths problem with which they were struggling. At the end of the lesson, he left the school with the girls and they all started to walk home together. The two girls were called Mary and Becky and they had been chums for a long time.

At a crossroads, he made a noisy point of parting company with them and went on his way in his own direction. Mary and Becky walked on and then separated as they lived in opposite estates. Mary walked on in the dark. Another five minutes and she'd be home in the warmth and enjoying her Mum's homemade soup. Suddenly, she realised someone was following her, well not exactly following her, but walking a few yards behind her. When she looked, she thought it was Becky who'd forgotten to tell her something, but then realised that, although the girl was dressed in the same school uniform, it wasn't Becky. In fact, the girl looked remarkably like herself but that was silly. Again, when she slowed down or stopped, so did the girl.

It seemed to get darker but that was probably because the street lamps didn't work on this particular stretch of road. Suddenly, a tall figure loomed up in front of her and it was her maths teacher who somehow had beaten her to this spot.

"I forgot to remind you there is an exam tomorrow and I thought you might want to revise tonight." He was putting on his gloves as he spoke.

"That's very kind of you, sir. You've come quite out of your way to tell me. Thank you. I'd better ring Becky and remind her too." He seemed taller in the darkness and they soon turned into the quiet path that led to Mary's home. The girl behind had stopped walking now and she felt quite alone with her teacher. He reached out and touched her hair. "You have lovely hair, Mary – I've always thought that." He was more familiar than he'd been before and he added, "I'll just walk you to the end of this path before I go," and he walked alongside of her. This was it! He'd made his mind up! She would be his next victim! He put his arm around her shoulders and pulled her towards him. She struggled and pushed him away, just as a very bright torch shone through the darkness.

"Mary – ah, there you are. Mother thought you'd be coming home at this time. I've come to meet you, darling." It was her father. Her beloved father. And she ran forward, out of the teacher's reach. "Here I am Daddy, I'm here. Have you been waiting long?"

The teacher said a quick goodnight and disappeared into the increased darkness. Phew! That was a close one. In fact, it was too close for comfort. He'd have to be more careful in his choice of victims. Mary did ring Becky when she got home but the girl emphatically denied that she'd followed Mary home. "And there isn't an exam tomorrow, it's next week." Both Mary and Becky never took another maths tutorial, they felt they already had enough knowledge.

Needless to say, the story spread about the teacher and suddenly no one wanted extra lessons. Mary told her father what had happened and instead of talking to the school, he went straight to the police, who came to the teacher's home to discuss the night in question. He was very plausible and told them young girls at the school were always trying to embarrass the male teachers and he denied touching the girl in an improper way. "I'd genuinely got the exam date wrong and wanted to tell her. It turned out it was the following week. I've got so much to remember sometimes."

His explanation was accepted but now he was within the police's radius – he'd have to be careful. He had no little reminder of this death, for which he was grateful. It hadn't been one of his best attempts.'

The next six weeks went past in a whiz of activities. It was exam time and he was extra busy. He began to feel a bit lethargic and realised he hadn't had the uplift of killing for quite a while and that he must do something about that. He turned his attention to the Night School in the town and decided to take an art class and see how well he could do. The first night was quite enjoyable and was mostly taken up with getting to know his fellow pupils. He noticed one woman in particular, a bit older than the ones he usually chose, but attractive enough with long brown hair and a nice rounded figure. The next week he joined her for coffee at break time. She was called Josie and was very easy to talk to. They chatted for a while and agreed that they'd use each other as models and produce a pencil sketch of each other, which would take a few weeks. He wasn't sure he could wait that long before addressing the problem of low adrenalin, something he needed to address very soon.

Another week later, she invited him to her flat after Night School was over. They could continue with their sketches there and perhaps have a glass of wine or two to keep their spirits up. She lived in a nice flat with some good quality furniture and fittings. "We like to call them apartments, rather than flats. It sounds more posh." She filled his glass for a second time and he could feel the mellowness creep into his body. Josie's sketch was very good – his, not quite so good – but she praised it all the same. She stood up and admired herself in the wall mirror but had to turn around quickly. "I really thought there was someone standing behind me. Do you ever get that feeling, that someone's watching you, like the feeling that someone's walking over your grave?" She sat back down again but kept glancing behind her shoulder. *Creepy, or what?* she thought. There was an ice bucket on the table, full of fresh chunks of ice. She held out her glass towards him. He crossed the room and used the steel ice pick to separate the pieces.

"Would you like some ice?" he asked.

"Yes please," she replied.

And that was her undoing. He came up behind her and leaned over her shoulder, ice pick in hand. He brushed her long hair from her face and bent down to kiss her cheek, but instead of doing that, he pointed the pick directly at her ear and slipped it into the opening. It took all his strength as it obviously hit some bone on its way in, but she only screamed once and her head fell to the side with blood streaming down her face. He looked at her with satisfaction and smiled. *Very smooth, young man,* he thought and pulled the ice pick from her head, not an easy task as it seemed firmly embedded.

He'd done his best to get it over quickly, for her of course, he told himself. His sense of satisfaction was immense and he could physically feel the adrenalin rise in his body. He wrapped the ice pick in a napkin and slipped it into his inside pocket. He left her then, going quietly out the door and down the stairs. He switched off all her lights before he left – that way no one would suspect anything – lights on all day would have been sure to attract attention.

He was out in the crisp night air and the need to pop into his Local for a pint was very strong. A nice cold pint after that was what he most wanted. The end of a perfect day. Then he spotted young Terry who was working behind the bar tonight. She was a pretty girl and he'd always liked her. He waited for her after her shift ended and asked if he could walk her home. "Course you can. Come on." She was completely unsuspecting and not afraid of him in the least. In fact, she'd always rather fancied him but believed she was too young for him.

It began to rain, but it was a gentle rain and they didn't get too wet. She still lived with her parents and told him the address. He said he knew it but knew a quicker way to get there. *Why not?* he thought. *So I do two on one night. It's sort of like two for the price of one.* He rested his arm gently on her shoulders and she smiled. A young woman was coming towards them. She was dressed in denim jeans and a blue sweatshirt, just like the one's Terry was wearing. She thought it strange but when she looked at him, he seemed to see nothing wrong.

"Don't you think that girl looked like me?" she asked.

"Not nearly as pretty as you." He bent and kissed her cheek. It was a dark street but there were houses on each side, so he'd have to be careful. He showed her his shortcut but Terry said she didn't want to go that way. Her dad had told her to keep to the well-lit streets. He pulled her down a path and shoved her in front of him. Terry saw the girl who looked like her was back and standing behind the man.

"You let me go," she shouted. "I thought you were a nice man but I was wrong." She pushed back at him and he stumbled over a rock, but managed to grip her arm and push her onto the ground. He was sweating, something he'd never done before. It was more difficult this time to subdue her and he put his gloved hand over her mouth to stop a scream. She managed to get away from him and started to run back down the path but he caught up with her and tried to put both hands around her neck. All at once, a gut-wrenching pain filled his entire body. He thought he'd been shot at first but knew it was something different.

Terry had a taser and she wasn't afraid to use it. She fired it straight into his stomach and he fell onto the path, gripping his heart as he did so. He felt useless and his body doubled up – could hardly move. The shock to his system was incredible. Meanwhile, the young girl ran away and this time, it was he who was left spread-eagled on the ground.

His luck had run out and the police found him five minutes later with an ice pick sticking out of his pocket. Was this to be his last souvenir, he wondered. They took him away in a black car and were none too gentle with him either. His interrogation took place the moment they arrived at the station. A duty lawyer was found for him and it was clear that, even he had little sympathy for the man caught in Flagrante Delicto. He almost said, *It's a fair cop, gov,* but knew better than to antagonise them. He sat there in front of a big mirror and wondered how many of them were watching him right now. He'd seen it on the television, they'd be crowded in there, to watch such a clever and important man. He felt so proud, he could have burst.

He told them exactly how he'd murdered the first girl, then the second, then the third. He couldn't be shut up and he even told them where they'd find the victims' scarf and ribbon. They'd already taken away the ice pick for analysis so he really was banged to rights. When asked why he had done it, he told them because he could. It was as simple as that. Gullible, stupid women deserved what they got. And one of the younger policemen couldn't resist saying, "And you'll get that too."

At the end of his trial, there was little doubt that he'd be found guilty of murder and the Judge even said that he was sorry he was no longer allowed to wear his black hat as life imprisonment was the most he could award. The formalities had to be done properly and the Jury came back into the court, after only minutes. He was told to stand up for the verdict and he saw quite clearly, himself amongst the members of the jury. The man was dressed in the same suit as he was and he'd even combed his hair in the same way. He wore a blue shirt too and a black tie, just like the teacher.

"Guilty" was the unanimous verdict and he was taken from the dock down the steep stairs into the cell below – but not before the judge had told him he would spend the rest of his life in a high security prison and there'd be no bail or time off for good behaviour. "You deserve no leniency, your crimes were inhuman and abominable. This sentence is too good for you."

The teacher smiled. He was proud at such an acclimation and he almost bowed as he left the dock. *Stupid women,* he thought and as he settled in the cell, the man in a suit like his, crossed in front of the open door, before banging it shut and pushing a heavy bolt across the lock.

For some reason, it caused him to think of his mother, perhaps from a sudden sense of needing her, something he hadn't done for years. She'd been a stupid woman too, always ordering him about and confiscating his comics and books. Oh yea, she'd brought him up on her own but that was because she could get no man to marry her. She really had been a bitch of a woman and he'd hated her. She'd only lived until she was 50 years old – he'd seen to that. He'd made sure she'd fallen off the train platform onto the track – where the rails were electrified. *A quick and satisfying death,* he thought as he pushed her.

Two weeks later, he was in the high security prison. Even the fact that it had to be high security pleased him as he knew it was for special criminals only. Strangely enough, he kept seeing the man in his suit, sometimes in the corridor, in the exercise yard or in the canteen. He was always someplace, he really was a stalker. The inmates didn't like him because they knew he was a random killer and made short work of innocent women. The guards didn't like him for exactly the same reason. He was a loner and proud to be that. The only thing that irritated him was the man in the suit, who seemed to follow him all over the place. When he approached him and asked who he was, the man always managed to disappear. He was an odd-ball right enough.

Truth to tell, a second matter irritated him too. He had planned his next murder when he was caught. As a maths teacher, he could easily gain access to the Science Labs, where he could steal a couple of flasks of Ether. He could knock the next victim out and then take his time to kill her. The police catching him spoiled that. Even at this stage, he was still considering how he could kill some more. If he hadn't been caught, there would have been no stopping him and heavens only knew how many other women would be dead.

He made a point of walking in the exercise yard every day. He felt it did him good but no one ever spoke to him. *Morons,* he thought. It was a crisp, cold day and he'd only been outside for about ten minutes when two men came up to him, one offered him a cigarette, which he took gratefully.

"Follow us for a couple of minutes," one of them said. "There's something on the roof we'd like to show you. We don't show it to everyone, only special people like you." He thought that was quite reasonable and he followed them up some stairs. At the top, on the roof, there were two or three other men, who joined them.

"Tell us," one of them asked. "How did you feel when you killed those women?"

He didn't even hesitate. "I felt marvellous, best feeling in the world when you see the life going out of their eyes." He took a drag on his cigarette.

"Did you know any of them or were they all strangers?" The men were curious.

"Oh, they were all strangers. I didn't know them. Best way really, then you can feel absolutely no remorse." He looked over the edge of the roof and saw the man in the suit standing below, looking up at the roof. He seemed to be mouthing something but the teacher couldn't understand.

"Who is that man? Can you tell me?" He asked, but they said there was no man there and he must be imagining things.

One man fetched a strong-looking rope from a corner and tugged it, to make sure the loop at the end was fixed securely. Another man brought a black bag from beneath his shirt and another man said, "I'm afraid your days are numbered, chum. You're the sort we don't even want in here. What you did to those women was bloody cruel and we're going to make you pay." Another prisoner pulled out a pair of handcuffs and put them on his wrists. He felt helpless. Then they slipped the bag over his head, but not before he had glimpsed the man in the suit still standing down there, smiling up at him. Somehow, he seemed to be fading away, less substantive than before. The man with the rope put the loop around his head and fixed the other end to a big, iron chest that sat on the roof. It looked like a boiler of some sort.

They moved him to the edge of the roof and lifted him bodily into the air, then dropped him. Of course he struggled but it was no use, the iron chest hardly moved. His weight did nothing to dislodge it. He kicked and struggled and thrashed about but no one could see or hear him. The rest of the men in the exercise yard made sure no guards were in the area.

Rough justice perhaps, but no rougher than what he'd dealt out to those women. The men casually walked back down the stairs and out into the yard, where their mates were waiting.

"Was it hard to do?" they asked, handing out cigarettes.

"Not at all hard," one replied, "and it needed doing. They'll find him tomorrow."

His peers had judged him and found him wanting. He really should have taken more notice of the man in the suit but he ignored him, just the way his victims had done just before they too had died.

However, he should have known better than them – he was after all, a very important man!

My Home Is My Castle

The heavy rain battering against the slate roof of the shanty woke Old Peter Bartholomew from a dreamless sleep and he stretched under the warmth of the thick blanket that covered him. *It's going to be one of those days,* he thought and checked to see if the dog was still asleep in the basket at the back of the door. The noise hadn't disturbed him and he kicked out in his dreams, as though running in circles, *Probably chasing some rabbit,* Peter thought.

He didn't really deserve his name as he wasn't all that old. He was about 60 years of age, maybe 65, and had lived in the shanty for the last 30 odd years. He looked older than he was but that was because of the long, shaggy beard and the uncut grey hair that went long past his shoulders. He was of slender build, in fact rather skinny, but he enjoyed his food, most of which he salvaged from the sea and the countryside. Peter got himself dressed and opened the door to fetch the bucket of fresh rain water which he liked to collect when he could. Nice, soft water made all the difference to a cup of tea, he believed. He usually had fried seaweed for breakfast – full of iron, calcium and iodine – he cooked red, green and brown vegetables from the sea, and anything else the sea produced from time to time. He poured some of the water into another bucket and put in some dried seaweed. It would be ready for cooking in about an hour.

He sat at the open door whilst the dog prowled all over the beach. Being rainy, it wasn't cold and he made himself comfortable and lit his pipe for which he also used seaweed, as good as tobacco any day. Life was peaceful and he felt calm – soon he'd go and find some more wood and sticks for the fire. The wind usually made this easy for him.

"Dog, Dog," he shouted into the wind and the dog appeared from behind the wet, shiny rocks. "Come help me find some wood." And the dog did as he was told. Peter followed him, after putting on his oilskin coat and boots. He'd always managed to find around the shore line, the things he needed to survive. His diet may not have been very varied, but it was healthy. He returned to the shanty and closed the door behind him, the dog was with him. He swung an old kettle, full of rain water over a tripod and built up the fire below. The room was soon cosy and the dog looked expectantly at the small cupboard built into the wall. Two things Peter had to go into the village for was meat for the dog and some of the baker's excellent bread, and this he did willingly. In fact, he liked doing it as he could always have a drink in the pub before returning home.

Happily frying the seaweed in a pan, he heard a knock on the door. He stopped what he was doing because no one ever came to his door. He shuffled over and opened the door and saw two men standing there, side by side.

"Good Day, sir – we have some business to put before you. I'm sorry we've come uninvited but you have no telephone nor proper address, so we had no option." Peter just stared at them. They were very well dressed, certainly not in clothes for a wet and windy beach. He stepped back and indicated that they could come inside. It suddenly felt very cramped in the shanty, as rarely was there more than himself and the dog inside.

"What do you want?" Peter sounded more gruff than he'd intended, but he had no idea who they were and what they wanted. The two men sat down on an old chest and shuffled their feet in consternation. One spoke up, "We've come to make you an offer. You are aware, are you not, that this part of the beach actually belongs to Clifford House at the top of the cliff? You may have lived here for some time but actually, you have no right to do so. We have been authorised to offer you a sum of money for you to vacate this shanty and move elsewhere to live."

The old man was dumbfounded and went on making himself a cup of tea. He didn't offer tea to the men as he felt they were not friendly. His suspicions were aroused and he didn't like the reason they'd come. He responded, "I have no intention of leaving my home and moving elsewhere – you can keep your offer of money. I've lived here nearly all of my life and no one has ever objected before." It was a lot for Peter to say as he didn't have many conversations with people.

The two men stood up and one of them said, "Well, if that's your attitude, we'll be back soon with the police and the new owner of the big house. Perhaps, they'll be able to talk sense into you. You know, you should think about it, there's no way out of it. Why not take a couple of days to think about it and we'll come back then – without the owner and police? Is that okay with you?" They didn't wait for a reply but left the shanty, briefcases in hand.

Old Peter slumped on the chair by the fire and held his head in his hands. He really hadn't expected something like this. It was his home and other than the orphanage years, it always had been. Outside, the day had dried up and a hint of sunshine had appeared. He got up and called for dog to follow him. He put on his warm jacket, muffler and gloves and set out along the beach. "It's time for a pint Dog, come on. I'll make the tea when I get back."

Sitting in his usual corner of the village pub, he nursed his drink for as long as he could. Not having much money, he could only have one drink. "What's wrong, Peter, you look bloody miserable," the landlord interrupted his thinking. Because he felt so low, Peter told him. "But you've lived there all your life – I thought you owned that part of the beach." Tom was angry but didn't know what to say to comfort the old man. He shouted across the bar to a young man having a laugh with his friends. They were a group of journalists from the next town.

"Nick, come over. I want to tell you something," and he explained to the young man what had happened to Peter that day. Nick looked down at Peter and asked if he'd like another drink. Two drinks were more than he usually had, but on this occasion, he felt he was justified, and nodded his head. Drinks in hand, Nick came back and sat down at the table. "So, the new owner of Clifford House has turned up at last. I heard he was coming to inspect his inheritance. He doesn't hang about, does he, to have his lawyers visit you already and give you your marching orders? Will you tell me how long you've been there Peter, are you a local man?"

They talked for a good two hours and Peter found that he liked the chap. "I was born around here but was brought up in a local orphanage until I was 16 and then I was given the boot. I had nowhere to go and I built myself a shanty in the shelter of the rocks on the beach. I lived in a cave there for a while until I'd gathered enough to build myself a place to live. At the time, the owner at Clifford House said it was all right and he had no objection."

"Have you ever tried to trace your family's whereabouts? Did the orphanage give you a birth certificate when you left them? If they did, what was your father's name or at least your mother's?" Nick was becoming more and more interested in the old man's situation.

"I asked at the time if they had something like that for me but was told no certificate had ever been given to them. I did try – honest – but in those days, official people were all powerful and I wasn't. I had to leave with no information about my childhood." Peter suddenly realised what a terrible position he was in.

"Hang on a moment. We're at the beginning of all this, there's much to learn yet. Can I ask you to let me do a bit of investigation and then come to you with what I've found? Don't give up Peter – when those lawyers come again, just stick to your guns and say you're staying put." Nick obviously had the bit between his teeth.

He had an ally, someone he'd never met before, but who seemed to care about an old man who lived in a shanty on the beach. He had a warm feeling and it wasn't the drink. He went out into the dark afternoon and made his way down the hill towards the shore. He knew his way in the dark but then, with the number of times he'd done it, he should know. Dog followed at his heels, his friend of many years. He slept well that night and that was because of the drink. The sun was shining next day and he got together his fishing tackle and he and dog made their way to the rocky shore. A nice fish for supper would be great and the fish would be biting today, after all the rain. He wore his long waders and made up his mind to be patient. He soon fell asleep with his back against his usual rock and began to dream of his time in the orphanage. He didn't remember all that much, strangely enough. It was mostly about some of the cruelties he'd had to endure. It had been run by some nuns who were very strict.

Unbeknown to him in the middle of his sleep, his new friend Nick, was walking up the front steps of the very orphanage where Peter had lived. He'd come to see what he could find out but knew that such places could be cagey about who'd lived there. He spoke at first with a young woman, who obviously wasn't yet a 'full-blown' nun and asked her where the office was. She took him along a narrow corridor and showed him the door. "Mother Superior is rather deaf; you'll have to speak up. She is quite old, you know." She smiled and left him standing in the corridor. He knocked and waited to be told to come in.

He went inside and saw the Mother Superior sitting at a large desk. "May I help you? I wasn't expecting anyone." It sounded like a chastisement. He didn't wait to be offered a seat but took it upon himself to make himself comfortable. The old woman said, "I would have offered you a chair but I see you've helped yourself." She had a bite to her, he decided. It wasn't going to be easy.

He told her why he was here and about Peter's shanty going to be taken from him. He thought he could see her taking more notice of him at the mention of the old man's name. She claimed not to remember him and also said she couldn't possibly talk about any of the children who'd lived there. She stood up and said, "If that'll be all, young man, I'll have one of the novices show you the door." But Nick had more back bone than that.

"If you don't help me, I'll go to the Authority who oversees you." He wasn't a journalist for nothing and knew how to deal with a bully, whether or not in uniform.

"I'll have to look at our records, I'm afraid. I'm an old lady and can't be expected to remember every child who passed through our hands."

She walked to the door and said, "Come back in one week and I'll see what I can find out for you."

It was the best he could expect in the circumstances and he left the orphanage. However, he'd started the ball rolling.

The two lawyers, complete with briefcases visited Peter a few days later. They were smart and official and again, Peter still didn't invite them to sit down, but they did anyway.

"When can we expect you to move out of here, and how much money will it take to make you go?" They named a sum, which to Peter seemed rather a lot but then he'd never had much money.

"Why does this new owner want rid of me so much? I don't do no harm to anyone. Why can't he just leave me be?" There was a loud knock on the door and one of the lawyers said, "That'll be the owner, he wants to meet you." A small, balding man came into the shanty and held out his hand to Peter.

"I've come to make sure you know I mean business. How soon can you leave here?" He got straight to the point. "I don't want tramps living on my beach. I own the place and you're trespassing." His words made Peter stand to his full height. He said, "I'm going nowhere and who are you to come in here and order me about?"

"I am Sir Clifford's relative and I have inherited the big house and its land." He looked at the lawyers and told them to come with him. "I'll expect you to come up to the big house – use the back entrance – and give me the date you'll be leaving. If you don't do that, we'll come with a digger next time and we'll pull this hovel down around your head." The three men left and Peter felt like a wet rag. It had taken it out of him. In fact, he sat down and cried. He had nowhere else to go, this was his home and he loved it. Peter felt the salt tears running down his cheeks and tried to pull himself together.

"Shall we go for a pint, Dog?" Dog agreed and they set off together. Peter nursed his drink for hours, the landlord wouldn't make his fortune out of Peter. As the sun went down, Nick came into the pub. "Ready for a drink Peter? I know I am," and he went up to the bar.

"Thank God, you've come Nick. He's been sitting there staring into an empty glass for hours. I swear he's frightened off my customers. I'll go out of business soon." Nick laughed and took the drinks to the table.

"Well, Peter – I've managed to find out a few things – mostly about you. You were delivered to the orphanage when you were just a new born baby. No mother came with you – just a man and his serving maid, apparently. I didn't learn much from the Mother Superior – I suppose you remember her – but she passed me onto another nun, who was much more willing to chat. She remembered you and told me when you left, she was the one who gave you a gold locket that had belonged to your mother. The serving maid had given it to her in secret. Have you still got it?" Nick was enjoying his beer.

"I do, young Nick. I still have it, but I didn't know it had belonged to my mother. I thought it had belonged to the serving maid. Well, don't you learn something every day," and he took a great gulp of his drink.

"I'll show you it, if you like."

"I'd like that very much, Peter. Tell you what, I'll pop down to your shanty tomorrow after work and you can show it to me. Right?"

And that's what they did. Peter had got out the locket from its hiding place and shone it up to show Nick. It seemed even more precious now, it had been his mother's. He actually had something of his mother's. Nick came and Dog was pleased to see him, he always got 'something' from the young chap. "Have you been crying Peter? You've streaks down your face?"

"Well, it belonged to me mother, didn't it? I never knew that. You've already found out something for me that I never knew. I'm an old sentimental fool, that's what I am." He swung the old kettle over the fire and made them both a cup of seaweed tea. Nick wasn't too sure about it but knew he'd have to drink it.

"I have to go back to see the nuns at the orphanage, Peter – there's something I have to ask. If you're up for it, I'll meet you in the pub tonight." And that's what they did. In the intervening time, however, Nick met up with the old nun he'd spoken with before and asked her if she could remember the young serving maid's name – the one who came with the man and who gave her the locket. "Oh no, young man. Her name's long gone but what I can tell you is that she stayed working at the big house all her life and only recently, when the new owner came on the scene, did she leave. She's living in a lovely, little cottage on the Shore Road – the last one in the row. How she could afford that place, I can't imagine – but she did." The old nun was in full flood now and enjoying herself. "I did hear that she was always very well paid by the master of the house, much more than the other servants got. She even ended up as the housekeeper and so earned even more. Makes you think, doesn't it? Is that helpful, young man?" She paused, put her finger to her lips and said, "Don't forget the Charity's records – something would have been written there when an illegitimate child came here."

He couldn't help bending down and kissing her on the cheek, she really was a mine of information. Another route he'd have to pursue. The Mother Superior must have known her deputy would be forthcoming with what she could remember.

He thanked her, looked at his watch and realised he could fit in a visit to the woman in Shore Road, before he was due to meet Peter. He knocked tentatively on her cottage door and after a wait, an old woman opened it only slightly. "Well?" she asked rudely.

He told her who he was and asked if she could spare a few moments to talk with him. "It might help someone you met a very long time ago," he said. She hesitated and then shuffled back a few steps and told him to come in. It was lovely inside, full of ornaments and paintings which had probable hung on more elaborate walls at one time.

He told her about Peter Bartholomew and what the new owner of Clifford House was trying to do to him. "I knew that old man was no good – as soon as he came, he gave me my marching orders although I'd been there since I was a young maid." She pottered about in the kitchen and came back with two china cups and saucers. Only the very best would do, it seemed.

"I've been waiting for someone like you to come and see me for years but no one ever did. No one ever asked any questions about what happened and I was being well paid for my silence, so why should I worry?" It was almost as though she was eager to get it off her chest. "I stayed with my master, but that was many years ago and then Master David took over when his father died. David was a good man and although he married a lovely lass, there never was any children. David himself died about two years ago and they spent all that time looking for an heir but there was none."

"Do you know, Peggy? May I call you Peggy?" he asked. "Well, it's me name right enough," she said tartly. He went on, "I honestly thought I'd have to beg and plead for you to talk to me but you really are forthcoming." The tea was good and he helped himself to a Digestive biscuit. "I really need to ask you some questions of a personal nature. Would that be okay?"

"I'm 76 years of age, Nick – may I call you Nick?" She smiled. "I don't have to hide my blushes any more. What do you want to talk about?"

"Before I ask anything, may I ask please if it would be all right to come back to see you tomorrow and bring someone with me you might like to know?"

"As long as you make it about this time, it'll be all right. This is when I make my afternoon tea." As she showed him the door, she added, "Actually, it's rather nice to have a young, gentlemen caller again. I've had a few in my time but none that would pay me as much money as did the old master."

When he reached the pub that evening, Peter and Dog were waiting for him. "My God, Peter, you've had a shave and a haircut? What made you do that?"

"No one made me do it, young Nick – I just felt like it. I wanted to smarten myself up a bit, so that I can deal with those lawyer men – they made me feel pretty shabby, I can tell you." Peter actually got up and went to the bar, whereupon the landlord looked at him in amazement as he ordered two drinks.

"Now then, Peter, I hope that's not Dog's meat money you're using." And Peter laughed.

They arrived the next day making a lot of noise as they came. A workman banged loudly on Peter's door. "Come on Ol' Yin – time for you to get out. We've been told to pull this shack down around your ears." He had the loud voice and the confidence of the bully. The two workmen started to pull away Peter's bits and pieces from around the door. Things he's found on the beach and used to decorate his house. They threw them into a heap.

Peter opened the door a crack and saw the obnoxious, little man who had introduced himself as the new owner of Clifford House. "Come on old man, let's get your possessions out of the shack so my men can get on with their work." He was smoking a huge cigar and wore a fur coat. He looked like a spiv. He tried to push open the door but Peter stood his ground and shouted, "I'll only get out if you bring the police here and they tell me I have to do it. I'll set my dog on you if you stay here."

Luckily, the arrival of Nick with the newspaper's photographer arrived just in time as 'Mr Bully' himself, threw a large stone through a small window. "Take photos of what's going on," he told his companion, who started snapping pictures of the bully and his workmen. "Either clear off right now or your picture will be in the paper tonight with the heading: 'MEN ATTACK OLD GENTLEMAN AND TEAR DOWN HIS HOUSE.' Then I'll go straight to the police and they'll soon stop you." Nick was furious.

"Look you, I own this land and he has been living here for years. I only want what's mine."

Mr Bully threw his cigar away as Nick shouted back, "He's always had the permission of the owner before."

But the answer was, "Well, he doesn't have it now."

The men left the beach but they left their digger there as a warning that they'd be back.

"Come on, Peter – we've got to visit your old orphanage before this afternoon – and then I'm going to take you to see someone you've met before, but not since you were a baby."

The old man wrapped up well as it was a frosty morning. He put on his muffler and old woollen hat and Dog was dressed in his collar and lead, not something that happened very often. They all piled into the photographer's car and drove off in the direction of the next town.

After much persuasion, they were allowed to see the nun's Mother Superior. She wasn't very willing to speak with them but her deputy appeared in the room as well and she realised if she didn't speak with them, then the other nun would. In the end, she agreed to look through old records until she found the day that Peter Bartholomew was left at the orphanage. There was no birth certificate nor details of any kind. He'd been brought in by a man and a young maid. The maid had left a gold locket with the baby and the man had given a £100 donation to the charity towards the baby's keep. They both denied knowing whose child it was but said that they'd found it on the doorstep of their house that morning. The child was admitted to the orphanage and had lived there until he was 16, when he was put out to fend for himself. All he was given was the gold locket.

Peter had been silent throughout the whole time but stood up then. "Can we leave now, Nick – there's nothing more to learn here." He had tears in his eyes, but now at least he knew the locket really had come from his mother. It made him feel like a real person at last – he had belonged to someone after all. They thanked the nuns and left.

That afternoon, just at tea time, they arrived at Peggy's cottage as they'd been instructed. As they settled in her sitting room, she already had all the delicate tea things ready to serve. "Well now," she said, "is this the baby I helped take to the orphanage so long ago? You've certainly grown a lot." The whole story came to light after all the years. Yes, she'd been the serving maid, whose master had paid her well to accompany him with the baby. He'd told her the gold locket had been inside the shawl and that he'd found the child lying outside his house. She added that she'd never believed him as she knew exactly where the baby had come from and that he was the father. However, she'd never learned anything about the mother.

"He paid me very well to keep quiet, which I always have. The money they lived on in the big house actually belonged to his wife, so the master could never tell her. He could never admit it, as he lived on his wife's money and they already had a son who was his heir. Not really a complicated story but one that got lost through the years." Peggy helped herself to more tea and offered it to the others.

Nick turned to Peter. "You do realise what all this means, don't you?" he asked the old man.

"Not really, but at least, I know now who my father was, but not my mother." He looked at Peggy. "Was my father, the old owner of Clifford House – not the chap who's just died but his father?" Peggy looked sorry for him and said, "You obviously had a half-brother, that's who's just died, but you were never allowed to know him, I'm afraid."

Nick stood up and so did the others. "Let's go home now, Peter. You and I have to talk."

He kissed Peggy on the cheek and strangely enough, so did Peter. The men then went their separate ways but, in the morning, they met at mid-day and Nick hired a car to go to see a lawyer. He'd rung him earlier to make an appointment and that appointment lasted three hours. When they left his office, he told them he was quite sure that Peter could claim to be the legitimate heir to Clifford House and all the money that went with it. He asked for some time to check on records and to take affidavits from the nuns at the orphanage and from Peggy, who could easily prove she'd worked at the big house since she was just 16.

Peter said, "When, and if, everything you think is true, does that mean I'll have to go and live at Clifford House. I don't want to do that. I want to stay in my home on the beach."

"But Peter, you'll be a rich man and you'll be able to live anywhere you like." Nick felt great, with that wonderful feeling that comes from helping someone less fortunate than yourself. Peter had needed help and he'd just come along at the right time. Peter went on, "One thing I would like to do, however, is to be the one who tells Mr Bully that he has to get 'out of my house'."

"You'll be the one to do that – I promise you. Now, one quick drink at the pub, then it's home to bed."

Old Peter Bartholomew slept well that night, it was probably the drink. He did have a vivid dream, however, and saw two men and one woman standing at the bottom of his bed. The older man said, "You're doing the right thing, Peter. I was the one who left you at the orphanage when you were a baby. I am the guilty party." Then the younger man told him, he was his brother whom he'd never met, but best of all, the woman stepped in front of the others. "I'm your mother and we only met once, when you were born. I was never allowed to see you after the first few minutes but I've had love for you in my heart all of my life. I did love your father but he already had a wife." She was rather a hazy figure but old Peter could see she had a beautiful face and a loving smile. It was a good dream, except that when he sat up in bed, it didn't go away. The room was dark but the light of the moon lit up the little group standing there all together. The rush of the sea pounded in his ears but he could hear their words clearly.

"Are you real?" he asked them, clutching the blanket tightly under his chin. "Or are you ghosts?" He started to cry, thinking what a strange way to meet a family.

The older man spoke up, "You must accept the family home and all the money that goes with it. You are the rightful heir, not that pip-squeak who's up there now. Never forget what he was planning to do to you – feel no pity. He certainly had none for you. If I'd had any backbone, I'd have spoken up when you were born or at least introduced you to your brother when my wife died. But there you are – we'd all do things differently with hindsight, wouldn't we?"

They began to fade away, the lady first, then his brother and then his father. The moon continued to shine on the spot where they'd stood. Peter's dream took over again and he fell asleep almost immediately.

It all happened the way Nick had predicted. The lawyer came through with irrefutable proof of ownership, signed by three High Court Judges, and Peter was given the letter for Mr Bully. The workmen were instructed to remove their machinery and to put back the items they'd moved earlier. It all took place so quickly. When he called at Clifford House, he simply told the man, "Get out of my house. You have one week and then I'll be back with the police." The butler had answered the door but had quickly fetched his master. Peter didn't cross the threshold but stared meaningfully at the man. He added, "An inventory will be taken tomorrow and then again when you vacate the house." He was feeling quite strong and in control. That was obviously Nick's influence.

He went back to his dear shanty, the only place he'd ever felt comfortable. It was raining, but he didn't mind. He fetched indoors his bucket of rain water and filled the kettle for a cup of seaweed tea. Life was good and getting better all the time.

Time passed with little immediate change, except that the owner-that-was left Clifford House as instructed. An inventory was taken and several valuable things were missing, but Peter said not to follow that up, as some compensation was only right in the circumstances. New builders moved into the big house and worked there for about a year, at the end of which, Peter and Nick had a look at their work. They were well pleased and after they'd left the house, Peter invited his friend for a drink. Sitting at their usual table, Peter said, "Nick, I want you to have half the money I was left by my brother, don't say anything until I've explained myself. I was a lonely, solitary man until you showed an interest in me and from that moment on, things got better and I have you to thank for that. I now know I did have a family and the reasons I was left in an orphanage. I never wanted a lot of money nor a grand house – you know I love my shanty – but I needed half the money to do what you've seen today. Clifford House is a new orphanage and the children there will be happy and well looked after. I won't be leaving my shanty on the beach but I'm not stupid, I'll keep enough money to live on. The rest I want you to take and if you try to turn me down, I'll chuck the money in the sea. What do you have to say to that?"

Nick smiled and said, "Thank you. I've never heard you make such a long speech before Peter and you've quite taken the wind out of my sales. But again, thank you."

Six months later, Peter was sitting on the beach, leaning against his comfortable rock, – fishing rod in hand and pipe full of dried seaweed in his mouth – a picture of peace and tranquillity, if ever there was one. It was raining hard however, but he enjoyed fishing in that kind of weather. His long wellington boots and stout coat kept the worst of the weather at bay and he always thought the fish bit better at this time of year. He caught two good size fish and turned to tell Dog to help him off the rock – but Dog had gone – and he was all alone now. Dog had just gone to sleep and never woke up again. *Just the way I'd like to go myself,* he thought when he found him. At home, he put a big pot onto the tripod over the fire and filled his belly with freshly caught fish. He fell soundly asleep after that and didn't wake up for hours.

The good weather was coming at last and Peter could hear the children laughing and shouting outside his shanty. It was June, a month he'd always loved and he gathered up his fishing tackle and made his way to his rock. He had to weave through some children, who called out, "Hello Peter, how are you today?" The way they spoke to him, you'd swear he was a child himself, but he liked it and felt he was one of them. He lay back against the rock and felt the warm surface against his skin. The kids were having a great time, jumping in and out of the water and giggling loudly.

He felt all was right with the world and yet he felt so tired, he couldn't even be bothered to cast his line. He just lay there and stared at the sea. Surrounded by the young laughter, he thought he'd seen someone coming along the beach. Then he was sure. There was more than one person, there were three – two men and a woman, but their forms were hazy. They called out to him gently, telling him it was time for him to come with them.

"We've come to collect you, Peter and take you to a place just like your shanty where you'll always feel at home."

He knew who they were and why they'd come. It was his family. He shuffled to his feet, feeling suddenly light and carefree. He moved towards them but turned back once to look at the rock, and saw himself sound asleep. His right arm had fallen to the side and his hand lay open-palmed on the rock, and the sun high in the sky, made something in his hand glitter and shine. It was his mother's locket; he took it everywhere with him. He joined the little group and all four walked through the laughing children but no one noticed them. One boy shouted to the others, "Oh look, Peter's fallen asleep on his rock. Let's go up to the big house and tell Nick. He's visiting today and planned to come to the beach later to see his friend."

So Nick was duly told and came down to the rock where Peter was lying dead. He put his arms around the figure and took the gold locket from his outstretched hand saying, "This will go with you Peter – as it always has." He closed those unseeing eyes and thought again of all the great things the old man had done in such a short time. He promised himself to make sure the old shanty stayed exactly where it had always been, after all his home really had been his castle.

Matilda Had a Little Lamb...

The children were playing on the village green. They called it Cricket but it was really Rounders. Whatever the correct name, they were obviously having a good time as the screams and giggles proved to everyone around. The village green was completely encircled by small, quaint cottages that had been there for many years – as had some of the people who lived in them. Today the sun was shining brightly and one cottage garden in particular was occupied by a frail, elderly lady, who was having tea from delicate china and using a lace-edged handkerchief to touch her lips after each bite of a Victoria Sponge cake she'd baked that very day. She actually made an idyllic picture of old-world charm and serene surroundings. Her name was Matilda Matthews and she was very popular with all the villagers who knew her – and that was almost all the people in the village, which was quite a small place to live. A school, a church, a general grocer with post office, a bakery and a village hall where all sorts of events were held throughout the year. There was also a farm in the centre of the village where you could get fruit, vegetables and flowers – not so many flowers however, as everyone took great pride in their gardens and there were always plenty of flowers around. The farm shop and the grocers were known to be serious rivals.

In the midst of the excitement, a little boy fell over and somehow landed on a stone. He was crying and the other children were comforting him. "Cheer up, Jeffrey, we'll take you over to Miss Matthews and she'll help." At the mention of Miss Matthews, the boy cheered up as she was known for her generosity and scrumptious cakes. He squeezed his knee a little so as to make sure there'd be blood when he reached her gate.

"Oh, dear Jeffrey, what on earth has happened?" Miss Matthews was already on her feet and opening her gate to allow the child to come in. His best friend Peter came with him but the other children stayed back out of the way. "Come with me child, into the kitchen and we'll clean your wound and find the plasters." Tending to limp in an exaggerated way, Jeffrey followed the old woman and so did Peter who was not going to miss out on what might be on offer. Miss Matthews sat the boy on a chair and washed his knee with hot, soapy water, dried it and covered the cut with a plaster. "There you are boys, that's done. Would you like a piece of cake before you leave?"

"Yes please, Miss Matthews," and Jeffrey swallowed almost half the cake in one bite. "Before we go, Miss Matthews, who is that I can hear singing in your sitting room? I've heard her singing before but she never seems to leave your house or talk to anyone."

"Oh, never mind about her, that's just my sister and she never has much to say for herself. Now get along and be more careful in future." She shooed them out the door and tided away the 'healing' bits and pieces. In the sitting room, her sister was still sitting, looking as if she'd not moved for hours. Miss Matthews or Matilda looked very annoyed and said, "Must you always choose to appear when someone new is around – you know it will only make them suspicious." She plumped up the cushions on the sofa and then sat down. The other Miss Matthews smiled and said, "Wait till you see what I picked up at the village shop today. You're going to be so pleased," and she reached for a box from behind her chair and plunked it in front of her sister. Inside was a bottle of perfume, in fact Matilda's favourite.

"Why, thank you dear, it's lovely. I hope you didn't pay for it?" She opened the bottle and squirted some of the perfume on her wrists. "Of course, I didn't pay for it. You know our agreement. When you're busy and being seen by several people, I can do what I like as long as no one sees both of us together and vice versa of course. When I'm in the garden or someplace I can be seen, you can make your own decisions as to where you go. We just have to be careful, that's all."

Actually, they were not sisters – although they dressed alike and looked identical – but one of them was a 'doppelganger' of the other. Amazing really as the original Miss Matthews never did anything to bring it about. One day, she was looking into a mirror combing her hair when someone appeared behind her. She turned around quickly to see who was there – and what she found was an exact duplicate of herself, even down to the hairstyle and the blue dress she was wearing. "Who the devil are you?" she asked. "And where have you come from?" To say she was astounded was to underestimate the situation. "I am your doppelganger, Matilda and I'm exactly as you are. I'm here for as long as you want me – and even if you don't want me – I may just stay around."

From that moment, they worked hard at getting on with each other – and had realised that there being two of them, could be a very lucrative addition to Matilda's life.

"After I came from the shop today, I strolled surreptitiously around the houses on the green. I could see you sitting in the garden having afternoon tea but obviously, I kept well away. The Jenkins are going on a two-week cruise, you know and they leave on Saturday morning. We'll be able to clear the place out and keep all their best things." Matilda 2 was excited at the prospect.

"Now Matilda 2, I've told you before that we mustn't ever be greedy as that's how we'll get caught." Matilda was far more cautious than her doppelganger sister. Although, even she was delighted that they could add some items to their hoard above the garage and the Jenkins were a very comfortable family and would have lots of lovely things.

"Coo-ee Matilda, are you there, dear? It's Jessie. Any chance of a cuppa?" And a very buxom lady appeared at the sitting room door. "Of course Jessie, come on in," and Matilda 2 disappeared as quick as a flash. Jessie was out of puff but managed to plonk herself on the sofa, arms and legs akimbo, before saying, "Have you heard that Mr Brown in the lane has been burgled and all his precious stamp collections have been taken. He's absolutely bereft."

"Oh dear, what are we coming to?" Matilda sympathised with Mr Brown. She liked him – he was a nice man – all she could think of was that it must have been Matilda 2 – 'cause it certainly wasn't herself. She'd have remembered if she'd 'done' his house. The women chatted on for quite some time and Jessie reminded her of the church coffee morning on Saturday and that she'd promised at least two of her Victoria Sponges.

"Yes, I'll get on to that tomorrow. What are you going to make – something for the 'Bring and Buy' sale?" Matilda began tidying up around her friend as she'd been here for almost two hours and it really was time she went home. "When did you say the Jenkins were going away on holiday – oh dear, they won't be here for the Coffee Morning, will they?" Matilda smiled to herself as she realised that would be an excellent time for either Matilda 2 or herself to choose at leisure what they'd most preferred from the house.

Just as she was leaving the house, Jessie turned and asked, "How did you know the Jenkins were going on a holiday? I'm sure I never mentioned it." She wasn't as green as she was cabbage looking and Matilda realised she must be more careful in the future. Matilda 2 had been here for two months now and strangely enough, her arrival coincided with the first burglary in the village. Still, no one else knew that.

The two ladies spent the next day quietly and to pass the afternoon, one of them sat in the garden at the wicker chair and table and the other worked on the inventory they were building up of all the stolen items they'd accumulated on various raids on local houses. "Pretty soon, dear, we'll have to take another trip into the city to sell some of the stuff we have. The spare room is quite full now. We have been busy, haven't we?" Matilda 2 stood at the bedroom window and called down gently into the garden. "I think you've been busier than I have, dear – but I'm not complaining as I know we'll share whatever money we make," her sister responded.

"Who are you talking to Miss Matthews?" A young voice filled the air over the hedge and young Polly Smithers appeared as if from nowhere. "They'll be taking you off to the Loony Bin, if you keep that up."

"I wasn't talking to anyone Polly, just reciting a poem I learned in school. You're a very nosey child, you know – you observe everything around you." Although she sounded gentle, her voice was unmistakably sharp and she was quite annoyed.

"I've come to take your cakes to the Church hall to save you the bother in the morning. And I wasn't being nosey really. You know how much I like you." Polly was a bit miffed. But when Matilda fetched the cakes from the kitchen, they were so lovely and creamy, the girl forgot about what she'd been saying. "See you tomorrow, Miss Matthews," and Matilda was alone again.

By the fireside that night, the two conspirators agreed who would do what the next day. They decided the original Matilda should go to the Coffee Morning, as she'd baked the cakes and could talk about baking. Matilda 2 would visit the

Jenkin's house and see what was there. Funny, but they always agreed with each other as to whom should do what, never a cross word was uttered. Not yet, at least.

Saturday morning dawned a beautiful, sunny day and the villagers flocked to the Church Hall. Poppy had placed Matilda's cakes in the centre of the table – pride of place – and many other cakes were distributed all over the display units and tables. There were scones of all types, fresh cream and pots of home-made jam. Of course, everything had a price but it was always so at country fetes. They sold Matilda's cakes in giant slices on paper plates and people sat around on the grass, munching greedily. The baker was at hand to answer any baking questions that arose and also to enjoy a well-deserved cup of tea. Meanwhile, Matilda 2 was visiting the Jenkin's house on the green. No one was around so she felt free to nose around as much as she liked.

She got inside the house through the conservatory, which was always unlocked, although, she knew exactly where the door key would be, should she need it. Inside, she went first into the study and helped herself to several desk pieces and a couple of silver frames. In the dining room, she emptied the sideboard drawers which were full of silver cutlery and then she went upstairs into the bedroom to rummage through two jewellery boxes there. As she was making her way downstairs, she heard someone in the garden and hid behind the curtain. Flossie Smith was coming up the garden path, making for the conservatory. She lived two doors away from the Jenkins and was obviously detailed to 'keep an eye on the house' whilst the holiday makers were on their cruise.

Flossie came into the house, making quite a noise as she did so. She checked upstairs first and then decided to sit in the kitchen and make herself something to drink. What was that? She heard something coming from the cellar below. She hadn't been going to check the cellar as it's quite dark and dank, but she knew she'd have to now, after hearing a strange noise. Downstairs, she opened the cellar door, using the big key that always hung outside the door. Inside it was a bit dark and she couldn't see very well but she crossed the floor towards the boiler and looked carefully in all the corners. A sudden sound made her turn around quickly, just in time to see and hear the cellar door being slammed shut. She was trapped inside and it seemed to be getting even darker. She shouted as loudly as she could. "Let me out please. You've shut me in here. Please let me out." She pushed at the door and banged on it with her fists and then with an old bat she found leaning against the wall.

Flossie started to cry. She looked at her hands and saw that her nails and knuckles were red and there was even blood there. She went over to the window but it was a very small one, only about a foot wide and long, so she went back to the door and started banging as loud as she could. But Matilda 2 just smiled. She'd gone back upstairs and gathered all the valuable items and cautiously made her way back through the conservatory., using a little trolley she'd brought with her. This time, she made sure she locked the door and put the key back where she'd found it. She knew that no one would ever hear Flossie as the walls of the cottage were about a foot thick and anyway, as she was the delegated house watcher, no one else would come near the place. The next-door neighbours, luckily, were an elderly couple, both very deaf. In fact, it was a perfect prison for Flossie Smith.

Both Matildas met at the house and both had had very productive days. Matilda said her cakes had been a great success and raised much money for the Church and Matilda 2 spread out on the carpet, all the lovely things she'd collected from the Jenkin's. They were so happy; they opened a bottle of Sherry and had several glasses each. Matilda 2 completely forgot to tell 'her sister' about Flossie Smith and that suited her very well.

The following day, they hired a taxi and went into the biggest town to sell some of their bits and pieces. The man in the shop asked them if they were downsizing their home and needed to get rid of stuff. He was an honest man and gave them a fair price and so, after having afternoon tea in the best tea room, they went home – again by taxi – as they felt they owed it to themselves as a treat. They'd opened a new bank account in the town as their post office savings were becoming too large of late and the village post mistress might become suspicious. They'd thought of everything and felt very pleased with themselves. Matilda 2 continued to forget to mention Flossie Smith as she thought Matilda would feel differently about what she'd done.

"Tell you what, why don't we go on a holiday together? We can dress in different clothes and people may not notice how similar we are – in fact, I could get a wig." Matilda was quite excited at the prospect of a holiday, something she'd never done before in her life. "I would love to see The Scilly Isles and we could take a ferry out of Penzance. It wouldn't be too far to get there and I'm sure we'd love it." As was usual, Matilda 2 agreed and they planned to go in a couple of days.

"You wear the red and I'll wear the blue – different shoes of course and one of us with a head scarf and one without one." They set off in a taxi, first going into the town to get some money from the bank. "We don't want to stint on ourselves, do we?" Matilda 2 wore a money belt. "You can never be safe enough, can you?" They boarded the ferry in Penzance and set off to enjoy the adventure. They'd booked a small hotel on the island, only for one night of course. "Mustn't squander money, must we?" They smiled at each other.

The sea journey was very rough and both ladies felt quite sick with the heaving of the waves. The sea was so wild that nothing could be seen out of the ferry's port holes as the boat was so deeply embedded beneath the waves, there was no daylight. Many people were sick and everyone seemed to be wandering around, staggering as they made for the toilets. Of course, there were some people who didn't suffer from sea sickness at all and sat around, looking smug and complacent. Unfortunately, the Misses Matthews fell into the former category and not the smug one. But they eventually landed on the island and almost ran off the boat. Terra Firma had never looked so inviting.

The hotel however, was small and cosy and they felt immediately at home. In the afternoon, and now that their tummies were settled, they ordered cream teas and a large pot of coffee. Life felt good now and tomorrow, they'd explore the island. Matilda 2 touched the sides of her mouth with a lace handkerchief and suddenly felt her conscience prick. Maybe she should tell what she'd had to do with Flossie Smith. Yes, she'd tell now. And she did. Matilda was speechless and choked on her last crumb of scone. "My God, she'll be dead by now – that was almost a week ago." She couldn't believe her ears. What had her doppelganger done?

"You realise she could be dead by now?" she said again. "Unless someone has found her and released her. She didn't see you, did she?" Matilda was getting worried.

"Of course, not," her companion said. "What do you take me for?" Now Matilda 2 was getting fed up with the conversation.

In bed that night, the real Matilda couldn't sleep. She tossed and turned until the early hours of the morning when she eventually fell asleep. However, she soon woke again and searched for a book to read until it was time for breakfast. The one she chose was the story about shipwrecks around the Scilly Isles. It was very interesting to learn that there had been more shipwrecks around the islands than anywhere else in the world. The wet and windy weather conditions were to blame, as were the winter gales and treacherous rocks that were mostly hidden beneath the waves. In 1875, there was a shipwreck. The ship was called The Schiller and 335 German people, men, women and children were lost at sea. It was bound for Hamburg and had recently left New York. Gripped with the tale, she almost missed breakfast but remembered to replace the book to where she'd found it.

As she sat opposite Matilda2, she knew she had to do something about her. She'd been a bad influence since she'd first arrived and encouraged the normally well-behaved Miss Matthews to do things she'd never considered before. Oh yes, she'd have to come up with a plan.

The two elderly women walked around the island that morning and called into the little gift shops that were dotted around. Martha 2 of course, couldn't resist helping herself to a couple of bracelets from a jeweller's shop near the harbour. She was bordering on being a kleptomaniac and just couldn't help taking anything she wanted, and of course, not paying. They boarded the return ferry that afternoon at two o'clock, by which time the weather had again become quite wild. As the ferry set sail, they went down into the lower deck and bought two cups of tea. Nothing seemed to stay still and the crockery on the tables slid across the surface, falling onto the floor with almighty crashes.

"It's going to be a similar journey to the one when we came out." Both ladies were already feeling sick and couldn't even drink their tea. "Let's go up on deck – they always say fresh air is better for you and that if you can see the horizon ahead, you'll soon feel better." Matilda took her friend's arm and guided her up the stairs and through the door onto the deck. They were quite far out at sea by now but they seemed to be the only people, brave or foolish enough, to go outside. Behind the door, there was a shallow cleft in the wall where they sheltered from the ferocious wind and rain. The sea, however, was a different story with enormous waves crashing against the ferry and there was no escaping from their whipping spray that felt sharp against their faces.

Martha spoke up at last but she had to space her words between the gusts of wind. "We're fast approaching the spot where a ship called the Schiller sank in the 19th century with a loss of 335 people. It was a large ship but there was thick fog around that day and several freak waves crashed against it." She was gasping between gulps of air but Matilda 2 was engrossed in the story and wanted to hear more. "Two lifeboats, which were full of people, were crushed, when two of the ship's funnels fell on them. The roof of the ship was blown off and a great number of passengers were washed out to sea." She was gasping for air and the rain was blinding her. "Do you know, the Scilly Isles were never bombed by the Germans in the Second World War because of Hitler's gratitude to the local people for their kindness to the 27 survivors who managed to get ashore after the shipwreck. Truly amazing, isn't it – what goes around, comes around."

"That's an amazing story – how dreadful for everyone on that ship." Matilda 2 was amazed. "And it's about here it happened, is that right?"

"It is – let's move over to the rail and see if we can see anything below the waves – maybe a shadow of the ship or something." The two women staggered across the deck and grabbed onto the rail. "See just there," and Matilda pointed into the black and grey swirling sea. Matilda 2 leaned further over the rail and stared hard at the waves. "Yes," she shouted above the wind, "I can see something down there and it looks like the hull of a ship."

Matilda stood behind her and bent down to grab her ankles. She hoisted her doppelganger into the air and pushed her violently forward over the rail. For about a minute, she watched Matilda 2 thrash about in the water, disappearing two or three times below the surface. Then she was gone. No sign of her any more. Matilda stepped back into the cleft in the wall and smiled. She'd got rid of her at last. There was no coming back from that hell. Inwardly, she cheered and went back down the stairs into the salon. The journey continued as before, wild and frightening, but she felt calm inside now that she was alone.

That night, Matilda returned to her cottage about eight o' clock. She had passed the Jenkin's house and saw that all the lights were out, so either Flossie was lying dead in the cellar or she'd been found already and taken away. It was lovely to be at home on her own with no doppelganger to spoil her solitude – but she was very aware of all the 'things' there were in the spare bedroom – things that had come from all over the village and would have to be dealt with before anyone found out. Most of the things had been stolen by Matilda 2 but she herself had helped, she'd made it possible for it to be done. She went to bed after a hot chocolate and slept better than she'd slept for many a night.

Next morning, she started to weed her garden border. It had been neglected for some time and was in a bit of a mess. She deliberately didn't go near the Jenkin's place in case she looked suspicious but, in the end, it didn't matter as Jessie arrived and invited herself in for coffee. How did that woman know she was back... she knew what was going on before it actually happened? "Of course, I can make us some coffee, come on in." She desperately wanted to ask about Flossie and where she was, but knew that wouldn't be wise.

Sitting in the garden at the wicker table, Jessie suddenly said, "Well, what do you think about Flossie then?"

Matilda looked confused and said, "What about Flossie?"

"She was found in the cellar room in the Jenkin's house where she'd gone to check that everything was all right. Apparently, she'd been down there, locked in, for about a week and she'd only survived by eating some vegetables stored there and drinking water from a butt. She's still in hospital and I don't know how well she is." Jessie was enjoying the telling as she always did – she was a born raconteur. "Now you're back, perhaps we could go and visit her – if we're allowed in, that is. What do you think?"

"Yes, I think we should." But just as they were arranging when and where to meet, a black car drew up at the front garden gate. "I wonder who that can be. I don't recognise the man at the wheel." Matilda stood up and went indoors to open the cottage door. Two men stood there and behind them was one uniformed police constable – they all looked a bit ill at ease.

"Are you Miss Matilda Matthews?" The older man came straight to the point. On hearing that she was, he asked if they could come in and speak with her.

"Of course, but I have a visitor in my back garden. I'll just have to ask her to leave, but do sit here until I attend to that. By the way, would you care for some coffee or tea." Matilda always remembered her manners, but she was beginning to understand that all the men were from the police.

Out in the garden, she told Jessie she'd have to go as the men wanted to speak with her. "But I can stay with you Matilda – you might be glad of the company." Matilda protested but Jessie insisted and the larger lady had to be evicted out of the back gate. She kept looking over Matilda's shoulder, trying to see where the men were.

In the kitchen, she made some coffee and put some biscuits on a plate. Good china of course, but not the best. She carried the tray back into the sitting room and put the tray on the coffee table. "Now then gentlemen, how can I help you? I've actually been away for a few days, so I don't really know what's been going on but if I can help, then I will."

"I'm afraid, madam, that we're here to ask you some questions. You may have heard from your friend that Mrs Flossie Smith has died in hospital after having been locked in a cellar for a week. When she was found, she was still alive but very weak and yesterday, I'm afraid she died. May I ask for your reaction to that?" He put his cup down and stood up which made him appear more dominating.

"Why should I have an opinion about that? Obviously, I'm very sorry for poor Flossie but as I said, I've been away from home for a few days." Matilda tried to hide her discomfort but she knew something was very wrong.

"What happened to Mrs Smith actually happened about a week ago and she was able to talk to us for a little while before she died. She claimed you were the one who locked her in the cellar – and although she shouted to you and banged the door – you deliberately ignored her. In effect, Miss Matthews, she claims that you're the reason for her death. As such, I'm afraid I will have to ask you to accompany me to the Town Station and we can talk more there." The other man stood up too and asked her where he could find her coat. Although he brought the wrong coat, she thought it best to say nothing and she fetched her handbag and gloves. As she got into the police car, she noticed several curtains fluttering, presumably to get a better view. *Let them look*, she thought, *I've done nothing wrong*.

Following in-depth questioning, the inspector spoke the dreaded words, "Mrs Matilda Matthews, I am arresting you for the murder of Flossic Smith."

"I didn't murder Flossie Smith, really I didn't. On that day, I was nowhere near the Jenkin's place. I was serving Victoria Sponges at the church coffee morning – why, you can ask Poppy Smithers, if you like – she'll tell you where I was all that afternoon." Now, she realised that her doppelganger hadn't been as careful that day as she'd claimed. "Ask Poppy please, she's a good and truthful girl."

"We have already whilst we were waiting for you to come back from the Scilly Isles – she confirms you were there that day – but she wasn't watching you all the time – and she said you could have slipped away for half an hour or so – and she wouldn't have missed you. Sorry, but Flossie's death bed statement carries a lot of worth and must be accepted as the truth." He felt sorry for the old lady but that wouldn't stop him from doing his duty. Soon, Matilda found herself in a cold and rather uncomfortable cell. A stranger visited her and said he was her lawyer. Several weeks passed and she was on trial in the court. She repeated and repeated that she hadn't done it, but to no avail. The judge sentenced her to ten years in prison and as she was already of a certain age, he hoped she would live to see her sentence through.

There was nothing more to be done. Her languid days working in her garden and stopping for the occasional cup of tea were over. She would spend the rest of her days locked behind iron bars, she didn't doubt that, and all because of her doppelganger. She'd never mentioned Martha 2 throughout the proceedings as she knew no one would believe her. Hating Martha 2, however, was like hating herself. She'd done the right thing to her – the bottom of the sea was too good for her.

She made out her will – something she hadn't done before – and left her cottage and possessions to Jessie and Poppy as they were her only friends, although everyone in the village liked her, they would want nothing to do with a murderer. Nice surprise for Jessie and Poppy as the cottage was very fine – it had been the arrival of her doppelganger that had spoiled everything. She had a small cell to herself, but it was so basic, she hated it. She asked for some of her books from home and this was done. She was even allowed a mirror on the wall, something not everyone was given, so she wasn't badly treated. She was allowed once a day to walk around the prison yard and this she always took advantage of, until the day she thought she saw someone she knew out there. She was sure it was Flossie Smith standing in the corner of the yard. She hurried over to her but when she got there, the woman had gone. *Well, I never...* she thought. *Must have been someone who looked like her.*

But that night in her cell, and after lights out, she felt someone's presence in the room and when she turned over in bed, there sat Flossie Smith on a small tool. "You murdered me, Matilda Matthews – you know, you did and I've come to haunt you until you give up the ghost." Flossie didn't get up – she just sat there and stared. Matilda pulled the blanket over her eyes and shouted, "Go away, Flossie Smith, you're not real."

"I'm real to you though and that's all that matters." Flossie was smirking.

From that day on, Flossie went everywhere Matilda went. And I mean everywhere. Matilda asked to change her cell but that did no good. She spoke with the prison chaplain who explained it was just her conscience creating the ghost in her mind. "You killed her, Matilda and your mind won't let you forget," he explained.

But she knew different, it wasn't conscience, 'cause she hadn't done it. It was Matilda 2 who was guilty. Then Matilda 2 appeared in her cell – she had both Flossie and her doppelganger in the cell – it was getting crowded.

"That's who did it, Flossie, she was the one. Not me," she pleaded with Flossie, who just replied, "She's just a part of you – in fact, she is you." And that was that. No one would believe her. She really couldn't take much more of his. Not two of them. That night after lights out, she tore her bed sheets into thin strips and tied them together. She hooked the rope around the ceiling light – which was just possible – and brought the little stool into the middle of the floor. She climbed on top and tied the rope around her neck and kicked the stool away.

She hung there until morning. It had not been an easy death, it was slow and painful but it gave Flossie Smith a lot of pleasure. They took her gently down and she was buried in the prison cemetery, she wasn't allowed hallowed ground as she was a murderer and also had taken her own life. She couldn't go to Heaven, could she?

However, she did go back to her cottage. She would live there with Poppy, who'd decided to live there as her home. She wouldn't be a nuisance, however, and Poppy would never know she was there. Or would she?

After all, everywhere she went, Flossie and Matilda 2 were sure to follow. In the end, the cottage could become quite crowded.

Twinkle Twinkle Little Star

He is a star! A real star! He's made of gas and dust. His name is Paddy and he is about 4000 years old. He lives as a star and is just one of the billions of stars that exist in the Milky Way. He is officially known as a white dwarf star, which means that he's not one of the very large stars but is of medium size – he does, however, shine and glitter with a very strong light. His home is made of dust and gas, as he is, and he loves it there.

If you've ever wondered where people's souls go when the physical body finally fades, then this is the answer – every star in the sky represents souls and depending on the sort of lives they'd led whilst on their planet – earth in Paddy's case, they could become a white dwarf star or a red dwarf star. The odd thing is that the white ones are of medium heat and the red ones of more intense heat, but although called red, they actually shine with a blue light. Confusing? It gets worse. I hope you'll agree that a soul can't just be allowed to peter out into nothingness – all that love, emotion and wisdom has to go on benefitting the universe.

Paddy has many companions, bigger and smaller males and females, who are of very differing ages. The stars in the earth's solar system all originated from a nebula, which is a cloud in space and is made of gas and dust. Actually, he's positioned not too far from the sun, which is a yellow star so he's able to keep a close eye on all of earth's doings. Venus is his closest planet and all instructions about his duties come from there. Other stars get their instructions from various ruling planets like Mercury, Jupiter, Mars etc, who look after stars who have come from places where life forms exist.

Paddy is a Samaritan star who is frequently sent to earth on special errands. He came from there originally and understands the people. In addition to Samaritans, there are many other stars who are responsible for everything and anything.

The hierarchy works quite well as even in Heaven, there has to be overseers and those who need to be kept in line – and this is how the star system works – the bigger stars deal with the dwarf stars and the planets and solar systems control them in their turn. The black holes have two roles, one is to oversee the major planets and one is to collect the burnt-out stars who haven't fulfilled their duties, either on their home planet or when serving as a star. Black Holes are important and are in charge of the constellations of all stars.

There are trillions of stars in the sky, all with their own specific role to ensure that the system works as well as it can. Not really a big surprise and very well planned by the 'Main Man' at the time of the Big Bang.

But let's pay more attention to Paddy. He hasn't been very busy for some time now and has just returned from visiting a neighbouring star whom he knows as Ernie. He and Ernie almost collided one time when he took his eye off the ball. After numerous apologies however, they formed a good friendship. Ernie isn't a Samaritan like Paddy but he's a 'Fixer' who is often sent to earth to settle matters where there is little flexibility between people and where a calming influence is needed.

One day, Paddy was resting and listening to gentle, heavenly music which is all around the Heavens. Suddenly, his communicator buzzed him and he received new instructions from the station on Venus. He was to head for a small village in Spain, where several children had fallen down a hidden mine shaft and couldn't get out. Paddy was off! He headed straight for the brush land where the children had been playing. He could hear them calling for help and he hovered over the mine entrance. The children saw the bright light above and fell silent, knowing help might be coming. He slowly moved in to the shaft and lit up the whole area. The children were dirty and a couple were bleeding but they were all right. They'd been there a long time and covered their eyes as he was so bright but Paddy dimmed his glare to a comfortable level. "Don't worry children, we'll soon have you out of here. Be calm and hold your hands over your eyes. I'm going to shine my brightest light up the mine tunnel so it can be seen clearly outside and attract someone's attention."

He did as he promised and told them to shout every now and again as that would help his light. They did as they were told and as time passed, Paddy asked them what songs they knew. He started them off singing and told them a couple of Christmas cracker jokes he remembered from his days on earth. They could hear a helicopter hovering overhead and a man shouting that he could see them. "Keep still children," he shouted. "We'll get to you as soon as we can." And the helicopter went away.

Paddy kept shining his brightest light as best he could and the children started to sing again. They felt safer now and one little boy asked, "What are you? Where have you come from? You're very bright, aren't you – in fact, I can't quite make you out?" Paddy sang 'Twinkle Twinkle Little Star' but said no more. In the fall, the children had bruised and cut themselves and the smallest one began to cry for his mother. Then it happened – a voice outside shouted, "Stand back against the sides – we're going to send down a basket for you. Get into the basket one by one and hold on tight – we're going to pull you up."

They did as they were told until there was only one boy and Paddy left in the shaft. He seemed to be the leader of the group and he stared in Paddy's direction and said, "Thank you for helping us – when I get to the top, I'll tell them to send the basket down for you."

"No need young man – I can get myself out without that," Paddy explained. The boy continued, "Do you mean you could have got out of here any time you wanted, but you chose to stay with us?"

"Yes," said Paddy, "I came to help you and I wouldn't have gone until I knew you were safe."

"Thank you, sir, you're a very kind man." And the boy climbed into the basket and was gone, leaving Paddy alone. He could hear the helicopter blades change their tone and he knew it was flying away. The children were safe and the Samaritan had done his job. He came out of the shaft and disappeared up into the sky. Remember, next time you see a shooting star, it's probably just a white or red Dwarf doing their job. But still make a wish, take the chance, it'll probably work.

Paddy was back in his comfort zone in the sky. Ernie had been watching for him and he shot over to find out how he'd got on. They were enjoying a snifter, a sort of honey drink, which every star drank. Apparently, it helped lubricate their parts, at least that's what they chose to believe. The buzzer from Venus rang loudly and both stars jumped to attention. Venus told them they had another venture to go on and that it would probably take both of them this time, as it was a bigger challenge than usual.

"Where are we going? Is it on earth again?" Paddy asked. It was earth he was told but this time it was on a small isolated island in the Pacific Ocean, where the local people needed help. It was also in a completely different era than before, it was to go back to 1015 AD and to dress accordingly. Paddy wondered what suitable dress was in the first millennium – but he'd find out when he got there. He and Ernie travelled together and soon arrived on the island, where there was a public meeting being held and many voices raised in frustration.

"But we've tried so many ways and come up with nothing I'm afraid we've started something we can't finish." A tall, broad shouldered man was standing in the middle of a circle. "It is a great enterprise and worth doing for the protection of our people – there should be a way." But it seemed there wasn't.

Following a long-ago volcanic eruption, a few of the village men had discovered how tough and stable the volcanic ash left after the eruption really was and they'd started to build with it. They planned to build many big figures which they would call Moai – these figures would protect the island and the islanders themselves. The people were called Rapa Nui and they'd lived in this paradise for many years – they were mostly farmers and fishermen and the island itself was located between Chile and Polynesia. Paddy and Ernie listened to the conversation and soon learned of the great problem – it was how to move the statues once they were completed. There were already two or three of them lying on the ground. They were statues of men with very large heads and were on average 20 feet tall and weighed about 20 tons. Moving them from the volcano to the shore line around the island was proving impossible. They were intended to stand guard with their backs to the open sea and ward off evil spirits. Sounded like a simple, straightforward plan but the weight of the Moai made moving them impossible.

Paddy and Ernie rubbed their chins and nodded their heads. As it was so long ago on earth and the island so isolated from the rest of the world, there was no equipment that could help. Trees used as rollers was an option but for some reason, there weren't many trees on the island, so the weight involved was still a major factor. The two stars thought long and hard and Paddy suddenly jumped up and brought back a broken piece of ash. He gathered some pieces of grass and weed from the ground and used his brightness to allow him to see what he was doing. He twisted the grass and weed into strands like a long, thin piece of string and tied it around the middle and top part of the ash lump – with several strands left dangling on either side. He laid the ash on the ground and gently pulled at the string on his side, giving Ernie the other to hold. By a miracle, the volcanic ash stood on end and the stars moved it in a walking gait, which moved it along the ground.

"That's how they're going to do it Ernie," he said. "They'll have to find the means of making long – and very strong – ropes out of tree branches and twigs and tying them in the same way as we've done. It's worth a try, isn't it? And that's why we've been sent here – to try and help them. Let's leave it till tomorrow after they've all had a good night's sleep and then we'll speak with them." Ernie agreed and both stars fell into a dreamless sleep.

The natives were sat around a blazing fire next morning – eating from bowls of what looked like porridge. Ernie and Paddy approached them, looking remarkably similar to them in build and dress. They sat down by the fire and were offered bowls of their own, which they accepted, although food was not something they needed. They tentatively approached the problem about moving the huge figures. The men listened but some laughed and said it would never work. At the stars' insistence however, they left the fire and began to gather the twigs and branches to make a rope, a good, stout rope. The search took many hours but they knew how important it was to the plan. 20 tons of volcanic ash was a lot to lift and move but they'd failed at everything else, so it was worth a go.

A native shouted that the Moai weighed too much and would probably break the ropes, but the others wanted to have a go. It had taken a long time to get this far, so it was worth a try in the morning. The two stars covered the area with soft, gentle light that seemed to make the natives drowsy and most of them fell asleep as though drugged.

"What do you think will happen, Paddy?" Ernie asked. "I hope, if we fail, they won't decide to kill us."

"We'll just have to move fast if that happens, Ernie – we can move pretty fast when we want to. Anyhow how would they kill us – in their time, we've not been born yet?" Both stars dozed off – it had been a busy day – but a positive one.

In the end, it took three days to forage around the area and collect what was needed to make the ropes, and then it took another three days to twist and make them as strong as possible. The women of the tribe helped with this and did a good job. All the men who were fit took part too, although none of them were really sure about what they were doing. However, they did it with gusto.

Paddy and Ernie helped them arrange the ropes around the torso of one of the Moai lying on the ground and up around the shoulders and head. Many of the men went to the one side and pulled carefully, the Moai moved slightly and the men cheered as it was more than they'd managed before. Using the ropes and covering their hands with animal skins, they worked with the ropes and the Moai was raised slowly, bit by bit, until the massive man stood proud and erect. Many of the men were scared in case he toppled onto them but he didn't, his feet were broad and solid and took his weight.

Paddy now had to explain the 'walking movement' that should work in theory. Again, there were disbelieving faces, but they were still keen to try. The huge Moai moved tentatively forward on one side and then on the other. He moved in a walking gait and as long as the men with the ropes were slow and careful, everything went according to plan.

The Moai was walking small steps and rolling from side to side. He was brought to the ocean, where a couple of men had dug a big pit for him. The ropes were used again, carefully, to move him over the pit and ease him down into the hole. Very quickly, the men filled in the hole and packed as many boulders as they could around him. He stood there strong and powerful with his back to the ocean – a protector of a people who never knew there was a world beyond the horizon, but who felt safer because of his presence. The people of Rapa Nui thought the world ended at the horizon and never knew anything different until the earth's 18th century, when a Dutch man visited the island and named it Easter Island as Easter Sunday was the day he first stepped onto the sand. After three or four centuries of the new millennium, there were about 800 Moai standing along the shore line protecting the people. I'm sure you've heard of Easter Island – now you know its story.

Paddy and Ernie had done their duty, in fact, more than their duty. But their job was done and it was time to leave Easter Island and go back to their other duties as stars. They didn't say goodbye but left the way they'd come, quietly and unobtrusively. The silent heroes.

"Oh, not again," Paddy said into his buzzer – it was another message from Venus, "I've already taught many children to ride their bikes. It's not easy, you know." He was of course heading for a reprimand, so he backed off a little. "Who is it this time? He lives in Russia, you say? Well, of course I'll do it, if you tell me to. Is there anything I should know about before I go? He's done what? Run away from home and lost himself in the forest – there's still bears in that country, you know. I see, you do know – and that's why you've contacted me?"

He was soon in a wild part of the country called Russia, it was pretty remote. He used his bright light to look all around. Lots of trees hidden in a forest. Is that where the child has gone, he asked himself? He could see the individual trees now and pushed his way into their midst. There, at the foot of a tree crouched a little boy. He was crying and very miserable – he saw the brightness coming through the trees and he scrunched his little legs even tighter, his knees under his chin.

"Hello Little Chap," Paddy said in a soft voice. "I've come to help you get home."

"But I don't want to go home – all my friends there laugh at me and call me names. They can all ride bikes, you see and I just can't. I wobble all over the place and they watch me and giggle." He was crying even harder. "My brother even joins them – he's in their gang, but I'm not."

"Well, we'll just have to do something about that, won't we? You know what I am, don't you? I'm a magic star come down from the Heavens to help you. Now, come along and we'll find a flat piece of ground so you can learn to ride your bike. Where is it, by the way?"

The boy pointed to a shiny red bike lying on its side. "I hate it," he went on, but he still stood up and went over to Paddy.

"Now, you're going to get on your bike and follow my light – you'll keep your eyes on me and do exactly what I tell you." He used his bright light and completely mesmerised the child. "Keep up with me – keep pedalling." He used his light in a flashing sequence and as he knew it would, the light helped the child, who was laughing now.

"Can you find your way home now – and show your brother and friends how well you ride?" The boy nodded his head but couldn't stop cycling. He was so excited.

Paddy heard his Venus buzzer go off in his head and he was told to move on quickly as he was needed in another town in that country. He moved very quickly and waved goodbye to the child. Now, he could hear voices, a woman screaming and men's course voices shouting at her. He pressed his nose against the window of a small cottage and saw the woman tied to a chair, with one of the men holding a hammer above her head, as though he was going to strike her. He shone his light as strongly as he could and then burst into the house through the window. The man dropped the hammer and lunged at Paddy, who side-stepped out of the way and grabbed the weapon.

"Drop it, I said," Paddy shouted. Then the other man pushed him aside and he too, made to strike the woman. She shouted to Paddy, "They've stolen all my valuables and locked my dog in that cupboard." Paddy dodged the men and untied the woman. He thrust the telephone into her hand and told her to ring the police whilst he dealt with the men. She did as she was told. The men were filling an old sack with everything they'd stolen and had obviously decided to get out of the house as they couldn't work out what Paddy was, and truth to tell, they were scared.

Paddy used his brightness to cover their hands. It burnt them and they dropped the sack, rubbing their hands together. His brightness also blinded them for a while and then in the distance, a police siren could be heard. The thieves tried to leave the house but their hands were so badly burnt, they couldn't use the door handle. The door was thrust open and two policemen came inside. They grabbed the men and went to grab Paddy too, when the woman said, "No, not him – he's been helping me."

Paddy looked at her and touched her cheek gently. "I must go now, before the police come back to talk to you. Are you okay?"

"Who are you and how did you know I needed help?" He told her that was their secret and he had to go now but she should look upon him as her guardian angel. "Thank you," she said and wiped her eyes with her sleeve.

Paddy was gone and speedily made his way back to his base. *What a night,* he thought, *I need a rest now. No more tonight please, Venus – I realise a Samaritan should always be ready to help – but could I just have a little sleep now?*

There was only silence, so Venus must have been listening. She wasn't so silent the next day however and she buzzed him at noon. This time, it wasn't a new job but rather a command to visit the planet. Venus wanted to talk with him. *Oh dear,* he thought, *what have I done now?* He went straight to the communication centre and presented himself at 12 precisely. On being told to sit down, he thought that perhaps she wasn't going to tear him to shreds at all.

"Well now Paddy, we've been keeping you pretty busy lately, haven't we? Some big demanding jobs and some not so big. Have you enjoyed your time as a Samaritan White Dwarf Star – or are you perhaps looking for a change?" She was just as beautiful as her planet – just the sort of woman that, had Venus not been a planet, she would have been a perfect beauty, long golden hair that hung in ringlets down her shoulders and with eyes as blue as the summer sky. Paddy sighed, the days when he thought of a woman as a woman were long gone, but he had a good memory.

Venus continued, "Paddy, we are going to move you from your present site – in effect, we want to promote you as a reward for the work you've done since joining your constellation. You're going to move to be a supporting star – within a special cluster – who support and care for the Dog Star, Sirius. You will form part of the Hunter, Orion's belt – you know the stars well, but Sirius is the brightest and strongest light in the belt; he is the middle star and is well known for being easily seen from the earth's surface – in fact, whilst living on earth, you probably stared at him many times. What do you think of that?"

Paddy was dumbfounded and couldn't speak at first, but then he smiled and said, "Thank you, ma'am, that is a great honour and I feel very humble." Paddy was almost crying and stared down at his hands. "When is this to happen, ma'am?" he asked.

"Literally as soon as you've gone back to your original site – to say goodbye to any friends you have there.""

"There are – I'd like to say goodbye to Ernie. He's been my friend for a long time and I'd like to tell him where I'm going – just in case, he ever visits the area and wants to pop in and see me." And so it was done!

Paddy said his goodbyes and travelled to the small cluster of stars surrounding Sirius. Venus had explained to him that he might still be needed in his role as Samaritan, as he is good at that. He was pleased about this as it made him feel really useful.

Now when you look up into the night sky and see Orion in particular, you'll know that Paddy is there. His duties may have changed slightly but he's still Paddy. When you next see a shooting star, remember it could be Paddy or one of his billons of companions, coming to earth to help some person or situation – that person could be you. Guardian angels are there to take care of mankind and on many an occasion, they have to come to the aid of those still alive and living on earth – and they are only too willing to do it. A shooting star could be Paddy, or Michael… John, or Belinda, – all obeying the mother planet and come to our aid. Guardian angels in the truest sense.

A Bad Start but a Good Life

She was pushed out of the door by her mother and onto the cold stairs of the tenement. It wouldn't have been so bad if she'd had shoes but her bare feet had no protection except for the permanent layer of dirt that was encrusted on them. She stood in the landing for a few minutes, it was almost as cold there as it was inside, but she convinced herself it was fine. She pulled her ragged shawl tighter around her shoulders and smoothed down her torn dress to just above her knees. Her basket, full of black and brown boot laces sat on the floor, whilst she blew into her hands in an attempt to make the fingers move. It didn't work very well but it was worth a try.

Basket over her scrawny wrist, she started down the stairs into the morning air and tried not to breathe deeply as there was still freezing snow falling around her. It was odd how pretty everything looked in its blanket of white whilst it was actually lethal – and many would die that day crouched in alley ways and gutters – too cold to move. The girl's name was Marigold and she was 13 years old. She had seven brothers and sisters at home, which didn't leave much room in the cramped room and kitchen with one bedroom, where her parents slept. All the others slept in the kitchen but at least they had the warmth of the range which still had a few embers alight after the day's paltry fire. John, her brother followed her out of the house with his bag of matches which he would try to sell to passers-by. His clothes were just as tatty as his sister's except that he wore a big muffler around his neck. He was incredibly thin but at least he wore a pair of old shoes, which unfortunately were falling apart.

It was good when the two eldest children were turned out in the very early hours of the morning to start selling their wares, Marigold, her boot laces and John, his lucifer matches. It meant the other children could move more in the bed. What the two eldest sold may only have brought in a few pennies but any money was welcome to help feed the whole family. Marigold reached her spot in the centre of the city where she hoped to sell to people on their way to work, a good time for people to break their laces, rushing to get to work on time. John's favourite spot wasn't near to Marigold's but they always met up at the end of the day to walk home together, in case any ruffians were waiting for them, knowing one of them might have a few pennies in their pocket. It wasn't an easy time in Edwardian England where starvation and deprivation were commonplace – at night, there were many people wandering around the worse for alcohol – as this was one of the only things where they found some degree of comfort.

"Spare a farthing, mister – go on – spare a farthing. Look, your laces are all shredded – you'll trip up if you're not careful." Marigold had a few lines she used to get the attention of people but that was a good one, as people actually believed their laces were coming undone, and had to buy some for as cheap as a farthing. She wasn't doing very well this morning, as the snow and bitter cold was making people move faster than usual. They would rather have tripped over their laces than freeze to death in the Winter weather. A woman stopped and bought two pairs which was a whole half-penny – she had her children with her and pushed them along the pavement in front of her. "Move you, kids, it's gone seven o'clock and you'll be late for your jobs," she scolded. It seemed to Marigold that everyone had to rush to a job, or they just couldn't live. What a world, it was.

Her feet and hands were red and blue. She couldn't tell which were colder but decided it was her feet. She bent down to rub her swollen toes and caught a glimpse of something glittering in the snow. She moved towards it and reached down. It was difficult to pick it up with her frozen fingers but she did it, and couldn't believe her eyes. It was a silver half-crown coin, heavier than she thought it would be. A very solid coin. She looked after the woman but she'd already disappeared into the crowd – anyhow, it may not have been dropped by her. She curled her fingers around the half-crown and looked carefully around to make sure that no one was watching her. They'd have slit her throat for so large a coin and she knew it. She was so busy thinking about her good fortune that she allowed several people to pass without challenging them.

She made up her mind quite quickly and walked in the direction of the market in Leatherhead Lane. She felt sure she could find some second-hand shoes there and they'd be good and cheap. She found a stall covered in tatty, old bits and pieces but there, in pride of place in the middle of the heap, was a pair of good quality lady's shoes – they were pink and shiny – just the sort a princess would wear. Too big for her, but she still managed to keep them on her feet – those cold and swollen feet that stared up at her from the snowy ground. The woman behind the stall said, "Cor, ain't they lovely, Ducks. Just threepence from you, I think. My, where did you get so much money."

Marigold bristled and told her to mind her own business. She checked the change the woman gave her and put it firmly in her little basket, covered by the laces. Trying to walk, she limped along the street and sat down in a shop doorway. Using swollen fingers, she tried to make the shoes fit better and stuck her feet out in front to admire her princess's shoes. If she could get these for threepence, maybe she could get a warm shawl to wrap around her shoulders, and there as though provided by fate, she saw the very shawl and it was bright red, just the colour she loved. Another threepence and it was hers, wrapped around those thin, bony shoulders.

Never once did she consider taking the money home to her parents. It was too magical a feeling and after all, she'd been the one to find it. Maybe she'd keep some to take home with her lace money at the end of the day. She'd see. She moved back towards the main road where all the carriages and horses were pushing past each other. She darted through a gap in the traffic and found herself standing in front of a very large and imposing building where every window shone with candle light. Peering through one of the down stair windows, she could see a grand fireplace where flames were reaching up the chimney. Although, she could feel none of their warmth, she thought she could, just by imagining it.

Marigold, the princess in the red shawl and pink shoes crept around the building to the back doors, where everything and everyone was a-bustle – yard boys and footmen carrying boxes of vegetables into the hallway and maids doing the same with smaller delicacies, such as cakes and sweets. She watched them in wonder and thought that was the kind of job she'd like, something so busy and pretty. She gave herself no time to think, but just marched up to the door and asked if she could see the cook or person in charge. After a few minutes, a woman, dressed all in black, appeared and asked her what her business was.

"Ma'am, please excuse my impertinence but I wondered if your establishment was in need of a maid of some sort – the lowliest sort, of course – but I'd work hard to please you." Marigold held her breath, whilst the woman looked her up and down. "What's your name girl? Marigold? That's no name for a maid. Have you ever worked in a hotel before? You haven't – well, that's not much use to me." And she turned to go back indoors, but Marigold jumped in front of her and said, "Please ma'am, give me a chance to show you I'm a good worker," and her trembling lip touched the heart of the housekeeper.

"Get yourself inside and have a good and thorough wash in that scullery sink." This time she went away to get on with the business of the day and Marigold did as she was told. Ten minutes later, she emerged into a huge kitchen looking like a different person. She'd used the washing soap to get really clean and the scrubbing brush to tidy her long hair. She still wore her shawl and shoes, as she was very proud of them but she knew the rest of her clothes were pretty dreadful.

"Well, that's a bit better." The housekeeper came into the kitchen. "You look more human now. Pity you never thought to do it before."

Marigold thought of the cramped kitchen at home with just a bucket of water fetched once a day and just nodded her head silently. "Is there something I could do for you just now, ma'am, to show you how well I can work?"

"You see that mountain of potatoes over there, well, they need peeling – and peeling well – so you get started on them and we'll see how you do." The girl moved towards the potatoes but stumbled as she did so. "Sorry ma'am," she said, "I'm just a bit hungry and cold. I'll be all right in a minute." She lifted up the sharp knife.

"Just a minute, eat this bread and jam and drink some water, then start on the potatoes. You're no good to me if you're ready to faint." The housekeeper pushed a plate towards Marigold with a heel of bread and a spoonful of jam. It tasted like heaven and she thought she was going to be sick for a moment, so unused was her stomach to food, but the moment passed and she ate the lot before falling with great gusto to the chore in hand. As she was peeling, she wondered where her brother John was and how he was doing but soon discarded the thought as it wasn't her problem at the moment. The warm water soothed her hands at first but then the chilblains from the bitter cold crept back; she ignored the pain and strived to finish the job, but it was a mammoth task and the next time the housekeeper came into the scullery, she had to ask if she could sit down for a few minutes.

"Oh my Lord, I forgot all about you. Of course, you can sit down – come on over to the kitchen table and I'll make you a cup of tea – better still, I'll get Jenny to make you one and some toast." She called to a little maid who came running over and took the order from the housekeeper. Jenny banged the plate and cup on the table in front of Marigold and told her to hurry up. She obviously resented having to wait on someone who was obviously her inferior. Marigold ate the toast and slurped her tea – it was so good. She jumped up and ran over to the scullery sink where she got on with the rest of the potatoes.

The last one peeled, she covered them all in cold water and dried her hands on a piece of rag. The housekeeper came up behind her and said, "Well, that's a job well done. I'm very pleased with that. You can go home now – it's dark outside – so hurry along now. Come back tomorrow at seven sharp and I'll find you some more tasks to do, but this isn't a proper job offer – not yet – this is just casual work until I see how we get on." She started to leave the kitchen but turned around and shouted over her shoulder, "Take half a dozen of those potatoes home with you and you can have them for your supper." And she was gone.

Marigold knew she was too late to meet John, so she just took a shortcut home and handed the potatoes over to her mother the minute she got in the door. "Here you are, Ma – some food for you and the kids." Her mother grabbed them and asked where she'd stolen them from. "They're not stolen Ma – I've found myself a little job in a swanky hotel in the city and the woman in charge there gave them to me. I've got to be there at seven in the morning to do some other work."

"Oh well, that means you can have a bit of a lie-in. Pass your laces to your sister and she'll have to try to sell them. High time, she was going out to work – she's ten now – quite old enough." Ma didn't really care how many of her children were on the street – even in the snow and bitter wind – as long as they brought some pennies home to her. Marigold gave the laces to little Mary and warned her she must wrap up as well as she could, 'cause it was cold out there. She taught her too, the phrases she always used and made her practice them. Mary lisped a little but Marigold thought people might feel sorry for her and buy the laces, even if they didn't need them.

At the hotel next morning, Mrs Meadows, the housekeeper, was already working in the kitchen. She was chatting with the cook and telling her about Marigold and what a good little worker she was. Marigold was even more determined to work hard for the housekeeper. Before starting her on the preparation of various vegetables, she beckoned the girl to follow her outside into another room. Marigold stared all around, taking in the huge place. Mrs Meadows pulled some clothes out of a chest and said, "Try these on Marigold –

even if they don't fit well, they'll be a lot better than what you're dressed in now."

Marigold felt very grand and chose a blouse and skirt in a sort of brown colour. There were even stockings – strong woollen ones – that she held up with pieces of string. With her red shawl and pink shoes, she felt quite like a lady and stood tall in the middle of the room. The cook came into the room and told her to get a move on and start on the vegetables. The lunches would need to be ready for 12 o'clock when the city workers and businessmen came in, looking for a good meal. Marigold asked the cook what the names of the vegetables were as she had never seen them before. Cook enjoyed teaching her and liked the way she was asking questions all the time working on the food. Today, her feet and hands were a little better and again, the warm water helped a lot.

And so, Marigold settled down to working in the hotel kitchen, only doing the most menial tasks, but she didn't mind. Mrs Meadows told her she could have a permanent position there and would earn sixpence a week plus her food. Marigold thought she'd died and gone to Heaven but when Mrs Meadows also asked her if she was comfortable at home – as there was a very small back room she could have if she liked – she really thought all her dreams were coming true at once. So, Marigold moved into the smallest corner possible in the grandest hotel ever and she felt better than she'd ever felt before. She had a pallet of straw to sleep on, and it was her own – she didn't have to share with anyone.

Marigold worked at the hotel for the next four years. They were good years for her and she'd managed to get her brother, John, a job there as boot boy. He was a hard worker like his sister and worked his way up the ladder as well. By 1917, she was an assistant to Cook, sometimes serving in the dining room and he was a waiter, also working in the very smart dining room. Due to the shortage of men fighting at the Front, their jobs were secure and they sometimes sent money home to help the family. The First World War affected everyone and Marigold had a plan to learn all she could from Cook and then use that knowledge to do something important. She wanted to go to the Front and set up a soup kitchen there to help do her bit for the War effort. She'd confided her plan to Mrs Meadows, who'd promised to see what she could find out from some of her acquaintances.

One morning, when Cook and Marigold were preparing the daily lunches – lunches not quite so grand as before the War, due to the shortage of food – when Mrs Meadows told the assistant cook to step into her office. She explained that she'd spoken with an Army Colonel whom she knew quite well and he'd told her there was such a Field kitchen being sent to France to help feed the lads and that a trained assistant cook would be most welcome to join them. She couldn't believe her luck and knew right away she wanted to do this. She went to the address given her by Mrs Meadows and spoke with the people there who told her exactly what would be expected of her. A month later, she travelled with half-a-dozen people she didn't know, to a place she didn't know and to cook for all sorts of people she didn't know. Life was exciting and she couldn't believe she was the same girl who'd been selling boot laces not all that long ago.

When they arrived, however, everything was bare and inhospitable. The kitchen which resembled an old barracks had two stoves and a cupboard of pots, pans and dishes – and that was all. Lots of work was needed and elbow grease was the first priority. The little group first made up straw pallets and covered them with blankets – they knew they'd have to work hard but they knew too that they'd need a place to lay their heads at night. They scrubbed and swept and washed down everything in sight – some of the soldiers who were on sick leave, were drafted in to help them – and soon, the kitchen and dining hall were as good as new. Then, the food itself had to be collected, but again the Army came up trumps and brought everything into the kitchen – and then into the cupboards.

Two days later, the first soldiers arrived for breakfast and Marigold, her long hair in plaits, dished up as hearty a meal as she could muster. The food was enjoyable – just the way Cook had taught her and afterwards, the soldiers cheered and banged their mugs on the table in appreciation. 'Three Cheers for the helpers' was a cry that was to be heard many times again. The work was hard and securing the rations not easy but somehow, they did it and Marigold herself was so pleased at what they were achieving, she could have burst with pride. One day, she was shelling peas into a big pot, when a polite cough made her look up from the task. There stood a familiar face in an Army uniform and big, shiny boots. It was John who'd sneakily joined the Army, lying about his age. He was still only 16 and too young to have joined up officially, but so desperate were they for new recruits, those in charge turned a blind eye on certain occasions.

"What on earth made you do it, John? If you'd waited, it might have been all over by the time you were 18. You're a mad boy that's what you are – come over here and give me a hug," and she took her young brother in her arms, hoping that no harm would come to him. They settled down at one of the tables and she fetched him some bread and soup which he wolfed down. "Thanks, Sis – that was good. Anything for pudding?"

"You cheeky young thing, be grateful with what you're given." But she still brought over a bowl of Jam roly-poly and custard and plopped it in front of him.

He had to get back to camp, but before he went, she introduced him to her companions and told him to come back next time he's allowed to leave camp. He agreed and went on his way whistling and with a pleasantly full stomach.

She never saw him again. The very next day, he was on patrol with some others, when a German machine gun fired on them and threw a couple of grenades for good measure. The British soldiers didn't stand a chance and her 16-year-old brother lost his very, very young life. Marigold cried and cried for him – he'd never had a chance to live – and she knew she must write to her mother now and tell her what had happened. She did this and in the envelope, she placed a Poppy head as they were in bloom at the time. Pointless gesture, she knew, as her mother wasn't the sentimental sort – but it made her feel better. A little bit of John's last resting place going back to England.

The next day was intensely hot and the kitchen felt like a furnace. It was hard to keep the food as it should be, but the kitchen staff did their best. As it got close to meal time, some of the soldiers arrived early and suggested they move two or three tables outside the building into the cooler air – and just for the look of it – light a small fire in the centre of a circle, where everyone could sit, plate and fork in hand. It was a great idea and accomplished as soon as it was said. Marigold and the others made sure there was plenty of bread and soup – as meat was hard to get and soup was a good filler-upper. It was soon dark and the bellies were filled when one of the soldiers brought out his mouth organ and started to play some of the day's popular songs. Soon, *Lili Marlene*, *Pack up your troubles, Over There* and especially *Keep the Home Fires Burning* – were all filling the air. Even with the sound of the guns firing at the Front Line, the music was soothing and many eyes filled with tears.

Then she saw him, standing outside the circle of men. He wasn't in uniform but in his civvy clothes that he wore at home. He was staring straight at her and mouthed the words,

"Goodbye Sister – don't grieve for me – the worst's over and I'm looking forward not back."

She could actually hear the words and she stretched out her hand to him. "Goodbye, John. What a brave brother you are." The soldier next to her looked at her oddly but said nothing. Everything here was strange and people did and said the oddest things.

One month later, Marigold was back in England – she'd been relieved after her stint of duty and strangely, she felt sad at leaving France – but she had to come back as her time there was over. Of course, she was taken back by the hotel. Her cooking skills had been missed and feeding the guests was increasingly difficult as rations were low in quantity and in quality. She had learned a few tricks whilst at the Front and her shortcuts and suggestions were well received by Cook and Mrs Meadows. After a few weeks, she was promoted to assistant housekeeper – to help Mrs Meadows who was getting old. Her mother had never written back to her when she told her of John's passing, so she never went home again as she knew she wasn't missed there.

One afternoon, she was helping in the drawing room where afternoon teas were served. There were many ladies there, sitting two and four at a table. They were all well-dressed ladies with tasteful little hats perched on their heads. Chattering was loud and continuous, and Marigold moved amongst them with dexterity, not wishing to disturb their conversations. Her manner was much appreciated by the customers who knew where she'd been and what she'd been doing. They admired her courage and sometimes left her little tips, which all helped to keep the wolf from the door.

She had just fetched a fresh pot of tea and some more scones to a table of four, when she couldn't help noticing one of the ladies was crying. The others were comforting her, trying to cheer her up. Her only son, Robert was serving at the Front and that morning, she'd received a telegram, telling her he was missing in action. She completely believed that meant he was dead, even though the others were telling her that wasn't so. When they saw Marigold, the 'bereaved' mother dabbed her tear-filled eyes and tried to smile at the girl. Marigold saw him quite clearly, standing behind his mother's chair – he was in uniform but had blood-soaked bandages around his head and shoulder. She crouched down beside the lady and put her hand on hers. "What's your son's name?" she asked.

"My son is called Robert," the lady replied.

"Robert is not dead, ma'am – he has been wounded in battle but he has not been killed." She didn't know why she had done this, but Marigold felt very strongly that the young man was safe and she looked up at the figure standing there. He nodded and smiled at her, then disappeared completely.

Two days later, the same ladies were having tea when Marigold hurried over to serve them. The woman who'd been crying stood up and kissed the assistant housekeeper on the cheek. "My dear – just this morning, I had another telegram saying my son was well and was in a Field Hospital. He would be coming home to convalesce in the future. I want to thank you for giving me a reason to hope – I slept that night for the first time since he left for the Front." The other ladies gathered around and made a fuss of Marigold who escaped from their suffocating arms as fast as she could.

The deed had been done, however, and the story was out. The number of ladies coming to the hotel for afternoon tea increased dramatically and extra staff had to be taken on in the kitchen to help bake the extra scones that were needed. They all wanted to talk with Marigold – especially those who had sons away at the Front. She had become a sort of heroine and didn't know how to deal with it.

On a dark, wintry afternoon, she came into the drawing room and to her great surprise, she saw about six young men standing around the tables – all behind the chairs of the ladies. Some were in Army uniform and some were in civvy clothes and she knew what the difference meant. The ones in uniform, were wounded but not dead and the ones in their home clothes, had unfortunately already passed over. Some of the women were begging for her to tell them where their sons were.

A hush fell over the room when Marigold held up her hand. "I have no actual knowledge of what's happened to your sons – I can only tell you what I feel in my heart." She wanted to give no false hope but she knew she'd have to say something All the ladies nodded their heads in understanding and Marigold really hoped that they did. She moved over to the first mother and asked for her son's name. Peter was in uniform so she felt safe in saying that he had been wounded only and that she must be patient for information. Unfortunately, the next table had a young man dressed in civvy clothes. She looked into his eyes and he smiled at her. He mouthed, "It's all right, tell her the truth." And Marigold did it as gently as she could. The lady laid her head on folded arms on the table and cried. Her friends comforted her as best they could but what could they say?

The assistant housekeeper moved quietly around the room, stopping another four times for brief words with the ladies there. When she looked back around the room, all the sad figures of young men had disappeared. She felt drained and Mrs Meadows came into the room to take her away. She fell fast asleep on Cook's big armchair by the hot range – and they let her sleep there for the next two hours. She woke with a start and wondered where she was – then she saw Mrs Meadows sitting opposite her and she felt reassured. Except there was something strange about what met her gaze – it wasn't only Mrs Meadows there but behind her chair, stood a young man with fair hair and very blue eyes. She sat up and shook her head to clear her vision, but nothing changed. The young man was about 18 or 20 and he was dressed in civvy clothes.

She hesitated. "Mrs Meadows, do you have any relatives serving at the Front in France?"

"I have a grandson of whom I'm very proud – he joined up the very day he was 18. I haven't seen him for a while now and I miss him dreadfully. I reared him, you know, his mother and father died of smallpox when he was only five and he came to live with me then. I've loved him all his life and I hope to see him someday soon, he must be due for a break from the fighting." She made to get up to make a cup of tea for Marigold, but the girl made her sit back down again.

"Have you had a telegram recently, Mrs Meadows?" she asked. The housekeeper said that she'd had nothing and certainly wasn't expecting one. "I'd know if my grandson was dead, he'd find a way to tell me," and she got up to fill the kettle. When Marigold looked again at the chair opposite, the young man had gone and she felt relieved – it must have been a dream, after all she'd already had a most strange afternoon.

Next day, the housekeeper came rushing into the kitchen, holding a brown envelope in her hand. "Just as you said yesterday. It says he's missing in action and they don't know where he is just now. What does it really mean, Marigold? Does it mean he's dead, do you think?"

Cook came bustling forward and grabbed Mrs Meadows by the shoulders. "Now it means just what it says – he's missing in action – not that he's been killed in action. Now, you sit down by the fire and I'll get you a cup of sweet tea – for the shock." She was a big, kindly woman who meant well, but didn't always understand what to do in certain circumstances.

"Marigold, answer me, why don't you?" She sat down on the same chair as on the previous night – and when the girl looked up, there stood the fair-haired boy with the incredible blue eyes.

"First of all, describe him to me and tell me his name." She knew what was coming but she had to be sure.

"Yes, the eyes were very blue – he got that from his father – and the hair always shone in the sunshine. His name was Jimmy." And Jimmy smiled at the young woman and nodded his head, asking her to go ahead and tell his grandmother. Marigold did as she was asked and the young man disappeared. Mrs Meadows slumped forward in the chair, her head on her knees – and she died, just as she'd lived, quietly and in control. Her poor old heart gave out at the news – and maybe it was a blessing, Marigold thought, as they carried the housekeeper into a small back room.

This time, she made the cook a cup of tea and sat her down in her big armchair. "Come on Cook – there's lots of sugar in there – drink it all up." Suddenly, Marigold was back in charge and knew what had to be done next.

A week later, she was sent for by the Hotel owner, who had a suite of rooms on the top floor. "I would like to offer you the late Mrs Meadow's position as housekeeper. How would you feel about that?" He was a big, gruff man who was obviously ill at ease in a woman's company. A handsome man though, about 40 years of age, who'd never married. He ran the hotel very well, probably because he had the spare time to do it.

"Well, Marigold – no one knows the job better than you and I know Mrs Meadows trusted you to always do a good job. She told me." He lit up a big cigar and settled down at his desk. "Well?"

"I would be honoured, sir, I really would and I'll work hard and show you you've made the right decision. I'm well acquainted with all the staff and know what to look for in any newcomers. When can I start? And can I tell Cook and everyone what's to happen?"

"You certainly can and as for when can you start, well start right now." He stood up and held out his hand. "A handshake is as good as a contract – but of course, we'll also get a contract drawn up. Off you go and get started on your new duties but remember, I'm always here should you need any advice." They parted and the new housekeeper felt taller than when she'd first come in. Everyone accepted the news – they knew it was the most logical thing to happen. Everyone liked Marigold but they couldn't call her Marigold any longer – or even Miss Lambert – so the new housekeeper of the hotel became Mrs Marigold, as a compromise. The one condition that the hotel owner made was that she went on appearing – and serving afternoon tea if necessary – in the drawing room. She had become a very popular figure there and had increased the hotel's income as many well-off ladies now came just to see her – but also to order tea, scones and cakes. She had become an asset to the hotel for her popularity alone.

Sometimes her duties drained her but following a session in the drawing room, she would go and sit in Cook's big armchair and rest for a while, before getting on with her other duties. It all seemed to work well. Even after the War ended, ladies continued to come as there was always sadness in someone's family at some time. The ladies dressed differently from the way they had before the War – their costumes were more severely cut and the skirts just a bit shorter. They wore small hats now and fox fur stoles were popular. In a way, the women dressed more like the men – a sign of the times of course.

The First World War was over and life was changing rapidly, especially for women. The men returned from fighting only to find that some women had taken over their jobs. Of course, the returning heroes were taken back into the jobs they'd left where it was possible but some found it difficult to fit in again and carry on as before. With the passage of time, however, things settled down well and Marigold was a great success as housekeeper at the hotel. Three years after the War was over, she married Damien, the owner of the hotel. They'd become closer, now that as housekeeper, she had to see him more often than before. They found they had much in common and the romance began on the day he asked her to have dinner with him in his suite. They thought it was an inconspicuous way to meet – but of course word soon got out and everyone knew they were becoming a couple.

Their wedding was quite a grand affair and he spent money like water. Marigold again couldn't believe her luck – from the freezing cold of the gutter to the beautiful Wedding Breakfast in the hotel – she took nothing for granted, however, and went on taking part in the afternoon teas in the drawing room. She was like a fixture at the hotel and brought in increased numbers of customers all the time. Damien loved her too – which was an extra bonus for her – and she loved him. He was a kind man and a true gentleman. They had one son, two years after the marriage and called him George. Marigold adored her son and he adored her – Damien adored them both. It was a good marriage and the years soon passed. George was 18 and talking about joining the Army. Hitler was determined to engulf the whole of Europe and would annihilate any country that got in his way.

George came home one day in full khaki uniform. He had joined up without telling his parents what he was going to do. But the surprise he gave them was even bigger than that – he'd also got a Special Licence and married one of the hotel maids. He realised if he had a wife, she could have his Army allotment and she'd be safer that way, throughout the war years until he came back home. Marigold almost fainted and Damien was furious but the deed was done and suddenly they had a daughter as well as a son. Her name was Elizabeth and she was a quiet, well behaved girl, whom they couldn't help but like. She was 18 like George – both a couple of children really – and everyone would miss him from the hotel – he was a very likeable young man always willing to lend a hand when needed. But he was gone – somewhere near Holland apparently but they knew no more than that.

Three months later, Elizabeth told her parents-in-law that she was pregnant and the baby was due late summer. She was no different from many young women at the time and she was luckier than most, living in comfortable rooms in a grand hotel, which had become bigger with the passage of time – Damien had bought both large houses on either side and joined them all together. Maybe it wasn't a great time for expansion but it was a great time to buy properties.

One evening, Marigold and Elizabeth were seated in the study, going over the menus for the following week. The young girl was quite large now and she had just read George's last letter which had been sent from she knew not where. "How do you think he's coping Mama?" she asked Marigold, who'd got up to ring the bell for a servant.

"We need some cocoa darling, don't we? As to how George is doing, who can tell? He won't be as comfortable as you and I are tonight." The maid appeared and Marigold asked if she would please bring some cocoa and biscuits. As she returned to her seat, she saw a shadow at the back of the room. Probably just the flicker of the fire in the grate but she still moved towards it, only to find that it had moved and was now behind Elizabeth's chair. It was George, of that she had no doubt. He had a hand on each of his wife's shoulders but was looking into his mother's eyes. He seemed to be pleading and she wasn't sure what he wanted. He was not dressed in army uniform.

"Elizabeth, when did you last hear from George?" she asked.

"Just a couple of days ago, Mama – why?" Marigold told her it was nothing important, she was just curious. But Elizabeth was insistent and said again, "Why do you want to know, Mama?"

Marigold got up again as the maid came in with the cocoa and biscuits. "Daisy," she said, "please, will you ask Mr Damien to join us here – sooner rather than later?" Daisy did as she was bid. Marigold sat down again and poured out the cocoa. She set it down on the desk beside Elizabeth, first making sure it wasn't too hot. Damien came into the room. "What is it, my dear?"

"I have some news for Elizabeth and I wanted you to be here when I gave it to her." He too sat down and reached for his cigar case.

She told her daughter-in-law as gently as she could and stressed until they'd heard from the War Office, they mustn't assume her premonition was accurate.

"Is George still there?" Elizabeth asked and turned around in her seat and put out her hands as though to touch him. "He is, my dear but he's beginning to fade now and I can just about make him out." Marigold crossed to Elizabeth's chair and took both her hands in her own.

Of course, the official confirmation came from the War Office in due course.

And that was how it happened. Another generation gone from another family. The second World War lasted for six years and thousands of young men died in a foreign field. George was just one of them. As with previous generations, he'd left a child behind to carry on his name. His little son was born not long after that but Elizabeth contracted Milk Fever after his birth and died within a few days. Another young life gone so suddenly. She had named him George, after his father and everyone who saw him, fell in love with him right away. He grew up into a fine, young man who helped Damien with the running of the hotel. He was intelligent and learned a lot from his grandfather – in fact, by the time he was 17, he attended meetings in Damien's place and saw to all the deliveries, the hotel needed. His grandfather was quite old now and needed more help. In Fact, George Jnr was a Godsend.

Marigold was still attending the afternoon tea sessions in the drawing room, but she was getting older and found that she needed to rest more and more with the passing days. One morning, she got up and dressed. She was fixing her hair at the dressing table when something caught her eye in the mirror. There she stood in all her finery looking at herself. She was wearing a red shawl and when Marigold looked down at her feet, she was wearing pink princess shoes. She knew what was afoot. She was tipping herself off that this would be her last day on earth and that she should say goodbye to all those she loved.

She did just that. She sought out some of the staff of whom she was especially fond and gave them a little token of her affection. No one knew what to say but bobbed curtsies or bowed. She went through the house like a queen and she kissed Damien on the forehead, first removing his cigar from his fingers. She wouldn't awaken him as he needed his rest more these days. When she eventually found George Jnr, she sat down opposite him and told him her days on earth were over and that she'd have to leave Damien and the hotel in his capable hands. Of course he protested and said he was going to fetch the doctor – but she was so calm and relaxed that he hesitated and knew he couldn't leave her at that moment. She leaned her head on his shoulder and took a great sigh – and he knew, she'd gone. His dear, precious grandmother was no more – and he alone would have to break the news to his grandfather.

He had a plaque put up in the doorway of the drawing room where she used to stand to welcome the ladies for tea and say goodbye to those who were leaving. The plaque said, simply:

'This plaque is in memory of Mrs Marigold who did so much for this hotel. It's been placed here as this was her spot for over-seeing that all was well in the room. She saw many amazing things and shared those things with the dear ladies, she'd come to know and love.

Placed here by her loving Husband Damien and Grandson, George Jnr who loved her dearly.

To mark the passing of a dear Lady.'

It has to be added before I end this tale that she has been seen since wandering around the hotel. No one is ever afraid of her as she has such a gentle expression on her face. It would be nice if you could visit the hotel in the city – one of the biggest hotels the city has to offer – and see if you can find Marigold there. The best place to glimpse her is apparently beneath the plaque in the drawing room, but don't be surprised if she's wearing a bright red shawl and pink princess shoes.

It's just her little joke.

A Good Manure Helps
the Roses Grow

She shook her long red hair over her shoulders and the ceiling lights were reflected in the shining lights of her curls. She was a tall, well-built woman and she enjoyed this time when preparing to allow many people's eyes to meander over her alabaster skin. She dropped her white robe to the floor and bent forwards to remove her shoes. The chaise longue on the raised platform in the middle of the room was rose pink in colour and set off her skin tone beautifully. She lay down on the chaise longue and slowly made herself comfortable on her side, with one arm raised above her head.

There was a lot of scraping of chairs on the floor as each artist tried to get the best view of the model. Yes, Clara was a life art model and came to this community centre every Wednesday to pose for anyone who would pay the tuition fee and who would try their best to capture her obvious charms. She also modelled every Friday evening in the next town and the money was quite generous and she had to do nothing to earn it, except to reveal her naked body to all and sundry. It made her feel beautiful and desired – so, she keenly looked forward to each Wednesday and Friday.

Of course, her mother believed she was at the library, helping to organise the books and to track down the misfiles people had been careless enough to put in the wrong places. She enjoyed to think about her mother whilst she was posing in this way. She was such a tyrant and watched Clara's every movement.

The clock ticked loudly but there was no talking amongst the artists – just a slight movement of chairs every now and again. She stretched herself languidly and her movement immediately caught the attention of the pupils. The tutor spoke at this point, to remind everyone that their hour was almost up – there were some disgruntled noises and clearing of throats – but the tutor was adamant. He knew that Clara would need to move now and he didn't want her to cramp up. She'd been a good model for a number of years now – she always turned up on time and stayed for her full hour. Yes, she was getting a bit long in the tooth perhaps, but she was still a good-looking woman and an excellent model. A very secretive person, she always disappeared very quickly after the session and never spoke about her home life. She was a spinster, he knew that much, and she lived with her mother still – but that was all he knew.

Now she was dressed in a heavy camel coat and wearing brown, brogue shoes – flat and with tie-up laces. On her head was a checked headscarf and her handbag was big and hung over her shoulder. She turned into her street and glanced at her watch. Mother would be watching out for her and sure enough, as her house came into view, she could see her mother, sitting in her wheelchair staring out of the downstairs window. The curtain was pulled back so she could see better. Clara hurried up the garden path. It was a big Victorian detached house that looked just as it must have done, when it was first built in the middle of the previous century. Sometimes, Clara felt like part of the stone work – it had always been her home even when her father was still alive. Her father had indulged her more than her mother ever had – he was a gentleman and she'd loved him. But mother was a different kettle of fish all together.

"Where have you been till this time, Clara? It's gone ten o'clock already. I hope you've come straight home from the library." Mother was old and couldn't walk any more. She used a wheelchair to get about the house and had a stair lift fitted so she could go up and down to her bedroom when she wanted. It also allowed her to search her daughter's room to make sure she wasn't up to anything she shouldn't have been. Clara had many hiding places all over the house. She'd had to do this ever since she was a young school girl.

"Of course, I've come straight from the library. Where else would I go?" She disliked her mother – more with each passing day. "Have you had your Horlicks yet?"

"No, I haven't. Do you want me to scald myself with that kettle? That's what I'm waiting for and then I can go to bed." She moved her wheelchair away from the window, where she'd been watching for her daughter and wheeled it over to the fireside. It wasn't cold tonight, but mother was always cold and needed a fire even in the middle of summer.

"Go on up to bed and I'll bring your Horlicks up." Clara avoided the old woman's eyes and went into the kitchen.

"Don't try to send me to bed as if I'm a child. I'll go when I'm good and ready. Get my drink – I want it in here." She held out her hands to the diminishing flames and tutted several times. The room was very old fashioned, the furniture and the décor had always been the same – right back to when Clara was a child. In a way, it was still Victorian – but not expensively Victorian – just very ordinary Victorian. Clara brought the drink for her mother and put it on the small table by her chair.

"Look what you've done, you, messy girl – you've spilt it in the saucer. Get a cloth and dry it up." Not a word of thank you left her lips, but then, Clara was used to that. She fetched some kitchen roll and mopped up the tiny spillage.

"That drink is stone cold now, you, clumsy girl – get me a fresh cup and carry it carefully this time. I'm going on up to bed now – bring it upstairs when it's ready. I can't wait here any longer." She wheeled the chair across to the door and left it at the bottom of the stairs, and climbed into the stair lift.

Clara sighed deeply and told herself to stay calm. She should have been used to mother's bad temper by now but sometimes it still took her by surprise. She did as she was told but then, she always had. Mother had never allowed her to get a job, even when she'd first left school. She'd wanted to be a nurse at one time, but Mother told her that wasn't a job for a lady and would never let her look for things that might have interested her and got her out of the house. She'd also said that about the doctor's receptionist job she'd looked into – not good enough for her daughter. In fact, anything she'd suggested throughout the years had always been dismissed as unsuitable. In the end, she gave up trying to find suitable employment and accepted that she had to stay at home and look after her mother and father – until her father died a few years before.

She had been weak, she knew that – but she'd always been a weak person. A timid school girl, then an awkward teenager and finally a shy woman of whom nobody took any notice.

Maybe that was why she'd applied to become a life model at the local community centre – and then at the one in the next town as well. The type of work was so unsuitable and she knew her mother would be furious but that made it even more attractive, and she went right ahead. Now, she was firmly established at both premises and life modelling seemed to suit her very well. She loved the fact that Mother knew nothing about it and that she'd managed to hold onto both jobs for so long. It was the only time in her life when she felt attractive and sought after.

A loud banging on the ceiling told her mother was impatient for her Horlicks drink and she hurriedly put it on a tray and took it upstairs.

"Put it on my bedside table Girl and then get out of my room. I have no further use for you tonight, but make sure my bell is working in case I need anything during the night."

She leaned forward to kiss her mother on the cheek and say goodnight, but the old woman tutted loudly and told her to get off. If Clara hadn't tried to kiss her goodnight, that would have been wrong too.

She closed the bedroom door and breathed a sigh of relief. Peace at last. She settled down in front of the telly and ate her freshly prepared salad sandwich. She knew people thought she was odd – they'd always thought that – but she didn't really care that she had no friends. She always passed the time of day with the postman and the milkman – and with any other casual callers who happened to ring the doorbell – but mother didn't like her talking to people and she made a point of always sitting in her wheelchair behind the hooked-up curtain, so she could watch what her daughter was doing.

Clara finished her supper, washed the dishes and put them back exactly where they belonged and then went up to bed herself. She always felt delightfully tired on the nights she did the modelling and knew she'd get a good sleep that night. She could hear mother's snoring coming from the other room and as she did often, she wondered afresh how much she disliked her mother or even hated her. She set her alarm clock as she knew the gardener was coming tomorrow and she'd have to be ready for him. Mother gave implicit instructions as to what she wanted him to do, but she wouldn't deign to talk to him herself. He was a workman after all.

The boiled egg had to be just right or Mother had been known to throw it out of the kitchen window and demand another one. It had to be between hard and soft – just the way she preferred it. Clara set the kitchen table and cut the toast into four triangles exactly. She put the knitted tea cosy over the teapot and turned around just in time to see Mother's wheelchair coming into the room. "Everything's just as you like it Mother." Clara turned the radio down as mother didn't like it too loud.

"I'll be the judge of that Girl. Where's my spoonful of marmalade? Have you forgotten it?" Mother was in her usual bad mood. She was not a morning person – in fact, she was not an evening person either.

"Here it is Mother – I had to open another jar," Clara explained.

"I hope you scraped the last bit out of the old jar before you threw it away." She pulled the tray over towards her and positioned her wheelchair close to the table. "Is that gardener here yet?"

"No, Mother – he's not late yet, you know." Clara finished the last of her coffee and looked out of the window. "He's just coming now. What do you want me to tell him to do today?"

"I want him to do a general tidy-up of the garden and of course, cut the grass. Clara, this egg is a bit hard, not the way I like it at all." Her lips were pinched and she looked annoyed – but she ate it anyway.

Clara went out to meet John, the gardener and had a conversation with him. However, she gave him an additional task that Mother hadn't asked for – Clara wanted it done for herself.

"Deep holes, Miss Clara? Six of them – just dotted around the back garden – in no particular pattern? Is that right?" John looked rather puzzled. He hadn't been asked to do that before.

"That's right, John but one of the holes needs to be right in the centre of the lawn." Clara had obviously been thinking about the garden. "I'm going to get some rose plants and I want a pure white one for the centre. Is any of that a problem?"

"Not at all, Miss Clara but I'll cut the grass first and then weed the edges. The deep holes I'll leave ready for you to fill. Is that okay?"

"Great." And she went back indoors and left John to get on with his work. Mother of course had left the dirty dishes for her to wash and clear away and had already settled herself in her wheelchair by the front window, and of course with the curtain hooked back slightly to see more.

"Mother, I have to do some shopping before I make lunch. Is there anything I can get you from the shops?" Clara tied her head scarf around her hair with her red curls tucked securely inside. She took the shopping bags and asked mother for some money to pay for the groceries. Of course, she had some money of her own, but mother liked to be in charge and give out the money – and she'd be sure to check her change when her daughter came back. Clara waited for her to sneakily open her purse, peer inside and count out the money.

"Just before you go, Girl – who is that man standing outside our garden gate? I don't recognise him, do you?"

"No, Mother, I don't," and she went quickly out of the house. She did recognise him, however – he was one of the artists who came to her two modelling evenings. He always sat in the front row and watched her intently.

"What are you doing here?" she asked as she passed him. "You'd better get gone before my Mother sends for the police. She would, you know." She walked away from him but he followed her. "Why were you hovering outside my house anyway? I don't know you." Clara felt slightly scared and she didn't know why.

"Oh yes, you do." The middle-aged man replied. "You've seen me at the modelling classes. I really do think you're beautiful, you know, and I'd like to get to know you better." He was well spoken and polite but Clara didn't want to know. She quickened her step and rushed away from him. He called after her, "I'll see you tomorrow night in the next town. Take care of yourself till then. By the way, my name is Tim – Tim Smith."

She did see him the next night, sitting in the front row as usual, but she ignored him and asked the tutor if he would walk with her to the bus stop. "There's someone I don't want to see and he won't speak to me if I'm with you." Of course, the tutor agreed and even helped her onto the bus running board. She got home safely.

When she got indoors that night, it was about 10.15 and Mother was waiting for her. "And what kind of time is this to come home? I've been waiting for you all evening and I've been on my own all day long as well. Starved for company, that's what I am." Her mood was even worse than usual. "Why do you have to go to the library so often? I must say I find it very odd. And wait till you see what that gardener has done to the garden – he could see I wasn't happy but he wouldn't stop digging."

"Did you speak to him, Mother? He's perfectly approachable and he knows you're the real boss around here, so you only had to give him your instructions, you know." Clara removed her coat and shoes. She felt tired tonight and knew she wouldn't be able to listen to much more of mother's moaning. "Do you want your hot drink now or do you want to go straight to bed?"

"No, I do not. I want my drink first," and she moved her wheelchair away from the window. "And those children have been watching me all day – they think I don't see them, but I do. You're going to have to speak to their parents again and tell them to keep their children away from this house." She seemed to be getting a bit of a cold and kept dabbing her nose with a tissue.

"Mother, if I'm late, why don't you make your own hot drink? You do it during the day, so why can't you do it at night?" Clara felt her temper rising and knew she couldn't listen to mother for much longer. She went into the kitchen and searched in the cutlery drawer for the sharpest knife she could find. It was long and very pointed and had a bone handle, which made it easy to grip. She put the kettle on, so mother could hear it starting to boil, but just before it did, she switched it off and came back into the sitting room. She walked behind the wheelchair with the knife still in her hand.

"Mother, do you love me even a little bit? Do you ever think about my happiness and how controlling you are about everything I do?" She just stood there, waiting for an answer. At first, no answer came, then – "No, I don't think I do. I never wanted a child but I've told you that before, haven't I? It was your father who wanted a child, not me." She stopped talking, then went on, "Tell me something, Clara – are you happy? Do you have a good life with me? It's okay, you can tell me the truth – I don't care what your answer is – it means nothing to me." Mother was quite ready to be unpleasant and enjoyed upsetting her daughter when she could.

Clara stepped closer to the back of the wheelchair. "No, Mother, I do not have a good life with you. I'm not happy. In fact, I hate you. You've always been mean to me and never generous." She raised the long, sharp knife and brought it down, across her mother's throat – from right to left. And it was done. Mother slumped forward with blood spurting all down her front. Clara just stood there, staring at the woman in the chair. She knew she'd done a terrible thing and that God probably wouldn't forgive her. But then he might, you never know. She had had a mean and horrible woman for a mother and all she could think of, was why on earth hadn't she done it before?

She let Mother fall onto the thick hearth rug and rolled it around her. Although there was a lot of blood, the rug soaked it up like blotting paper. Although she hadn't intended to do it this night, she wasn't sorry that she had. She knew she was going to do it sometime soon – and now she had. Also, she'd had the gardener do his bit by digging those holes. It would be all right – she'd just have to stay calm.

She pulled the heavy rug onto the wheelchair and moved it into the cellar. The big chest freezer was empty – she'd made a point of letting that happen – and she'd cleaned it out a few days before. She wondered why she'd bothered to do this as it didn't really have to be sparkling fresh, but then Mother had always taught her to keep everything clean and tidy. She tipped the chair onto its front wheels and let Mother fall into the chest. She pulled over a small, wooden block to stand on and reached down as far as she could. It was going to be easy. The height was just right.

She'd let Mother cool down a bit and the blood would stop flowing. She mustn't actually let her freeze or that would make the dismembering too difficult. Yes, she'd be perfect about 2 in the morning. She closed the lid and went upstairs to take a shower and to collect all the spare sheets and towels that were more than she needed for herself. Although, she'd actually done it in the spur of the moment, she'd planned a lot of things well ahead and everything seemed to be going well.

In the shower, she felt relaxed and relieved – something she hadn't felt for a very long time. That night, she slept better than she had before but she remembered to set her alarm clock so that she could get up at 2. Mustn't forget that.

The ringing of the lock made her jump but then she remembered what she had to do and she got out of bed. From the bottom of the wardrobe, she took a new shower curtain, a shower cap, rubber gloves and a new set of carving knives – plus a book that she'd been studying for a few weeks now.

In the kitchen, she made a cup of strong coffee and fetched some cigarettes from her handbag. She'd smoked for a long time now but always at the bottom of the garden or someplace far away from Mother. She made sure the curtains were tightly shut and she opened the book at a specific page – on surgery. Re-reading the pages, she felt quite positive. The coffee and cigarette fortified her and she cut a circle in the shower curtain and fitted it over her head – it went all the way to the floor. Shower cap and rubber gloves fitted; she went down to the cellar where the chest freezer was.

Mother looked so comfortable as though she was just asleep but Clara knew she wasn't and began her grim task. Strangely enough, she didn't find it too grim. Mother hadn't been happy for a long time and look at her now – there was almost a smile on her face. Mind you, Clara sniggered – it had been so long since she'd seen mother smile, she wasn't sure if it was a smile or not.

Book propped up in front of her, she hauled Mother from the freezer and laid her on the plastic table cloth on the floor. First, cutting off Mother's clothes, she first removed the legs at the hip joints, then both arms at the shoulders, then the head from the torso. Just the right number to fit the six holes the gardener had dug. She rolled the parts into bubble wrap and placed them back in the freezer. Surprisingly enough, there wasn't a great deal of blood and it was easy to roll the plastic tablecloth into a ball, first putting the cut off clothes inside the parcel. She would burn it in the brazier in the morning – it would attract too much attention to do it then.

She closed the freezer and climbed the stairs to bed. It had taken longer than she'd anticipated and she set the alarm clock again – this time for eight o'clock. The Garden Centre was delivering the new rose bushes at nine and she must have burnt the cloth before they arrived.

Oh, it was lovely to come down to breakfast and put the radio on as loud as she wanted. No one to grumble or criticise or change her mind about what she wanted for breakfast and then change it back again, blaming Clara for making a mistake in the first place. She lit a cigarette and made a coffee. She sat by the kitchen window looking out at a glorious morning. The sun was high and bright and all was well with the world. At least, that's how she felt.

On the dot, the Garden Centre's van turned up and began to unload the large shrubs. "Just put them round the back, will you. I'm going to plant them myself." Clara waved to the milkman and beckoned him to come over to the door. "Just one pint from now on Bill – mother has gone to New Zealand to stay with her sister for a few months."

"That's nice, dear – I'll miss her friendly wave from the window. She was always there, watching for me." Bill handed her the milk and went back to the milk float.

She paid the Garden Centre man and thanked him. He'd asked, "You don't want me to put the plants beside the holes – good big holes, too. They're pretty heavy you know."

"No, don't worry – I've got one of those little wheelbarrows that can take them – but thank you for the offer." Funny how nice everyone seemed when

Mother wasn't there to find fault. At least, the milkman thought Mother's waves were friendly – he didn't know she watched him, hoping he would do something wrong, like being late with the milk. She went into the garden to examine the roses and was pleased with what she'd chosen.

Two pink, three yellow and one pure white. She'd told the gardener to put one hole in the middle of the lawn and that was for the white one. She planned to put Mother's head there as the centre of the garden and it wouldn't be difficult to do. Mother had always liked to be the centre of attention and in charge and so, would continue to be just that. The legs, arms and torso were planted one by one and when finished, everything looked beautiful – the roses were just coming into bloom and the rest of the garden was very alive too.

A week later, she'd been to the GP Surgery and told them Mother had left the country for a few months and she wouldn't be needing a doctor. She'd always had Power of Attorney – but not because her mother had trusted her, but because it meant she had to look after everything. Father had always done it before he died and mother never really learned how. So Clara had planned well – she went on receiving Mother's Pension into the joint bank account and had enough to live on. The house was fully paid for and she also had a copy of Mother's Will, leaving everything to her. Who else was there? Of course, she also had her salary from the life modelling classes – not a lot perhaps – but on top of Mother's pension, it was more than enough.

As she disrobed at the Wednesday class, she felt Tim Smith watching her and she deliberately looked around at the artists who were there that night. It was an odd feeling but he made her feel more self-conscious than ever before. Normally, she felt nothing as she knew the bulk of her audience were aspiring artists, some were dirty old men who may have had ulterior motives for attending the classes. He was one of the second kind, she felt sure. She didn't ask the tutor to walk her to the bus that night as she didn't want him to think she'd become increasingly nervous so she walked to the bus stop by herself. He was following her; she knew he was but she didn't look back – just stared ahead. He stood behind her at the stop and said, "We're catching the same bus, isn't that strange?"

He wasn't a bad looking man in his middle years but he seemed creepy and she knew he never usually caught this bus – he was following her. She climbed aboard the bus and sat near the door. He sat beside her but she didn't look at him. Journey over, she stepped off the bus, with him a close second. She turned to him. "Go away, can't you? If you follow me home again, I'm going to speak to the police." She was angry and scared at the same time. She walked towards her gate and of course, he followed. "May I come in for a coffee?" he asked. "I only want to talk to you and find out a bit about you and about your mother." She froze at that. Why would he want to know about her mother – he'd never seen her before, she was sure of that. Mother had stopped going out years before. She thought about it and decided she'd better hear him out.

"Okay, just a coffee and then you'll have to go." She opened the front door and switched on the hall light. "Come inside." And he did.

Over coffee, she asked, "Why did you want to talk about my mother?"

"She often waved at me as I passed your house. She always seemed friendly but I've not seen her for a few days now. Is she ill?" And Clara told him her Mother had gone to New Zealand for a few months and she'd left a few days ago. He seemed to accept this and finished his coffee.

"May I walk you home from the bus on other nights? It's safer if you're with someone." To get rid of him, she agreed and closed the front door behind him. As she turned towards the sitting room, she bumped into Mother's wheelchair, which she couldn't get rid of yet – in case it looked suspicious. *How did that chair get there?* she thought. *I'm sure it was by the front window where she used to sit.* And she wheeled it into that room. She wasn't sure yet what she was going to do about the man, but she had time for that. She should have asked him what he did for a living but she'd forgotten. Not that it was important as she didn't want to get entangled with him in the future. But who knew what the future held?

Clara loved flowers and roses in particular. She picked some of the pink ones as they were a bit further on than the others and they looked beautiful in the cut glass vase on the table. The gardener had called to cut the grass the day before and he remarked, "My Miss Clara – those roses have settled in well. They're going to be beauties." And he went about his business.

Clara still attended the life modelling classes and over the next few weeks, the man did follow her home but she never invited him in for a coffee again. She was very happy. Even coming from the classes, she loved coming home to a house without mother. No one moaned at her or accused her of doing everything wrong.

However, the next Wednesday, she did invite him in for a coffee. She supposed she was feeling a bit lonely or something and he was all that was available. This time she asked him what his job was.

"I'm a policeman," he answered and she froze again. She really shouldn't have a policeman in here, so she made the coffee quickly and started to say goodnight, when he said, "I'm not ready to go just yet. I'll go in a moment. May I have another coffee please – you make very nice coffee." She found that she couldn't refuse so she took the cups into the kitchen and made some fresh coffee.

"How is your mother getting on?" he called out. "When is she due back? Do you mind if I smoke and would you care for one?" She put the coffees on the table and took a cigarette. "Mother actually detests the smell of smoke but I can have one as she's not here."

"I know. She told me. You see, I wasn't exactly truthful with you before. I have met your mother. For some reason, she seemed to like me and would often open the window and have a conversation with me. I think we became friends – but it only happened on the days you weren't home – for some reason, she didn't want you to know we knew each other."

One bombshell after another, he kept right on dropping them.

"One day she invited me into the house for tea and from then on – every Wednesday and Friday – the pattern was repeated. We did become friends then but she really didn't want to involve you. I hope you won't mind my saying this, but she didn't like you, did she? We spoke about everything under the sun you see and seemed to have some sort of rapport with each other."

"I'm sorry I don't know what to say. I never knew. She never told me. My mother was a recluse and had a very bitter attitude to everything and everyone but obviously not where you were concerned. You're right – she didn't like me but I didn't like her either." She stood up. "I'd like you to leave now, if you don't mind. I'm feeling quite exhausted." He left the house without saying another word.

As Clara closed the front door, she tripped over Mother's wheelchair again. "I know you're trying to tell me something Mother – but don't bother. You won't upset or scare me – I'm my own boss now." When she went into the kitchen, the coffee cups had been put into the sink – she hadn't done it so it must have been mother again. She was being haunted, she realised. What next? Who knew?

Mother was becoming more visible about the house. Things kept being moved and Clara kept losing things. Well, she didn't really lose things – it was just that they never were where she knew she'd left them. She came home one evening and could have sworn she heard a man's voice and her Mother's voice. It really shattered her nerves and when she went into the sitting room – first tripping over the wheelchair – he was sitting on the sofa all by himself and with a drained coffee cup on the table.

"Who were you talking to? And how did you get into this house?" Clara dreaded the answer but had to ask.

"Why, your mother invited me in and we had a nice chat. I know now that she's not in New Zealand at all – but all over the garden. My God, that was wicked, Clara. Your own mother. She needed to speak to me so that I could help her – and I'm more than willing to do that." He stood up and moved towards her. "My, that's a pretty scarf you're wearing – a lovely shade of pink." And he moved even closer.

She struggled, of course, she did. But it was no use. The wheelchair was suddenly behind her and he forced her against it. His big hands went round her throat and he squeezed as hard as he could. She kicked out and scratched his face, but he was much stronger than she was. She blanked out and fell back into the wheelchair, dead as a doornail. My, he was a strong man, but he'd hurt his hands because she was wearing pearls and they bit into his flesh. He couldn't stop though till she was dead.

"Well, Mother, what do you think? Are you happy with that? I thought you would be." And he sat down on the sofa again. Clara lay in a crumpled heap at his feet, still looking beautiful with wide open eyes staring up at the ceiling.

He pulled her into the wheelchair and she sat there slumped over. He fetched a couple of sheets of writing paper and put it into her hands. He needed her fingerprints on it as he planned to leave a note from her, explaining why she'd had to go away. It was a plan he'd agreed with the old woman, whom he liked to address as Mother. He would bury Clara also in the garden and cover her in shrubs. He took the chair down to the cellar and left it there while he gathered up a spade and pick. He'd brought wellington boots with him and he'd hidden them behind the door. It was good and dark then, but there was a moon, whose light fell like a blanket all over the garden. Some light from the street lamp, out the front, helped as well but not too much as he didn't want to be spotted. He felt quite safe going outside as the house was surrounded by good solid walls. He was sure he wouldn't be seen.

He spent the next three hours working by the tall hedge which stood against one wall – he dug a trench about five feet long and as deep as he could make it. The soil was left in a heap, ready to fill in the trench when he was ready. He was sweating and tired although the night was quite chilly. He'd ring the Garden Centre early next morning and have them deliver at least six shrubs, all white roses. He'd tell them they all had to be white roses or he wouldn't buy any of them. Mother had been insistent that they be white. Returning a favour, she'd reasoned.

He went back into the house and switched on one of the lamps. Mother was sitting on the sofa, she had no need for the wheelchair, as she could move around quite freely now that she was a ghost. "We're all ready now, Mother – your plan worked well – I've even got the will you signed in my favour, leaving nothing to Clara. She got what she deserved, didn't she? Our will supersede the one she had – and the one she gave to her lawyer. Everything will be all right. I am the sole beneficiary."

Mother smiled at him. After what Clara had done to her, she didn't care who got the house and estate. He may as well have it, Clara didn't deserve it. "Get your head down for a few hours or you'll never be able to finish your gardening in the morning."

He did as he was told and fell asleep almost at once.

It was the doorbell that woke him the next day, he'd slept right through the alarm clock. The man at the door was from the Garden Centre and all around his feet, were potted plants of sweet smelling rose shrubs. All white of course. He asked the man to carry them round to the back of the house and he went back indoors after paying him. The man shouted through the kitchen window as he was leaving, "You've got a good trench ready for your roses – don't forget to put in plenty of manure – they love that."

"Oh, I've got plenty of manure ready, don't you worry." And he closed the window, before sitting down at the kitchen table to write the all-important letter, which he would subsequently find tucked behind the mantlepiece clock. He fetched the sheets of paper he'd squeezed into Clara's hands the night before and put one piece into the typewriter. He typed a date from the week before and started to compose.

To Whom it May Concern,

I've gone to New Zealand to see my mother's grave. I've recently heard that she died there and has also been buried. I'm fed up with my life here and have recently heard that Mother has bequeathed the house to another person and that the Will I have is no longer valid. I have checked this with the solicitor and know it's true as he has a copy of the new Will. So, I'm off to New Zealand to end up,

88

I know not where, but it can't be worse than here. Give away anything you want. I don't care.

Yours,
Clara

He signed the letter, just writing Clara several times before the final one. It looked good, he thought. Using his rubber gloves again, he put the letter into an envelope and placed it behind the clock on the mantlepiece, 'To Whom it May Concern'.

Now he had to get rid of most of her clothes, jewellery, shoes etc. He bagged everything up and took it to the landfill site just outside of town. He took some of Mother's things too so as to not look suspicious. He felt cleansed and had a sudden spurt of energy, a job well done, he thought.

The day was passing and it was evening already. He went down into the cellar, although, he wasn't looking forward to his next chore. Clara was standing in the cellar. She was dressed just as she had been the previous night, pearls and high-heeled shoes. Behind her, stood mother who obviously had no need for her wheelchair. The two women looked at him disapprovingly, although, he couldn't work out why Mother was displeased. They watched his every movement and Clara told him to be careful with her as he pulled her into the wheelchair. Having done that, he suddenly felt hungry. It had been a very full 24 hours. The cheese in the fridge looked okay so he made himself a cheese and chutney sandwich, although he didn't enjoy it, as the women were now in the kitchen still watching him.

That night, he had to give all his attention to Clara.

Obviously, he waited till it was dark and then he took her into the back garden on the wheelchair. He tipped her body over the edge of the trench and she lay there, rather like the way she used to stretch out on the chaise longue at the art centre. He couldn't quite straighten her body as she had stiffened in the meantime but in a strange way, it made it easier for him to cover her with earth. He began shovelling the soil into the trench but he didn't look at her once as he couldn't bring himself to do that. He brought over three of the rose bushes and filled the first half of the grave, then he brought over the rest of them and placed them equally along the trench. It was about three o'clock in the morning when he finally straightened up and arched his back. The freshly planted roses looked pretty good, he thought and wheeled the chair back into the cellar, with Clara and Mother following close behind. He was sweaty and dirty, he went upstairs to have a shower and put on the fresh clothes he'd picked up earlier that day – when he'd gone to the landfill dump.

He sat there with a steaming cup of coffee in his dirty hands and thought about the past few weeks and how much had happened in that time. Next day, he went back to his own small home where he waited patiently till he thought it was safe to come out of hiding. Clara's milkman had reported that several bottles of milk had been left on the doorstep and that he thought something might be wrong in the house. He told them he hadn't seen Clara for at least a week.

The police were involved now and in trying to trace Clara, they visited the community centre where she had been a model. No one had seen her for quite a long time and although the tutor had tried to ring her and had even gone around to her house, there was no trace.

In the meantime, the lawyer had contacted Tim Smith and told him about the Will. Tim said mother had given him a copy and he had known he was to be the beneficiary. Everything worked out slowly and the lawyer contacted the gardener who'd worked for the two ladies and asked him to keep an eye on the garden as the house would have to go on the market soon and it should look good. It seemed that no one would come back from New Zealand and they may as well, get on with the business in hand. Tim's job allowed him to learn what was happening about the disappearances. He went around to the house with the lawyer – a list of everything in the house would have to be drawn up – everything had to be done properly. Tim 'unexpectedly' found Clara's letter behind the clock and the mystery of her disappearance was solved. She wasn't coming back. He smiled at how the police had 'missed' the letter.

Tim Smith was a very lucky man. He was also a very bad man. He visited the house another two times but Clara followed him about, looking at him with evil in her eyes. Mother just followed her daughter around the place, looking, and probably feeling, lost. Tim was not welcome, that was for sure. The sitting room and the kitchen also affected the way he felt, there were vases of roses everywhere and the perfume was overpowering. Even when they weren't there, they were there. He told himself it could have been the gardener who picked the flowers and left them there but he knew that wasn't likely. "They' were doing it.

Two men from the Estate Agents' Office put up a 'For Sale' sign in the front garden. Tim was excited about the price they were asking and was looking forward to the sale. The garden looked beautiful and the gardener was proud of it, particularly the rose bushes, which were growing fast. The perfume was so lovely, people actually came to the street just to smell the roses. Tim Smith was proud of them and one of the photos in the sales brochure was actually of him, standing amongst the roses, beaming at the camera. He was standing by the single white rose – the bush in the middle of the lawn – the one whose roots must be intertwined with Mother's severed head by now – something of which Tim put out of his mind.

One young couple in particular were interested in the property and put in an offer very near the asking price. They were standing in the back garden one gorgeous summer's day in Autumn and the Estate Agent was waiting for them in his car. The young man, Michael, said to his wife,

"This is the loveliest garden I've ever seen – we've got to get this house."

"Oh yes, Mike – we must live here. Can you imagine all the lovely days we'll be able to spend out here – smelling all these perfumes." She was just as excited as he was.

"Well, let's go and tell the Estate Agent that we'll offer the full asking price but one thing I'll want to know before we do anything else, is what kind of manure they've used. It must be quite magic, mustn't it?"

And it was, but not quite in the way he thought. Clara and her Mother just smiled at the couple from the kitchen window. They watched as Tim arrived at the garden gate to have a word with the Estate Agent and they watched as two policemen approached him and asked if they could have a word.

"Of course, gentlemen but I hope you're not going to make an offer on the house because I've just accepted one from that young couple standing with the Estate Agent." Tim felt exhilarated and happier than he'd felt for a long time.

"Oh no, sir, we're not here to buy a house – we're here to find out what you've been up to for the last few months."

And so the investigation began and Tim's happiness began to ebb away. It was only just after all.

The Orphan Girl

She stepped outside onto the stone step and the heavy, wooden door slammed shut behind her. This was to be the first day of the rest of her life. She put her small portmanteau by her feet and clasped her hands together in front of her. She was slim with an olive skin and her brown hair was sleeked back behind her ears and piled on top of her head. She was 18 years of age and she'd lived at this Charity School ever since she could remember – in fact, she even learned to walk and talk here – she was educated by the nuns here and learned all there was to know about morals, chastity and truthfulness, but perhaps little about the world in general. She looked down at her plaid skirt and black boots, both items which had belonged to a young girl, who'd been unfortunate enough to die of a fever, but whose clothes were too valuable to dispose of carelessly. She'd been called Catherine and had been a bonny girl but not very strong in build. She'd been a friend for a long time and she would be missed at the Charity School as she always had a ready smile for everyone.

Sarah was proud of the shine on her boots and pointed one upwards so she could see it more clearly. She was waiting for the cart that would take her to the coaching inn in the nearby town. She'd never been so far before and was worried how would she manage it – she had no choice but to try, so she straightened her back and tapped her foot impatiently. In the distance, she could hear the cart's wheels rumbling along the ground and the horse neighing loudly. He knew he was coming to the end of the first part of his journey and would be given a treat by the driver. The horse and driver were used to coming to the school, either delivering parcels or new pupils – it was a well-trodden road. She climbed up on the cart and gave Old Bill a shilling for the fare. She'd been given several shillings – not too many despite all the years of work she'd done for the nuns – but enough to give her independence.

"How many times have you travelled this road, Bill?" Sarah was genuinely interested although some people called it nosiness.

"Too many times, girl – I never learned to count, so I couldn't tell you anyway." He pulled his cap further down on his forehead, which was a sign that he didn't want to chat. It was beginning to rain and Sarah pulled her collar around her face. They soon arrived at the coaching inn, the Sleeping Swan, and this was where he let Sarah down and where she would wait for the big coach to take her into Truro.

"Now don't you talk to any strangers, girl and keep yourself to yourself. Remember to eat the bread and cheese I'm sure the nuns gave you." And he was gone, waving goodbye as he went. She tucked herself under the eaves to miss the worst of the rain and heard all the laughter coming from the inn. The coach arrived two hours later and Sarah clambered up to the seat beside the driver. She was very wet but not as bad as she might have been had the eaves of the inn not protected her so well. The driver dropped her in the middle of a village just outside Truro, beside the old Market Cross, not too far from the house she was looking for. It was the doctor's house and she knew he had two children, for whom she would be the governess. She looked at her shoes and they weren't shiny any longer but she forced herself to straighten up and look for his house.

She knew too that his wife had only recently died and that she'd have to care for the children as much as she could, with them being motherless so suddenly. It had been a quick death, the nun had explained before she left the Charity School and she would be expected to do a bit of mothering, as well as being a governess. Unfortunately, she arrived just after the funeral service had taken place and the doctor's house was still full of people, all dressed in black. The little maid had opened the door to her and invited her inside. A tall man broke away from a circle of people and stretched out his hand. "You must be our new governess – it's Miss Middleton, isn't it? How do you do, my dear?" He didn't invite her to stay as he sensed she would feel uncomfortable, not knowing anyone. "Lucy will take you to your room and you can meet the children in the morning."

"Thank you, sir – that will be excellent," and she followed Lucy the maid up a long Victorian staircase. Sarah's room was next to the children's room and she felt comforted by this, as it made her feel not quite so lonely

She did meet the children next day when she came down to breakfast. William and Sophie were still having their food and looked at the new governess with shy smiles. William was eight and Sophie five, she discovered. The girl was quite chatty and easy to like. William had dried tears on his face and his eyes didn't meet Sarah's.

A stout jolly woman came into the room. She wore a voluptuous apron and had the rosiest cheeks Sarah had ever seen. "Well now, Miss – how was your journey and have you had enough to eat?"

"My journey was fine, if rather wet and yes, my breakfast was quite sufficient, thank you for asking." Sarah wasn't sure how important the cook was but she acted very importantly and told young Lucy, who'd followed her into the room, "Get those things cleared away Lucy. The doctor's been called out to see a patient but he'll be back soon and expect to see this room ship shape and Bristol fashion." Sarah made to get up and help the little maid but cook told her not to trouble herself as it was Lucy's job.

"The doctor said I was to tell you the schoolroom is ready for you and you've to do what you want with it. He did suggest that you start them off with geography but go gently with them and he'll come up to see you as soon as he's between patients." And she disappeared back to the kitchen.

Sarah looked around and liked what she saw. It seemed a comfortable home with very nice things all around. She had expected it to be rather sombre, but it was quite bright and cheerful. Well, as cheerful as a house could be where the mistress had just died. She took Sophie's hand and tried to do the same with William but he would have none of it, after all, he was a big boy of eight. The schoolroom was nice as well with two desks and chairs placed before the window. A bigger desk was in the corner and that was for her, she supposed.

"I hate geography." William pouted and threw his slate on the floor. Sophie gasped and said, "Mummy would have told you off for doing that, William." His reply was to tell her he didn't care 'cause Mummy wasn't there anymore. And as he said the words, the tears began to well up in his eyes. He was a handsome young boy with dark hair and very blue eyes, whilst Sophie was fairer with the same colour of eyes and blond, curly hair. Sarah knew she must maintain her coolness and not become over familiar with the children but she couldn't help putting her arms around the bereaved children. Dr Phillips chose this moment to come into the room and he had to admit to himself that he wasn't displeased to see the new governess had a sympathetic side.

"I'm glad we meet properly at last, Miss Middleton – it was unfortunate you arrived on the day of the funeral – my wife had only died the week before." He shook her hand again and said she was welcome in the house. "My children are very special to me and I want you to treat them well – but also teach them as much as you can." He ruffled William's hair and tickled Sophie under her chin. Sarah thought he seemed a nice man but time would tell and she'd reserve her judgement until she knew him better. He must have been about 50 years of age so he must have married quite late, taking his children's ages into account. William soon came around to liking Sarah and Sophie actually liked everyone, cook and Lucy were pleasant, generous people and Sarah began to feel as though she'd fallen on her feet by coming to this house.

It was a bright spring morning, when governess and children returned from a walk around the village. They'd been looking at the age of some of the cottages and Sarah had explained why there were so many villagers with the same surname – and how long some of the families had lived there generation after generation – how some of the cottages had been built in one night. Four walls and a smoking fire on a piece of roadside, all built in one night, could belong to the person who built it. – as long as there was smoke coming from the chimney. It was a challenge but a very worthwhile one. William was fascinated with the local history, a lot of which Sarah had discovered in local church records. As for Sophie, she just wanted to reach home to ask for one of cook's lovely, creamy buns. The children still missed their dear mother, especially William who still cried at bedtime, longing for his mother's goodnight kiss.

They came in the back way through the kitchen, just in time to hear cook say, "Yes, she died in her sleep, the doctor said. Maisie Snell was not all that old but she was a true villager, one of the oldest families around." She was smacking a big piece of dough, something she always seemed to enjoy doing.

Lucy added, "I saw her only last week and she looked so well, it's hard to believe. Still, the Lord giveth and the Lord taketh away. It's only been a month since Robert Pascoe passed away and he lived in the same street as Maisie. What a sad time." She finished making the custard to go with the plum pie that had been baked that morning. Sophie was licking her lips as she came into the kitchen, the smell was so lovely. Sarah told the children to go upstairs and wash their hands. William went slowly and Sophie ran.

"What was wrong with Maisie Snell – was she suffering?" Sarah joined in the conversation. She hadn't known Maisie but she felt she should show interest in the village happenings.

"I never knew there was anything at all wrong with her and she could only have been about 50, I think." Cook was cutting the dough into quarters to go into the oven. "In fact, I did ask the doctor what actually killed her in the end. He obviously didn't want to talk about her, he said something about patient confidentiality, or something like that. I must say that I thought when you were dead, confidentiality went out the window but then I'm just a cook. Lucy, there's someone at the front door, go and answer it." The maid disappeared quickly and Sarah could hear the deep voice of a man, saying he'd like to see the doctor.

"I've put him in the study to wait there," she said. "The doctor's due to return soon and the lawyer said they'd agreed to meet at three." Sure enough, they heard the doctor's key in the lock and he put his head around the kitchen door. "Cook, bring some tea and scones into the study please. I have some business to discuss with the lawyer."

Cook busied herself with the tea and quickly took it into the study. It should have been Lucy's job but the doctor seemed a bit flustered, so she didn't want to add to his problem.

All she heard was, 'I've still not concluded Mr Pascoe's instructions and now I have Maisie Snell's to deal with.'

She reported what she'd heard back in the kitchen and then they all sat around the big kitchen table and ate a tasty tea, especially Sophie.

Time passed and the children settled down well with their governess. Lessons filled more than half the day and they took regular walks around the hills and the village, learning as much as they could of the local history.

"Why did Mummy die?" William still fretted and it was obvious that he missed his mother dreadfully. Many times, she had to go to his bedroom and settle him down, his crying was quite loud. It never disturbed Sophie, however, but then nothing ever did.

"Mummy was quite sick, William and although your daddy tried his best, he just couldn't save her, I'm afraid." They were just passing the church and heading for the children's mother's grave. They'd picked some wild flowers in the fields and had brought them for Mummy.

"Mummy always preferred wild flowers to garden ones – she told me that once." He knelt down at the headstone and placed the flowers in the holder there.

"That's nice, William – she'll like those. I wish I'd brought her some too." Sophie looked sad. He gave her two pretty flowers to give to Mummy.

"Mummy hadn't been ill before she died. I heard some of the people who came to the funeral say that – they wondered what actually killed her." William was looking at Sarah with a puzzled look on his face. "What do you think,

Sarah?" He was allowed to call her by her first name, as Miss Middleton sounded too cold. She didn't know how to answer the boy and luckily, they saw the woman from the village shop come out of the church door. She waved cheerily and went on her way. William lost interest in his question then and made his way into the church.

"Would you like to try some brass rubbing, children? It's rather nice to do and you end up with some pretty patterns that you can keep."

"Yes, please," was the quick answer and she promised to get the necessary tools to do it.

Sophie suddenly asked, "Where are your mummy and daddy, Sarah? Do you ever go to see them?"

She wondered how to explain her position. Sophie was very young but then she'd had a traumatic experience of her own with losing her mother. "I don't know where my mummy and daddy are, Sophie. When I was a baby, they weren't in my life and sadly, they chose to stay that way. I never knew them and I grew up in an orphanage, a charity school, where the children were looked after by holy nuns." Strangely enough, Sophie seemed to accept this and quickly asked, "What's a nun?" She'd asked an awkward question but saved the day by zoning in on nuns. So, Sarah changed the subject and talked about nuns.

Dr Wilson finished his breakfast and wiped his mouth with a napkin. "Cook, will you remind Lucy that I've put some arsenic down in the cellar – along the wooden shelves. She will have to be careful not to touch them just yet – until they do their job and get rid of the rats that persist there. And you too Cook – don't go down there unless you really have to."

"Yes, doctor – now would you like some fresh tea?" She cleared away his plates and he left the room, turning down the tea.

"Ah, Miss Middleton – I was hoping to see you before I left – how are the children doing?" He was putting on his coat as he spoke.

"I believe they're doing very well, sir. They're bright children and I think William will be a good scholar. Sophie is fine for her age and a joy to look after." It was the right answer and she got an "ah good" out of him before he went out the door. Sometimes, she wondered if he was as fond of the children as he implied – his interest in them seemed weak sometimes.

"Oh, Miss Sarah, when the doctor comes home, will you tell him that Lucy is quite ill. I've had to send her back to bed – her stomach is hurting dreadfully." Cook looked really worried and Sarah made her sit down on the big chair by the fire and made her a cup of tea.

The doctor went straight upstairs to see the maid and gave her some medicine to settle her problem. He knew she must have touched the arsenic covered shelves. "I gave clear instructions that you were to be careful in the cellar, because of the arsenic I've put down." He was quite sharp with the girl, who was holding her stomach to ease the pain.

"Oh sir – I didn't touch the shelves where you put the poison – I just moved a big jar that was in my way. Could it have been that, sir?" Lucy was very tearful and quite scared.

"Certainly not, girl – you must have touched the shelves – that's the only place I put it." He left the room and told Cook to let her stay in bed for a couple of days and then, let him know how she was.

"Will Lucy be all right, Papa?" Little Sophie was fond of the maid and William was waiting for his father's answer as well. "That's how Mummy started to be ill, Papa – do you think she could have had something she shouldn't have, like Lucy?" William's question was more serious than his sister's and the doctor knew he had to respond.

"No, William – I don't think that's what happened with your mother. She just became very ill and wasn't strong enough to beat the pain. Now, Miss Middleton will take you both upstairs and tuck you in bed. Off you go." And he was left alone in his study. He sat in the fireside chair and poured himself a brandy from the decanter. He was very sad and said to himself, "I miss my wife as much as the children do but there was nothing that could be done."

He heard his wife's voice quite clearly. "Oh yes, there was, dear – you could have given me an antidote but you chose not to." He looked in the corner of the room and there, she stood, looking remarkably well for a ghost.

"Go away wife and leave me alone. I've done all I could since you died – I've been good to the children and found a nice governess to look after them. And you had a lovely funeral." He was very agitated.

She laughed – a gentle laugh that made the lit candles flutter. "Oh, Thomas, you are such a hypocrite – we both know you had to get rid of me or I'd have left you. Our marriage was over. And you've got my fortune now, haven't you?" He was going to reply but she disappeared as quickly as she'd come.

"Sir?" Cook looked around the door. "Before I go to bed, would you like a cup of cocoa? I'm making one for Lucy." He accepted the drink gratefully and was glad her appearance had had such a detrimental effect on his wife's presence. He went straight to bed and told her to bring his drink upstairs.

The children and Sarah were down on their knees making brass rubbings of a grave stone, set in the aisle of the village church. William was working hard and had black smudges all around his eyes. Sophie on the other hand, was day dreaming on a nearby pew. She saw no point in the hard work with which the other two were engrossed.

A man's voice rang out, echoing in the high vaulted ceiling, "That's amazing, so much work but worth it. The results are beautiful." It was the young curate who assisted the vicar in all his duties. Sarah looked up and saw one of the most handsome men she'd ever seen – not that she'd seen many men in her isolated upbringing at the Charity School – but he really looked like a saint from a medieval religious painting. "Where did you learn to do that?"

Sarah stood up and smiled at the man. "I learnt about it in the school I attended before I came here – my name is Sarah and this is William and Sophie, the doctor's children, whom I look after." She held out her hand and he took it immediately. She felt she was going to swoon, but pulled herself together and stepped backwards.

"Would you like to try it, sir?"

William smiled at the curate and Sophie piped up with, "Why are you wearing a long dress – you're a man, aren't you?"

He took the rubbing cloth from William and got down on his knees. "Yes, I am a man, young lady – and what are you, pray?"

"I'm a girl, silly," she replied and was rebuked by Sarah for being cheeky. "Sorry, I didn't mean to be cheeky, sir." He laughed and ruffled her hair.

That first meeting led to many more and the governess and her charges regularly walked near the church. In Sarah's case, with the hope that they'd all meet up together. Back in the house, she made enquiries of Cook and Lucy in the hope they knew about the curate. Always happy to oblige, Cook told her he'd been with the vicar for at least two years now. He was popular with the village people and always ready to lend a hand wherever it was needed.

"Do you like him then, Miss Sarah?" Lucy asked slyly and laughed at Cook's shocked expression. "His name's Peter – Peter the Angelic, the locals all call him."

"Of course, I like him – why should I not?" The governess was blushing and suddenly needed a drink of water.

"'Ere, have you heard that Billy Smithers is dangerously ill – apparently, he collapsed in the fields and had to be carried home in a cart. I wonder what's wrong with him?" Cook was making Coconut Tower cakes that the children loved. "The doctor went straight over there to help him, so I'm sure he'll be all right. By the way Miss Sarah, before I forget, the doctor's lawyer is coming round at four o' clock to discuss business with him. Will you be here to make him welcome – I have to go to market to get fresh supplies and Lucy has to come with me to help with the load?"

Sarah said she would listen out for him and make him some tea when he came, before taking the children upstairs to the schoolroom. To-day was history, which William loved – Sophie, not so much. She soon heard the doorbell ring.

"Come in, Mr Babcombe. The doctor told me to expect you." Mr Babcombe was a round, quite jolly man whose whiskers almost reached his chest. He handed her his hat and cane as though she was a servant but Sarah didn't mind, the nuns had always taught her humility was a virtue. "Will you take tea, sir?" He nodded and sat in one of the armchairs, reaching for a magazine from the nearby table. Sarah made tea for two as she knew the doctor would arrive soon and as she took in the tray, the doctor's key clicked in the lock. She hung around in the hall and found that she could hear their conversation quite clearly. She didn't mean to listen but she couldn't help it. Mr Babcombe's voice was quite loud.

"Look Thomas, I want to get this business over and done with as quickly as possible. Both Pascoe and Snell have left you their whole estate – house, land, valuables and money. I hadn't realised you were so close to them?" He helped himself to a buttered scone Sarah had generously heaped with strawberry jam.

"Yes." The doctor spoke more quietly but she could still hear him quite well. "Both of them thought very highly of me – and of my wife, of course. All I can think of is that she must have suggested they make their wills in my favour. It's not unusual for a patient to do that sometimes." He too helped himself to a scone and jam.

"The police came to see me last week – they were curious as to what killed them both. Of course, I didn't mention the wills as I couldn't see how it concerned them."

"Quite! Quite!" The doctor quickly changed the subject to the safe one of the weather.

Sarah went back upstairs but looked very thoughtful. Two people who died suddenly and left all their possessions to the doctor. She made up her mind to quiz Cook and Lucy more, about the mistress's death. It wouldn't do any harm to know what had gone on before she'd arrived in the village. Peter 'the Angelic' would be a good person to learn things from as well and it would give her an excuse to seek him out.

When Mr Babcombe left, the mistress herself paid an unexpected visit to the study. "Be careful, Thomas – they're watching you, I fear." She didn't stay this time but she'd dropped her 'poison' in his ear. "Perhaps, I'll bring some friends next time I visit you – you'll know them, of course."

Peter was very interested in what Sarah had to say and promised to find out what he could about the doctor's earlier years. The church records would be a good place to start and then the county records to follow.

They met in the meadow to talk further, without the children being present – the governess and the curate. Peter settled down on a fallen tree and Sarah sat beside him. "The doctor came to this area about 25 years ago and has moved between three or four villages over the years. He came from a Charity School a distance from here and was befriended by one of the local matrons, a widow who paid for him to train to be a doctor. Unfortunately, just when he qualified, she died and never saw the product of her investment. I don't think we have to guess what killed her, do you?" He paused for a moment as he thought he'd shocked the governess. "Why are you looking at me like that, Sarah – it's not really an unusual story?"

"It was my Charity School, wasn't it – run by the nuns?" She was very interested now.

"How could he be so evil? The nuns taught me to always do the right thing – to love people and always be grateful to have them around. What turned him into such a bad man, I wonder?"

"Why, yes, apparently it was your Charity School – but it seems he was a bit of a womaniser even then. She left everything to him and a few short years after leaving the Charity School, he was a rich man and owned a lovely house, not a mansion, of course, but a decent property. He stayed there for a while but then moved to another village as their doctor – but the local people didn't care for him – too many people were dying – so he moved on again. It was easy to follow his movements as a doctor – he would have had quite a high-profile. He's never been short of money since that first woman – and as he's become older, he's become even richer."

"The nuns really failed where he was concerned, didn't they? I'm sure they'd be aghast if they knew what he's done. My God, Peter – that's an incredible story," and then apologised for taking the Lord's name in vain. He just laughed and reached for her hand. They'd already reached this stage and he was trying to pluck up the courage to kiss her, when Lucy came flying over the fields, calling for Sarah.

"You've got to come quickly, Miss – Cook's taken a queer turn and looks quite grey." She was breathless and tugged at Sarah's hand.

Peter left them then and back in the kitchen, Cook was stretched out on the armchair. The kitchen was very hot but not hot enough to turn Cook that fiery colour. "Come on, Cook, you're going to bed for a little rest. Is anything hurting?" Sarah took her arm and helped her up to her room.

"My stomach 'urts, Miss – oh, it 'urts so much." Sarah told Lucy to go and get Cook a big glass of milk – not water, but milk. The nuns had always believed in the healing properties of milk and had taught her the same. Cook drank it quickly and said it did seem to ease the pain.

"No solid food for her, Lucy – just keep giving her drinks and help her to the toilet when she needs to go." Sarah automatically took charge and Lucy asked if she should go and find the doctor.

"Let's just keep things as they are, Lucy – no need to bother the doctor for a stomach ache. Let her sleep for the rest of the day, you and I can manage the meals, can't we?" Lucy went straight down to the kitchen and took charge. Sarah thought what a good girl she was. "Remember Lucy – give her no food or it'll make her worse."

That evening, Lucy took a drink to the Cook's room, only to find the doctor already there. "Where's her supper, girl – we have to feed her up to get her strength back." He was putting some small bottles back into his case and handed the maid one of them. "See that she has a teaspoonful three times a day." He took his doctor's bag and left the room. However, Lucy remembered what Sarah had said and decided not to give Cook any medicine until she'd cleared it with Sarah.

When he got to his study, his wife was there. She was sitting on the sofa and with her, were several people, some of whom he thought he knew. There was Pascoe and Maisie Snell and old Jacob with Mary Patterson and Josiah Morgan. Others were grouped around the sofa, all a bit fuzzy around the edges but they all seemed to know him.

Bill Pascoe stood up. "So, now it's Cook's turn, is it? What have you given her – the same as you gave us, I suppose? Why change things when they're working so well?"

The doctor turned away and put his arm over his eyes. "None of you are real – get you gone and stop bothering me." He left the study and went into the garden. But they were there too, standing amongst the flowers and staring at him. His wife stepped to the front and said, "Bill Smithers down at the farm is very ill we hear and now so is Cook. How could you do it to your own cook – she's been with us for years. I know she's got a bit of money put aside but it can't be as much as you're used to." She laughed suddenly as though she'd just thought of a joke. "Mind you, why am I surprised about Cook – you did it to me, didn't you? Your own wife. I know I was fed up living with you but you really shouldn't have poisoned me. Mind you, my money must have seemed attractive and worth taking the risk for."

"Cook was a mistake – she almost did it to herself by carelessness – nosing about in the cellar where she had no business to be – and now I'll have to finish it for her." He was smiling now, almost relieved to be able to talk about it.

Sarah had gone to the church to find Peter. She wanted to tell him about Cook and she wanted to see him.

"We've got to go straight back, Sarah and make sure she's okay." They arrived at the garden gate and saw the doctor still in the garden. He was sitting on a garden bench beneath a huge Magnolia tree that was in full bloom. The garden looked lovely, full of colour and of roses that smelt beautiful. In fact, it was a picture. The doctor actually seemed to be talking to someone but he was alone in the garden. Sarah and Peter crept closer to the tree just in time to hear him say, "Why don't you all clear off and mind your own business. You're all dead and can't hurt me now."

But his wife said, "Don't be so sure of that Thomas Wilson – we're here to stop your evil killings." He just laughed loudly, but he was scared.

Lucy came out into the garden through the French windows. She was carrying a tray holding cups and saucers and a big pot of tea. "Some tea, doctor?" She couldn't see the ghosts all around him but she did spot Sarah and Peter, although she said nothing to them. She poured him a cup of tea and put the tea pot closer to him so he could have a second cup.

"Thank you, Lucy – you're a good girl," and he drank the tea thirstily, before pouring himself a second cup. Lucy looked over at Peter and Sarah and just smiled. "Come on in and see Cook, Miss Sarah – she's been asking for you. She's feeling a bit better, I gave her nothing to eat, just like you told me." And the maid went back indoors with the governess and curate behind her.

Cook was on the mend and William and Sophie were visiting her in her room. "Sarah, Cook's hungry but Lucy said she can't have any food. Shall I go and get Papa and he'll make her something to eat." William still remembered how his mother went downhill before she died and he didn't want that to happen to the cook.

"You can't do that, William." Sophie was looking out of the bedroom window. "Papa's fallen off his chair in the garden and is lying on the lawn." She didn't really mind what Papa was doing but she didn't want William to have a wasted journey down to the garden.

Lucy had removed the tea tray and washed up everything thoroughly. The doctor was still lying on the grass, but she ignored him and went into the village to get the local policeman, whom she told that the doctor had died.

"Just sitting in the sun, he was. He's been so busy lately – I bet his poor old heart just gave out. Even doctors can't live forever, can they?"

"No, Lucy, that be true – bad luck always seemed to follow that man around – I'm glad I never needed his help or I might not be standing here talking to you."

He made arrangements for the doctor's body to be moved and told his superiors an unfortunate accident had happened to the village doctor. And believe it or not, that was that! But then arsenic was an undetectable poison.

Everyone knew that Lucy had brought some arsenic from the cellar and laced the doctor's tea, everyone who was dead, that is, and they weren't snitching on her. She'd done what had to be done and had probably saved many lives by her actions. Cook knew, Sarah knew, Peter knew but they could never be sure, so they kept quiet. Only Lucy knew and she was much smarter than to mention it. In fact, even the village policeman might have known, but then, he'd always liked Lucy, but not the doctor.

Had all the ghosts surrounding the doctor in the garden and blaming him for their early deaths, have caused an actual heart attack that finished him off? Or was it all in his mind? Either way, it could have been the reason his body let him down. But the arsenic couldn't have done him much good. He had believed they were all there, watching him, people he'd murdered throughout the years and people whose money he'd taken by coercion. He'd only murdered those who finally gave in and agreed to leave him their estates, except his wife, whose belongings came to him as a matter of course. The doctor had however done one decent thing in his life, he'd left all that he owned to his children, who would be well looked after for all of their lives.

Sarah and Peter married a few months later and the vicar gave his permission for Peter to live at the doctor's old house and not at the vicarage. Cook stayed with the newlyweds, as did Lucy who remained unmarried and was proud to be known as the village spinster. Peter and Sarah set up home as a Charity School, but with no nuns. The doctor had left lots of money – none of it earned by him – but by all those people who'd trusted him as their doctor. When William reached 18 years of age, he bequeathed the house and some of the money to Sarah and Peter to keep the school running, and of course to look after their two children.

It looks like a happy ending, doesn't it? None of the ghosts who visited the doctor, ever came to the house again, they'd done what they intended, and stopped him from killing more innocent people. But what do you think happened to the doctor's ghost? He was last seen lying on the grass. At night, when the moon is full, his ghostly outline can still be seen lying on the grass. He has nowhere else to go, you see and his wicked life prevented him from going with the other ghosts to a more pleasant place. He had been too bad a man all his life and suffered the consequences.

Little Ladies Aren't Always What They Seem

"Hot teacakes with lots of butter, please." The two little ladies settled themselves in a secluded corner of the tea shop, but not so secluded that they couldn't see who was coming in and going out of the shop. It was their regular visit to the tea shop, every Wednesday and Friday, their two shopping days in the city. They lived on the outskirts of York and were very proud of the beautiful city that had always been home to them. Two little, elderly but not old ladies who believed they were dressed in the height of fashion, but perhaps a fashion of many years before. Elsie, the waitress brought over fresh cups and saucers and set them down for the ladies. She added side plates and cutlery, and very important for afternoon tea, white linen napkins and a big dish of creamy butter.

"There you are, Ladies – all set. Is there anything else I can get you?" she asked her usual question.

"Just the teacakes please, Elsie," the younger of the two, Rosemary, said giggling. She didn't make many jokes but she always liked to giggle when she did, so that the other person knew it was a joke, and laughed accordingly.

As soon as the hot teacakes arrived on a silver-plated dish, covered by a matching lid, Rebecca made haste to get hers. Rosemary could be so greedy sometimes and she had to ensure she got her fair share of whatever was on the table. The ladies nibbled the cakes, breaking off now and again to wipe the corners of their mouths, with the linen napkins.

"It's your turn to leave sixpence for Elsie, Rebecca – I did it last time." Rosemary was always fair.

"Shall we stroll down by the river and feed the squirrels? They're always hungry at this time of the year."

"They're hungry whatever time of year it is." Her sister replied. "Yes, let's wander that way – it's a fine day." She slipped the sixpence under her saucer and bought two dry teacakes from the counter to give to the squirrels – and the swans, of course.

Down by the banks of the River Ouse, the ladies settled on a bench and tore open the paper bag. Immediately, the squirrels were interested and gathered around the bench. The swans probably knew a treat was coming but swam on in circles – seemingly disinterested.

"Have you brought Alice with you, Rebecca?" The sister bent down and took a small doll from her shopping bag. The doll had long, brown hair and wore a pretty blue dress. She sat between the two ladies on the bench and Rosemary straightened her clothes over her knees. They all sat for a while in companionable silence, a couple of people gave them funny looks, but they didn't care, they were happy.

"Tell you what, Sister – let's wander up to York Minster – I do love looking around there and the sun – if anything – is getting hotter. The cathedral will be lovely and cool." Off they went, doll fitted comfortably in the bag and climbed the steps of the Cathedral. The peace and tranquillity immediately calmed them down, no matter how many times they came here, it was always like the first time. The majesty of the high arches caused an echoing silence to invade the aisles and the sisters slowly walked down the centre aisle. At the side, they came across a young girl with long blond hair and wearing a cherry red sweater – her trousers were like those Rupert Bear wore. She was an artist and she was drawing the 'Rose Window' famous for its beauty and historic background. It was a very old stained-glass circle of beautiful glass mosaic and it was to commemorate the Wars of the Roses, white for York and red for Lancaster. It was an intricate thing to draw but she was making a good job of it.

Rosemary touched the girl gently on the shoulder and she turned around, startled and with a quizzical look in her eyes. "Who do you think should have won the war then? York or Lancaster?" The girl looked back at her drawing. "Oh, I don't mind – one of them had to win, didn't they?" She obviously wasn't interested in history – but just in the beauty of the Rose Window.

Rosemary went on, "Do you know, it was burnt very badly when someone started a fire. The window smashed to pieces in the intense heat – there were forty-thousand pieces of broken glass, which with painstaking patience were gathered up and after four years of hard graft – and a cost of two million pounds – it was as beautiful as when it was first made, perhaps, even more beautiful. What's your name then – it's not Rose, is it?" Rosemary was smiling at the girl, but Rebecca could see she was losing patience with the old lady who wouldn't leave her alone to get on with her work.

"Come on, Rosemary, let's move on and let the young lady get on with her labour of love. Are you an art student, my dear?" she couldn't resist asking.

"I am and my name's Janet. It's been nice talking with you but I must get on." She turned her back on the ladies and Rebecca immediately walked further down – deeper into the cathedral. Rosemary dawdled for a bit and then waved goodbye to the girl and followed her sister. "I think she was a bit rude, don't you?" she said. "It's a good thing my 'voices' spoke to me and told me what needed to be done." Rebecca tried to ignore her, as she always did when Rosemary mentioned her 'voices' – it was usually a cause for some concern.

They spent a good hour wandering about and reading the inscriptions, even Alice was allowed to come out of the bag to see the magnificent building, especially the Rose Window. Back in her bag, they took Alice home and sat her on the big chair by the fireside. She'd be tired with all that walking, they knew but the fresh air would do her good.

Next morning, Rebecca was first downstairs. She filled the kettle and then noticed that Alice had moved from the armchair and was sitting at the table, obviously expecting breakfast. "Oh no, Alice," she told the doll, "this isn't your day – you had yours yesterday," and she carried the doll into the spare bedroom where the rest of the dolls were.

There were eight of them, sitting around the room; beautiful dolls dressed in pretty clothes. They were the sisters' pride and joy – two lonely old spinsters who loved the dolls as though they were children. Well, they were children to them.

"I think it's Catherine's turn today," and she took a very cute, blond haired doll into the kitchen and propped her on a chair by the table. Rosemary appeared at this point, a very grumpy Rosemary but then she just wasn't a morning person. She did manage to say however, "Good Morning, Catherine – your turn today, is it?" And she patted the doll on the head.

"That's the paper boy, Rosemary. Fetch the paper, will you?" Rebecca was preparing homemade soup for lunch. Reluctantly, Rosemary went into the hall, scooped the paper from the floor and, without looking at it, brought it into the kitchen. Rebecca stopped what she was doing and without drying her hands, opened the rolled-up newspaper.

"Oh my God, Rosemary – look at the front page." Rosemary peered at it through half-closed eyes.

'YOUNG STUDENT FOUND STABBED TO DEATH IN YORK CATHEDRAL'

A young girl was found yesterday in York Cathedral. She'd been stabbed to death by an unknown hand. Janet Jones was 18 years of age and an art student at the University. She'd been sketching the Rose Window, one of the most popular attractions in the cathedral. There is nothing known as to the reason for the attack so if you were around the cathedral at any time yesterday, you should contact the police immediately. You may think you saw nothing, but what you did see, might help in finding the killer.

Rosemary's eyes were wide open now and the two sisters stared at each other. "Well, I never..." Rosemary didn't know what else to say and Rebecca just plonked herself down on a chair and covered her face with her hands.

"What should we do, Rebecca?" Rosemary poured herself a cup of tea and fetched another cup for her sister.

"Well, it's obvious, isn't it? We'll have to contact the police and tell them we were there in the afternoon." She got up and made for the telephone in the hall. Rosemary could hear her saying, "Yes Officer, we'll be here this afternoon. We'll look forward to seeing you then." And she hung up. Rosemary had already left the kitchen to get dressed so Rebecca turned to Catherine and lifted her from the chair to cuddle her. "What is the world coming to Catherine – in a church, of all places. Poor young girl – she was so young and pretty." Catherine just stared straight ahead.

A young policeman arrived at three o'clock that afternoon and Rosemary hurried to make a pot of tea. "Biscuit, Officer?" She held out a plate of chocolate fingers. Rebecca plumped up the cushion behind him and managed to knock his notebook from his hands onto the floor.

"I'm so sorry, Officer – now, how can we help?" She sat opposite him on the sofa. "My sister and I were both in the cathedral yesterday and we even spoke with the young girl who's been murdered. She was very nice, wasn't she Rosemary?"

Rosemary sat down too and said, "Well, I thought she was a bit standoffish – she obviously wanted us to go away." She didn't like being slighted by anyone or thinking she'd been slighted.

"Don't be silly, Sister – she was busy with her sketch and we were interrupting her."

"Why do you think she was slighting you?" the policeman asked Rosemary. "Did she say anything unusual to make you think that?"

"No, it wasn't what she said, so much as how she looked at me. The spotlight was on her and she rather enjoyed it." I was just about to show her Alice but decided against it as she didn't deserve it." Rebecca laughed and explained to the policeman that Alice was a doll not a person. "We always take one of our dolls with us when we go out for the day. They're such a comfort to us."

The policeman coughed in an embarrassed way and stood up, after finishing his tea. "Well, thank you ladies for contacting us in the first place and for seeing me today. If I need anything else, I'll get in touch with you." He left the house quickly, believing he'd just been with two, old harmless eccentrics.

"No, Sergeant," he said when he got back to the station, "nothing there. Just two old dotty women who happened to meet the girl in the cathedral. They'll not be of any use to us, I'm afraid." And he filed his report.

Back in the sun-filled room, the two sisters were watching a television programme. Rosemary suddenly piped up with, "I think it's time for one of your visits to the shop in the Shambles. Perhaps we could go on Friday and have tea from Elsie again. I always enjoy that so much."

"Of course, Rosemary, we'll have to visit the York Shambles for one of our purchases." Rebecca always tried to agree with her sister. It made life easier in the long run. "You can choose which one of our little girls to take. We can have a wander afterwards and show her the city."

On Friday, they did just that and Rosemary stayed down by the river with Belinda, whilst her sister went to the shop at the top of the Shambles to order a new doll for their collection. She loved the Shambles. When she walked up that twisted lane, she could almost hear the voices from the past selling their wares and smell the meats that were being sold, after slaughtering the animals out the back. Apparently, the Shambles used to be called 'The Great Flesh Shambles' for obvious reasons and she'd read somewhere that Harry Potter's Diagon Alley in the book was based on The Shambles in York, easy to believe really, it truly looked the part.

She reached the shop and was looking forward to ordering the new doll. She knew exactly what she wanted and she was sure Rosemary would approve. "It'll take about three weeks to design her, make her and dress her. Is three weeks okay?" the lady in the shop asked. She knew the sisters as they'd had lots of dolls made in her shop and they were good customers. "Have a seat over there, Miss

Rebecca – and I'll just get my notebook and patterns so we can make up the order." Rebecca settled herself and wondered what Rosemary was getting up to by the river. Well, at least she had Belinda with her, to keep her out of mischief. She smiled to herself.

Business over, she made her way down through the Shambles and could see Rosemary and Belinda in the distance. They were chatting to a young boy and girl. *Oh God, I wonder what she's saying,* was her first thought.

They were actually talking about the Shambles and Rosemary was showing off her knowledge to her heart's content, she knew all about the Shambles. "It was already there in 1475, in fact, it was mentioned in the Domesday Book in 1086 when William the Conqueror invaded this country. Doesn't that make it old, children?"

Rebecca interrupted with, "Have you told them about No. 10 in the middle of the Shambles?"

"I was just getting to that when you interrupted me." She turned her attention back to the children. "Yes, about No. 10 – there is a shrine in that house to Saint Margaret Clitherow, who used to help priests escape from the authorities in the middle ages, when Catholics and Protestants fought with each other. The shrine stands exactly on the spot where the 'escape' fireplace stood. She hid the fugitives there, you see. Remember the time when Guy Fawkes tried to blow up the Houses of Parliament? Yes, I thought you'd remember that. Bloodthirsty, like all children."

A woman's voice was heard calling to the children, telling them to come over. "We've got to go, Miss but thank you for telling us all those things." They were polite children and even if they weren't interested, they pretended they were.

"Why do you always lecture young people? You frighten them off sometimes, you know."

Rebecca sat on the bench beside Belinda. "I know you were a teacher and it's how you choose to communicate with children but can't you forget your teaching years now and again?"

On being told the new doll would take three weeks, she glowered at her sister and said, "You never do anything right, do you?" She liked to have the last word and Rebecca usually let her.

The days passed, the police hadn't caught the murderer from York Cathedral but then they hadn't had much luck in finding the perpetrator of several other murders that happened over the width and breadth of North Yorkshire. Despite a much larger police presence than normal, and constables and detectives borrowed from other areas, they'd had no luck so far. The two little ladies had been questioned again in case they'd spotted something of which they weren't aware, but that fell flat too. Well into summer, the gardens were beautiful and the two sisters often wandered around the city, searching for plants they hadn't seen before. They always took a different doll from the Doll's Room to get some fresh air and see different things.

The Doll's Room was the prettiest room in the house and the sisters loved sitting there with them all. Sometimes, they took afternoon tea in the midst of their little girls. There was even a doll's tea set which was laid out as though for tea but they never did anything like filling the small teapot for the girls. They were eccentric, but not mad, as they liked to tell each other. They changed the dolls' clothes regularly as it was the right thing to do and they needed washing to freshen them nicely.

They were sitting in the Dolls' Room one afternoon when Rebecca said, "I'm to pick up our new doll tomorrow. We should do something to celebrate, don't you think? Once we see her, we'll know what to call her – a very important thing to get right."

"I think we should, in fact, I was just reading an interesting article about Mother Shipton's Cave in Knaresborough – you know where the well there turns everyday items into stone – and you're supposed to make a wish when you visit. Shall we Rebecca – shall we? We could take a coach trip and a picnic tea – apparently there's beautiful woods all around the area. What do you think?" Rosemary was getting quite excited and lifted Mary, a sweet little doll, and twirled around the room with her.

"I think that's an excellent idea, Sister – I'll book the coach tickets on the phone," and she left the room. Rosemary stayed and talked to all the little dolls – she talked about the weather and about the state of the economy. Nothing was too high brow for her little pupils.

Before going to the coach station, the sisters went up the Shambles to the Doll's Shop at the top. The lady assistant was expecting them and she'd laid on some tea and biscuits. They were very special and regular customers who spent a lot of money on their dolls. She came from the back of the shop with a large white box.

"Well, here she is, ladies – dressed just as you instructed." She opened the box and lifted out a most beautiful doll with very long, blond hair that hung half way down her back. With Rupert Bear trousers and white sneakers, the doll wore a lovely, hand-knitted cherry red jumper. She looked amazing. Rosemary gasped and reached out for her. "What a pretty face – she reminds me of someone but I can't think of whom." Rebecca paid the shop owner and the sisters left the shop, proudly carrying the new doll.

"Does she remind you of anyone, Rebecca?" Rosemary asked.

"No, I don't think so – but strangely enough, when I described what I wanted to the lady in the shop, I realised I was describing someone I'd seen." Rebecca looked puzzled.

"I know who it is – it's that young girl we met in the cathedral last month – the one who was murdered."

"I do believe you're right, Sister – now, I wonder what made me do that. Strange, isn't it?"

The conversation came to an end as they reached the coach station and climbed aboard, carrying the doll very carefully. Settled in the comfortable seats,

Rosemary said, "Do you think it would be callus of us to call her 'Janet' after that girl? We haven't got a Janet yet."

"I don't think so, Sister – in fact, it's really a compliment, I feel." Rebecca patted the new doll's long, shiny hair, sat back in the seat and closed her eyes. Rosemary cuddled the doll to her chest and opened a chocolate biscuit.

On getting off the coach, the first thing they noticed was the beautiful woodland trees that greeted them. It really was a beautiful part of the Royal Forest of Knaresborough. The actual cave, known as Mother Shipton's Cave and the Petrifying Well stood alongside the River Nidd, as did the Wishing Well where you must make a wish before leaving the area.

The guide went on:

"See all the objects hanging from rope and tree branches – these have been left there by previous visitors, who tend to come back some time later, to see what the mystical powers of the water has done to their possessions. You'll see hanging there, baby's rattles, little teddy bears, keys, pretty dolls, books, plastic ducks and many more things that people just happened to have with them when they came here. It really is magical and has been working its magic since medieval times – and perhaps before that.

"This cave is where Mother Shipton was born in 1488. Even as a child, she looked most odd but as she grew to adulthood, things got worse. She had a large and crooked nose; her back was very bent and her legs were twisted – very much like a picture of a witch. She lived here, season after season – braving the elements and making prophecies which came true as the years passed. In this backwater place, she thrived and became famous throughout England. She prophesised the Defeat of the Spanish Armada 1589, in Elizabeth I's reign – although she'd lived many years before then. She prophesised that the Great Fire of London would happen and that didn't happen till 1666. She foretold many people's fortunes and she was so accurate that people came from all over England to see her. And this was how she made her living by allowing people to make donations for her comfort, such as it was."

He then invited the visitors to look inside the cave to experience the atmosphere where she'd lived and also to throw some money in the Wishing Well. "It does no harm to hedge your bets – that wish just might come true." The guide was good at his job.

Standing in the eerie blackness of the cave, Rosemary clutched Janet close to her chest. "Don't worry, dear, everything will be all right. I'm with you." Rebecca was examining the hanging tributes to Mother Shipton and she exclaimed, "They really have turned to stone – how amazing is that?"

A young voice spoke from the back of the cave, "I don't think it's amazing at all. It's called calcifying, that's all. Any idiot knows it's not mystical – just a natural event." She emerged into the light of the cave entrance and looked haughtily at the two spinsters. "Were there no schools or education in your day?"

"There were most certainly schools and education – but also manners – which your school obviously didn't specialise in." Rebecca chastised her but the girl just smirked.

"She's not on our coach, is she?" Rosemary asked later. "Best make sure we don't sit near her, or I just may have to kill her." Rosemary was cross at the girl's lack of manners.

Down by the Wishing Well, the girl was showing off again. "Old Mother Shipton's not getting my money, I'll tell you that for nothing."

Rosemary sidled up to her and said, "My dear, didn't you have a red scarf when you were in the cave?" The girl rushed back to the cave and went inside – Rosemary and Janet followed her more slowly – but in time to catch up with her there. It was most probably the echo inside the cave, but Rosemary thought she heard her 'voices' whispering in her ear. But perhaps not.

"Come along ladies – all together now. Just time for our stop for tea at the Service Station."

The coach left the enchanted woodland and made its way to the Service Station, half way from their home. "A good thing that rude young girl is on the other coach – with luck, we'll never have to see her again." She'd obviously irritated the guide as well.

Kicking their shoes off that evening, the sisters discussed what a good day it had been. "I believe she could tell prophecies and what a magical place to live." Rosemary was quite excited still. Rebecca looked at her closely. "Rosemary, you haven't done anything wrong today, have you?"

"Certainly not, Rebecca – please will you take Janet back to her room, so she can have a girly chat with the others and tell them about Mother Shipton's Cave? I know they'll all be interested." And Rebecca lifted the doll, and again, the cherry red sweater reminded her of the girl in the cathedral.

The television news that night was interesting, especially when the newscaster got to his last item:

'A young girl was found in the cave at Mother Shipton's site at Knaresborough tonight. She'd been viciously murdered, attacked and left for dead. The police are searching the countryside for clues and trying to contact everyone who'd been in that location today. The murder instrument was found with the body.'

Rebecca looked directly at her sister. "Rosemary, what have you done?" But Rosemary just smiled and said, "I think you should pay a visit to the Doll's Shop at the Shambles, don't you? They take so long to produce one, don't they? It would be best to make the order now."

"Golly," said the lady in the shop, "you lose no time, do you? Are you ready for another doll already? I wish more of my customers were like you and I'd be able to retire." She made notes of the kind of doll that was wanted.

Rebecca walked slowly back down the Shambles to the city centre. She was very deep in thought and knew she had to make a decision one way or the other. She went into the tea room and Elsie served her as usual. "Just one teacake today, Elsie – I've left Rosemary at home." When she'd finished her tea, she gave Elsie her usual sixpence for a tip but Elsie caught her arm before she got to the door. "Miss, I hope you'll forgive me for talking about this, but I've known you for years and I thought you'd like to know. The police were making enquiries in here yesterday and they spoke with me. They asked me about you and your sister and I told them what lovely ladies you were – and that's all I said. But I thought you should know."

Rebecca was shocked but thanked the waitress and went on her way. She arrived home after paying a quick visit to the chemist. It would save her having to go out again later.

Rosemary was pulling some weeds from the cracks in the front path and she went straight into the dolls' room. She thought she'd heard whispering from the room before she turned the door handle. Sure enough, some of the dolls had been moved. She asked, "Has Rosemary been in to see you girls and moved you about?" She heard soft giggling in her ears and knew that they were all listening to her.

"I don't know what to do, girls. I have to do something, you know – I can't let the police come here and question Rosemary. I could cope with it, but I doubt she could." She lifted one of the dolls onto her lap and lay back against the upholstery. "Tell me then what do you think? I need help."

For the first time ever, she heard the 'voices' that Rosemary regularly heard. "You've got to do something about her, you know that, don't you?" Little Mary spoke from rosebud lips and slid down from her chair onto the floor. "She can't be allowed to go on doing what she's doing."

"I know that Mary, but what am I supposed to do?" Rebecca was crying because she really knew the answer to that. She stood up and said goodnight to the dolls, before she joined Rosemary who'd come in from the garden.

"Would you care for a cup of cocoa, Rosemary?" she asked.

"Oh, yes please, Sister – that would be lovely. Whilst you're making it, I'll just nip upstairs and get changed. These trousers are all muddy." On coming back downstairs, two steaming cups of cocoa were sitting on the coffee table, with a plate of Chocolate Digestives of course. They sat on the sofa together and Rebecca put her arm around her sister's shoulders. "Oh, do get off, Rebecca, you'll make me spill my drink." Rosemary was getting tired and grumpy.

"I'll leave you alone if you tell me what you did yesterday," Rebecca insisted.

"You know what I did yesterday – you were with me. You're being quite tiresome, Sister – I think I'll take my drink upstairs to finish." She made to get up but Rebecca held her back and said, "I want to know the truth, dear – when you followed the girl into the cave to help her find her scarf, what did you do?" Rebecca was insistent.

"Well, she was a horrid, rude girl, you can't deny it. I crept up behind her and took my hat off – I used the long hatpin with the pearl end and pushed it right through her ear. It wasn't difficult, it was very sharp. I don't think she suffered 'cause she just sank to the floor and gave a long sigh. The only thing was, I couldn't get my pin out of her ear and I had to leave it there. *Bother,* I thought." And she finished her cocoa, every last drop and stood up. "Goodnight, dear – see you in the morning."

"Goodnight, Rosemary – have a good sleep. That hot drink will help." Rebecca knew she'd have a good sleep because she'd crushed a handful of sleeping pills she'd got from the chemist and stirred them into the cocoa. Lots of sugar hid their taste and the job was done.

She went up to bed herself then and crawled under the covers, exhausted. She wasn't ashamed of what she'd done – she knew it had to be done – but she was very sad at the thought of losing Rosemary and that it had to be done by her own hand, or more young girls would have died in the months and years ahead.

She was awoken next morning by a loud banging on the door. She put on her dressing gown and went downstairs. It was two detectives standing on the step with a young constable in uniform by the gate. They asked where her sister was and on being told she was still asleep, they asked her to go and wake her. Rebecca was only gone for a few moments, before returning and saying, "You'd better come upstairs with me. I can't seem to waken her." They all went upstairs to the bedroom.

"Yes, she's dead, sir," one of the men said, "and I've already phoned for the doctor and for forensic. It looks as if she died in her sleep but of course, that will have to be established later. And there were several long hatpins lying on the dressing table, one very like the pearl one that was used to kill the girl. Best come on downstairs with me, Miss." He said to Rebecca and took her arm.

"I'll just have to see the girls are all right and I'll follow you into the sitting room. Would you like some coffee, by the way?" She asked as if everything was normal.

He followed her into the dolls' room and was astounded to see so many dolls on display. They were beautifully dressed and seemed to be having some tea with a small set of cups and saucers. "Aren't they pretty?" She touched one of the doll's hair. "And there's one for every young girl she killed. She only picked unpleasant or rude ones – she used to say the world was a better place without them. And we did replace the dead girls with a newly made doll – as a replacement, you see." She opened a closet door and told him to look inside. "You should see them all so you have a true picture."

There were shelves inside the closet with several more dolls sitting in lines, all looking straight ahead. "We change them about, you see and give each one a chance to come out for some fresh air – and sometimes, we take them for a walk – it does them good." Rebecca loved her dolls – just as Rosemary had done.

"Get dressed, Miss please. I'm going to have to ask you to accompany me down to the police station where we'd like to ask you some questions." He felt awkward telling this to an elderly spinster.

"If I have to leave the house, I'll have to get one of my little girls to take with me. I very rarely leave the house without one of them." He told her, "Just one of them – and these mugs on the table?" He had spotted the mugs, still with some sediment at the bottom. "Oh, that's just our mugs from last night when we had our cocoa."

"We'll take them along too," and he put the mugs into a plastic bag which he took from his pocket.

The trial followed Rebecca's arrest and she was found guilty of being an accessory after the fact – she was always aware of every murder that took place – and doing absolutely nothing to stop them. She was as guilty as her sister. In fact the case blew open a very wide investigation into murders of girls all over England – spread over the country from John O' Groats to Land's End. There was a high number of unsolved murders that the police were now able to link with all the schools where Rosemary had been employed. She'd been a mobile teacher with no fixed contract, so she'd seen a lot of the country until such time as she retired. And of course, her sister always went with her.

When she was sent to prison, it was to be for the rest of her life and she was allowed to take her one doll with her. This wasn't usual but she was an eccentric, elderly woman who had no friends or relatives. The dolls were auctioned off, and the house as well, with the money going to a charity for the victims of murders. In fact, the value of even the smallest doll increased dramatically once people realised its association with a serial killer.

The whole business was wrapped up quite neatly and Rebecca actually came to like her cell and her daily walks in the prison yard. She always took her doll with her when she left her cell.

She allowed the little girl to sit on the window ledge when in the cell and watch the world go by through the iron bars. She held conversations with her and was quite satisfied with the answers she got. Sometimes, the warden would listen to the conversations and on a couple of occasions, he was sure he heard the doll answer but he never told anyone about that, or they'd have called him eccentric as well.

"Come on, Miss, time to stretch your legs in the yard." He called to her through the open slit in the door.

"Yes, Officer, I'm just putting on my little girl's coat – it's cold today." A voice whispered in her ear, "Put on your coat too, Mama – or you'll catch a chill." When they left with the warden, they were both dressed suitably for winter – mother and daughter together.

What Goes Around Comes Around

Her ivory silk dress swayed gently to the floor. It was a creamy soft colour as were her shoes which peeped out from beneath the hemline. Her dark hair was dressed in a chignon with glossy tendrils cascading down her cheeks, all falling from a small silver tiara and her pearls were glowing with a bright, shiny lustre. She really was a beautiful bride, married only for two hours, she felt her happiness could know no bounds. She smoothed the folds of the dress across her hips and looked at the large, oval mirror fixed to the wall. She saw nothing; no bridal image, no silk dress and no happy smile. The mirror was empty except for the reflection of a chair at the top of the winding stairs of the hotel, reaching down to the lobby below. She looked down at her shoes and fingered the lovely dress. Everything was clear as she looked down at the soft material but when she looked again at the mirror, there was nothing. It was as though she didn't exist.

At the bottom of the long winding staircase, she could see a group of wedding guests gathered round in a circle and all chattering at once. She could hear the words, 'How could it happen? She must have tripped on her long dress. Poor girl.' And she realised they were talking about her. One man left the circle and she could see herself then, lying in a crumpled heap with her limbs bent at awkward angles. What on earth has happened, she wondered. She couldn't remember falling down the stairs and she'd known to be careful of her dress. Her new husband, Tom, suddenly came flying out of the first bedroom along the corridor. "What's happened? Where is Lucy?" He rushed right through his bride as though she didn't exist; as it appears, she didn't. He ran down the stairs and threw himself onto the floor by her side.

"Lucy?" he shouted and tried to lift her up but a couple of men stopped him. "We've already sent for the ambulance – don't move her just yet." Tom was frantic and looked ashen. He was pulling at his own hair and brushing tears from his face. "How did she fall? Why did she?" He kept smoothing back her hair from her forehead until a lady bent down and took his hands in hers. Someone had brought a brandy for him and made sure he drank it. The ambulance arrived. It had been quick and two paramedics jumped from it and crossed the hotel lobby. They tried everything to resuscitate her but to no avail. Lucy was dead and her husband of two hours was broken-hearted.

The other Lucy at the top of the stairs watched, as they lifted her body onto a stretcher and carried her from the hotel. Tom was left sitting in an armchair with several people around him. They'd only met each other six months before and it had been a whirlwind romance. They'd decided they were right for each other and saw no reason to wait. They were both in their mid-twenties and had had earlier romances, so what was there to wait for? Money wasn't a problem as Lucy had a Trust Fund set up by her late uncle and she'd also just inherited a goodly sum. Life was their oyster and they'd have many happy years ahead, so why waste time now?

She turned to the mirror again but could still see nothing. A young maid ran straight through her, hurrying to tidy up the sad bedroom. The hotel manager walked through her then and ran down stairs to check on Tom. Lucy had never felt so alone. No one could see her and she knew now, she just didn't exist. She ventured down the stairs and circulated amongst the shocked people, who'd been her friends. She caught snatches of conversation like, 'What on earth could have happened? Where was Tom when she started to come downstairs? He must still have been in the bedroom.' Many voices were talking at once and one man, the best man, said, "Tom will have to come back to our house. We can't leave him here after what's happened." He walked over to the groom and told him what was going to happen. Tom appeared to be in a daze and allowed decisions to be made for him without question.

Lucy knelt down by his side and stared into his eyes. Her memory was beginning to be clearer – she vaguely remembered his coming up behind her and putting his hands on her shoulders, but instead of hugging her as she'd expected, he swiftly turned her around and pushed her to the top of the stairs. He forced her down and she of course, lost her footing and fell headlong down the stairs. She remembered now – it was a most scary experience and then she blacked out and lost consciousness. When she'd finally arrived at the bottom, her mind told her she was dead – she hadn't survived the fall and now there was nothing. She saw herself however, at the top of the stairs with Tom still standing behind her. He turned quickly and fled along the corridor, presumably back to his room.

Downstairs, Lucy's ghostly eyes stared into his and he began to shiver and shake. His friends gathered even closer around him and got him to his feet and away out of the hotel. If he couldn't see her, he certainly had felt her presence. Amazing that. Although she was a ghost, she could still affect some people, Tom being one. Why had he killed her? They'd been married for such a short time and she had genuinely thought he loved her. He'd taken a bit of a risk really as she might not have died in the fall, but when she looked up at the height of the staircase, she realised there was a pretty strong chance that she would. And if she hadn't, who would believe that he'd pushed her, more likely that she'd tripped on her dress.

She thought herself back at the top of the stairs and suddenly she was there. Being a ghost had some compensations. She saw the little maid going into the bridal bedroom and thought herself inside with her. The maid was tidying up the room as it had been left in a bit of a mess and Lucy watched her folding some clothes and towels and then she saw her picking up some jewellery that had been left on the dressing table. Two large-stoned rings disappeared into the maid's pocket and so did another pearl necklace – similar to the one the bride was wearing – but not before she'd rubbed it against her teeth to make sure it was worth stealing. Yes, it was, and so it went into the pocket too. She then got on with straightening the room and went outside into the corridor. The hotel manager was there, looking for her. "Oh, good girl, you've already tidied the room – her husband or a friend will be coming back tomorrow to collect the bride's things, and we mustn't let them see the room in disarray. Well done – now off you go down to the kitchen – the cook has prepared some tea for those involved in the incident – they're all very jittery." He followed her downstairs.

Two other maids were seated at the kitchen table and were already well through the scones and cake served by Cook, Grace joined them and helped herself to some food. Cook poured her a big cup of tea. The hotel manager decided to sit at the table too. Although normally, he had meals in his office but today had been so strange, he didn't want to be alone. The old grey cat was asleep by the range but got up when Grace came in. He crossed from the warm spot by the fire and stretched his paws up towards Grace's dress. She tried to scat him away but something was driving him to scratch at the maid's dress. What no one could see was the bride in all her finery bent down towards the cat and stared directly into his eyes. She was goading him to do something and he wasn't sure what, but he kept on tugging at Grace's dress. Suddenly, a load of beautiful pearls spilled out of her pocket and ran all over the floor. She jumped up and started to gather them, but it was too late and it was like a snow storm with flakes falling everywhere. The hotel manager jumped up and said, "Where did you get those, Grace – they look like real pearls to me. They must be very valuable." He picked one up and rubbed it across his teeth. "Yes, they are real pearls. Where on earth did they come from and what else do you have in that pocket?" It didn't take him long to work out they must have come from the bridal suite, where he'd last seen the maid tidying up. He spoke to one of the other girls, "Put your hand in her pocket and show me what else is there." The maid did as she was told and pulled out two lovely – and very large – golden rings, one with an emerald stone and the other with a ruby. Worth a lot of money, he was sure. "Ring for the police," he told one of the girls, "and tell them we'll hold onto the culprit until they arrive."

Lucy stood up and smoothed down her long silk dress. That was a job well done or else the little thief would have got away with everything. She thought for the second time that being a ghost had its good points. Then she spotted a little girl dressed in pink pyjamas and a long dressing gown; her hair was in two pigtails and she looked about seven years old. They were both ghosts and no one else in the room could see them. The girl smiled at Lucy and said, "Hello." Lucy could hear her clearly and she walked towards her as she leaned against the kitchen door. "Who are you, child and what are you doing here?" The folk in the kitchen were still in a turmoil and trying to pick up the rolling pearls. Grace, the maid was sitting on a chair by the table. She looked very frightened and her skin was ashen. She was suffering because of being caught or because she'd committed the crime in the first place. Either way, the police were on their way.

The young girl looked directly at Lucy and said, "How did you know she had the jewellery in her pocket and how did you get the cat to do what you wanted?"

116

Lucy explained that she'd been in the bedroom when the girl pocketed them, and that she'd been the bride who fell down the stairs. "Yes," the girl replied, "I saw that happening. Poor you! That man was very cruel to push you like he did – I watched him and he seemed to be enjoying it. Who was he and why did he do it?"

"That man was my husband. We'd only been married for a few hours and why he did it, I don't know but I remember it all now. I didn't trip at the top of the stairs – he took me by the shoulders and pushed me over the top stair." She sat down on the floor beside the girl.

"Why are you here? Did you die in the hotel – how did it happen?"

"Oh, my nanny drowned me in the bath. She was left in charge one night while my parents went to a dinner party and she just went mad. She liked to drink my dad's whisky and it seemed to make her behave very strangely. That night, she got very angry and pushed me into the full bath, still in my pyjamas. I don't know why – but she told everyone, I'd climbed into the bath and hit my head on the taps. To make it look real, she even hit me on the head with a heavy lamp. Now I have to stay in this hotel until she comes back here and I prove what she did." She nodded her head wisely. "You're going to have to haunt this hotel until your man comes back and you get the chance to deal with him."

Lucy felt even more depressed and sad. What a future! "Cheer up," the girl told her, "Being a ghost here is not so bad. You know everything that's going on and you can even get involved in different things. I'll show you the way, if you like."

The girl was called Elizabeth and she was indeed, seven years old. The two ghosts – although so very different – appealed to one another and formed a friendship then and there.

"How will I ever make my husband come back here so I can deal with him?" Lucy was not optimistic.

"You'd be surprised – time passes so quickly – and your chance will come." It was impossible not to feel better when the girl spoke like this – she had obviously been a happy child.

Next day, the two ghosts were hanging around the hotel lobby when Tom and Lucy's mother came down the stairs. They'd been clearing out the bride's belongings and were looking for the manager to thank him for his help. They were discussing Lucy's fall and her mother was saying, "I can't believe it, Tom, she was always so careful – to trip over her own dress seems so out of character." She was dabbing her eyes with a handkerchief and Tom put his arm around her shoulders. Lucy darted forward and tried to push him off but of course, she could make little difference. She stared into his eyes however, and truth to tell, he looked most uncomfortable and removed his arm from her mother.

"We'll have to see the lawyer. Tom – and get everything sorted out. Her Trust and will, I mean."

"Of course, we will, Mother – but we'll get to that in due course." He looked smug when he said that and then Lucy knew. He'd killed her for the money – she should have realised that – only two hours after the ceremony. It had been he who'd insisted they sort out their finances before the wedding, and everything went to him. She was supposed to live with him for the rest of her life and it was right that all her money and belongings would be his. He even had the audacity to call her mother, mother. This made her even more furious and she vowed to get her own back on him. He hurried the older woman out of the hotel doors and into a waiting taxi. He was gone, with everything that had belonged to her, even controlling her dear mother.

A few months passed and the bride and the child wandered all over the hotel, peeping in some rooms and listening to many conversations. Elizabeth taught Lucy some of the tricks of being a ghost; things she'd learned to do in the years when she was alone as the hotel ghost. There were times when some people caught a glimpse of them as they ran up and down the corridors, giggling as they went, but mostly they were invisible to all the people and they could keep a watchful eye on what was going on in the hotel. Lucy had tried to go out into the street a few times, but a barrier stopped her just at the revolving door. Elizabeth was right, they couldn't leave the place where they'd died until they'd achieved a just punishment for their killers, i.e. their deaths.

One afternoon, they were resting in the lobby, watching everyone come and go when Lucy caught sight of two waiters whispering in a corner. She moved closer so she could hear them.

"Is Mary in the room now, waiting with the baby?" One of them said.

"Yes, she's there and she has the baby. She's got nappies and food too – so everything is going all right," his friend whispered back. "I told her we'd come up and give her a break at five. Okay?"

They smiled and walked away from each other. Lucy thought what a strange conversation it was. A baby in a hotel room. How odd! She told Elizabeth and they both made their way up to the attic floor where some members of staff slept. They went along the passage, popping their heads through the doors to see who was inside. It was a ghost's prerogative after all. Not being nosey, just watchful. And there she was, young Mary with a sweet little baby of about six months. It obviously wasn't her baby as she was only a girl and she was holding the baby awkwardly, as if she wasn't used to it. They hung about only long enough to see everything was all right and then thought themselves back to the lobby, where the waiters were still serving afternoon tea in the lounge.

As the two men passed each other, they continued a very broken conversation. One said, "It's okay, Billy has delivered the ransom note to the parents – now we just have to wait."

My God, they'd kidnapped a baby and were demanding money for its return. The two ghosts didn't know what to do but they knew they'd have to do something. The daily newspapers were still lying around the lobby table and they started to read. They didn't have to read too much before they found it, 'BABY KIDNAPPED FROM HER OWN COT'.

They stared into each other's eyes. Elizabeth asked, "What shall we do?"

The other waiter came up to his friend and said, "It's not going all right – the ransom has been refused – they say they don't have the money." The other man kicked the table and swore. "Let's give them till tomorrow and see what happens. We can't keep the baby here for too long or someone will find out. We'll just have to get rid of it if the parents don't pay up. Okay?"

"Okay," was the reply. "But when you say 'get rid of it' – what exactly do you mean?"

"You know what I mean," and he made a thumbs down sign.

The two ghosts were desperate now to tell the outside world that the baby was in the hotel – but how to do it? "A message," Lucy said. "We've got to get a message outside but neither of us can go outside." She looked at Elizabeth who'd only been seven when she died but she was a smart child and she was looking thoughtful.

"Lucy, I think it's time to show you how to move things with just willpower. It will take a while to perfect it, but it's quite possible. You have to focus on an object – a light object, that is – and keep focusing on it, willing it to move – and after a while, you can do it. It'll move – not very far but at least it'll move. Watch me and I'll show you." And the little girl bent over the coffee table and stared at the small magazine lying there, she stared and stared, and the magazine actually fell off the table onto the floor.

"Did you really do that, Elizabeth?" Lucy was amazed. "Let me try, will you?" She chose a journal lying on the same table and stared at it, focussing with all her might. Nothing happened and Elizabeth told her to focus even harder. The journal moved slightly and then just flew off the table. "Cor blimey Lucy, you must have been strong when you were alive." Elizabeth praised her friend.

"Okay, I understand but what's the rest of your plan?"

"Well, we come down during the night and go to the reception desk – move the pen and write a big message across the register – something like, 'Missing baby is here – fetch the police'. I'm sure between us, we can manage that." Elizabeth was quite excited and put her fist to her mouth with excitement.

"That's absolutely brilliant," Lucy said. "Let's do it tonight." And the two girls took a final look in the attic room, to make sure the baby was still all right. The plan worked beautifully and soon they were in the dark lobby, pen in Lucy's hand. The register was lying open and much of it was still blank. The focussing began and soon the message was scrawled across the page – just as they had planned.

'Missing baby is here – on the attic floor – fetch the police'. And that's exactly what happened. The receptionist arrived for work and rang the police immediately. The ghosts were settled in the lobby watching the excitement. The two waiters were there too and were whispering together. They fetched their coats and a few odds and ends and left the hotel the back way, never to be seen again.

"Dammit," Lucy said, "they're getting away." Elizabeth covered her mouth with her hand. "You're not allowed to swear, Lucy," she admonished her friend.

Soon, the police arrived and went straight up to the attic room. The baby was crying so it wasn't difficult to find the right door. The ghosts were just behind them and the young girl in the room looked scared out of her mind. The police took her away, and also the baby, wrapped in a bedcover and looking none the worse for the adventure. In fact, she was fascinated by the uniformed officers and started to smile.

That had been quite an adventure and the ghosts felt pleased with what they'd managed to do. "Whatever will be next?" Lucy said. And they had a few more adventures over the next few weeks, trivial things though, not like the kidnapped baby or the maid who'd stolen Lucy's jewels. It was more like – 'why is another bag of sugar missing from the larder' or, 'who's been helping themselves to the eggs?' or, 'why has some of the silver cutlery from the dining room gone missing?'.

Then, another 'biggy' happened. A family arrived at the reception – a mother, father, one little girl and a nanny, all dressed in black. Elizabeth jumped off the sofa where she'd been lounging. "It's her, Lucy, it's definitely her." And she ran over to the woman and stared into her face. The woman fidgeted and ran her finger around her collar.

"Is it the woman who drowned you, Elizabeth? Oh my God, what are you going to do?"

"I don't know yet but I'll do something. It's my chance and I'll have to take it. I may not get another one."

The family had been shown up to their room and the two girls still sat on the sofa, thinking aloud. "Let's find out how long they're staying." She went up to the register and looked at the last details. "We've got three days Elizabeth – plenty of time to come up with a plan. Now we can move things, it'll be all the easier." Lucy was very keen to help.

But things weren't as easy as they'd thought. A day and a half had passed and they hadn't thought of anything. That night, the mother and father were going to the opera. They'd heard them ordering a taxi and after they'd left for the evening, the ghosts went up to the bedroom. The little girl, about five years old, was already in bed and seemed to be asleep. *At least, they're not drowning her,* Elizabeth thought.

"Let's start by teasing her a bit. We'll move things about the room and move the curtains as though there's a draught in the room. Things like that." Elizabeth agreed and immediately began to annoy the Nanny. They stole her handkerchief, blew into her ear, moved the footstool around the room. Harmless things, but quite scary when you don't know what's going on.

Then it struck Lucy. "We can't drown her, that's not possible – but we can cause her death and that's all you need to be free from here. Let's entice her out onto the balcony – we can both focus on her at the same time and that should be enough to make her obey. It's like a form of hypnosis really, isn't it?" And they set about their task. The nanny had gone into the little girl's room – just to be near someone as she knew things weren't right in the apartment.

The child was asleep and the nanny was sitting in an armchair by the bed. She looked nervous, as well she might, the curtains were moving and the cover on the bed was slipping onto the floor. *What's going on?* she wondered but she just sat there, as she couldn't work up the courage to move. Both ghosts crouched by her feet and both blew into her face. Lucy said, "Get up Nanny, it's very warm in here, isn't it? You need some fresh air. Open the window to the balcony and a lovely breeze will come inside and cool you down."

Elizabeth joined in, "Hello Nanny, do you remember me? I'm the girl you drowned in the bath – and I want to repay the favour now. Follow me over to the window."

And the woman in black stood up hesitantly, turning around to face the window as she did so. The ghosts escorted her across the room and she obediently opened the window. Fresh air floated into the room and the child stirred in her bed. Nanny stepped out onto the balcony and looked down into the street. Vicious looking iron railings stared back at her and she took a quick intake of breath, before bending over the ledge.

The two ghosts used all their focussing power and told her to climb onto the ledge and then just let herself fall to the ground. She stood up and was standing on the ledge, then she just fell into the air, arms stretched out to each side – then she was no more. Elizabeth had achieved what she needed to and she looked down at the woman, who'd been impaled on the sharp railings. It was clear, she was dead.

Elizabeth began to feel a bit dizzy and knew something big was happening to her. "I think I may be passing over Lucy – and after all, this was what I wanted. To feel at peace and go to my rest – but I'm going to miss you – I've grown very fond of you." Lucy took her hand and said, "I'm going to miss you too, Elizabeth – I don't know what I'd have done without you. You taught me so much. I'll miss you a lot," and suddenly she couldn't feel her friend's little hand, it had disappeared. The young ghost was fading and suddenly disappeared from the room. She had gone. Her friend had gone and Lucy was alone in the hotel. She shivered and went down to the lobby again where she herself had originally died. There was a crowd of people outside the door, the nanny had been found, it seemed. Her job was done for that day.

The next six months passed. She still missed her young friend, but she could do nothing about that. Many more small incidents helped pass the time and she actually enjoyed most of them. She even enjoyed when certain people could see her and know her for what she was, the hotel ghost. She had never adopted a scary image and when people saw her, they didn't scream or run away, they just got on with what they were doing and Lucy soon disappeared. Cook was one of her favourites and was the one who saw her often, but wasn't in the least bothered by her.

One afternoon, she was resting in the kitchen and Cook was busy preparing some sumptuous meals and putting the finishing touches to a large, three-tier cake – my, weren't the couple lucky? Lucy always enjoyed the days when the hotel was hosting a wedding breakfast and the party that followed. Cook looked across the table and said, "Look now, you had better make yourself scarce – you'll frighten the bride and groom. I know you like weddings – they probably remind you of your own when you had that dreadful accident." She talked as she worked – nothing fazed her, it seemed. Lucy thought herself into the lounge where champagne was being drunk like water. Two waiters brought in the wedding cake and put it on the table in the place of honour. The bride and groom turned around and a shower of confetti fell to the floor – everyone laughed and cheered. Lucy felt she was part of the breakfast ceremony and although no sound came from her, she cheered with the others.

Then she looked closely at the happy couple. The bride was still very young, younger than her new husband, and quite plain looking, but she was wearing a sumptuous dress that cascaded to the floor. The groom was familiar to Lucy and she went over for a closer look – it was Tom – her Tom. He was getting married again. Perhaps, he'd used up all her money and was looking for another, rich wife – well, he'd obviously found her or he wouldn't be marrying her. His best man was a different person which seemed right, considering what had happened before.

She stared at Tom for a long time. He was still very good-looking but she viewed him quite differently than she had before. Now she was able to see the evil in the blue eyes and the determination of the chin – to get exactly what he wanted. She had loved this man once, just as this young bride probably did now, but she knew that to be set free from haunting this hotel, she must seek retribution for what he did to her three years before. She had had plenty of time to think about it, so she had a plan of sorts in her mind.

The couple were booked at the hotel for one night only, so she had to move quickly. Tom and his new wife were dancing in the middle of the room. The bride was hardly more than a child, perhaps 19, but Tom would have managed her perfectly, just as he'd managed Lucy herself. She was wearing some magnificent jewels which implied her family was quite well off, just the sort of family Tom would have chosen. They had better watch out for their little girl as he would only use her to get what he wanted – or even worse.

Lucy stood very close to them. The bride was unaware of her but she knew Tom wasn't. He stumbled a couple of times, although he'd always been a good dancer and he made his excuses to his wife, saying that he must sit down for a few minutes. "All the excitement of the day," he explained to her. Lucy followed him to the top table and sat on the next chair. "You know I'm here, don't you, Tom? I've been here all these years since you pushed me down the stairs and caused my death. Everyone thought I'd tripped on my dress hemline, but you and I know what really happened." She waited for him to respond but he said nothing. She knew he was aware of her and just to spook him, she moved the cutlery and his napkin – actually she lifted the napkin and dropped it onto the floor. Tom was sweating profusely – he really hadn't expected this. He hadn't chosen this hotel, it was his bride's family, but he had no reason to object. At least, that's what he thought.

He got up and crossed to the bar ordering a brandy to steady his nerves. She followed him and knocked his arm so that the brandy dribbled down his chin.

He spoke at last. "Leave me alone, damn you – I know who you are – but you're not real, are you? You're just a figment of my imagination – perhaps, I've eaten something that's upset me." He shook his head, trying to clear the unpleasant thoughts. But they wouldn't go away. There was a breeze around his face and the candle on the bar was flickering. He jumped up and knocked his chair onto its back. Everyone looked at him and he tried to smile. "Think I need some air," and he made his way to the front door. He sat in the front garden and lit a cigarette. He didn't realise that Lucy couldn't follow him, but she'd wait patiently for him to come back inside.

In the meantime, she went over towards the bride, who was sitting with her mother and father. It seemed so familiar to her and she wondered what the future plan was for the bride. They were talking quite quietly. The father said, "You mustn't do that child – to leave him everything is too much. You've only known him for six months after all."

"Yes, dear, I quite agree with your father. We've let you marry him with such short notice – but you're being rash now and rushing things too fast." Mother was obviously upset. They were rather nice, ordinary people with no airs and graces, who looked quite uncomfortable – as though they'd rather be anywhere else other than at this wedding reception. Their daughter, however, remained adamant.

She replied, "I love him and he loves me – he's all I'll ever want – so don't try to change my mind about my money. Grandfather left it to me to do with what I want." And she went off defiantly to join some friends at another table.

Now Lucy knew. It was exactly the same story as her own. *How long did the young bride have,* she wondered. Not long after the will was signed, if it hadn't been already. She knew what Tom's plans would be, although, this bride might get a longer time married, than the two hours she'd had. She sat in the lobby, first checking the register to see what room they were in. Of course, it was the bridal suite. The same one as she'd had for her wedding. She thought herself upstairs and into the room, it was almost the same as she'd left her own all that time ago, jewellery and make-up all over the place and the bride's going away dress hanging on the wardrobe handle. So different, yet so familiar.

Downstairs, the wedding reception was still in full swing, couples were dancing, drinking and laughing. Tom was back inside the hotel and dancing with his bride. He looked normal now – although still a bit grey around the gills. He bent his head and kissed his bride. It all seemed so normal. They finished their dance and he said, "I'm just going to pop upstairs and get some cigarettes – I seem to have lost the packet I had." He didn't know that, that packet was actually hidden in Lucy's dress pocket.

The first thing he saw when he went into the room was Lucy. She was standing by the window and she looked as beautiful a bride as she was when he'd seen her a few years before. He just stood there, staring. He could see her quite clearly. She'd used all her skills to make him see her – and it had worked.

She suddenly said, "You killed me Tom. You pushed me down the stairs on our wedding day – and you took all the money I'd inherited. How could you do that? You sentenced me to stay in this hotel until I'd achieved one final thing – and that's what I'm going to do now." The silken folds of her dress swayed in the breeze from the window. He tried to turn away and get out of there but his feet were stuck to the ground. He started to say that he hadn't done that – that she'd tripped on her long dress – but she cut him short saying,

"Stop right there, Tom, we both know what you did and why you did it. You're inhuman and I bet your new, young wife will meet a similar accident in the not too distant future – is that right? Is that your plan?" Strangely enough, she almost felt sorry for him as she had already made up her mind that this was to be the moment – the moment she achieved retribution – and finally get the peaceful after-life she deserved.

"Go back to your bride, Tom – at least make this day a happy one for her," and he hurried out of the door. She followed him to the corridor outside and stood by his side at the top of the stairs. She looked intently into his eyes and put her ghostly hands around his neck. At first, she squeezed and squeezed, then she lifted him bodily over the top of the long, winding staircase. He looked down at the ground and could see his own feet dangling over the edge – he was about six inches up in the air. Her ghostly strength was amazing.

"Goodbye, Tom – it's not been nice knowing you," and she let go of him and dropped him over the stairs. At first, he rolled and then bashed himself against the bannister – then against the wall – head over heels, he crashed down the stairs. The noise of his fall scared all the guests below and they looked up together. He reached the bottom and lay there motionless, in front of them. His arms and legs were spread-eagled across the floor. He had broken his neck.

He got up from the floor and looked upwards. Lucy was sitting on the top stair, watching everything that had happened. She was looking very relaxed and she could feel a strange sensation creeping over her body – she'd finally got her retribution and punished the man who'd taken her life so long ago. He mounted the stairs towards her and sat on a lower stair.

"Have you been waiting to do that, Lucy?" he asked. She nodded and smiled at him.

"It had to be done, Tom – I had to seek retribution from the person who'd taken my life – and now I've done just that. You know what it means, don't you? No, I don't suppose you do – but I'm going to enjoy telling you. Just as I've been imprisoned in this hotel since our wedding – it's going to happen to you now – you'll be the resident ghost here from now on. I'm going to my rest and you – you'll take my place. The only difference is that for you to escape, you'd have to achieve retribution against the person who killed you – but that was me – and I am fading fast, I can feel it in every bone in my body. You'll never be able to deal with me as I've done with you – you're here forever. Am I looking hazy to you? You're not hazy – you're a good, strong ghostly colour. You'll have no friends – unlike me – and it'll take years before you can make anyone even see you. Goodbye, Tom – it's been no fun being your wife," and her fading, silvery figure went down the stairs towards the concerned circle of people.

The new bride was sitting on a chair crying her eyes out. Lucy still had some power left and she knelt down beside the girl. "It'll be all right, dear – you won't think it now, but this is the best thing that could have happened to you. You have your life back."

And the old bride kissed the cheek of the new bride before she completely faded away to the best rest, she'd ever had in her life, or in her after life.

Boudica – Warrior Queen

This is a tale of an amazing woman. She was an aristocrat, a queen, a wife and a mother. She was afraid of nothing and no one – a leader, a warrior, a Celtic noble, who stood up to the all-powerful, oppressive Romans, who had made up their minds to conquer and plunder all they wanted from Britain. She gave Rome much to worry about for a time.

Her name was Boudica which was from the ancient British word for victory and her husband was the king of the Iceni tribe, a rich and powerful Celtic people. He was, however, a puppet king of the Romans and was allowed to govern in name only, all major decisions being taken by the Romans.

This tale takes us back to when Boudica was a young woman. She was rich and lived a luxurious life, as did her two daughters. She didn't like the way her ruling family weren't allowed to rule at all and she greatly resented the way the invaders just took what they wanted and brushed aside whoever got in their way.

My name is Breagha and I was a servant and companion to the queen. I also was allowed to train beside her in war tactics, as did all Celtic women in ancient Britain. She was a physically strong woman who seemed to fear no man and I, Breagha, tried to be as much like her as I was able; but not being of noble birth, I was limited in this.

One day in the palace house, where Boudica lived with her husband, Prasutagus, I was combing out her long, red hair and two other servant women were feeding her sweetmeats. A male messenger entered the room and asked to speak with his mistress. She was dressed in a long, flowing, green dress which was made of a gauzy material. She got up from the couch and stood to her full height, which was considerable.

"Why do you disturb my rest this day – I have been training all morning and feel exhausted." I quickly stood up with my mistress and faced the messenger with a stern look.

"Speak up, my man – the lady has asked you a question." I liked to appear more important than I actually was.

"My lady, I come from your husband who has become bed-ridden of late and would have you visit him in his quarters. I fear he is very ill – and may not last the night." The messenger lowered his eyes and hoped he hadn't said too much.

I accompanied my mistress to Prasutagus' room and was surprised to find him lying on his bed, with several courtiers standing around him. They moved back to allow Boudica to come forward. "My dear, I'm afraid I am breathing my last, as I speak. My weakness has overcome me. You must prepare your kingdom for after I have gone – we have no male heir, so I fear what the Romans will do to you and to your people." He coughed and looked down on the blood splattered sheet. He was breathing very shallowly.

"I am sorry to hear that, my lord," Boudica said, "I had no idea you were so ill." She turned to the doctors and asked, "How long does my husband have to live?" The forthcoming answer was that he had very little time left. She did not cry as she had never been very close to her husband but she knew what his death could mean to her and her two daughters. The Romans were not known for their sympathetic ways and generous acts. She did not even wait for Prasutagus to breathe his last but turned swiftly and left the room, telling the doctors to come to her when he had passed. I quickly followed her.

"My lady, I am truly sorry – may I help you in any way," I asked.

"Breagha," she said, "Fetch my daughters – I must speak with them." She crossed to a writing table by the window and pulled some paper towards her. She knew that when she became the sole leader, the Romans would not like it. They didn't have the same respect for a woman as did the ancient Celts. She sent messages to other tribes, telling them what was happening and asking that they join her rebellion to defeat the Romans. It was an ideal time to do this, as the Roman Governor was away from the area, fighting the Druids in Wales – and the Emperor Nero was too far away to get involved with petty issues – as he saw them. Prasutagus' will did not leave his estate to his wife, nor to the Romans, but rather to his two daughters. He had often told Boudica that he didn't trust her as she would never do as the Romans wanted and he believed that would be the kiss of death for his people.

However, the tribes rallied to her cry and sent messengers to say they would fight alongside her. They were tired of Roman rule and how they confiscated everything they wanted. Prasutagus died that night and a few days later, a Roman legion arrived at the gates of the palace house.

I was scared but stood my ground with my mistress. She told me I could be released and return to my tribe, but I refused as I greatly admired her and wanted to be by her side when the Centurion leader came to her room. He said, "I have come, madam – at Roman instructions to relieve you of all you possess and all of your properties around the area. You have no male heir and therefore, are unable to rule."

She knew this was coming but she stalled him and plied him with drink and meats, assuring him that she would comply with all he asked. That night, she called out to me and when I went to her, she told me I must go to the other tribe leaders and tell them she was going to need their help now. "Tell them to use their chariots, as I will do – the chariots with the scythes fixed to all four wheels. We'll deal with these Romans, Breagha, and then we'll be able to rule our country as we would want."

I, Breagha had been given a very important role. I dressed in animal skins and woollen garbs and had the servants get ready the fastest horse in the enclosure. I rode off into the night – my sword and dagger on my belt. My first port of call was the Iceni overlords themselves who lived closest and who had many reasons to hate the Romans. They worshipped Boudica as a Goddess and she knew they would die for her. They were tired of having to pay dues to the invaders and to pretend to accept the political decisions made by them.

Whilst I was travelling between the ancient tribes, Boudica was faring worse than I. Two days after the arrival of the Roman Legion, Boudica was in her palace, trying to hide her most valuable treasures and get the Iceni people ready to take up arms against the Romans. She heard a great noise, of crashing and screaming and suddenly, the palace was full of servants running in all directions. There were Roman soldiers everywhere, flailing their swords as they ran. They didn't care who they struck as one dead Celt was as good as another. Boudica drew her small dagger, but knew there was little point. The Romans were all powerful and the killing spree lasted for two full days. It was a catastrophe and many innocent people died for nothing. The soldiers looted and sacked the palace; they raped and pillaged and sent messengers all around the area, telling the ancient Iceni leaders that their lands were confiscated. They also demanded the repayment of money loans they'd made to the Celtic overlords and that panicked them beyond words. All Boudica's relatives were imprisoned and her two daughters held in captivity.

Worst of all, however, they took Boudica herself out of the palace and tied her to a wooden stake. She said nothing. Her bravery was incredible. Several Roman soldiers flogged her to an inch of her life. She couldn't stand upright and was covered in blood and wounds. Her matted, red hair clung to her body and the soldiers jeered. For Boudica, even worse was to come. They collected her two daughters and in front of their mother, they gang-raped the girls. At first, the girls didn't know what was happening – they were virgins, they were royal and they were holy, as many believed their mother to be a Goddess. The girls screamed loudly and shouted for their mother. They lay on the ground in front of Boudica's stake, they were both rolled into balls, searing pain stopping them even from screaming.

That night, Prasutagus appeared to his wife. He looked down at the weeping woman and told her, "My dear wife, I asked you not to go against the Romans. They are all powerful and whatever you do next, you will not triumph." He crossed the room to be closer to her.

"Are you listening to me, wife – I know you've always hated the Romans – but please listen to me." Boudica fainted, from pain and from fear of the apparition. She told herself in the morning that she'd had a dream, nothing more.

The news of what had happened reached Breagha's ears very soon. She immediately turned her horse and made her way back to the Iceni lands. She didn't know what she could do to help, but she knew she had to be with her mistress. In line with Breagha's visits across the tribal lands, Boudica rallied the Iceni overlords and the leaders of several other Celtic tribes, including her close neighbours the Trinovantes, and told them to join the army she was amassing to run the Romans out of Britannia. They were all willing to do this and soon, Boudica had a growing army. They came in scythe bedecked chariots with all the weapons they could muster. Breagha joined this army but found her mistress much changed. Still with the long, flowing red hair, she now dressed almost as a man, in leggings and a hooded jerkin made of animal leather. She now looked like a General, which she was.

What the Romans had done to the ruling Iceni family was something the Celtic overlords could not accept – nor could Nero and the Senators in Rome. Roman or Celt – if of royal blood – they should not have been treated as Boudica and her daughters had been. Royal blood was almost holy to all civilised peoples.

Breagha rode with her mistress at the head of the army. She dressed as her mistress and carried a heavy sword to defend herself. Boudica had said, "Come ride with me Breagha – you have been my most loyal servant and I value your presence." The two women rode side by side towards the Roman capital, Colchester, and slaughtered and plundered wherever they went. The Iceni and compatriots showed no mercy to either the Romans in the city, or to the Romano-Celts who had supported them. The small number of Roman soldiers who were in Colchester gathered with the local civilians in an enormous temple in the centre of the city and barricaded themselves inside. The Iceni surrounded the temple and burnt it to the ground with the people inside. No mercy was shown and those people who left the temple to escape the fire, were executed in the most vicious ways.

Colchester was flattened and couldn't be called the Roman capital of Britannia any more.

"Mistress, you have done well here – the Romans are on the run." Still, I cautioned Boudica, saying the vast numbers of Roman soldiers fighting the Druids in Wales would return to the area.

"Then, we shall finish them off too – we are invincible." Boudica climbed onto a chariot and spoke to her army – encouraging them to help rid the country of Romans.

"Come my champions, let us rid this land of the invaders. We can take our country and independence back again. Will you follow me?" she shouted to the men.

"Hail Boudica," they shouted, "hail the Warrior Queen. We will follow you to the death," and they cheered loudly.

Boudica and Breagha spent the night in Colchester. Boudica called her two daughters to her side. They were getting stronger every day and they now hated the Romans as much as their mother did. Boudica lay on a rough mat as did her army. She would always rough it out as did the Iceni tribe. She woke with a start and there, in a sort of halo, stood Prasutagus. Again, he had come to plead with her to stop fighting with the Romans. "You will never win, Lady – my heart is breaking for what you have already suffered and what you have still to suffer."

But Boudica would not listen to him. Even I, her loyal servant tried. I spoke to her softly and tried to make her change her mind. I was tired of the killings and had heard that the greater part of the Roman army was to return from Wales to deal with Boudica, the upstart. I tried to tell my mistress but she was not for listening.

Next day, the Iceni army marched towards London, murdering all who got in their way. They massacred the Romans and the civilians and again burnt London to the ground. No mercy was shown and some of the mutilations they left behind spoke of no mercy to either men, women or children. I, Breagha, found it a terrible time.

We marched North West towards St Albans, another Roman stronghold but one held by Celtic collaborators who admired everything Roman. This upset my mistress more than anything, her own culture to turn their backs on their own people, infuriated her beyond words. The Romans had given St Albans total ruling rights and therefore, had no army garrisoned there. Boudica swept into the town and destroyed all who got in her way. The town ended up deserted, the inhabitants fleeing to the countryside and hiding there.

My mistress was all-powerful and her eyes looked almost mad. She felt she was invincible.

Prasutagus followed her more than ever but she chose not to see or hear him. "Get away from me, My Lord, you are no longer of this world and hold no power over me." Prasutagus said, "Listen to Breagha then – she tries to warn you. There are more and more Romans coming to this land – and you are the reason for that."

I had told my mistress of what I had heard. The Romans were marching the 300 miles back to the region. She again took no notice of me and I wept for what I feared was coming.

I had heard that the Roman Governor of Britain, Paulinius, was leading the army. He was known for his prowess as a soldier. He was to be feared greatly. Towards the south east they came, looking for Boudica and her men. And they found them. We had camped in a low valley with woods to one side and an open plain in the front and it was there, one early morning, that the Iceni looked up and saw thousands of Romans at the top of the valley.

I know my mistress wished she had listened to either Prasutagus or to myself, but she was almost mad now with power and rallied her army to face the Romans. I rode my horse close to Boudica's side and brandished my sword above my head. She sat on her chariot well, proud and upright, and was followed by the large army of Iceni.

It was all to no avail, however, the Roman soldiers advanced in straight lines, giving no quarter to any who got in their way. They fought as only Romans could and they massacred the Celtic army. They swept into the valley like great clouds of bees. My mistress's forces could move neither forward nor backwards and they were crushed by the Romans. I raced forward and pulled Boudica onto my horse and rode hard to leave the battlefield. She fought me like a mad person but my horse was swift and sure-footed and we emerged from the woodlands into an overgrown and rocky crop. I helped her down and took her to a small cave on the hill. She fell to the ground and I reached for my water flask to wet her lips. I went outside again and hid my horse as best I could. When I returned to the cave, I was not surprised to find Prasutagus there and alongside him, were his two daughters. All three were now ghostly apparitions. The daughters had been killed, not by the Romans, but by the Celts, who feared what the Romans would have done to them had they caught them.

Prasutagus turned to me and said, "You have been a good servant to your mistress and I applaud you for that. However, it is now her time to join my daughters and myself before the Romans find the cave." He held out a flask of liquid and told me I must give this to Boudica as a last loyal and kind act on my part. I shrank from the flask as I knew it was poison and was to be the last thing my mistress ever drank. The Iceni had been annihilated by the Romans resulting in a genocide of its people and a confiscation of all its lands and valuables. In place of Icemi roundhouses, the Romans eventually were to build a series of military forts that covered the land.

I took the flask from Prasutagus' hand and looked into my mistress's eyes. I removed my sword and lay down beside her. Her breathing was shallow and there were tears on her cheeks. She whispered, "Breagha, if the Romans find me, they'll do unspeakable things to me. Help spare me that and hold that bottle to my lips. It will be your last service to a mistress who has always valued and loved you."

That was it. I held the flask to her mouth and she drank deeply of the contents. Her head fell back and she sighed. I put my arm around her shoulders and waited patiently. Her eyes fluttered and she breathed her last. I gently closed her eyes and kissed her forehead. The great warrior queen was no more. I cried and allowed my tears to fall onto her face. I slept then. I don't know for how long but when I woke up, it was to the morning brightness.

I left Boudica there and went to find any of her countrymen that were still alive. I brought them back to the cave and between us, we started digging a pit for the foundations of her death barrow. I had to bury her as I couldn't let the Romans find even her dead body as they would have desecrated it. We placed her in the pit with just her little dagger by her side and we piled the earth and any boulders we could find on top of her. It was a barrow fit for a queen. My helpers disappeared from my side as I was too well to the Romans for them to stay around me.

I went back into the cave and found the half empty flask. I drank the remaining fluid and knew that a gentle sleep would soon claim my mind and body. I lay there and thought of the many days I had shared with Boudica, and I smiled. It had been a good life and I'd tried to help rectify the greed and power lust of the Romans. As death was coming on me, I looked to the mouth of the cave and there stood Prasutagus with his daughters, and with Boudica herself. They beckoned me to join them and slowly turned towards the sky which was cloudless and beautifully blue. I left my body and followed them to their spiritual home. Five misty figures disappearing towards their final rest.

I had no regrets. Alongside Boudica, I had done my best and I knew that, although, she may have failed to rid her country of the Romans, she had ensured her name would be spoken of for centuries to come. Whereas the Roman Governor Paulinus's name died in history from the day he was victorious in his battle with Boudica.

Down with the Romans! Hail Boudica!

How to Pass a Boring Day

Zeus and Hera were relaxing around the mist pool. Today, the visibility was very clear; sometimes it could be quite hazy, but not today. Their view of the world below was clear and colourful. They were stretched full length along the whiteness of a cloud and were sharing a meal of nuts, wine and grapes. A feast for the Gods, which was very apt as they were gods. Their boredom, however, was apparent – what did the king and queen of the Greek Gods do to lift their moods? They both had the power to do exactly what they wanted, but now and again, their time was spent being idle, such as today. Hera leaned over the pool and trailed her long fingers in the mist. The movement was slow and deliberate, but as queen, she didn't care. She sighed repeatedly.

They hadn't long returned from a successful revolution against Kronos, Zeus's father, and now, with his father out of the way, he owned the heavens and the earth and was the king of the Olympic Parthenon. He was a brave man and afraid of nothing; all powerful, he took his role seriously. He was however, a great womaniser and made Hera, his wife and companion, very unhappy with this character weakness. He also had many children, some of whom were Gods in their own right – some were Demi-Gods and half mortal and some were entirely mortal, depending on his partners at the time of conception. Hera was a very astute woman and could also be a very mean one, who liked to tease and plague her husband in order to show her anger. Between them, they always played out healthy competitions, which helped to ease any tension between them. They were both perfect and had to relieve the boredom that came with perfection. Complete control of the weather and of the seasons was particularly enjoyable for them both and they used it to remind the mortals on earth of what the Gods were capable.

Today, however, they decided to leave the weather alone – no hurricanes, no tsunamis and no vicious storms. "How shall we pass the time, Hera?" he asked in a languid tone. "Shall we open our view of the world perhaps and see what the people are doing just now – and if we don't like it, we can always change it? What year shall we go for?"

Hera looked thoughtful and leaned over to paddle the mist ferociously. Everything magically opened up and the world below was clear as a bell. "I think we should go for their 20th century – around the man, Hitler's time in power. His reputation was not good and he seemed to bring great unhappiness to the people of the world – but let's not judge – let's just look." She rolled onto her tummy and stared into the clouds. Zeus did likewise.

Zeus liked to give a little background information so he said, "It seemed to begin when Hitler marched his troops into a country called Poland and from there on, disaster snow-balled all over Europe. Look, there he is speaking to crowds of people – actually, he's ranting – he really can shout, can't he? And he uses his arms and fists to good advantage – a born orator, I should say."

They moved the vision on for a few more years and saw the trains and lorries full of Jewish people, being taken to the concentration camps, specifically built to annihilate their race. He thought the Jews were useless and a blight on society, in fact, really harmful to all with whom they came in contact. The two Gods watched the fighting, the bombs and the ultimate deaths all over Europe – the homes in all countries were flattened and left derelict, no longer to be used for sheltering people. They saw murderous killing of servicemen and civilians – men, women and children. The horror that went on for many years seemed to be because of this one man. This Hitler, the German Fuhrer.

Zeus asked, "Why would one want to eradicate a complete race of people – they must have been good for something. I heard they were good business people and could make lots of money – perhaps, that's why he didn't like them – he wanted their money."

"Money does seem to be the root of all evil, doesn't it? This kind of thing has happened before in different times and places." Hera was sitting up now, paying closer attention.

"Tell you what, Hera – let's have him come here to us and explain his actions. It may help to understand his motives and you never know, we might even like him." He snapped his fingers and Hitler stood in front of them. He was completely bewildered and kept blinking against the brightness of the Heavens.

"He looks rather ordinary, doesn't he? In fact, he's quite an ugly specimen of a mortal man. That silly, little moustache doesn't suit him at all." She looked Hitler up and down and observed he was dressed in full military uniform. He suddenly raised his right arm and shouted, "Heil Hitler." It sounded like an order and the two mighty Gods looked at each other in surprise. No one ever spoke to them like that.

Zeus pointed his first finger at the little, dark-haired man. "Sit down, Hitler – on the clouds please. Don't worry, they'll hold you safe – until we've finished with you." The man, who called himself, the Fuhrer, did as he was told. He too was not used to being ordered about and he didn't like it.

"Well now, the world of your time seems to be a disaster zone and all because of you. Is that a fair observation?" Zeus was being deliberately antagonistic.

"No, indeed – it's not my fault. I am attempting to correct the balance between good and useful people and those who are useless parasites. It's the fault of some of the scum filled countries in the world." Hitler stood to his full height, which was not much. The two Gods also stood up. Both were amazingly tall and well-built – and they looked down on him with ease. He banged his fists on the soft couch but to no effect. Everything in this world was made for comfort and gentleness – something Hitler was not used to.

He banged his fists again but to no effect. He went on, "They needed straightening out and, in some cases – particularly the Jews – they needed to be eradicated completely. I want an Aryan race to rule the world – pure, brave and intelligent people – completely unlike the parasitic vermin that are Jews." He was becoming more angry as he spoke and obviously felt no remorse at what he was saying.

"I did not cause the mess the world is in – blame it on the British nation, who couldn't keep their nose out of what didn't concern them. The result is that all countries are now mixed up and it's my duty – and that of my loyal people – to put things right, and make the world a better place." He was shouting at the end of his speech – it was as though he was addressing a crowd and not just two people.

It was Hera's turn to speak. "We watched 'your loyal people' murder, maim and rape innocent people, who had done nothing to hurt you or your country. You pack human beings into gas chambers and pretend to shower them with water, but you are actually spraying them with poisonous gas. Is that the act of a man who 'just wants to put things right'? What kind of a man are you, I wonder."

"I have nothing to say to you, madame – I've only done my duty." He paused and looked thoughtful for a moment and then said, "Anyway, who exactly are you to question me in this way? I am the Fuhrer, you know." Hera hid a smile and thought, *Oh dear, his arrogance has tripped him up nicely.* Zeus would not like that, she knew. To speak to the Gods like that was quite unacceptable. Zeus was angry and waved his hands above his head. Thunder and lightning lit up the sky and two other, huge men appeared as if from nowhere. "We are here, Father. How can we do your bidding?"

Heracles and Perseus stood side by side. Zeus had fathered them of mortal women and knew they would understand the condition in which the world was. They had had involvement with the mortals on earth many times before. They were famous in their own right, known for strength in Heracles' case and fame for killing the Medusa and cutting off her head in Perseus's.

"Look deep into the mist and see the condition of the world, this man has come from. Everything you see has been caused by his greed and self-importance which he believes he has over his fellow men. Take a few moments to study the earth." Zeus and Hera sat down again on the clouds and waited for Heracles and Perseus to look through the great gap in the clouds. Hitler stood alone – but still straight and proud of his achievements.

Perseus was the first to speak. "I could take his head between my hands and squeeze until my fingers touched. He deserves nothing less," and he made to grab Hitler, but his brother intervened.

"No, let me brother – I could force him down into the ground until his whole body disappears – all the way over his head." Heracles was champing at the bit to get hold of the little, dark man.

Zeus held his sons back and cautioned them to be patient. He turned to Hitler. "You are not of the Aryan race – surely, we could start with you and pack you off to the concentration camps." His wife nodded her head in agreement. "I am of a pure race and I intend to produce many more Aryans to rule the world in the future." His hands were twisted into fists and his forehead was creased into deep lines.

The Gods sat in a semi-circle, with Hitler standing in the middle, they were thinking of the best way to deal with the situation. Zeus looked again at the world below, in the year 1941, and saw horrific death and bloodshed wherever the German nation marched.

"Let's put him back from whence he came and see if he can sort out this muddle. He obviously thinks he is all powerful and capable of doing anything." Zeus spoke quietly so the dictator couldn't hear. "The Japanese are just about to attack the Americans at Pearl Harbour and that will bring them into the war on the side of the Allies. That should have a huge effect on his next action." The other Gods agreed. "Let's see how he gets on."

Zeus placed Hitler back on the earth just after December 1941 when the attack took place. Hitler's first move was rather a foolish one. France had already surrendered, but he also now lost the Italians, who had not been, it has to be said, the best fighters or strategists in the campaign. Then, he decided to march into Leningrad where he intended to starve the Russians by shutting them up in their own city. This siege lasted a year and the people in the city were dying in huge numbers, but they stood firm against the force of the invaders.

All the Gods were silent, thinking about what had happened and wondering what Hitler would do next.

Hera broke the silence. "That seems rather foolish – now the little man is fighting on all sides – how can he win?" Her husband responded, "Let's hope he can't. Let's whisper in the Japanese ears that – now they've had the atomic Bombs dropped on them – it's time they surrendered to the Allied forces. A suggestion and a nudge is all it will take – especially the way I'll do it."

And so it happened after five long years of war – and with the Japanese having surrendered and the Russian Army on the doorstep of Berlin – Hitler realised his days were numbered and his great plans to take over the whole of Europe, were no longer viable. After the death and destruction, the cruelty towards all who stood up to him and the near annihilation of the Jewish race, he found himself shut in an underground bunker in Berlin – in the basement of the official Chancellery building, where once, he himself had been the Head of Department. That, of course, was when he was still on the rise to power.

Zeus stood up and said, "I am going to earth – Berlin, in particular – I want to see from close quarters, how these people deal with their last days on earth. Stay here and watch me – as it could still be dangerous down there." And he was gone. In the mist of the pool, the three spectators watched closely. They could see Zeus clearly but no one on earth could.

Hitler was sitting on a bunk bed and at his side was Eva Braun, his wife of two days. At their feet was the dog Blondi and her new pups. Amazingly, he was holding Eva's hand in a gesture of love and compassion – something he'd never considered for the people whose hearts he'd broken over the last five years. *The man does have a heart after all,* Zeus thought.

"Our time has come, Eva – we must end it now before the Russians break through and arrive at our door." Hitler stroked the dog's head as he spoke. "There's no telling what they will do to us if they capture us alive. I believe they will treat us abominably. They will use us to ease their own consciences and to justify all the things they did to try to stop us."

"I fear so, Adolph, we must take our own lives before they come. How will we do it? And what about the dogs – we can't leave them here? They will do to them what they'd have liked to do to us."

Zeus was astounded to see how they felt for each other and for their animals and yet, so many innocent people had died because of their cruel decisions. He stared at Hitler. *The man with the little, black moustache had never batted an eyelid in concern or regret for the thousands of deaths he'd brought about.*

"Eva – there may be a way out of all this. Yes, the Russians are very close to this building but there is still a way to escape. We could arrange for a small plane to land at the back of the building and we could change our hair colour and certainly our clothes. I shall shave off my moustache and we will no longer have the dogs." Hitler was quite excited at the possibility.

"What do you mean about the dogs – how can we leave them here without us?" She loved her animals more than she'd ever loved any person she'd ever known.

"We have spare cyanide capsules, don't we? We can try them out on the dogs." At this point, Zeus realised the man hadn't changed at all. There was no heart in that chest. Hitler went on, "Come now, you know we can try to escape – Argentina is waiting and has prepared a new life for us there." He fetched some capsules from a small, wall safe and broke two of them in half. He shook the poison into a bowl and covered the powder with milk. The dogs lapped up the liquid and Hitler and Eva watched them sadly. Nothing happened at first, then, moments later, the small pups began to squeal and fall onto their sides. Blondi, the mother, fell onto her side very quickly and gasped her last.

"There you are, Eva – at least we know the capsules work. But about our escape – I can begin the preparations now. We don't have much time – you know what the Italians did to Mussolini – not a straightforward execution – but a cruel and degrading death for their leader. I think the Russians and whichever of the Allied forces come along next, will treat us in the same cruel and degrading way – and I don't want that for us. We can ask our servants to fetch what we need to change our appearances. My officers have even suggested this to me and have arranged for us to go to a small Bavarian village in the hills – and from there, on to Argentina."

Zeus was on his feet. He couldn't let this happen. He couldn't let this man and woman escape. He looked up into the mist of the pool and saw his wife and two sons standing there. All three had their thumbs pointing downwards. Their message was clear and Zeus crossed the room and whispered into the ear of Hitler. "Your life must be over now – you have damaged too many people over the last five years. Get the capsules and give one to your wife." The power of his words and the clear instruction he gave, made Hitler return to the wall safe and fetch more cyanide capsules. He gave one to Eva and nodded to her to swallow it. He was almost in a trance. Zeus had him in complete control. .

Eva swallowed the pill and stared into her husband's eyes. "It's the only way for us, my dear. I know you were clutching at straws talking about escaping. But this has to be. Goodbye… Goodbye… it was fun while it lasted," and she lay down on the bunk bed and closed her eyes. She curled up onto her side in a sleeping baby position. He watched her and looked at the capsule in his hand. He put it to his mouth and swallowed it, but then got up before it took effect and fetched his pistol from a desk drawer.

For a moment, Zeus thought he was trying to change his mind so he spoke again to Hitler and told him to do it, there wasn't any other way. In fact, he commanded the man to do it.

Hitler pointed the pistol at his head and with one last look at Eva, he pulled the trigger. Blood gushed from the open wound at the back of his head and some brains fell onto the floor. Zeus looked at the brain matter and wondered how this substance had made the man think so differently from other human beings.

Zeus left the bunker then, it was all over and the war too, was over. He went back to his heavenly kingdom in the sky and sat down beside Hera and his sons.

"Well done, Father," Perseus said, "you stopped the war from going on – possibly for many more years. Had he escaped; he would have begun everything all over again. He showed no remorse for what he'd done. He would be able to find some group of powerful people to help him to take over the world – unfortunately, there are probably more like him than you'd think."

"Come, let us call for fresh wine and drink the nectar to us, the Gods." Heracles agreed with his brother. "Our intervention has ended a war of great, pointless destruction, which could have gone on for many more years."

A servant brought fresh wine to the table and poured it into goblets. Hera sipped her drink and said, "I wonder what the first thing he'd have done if he had managed to escape from the Russians and had reached the country Argentina. I really believe he would have started it all again – as you say, Perseus, he obviously felt no guilt."

"I believe that too," Zeus said. "He was originally just a house painter from Austria, who was apparently too fond of his mother. He couldn't bring himself to leave her and so he achieved nothing in his young life and stayed with her for a long time. He eventually woke up to the fact that he'd had no life and then worked his way upwards and outwards in all directions. His personality was so strong that the people of Germany would, and did, die for him. He came along at just the right time as the country was in a mess and people needed a strong leader. He really believed in an Aryan race and that Germany was the place to produce it."

Zeus stretched his long frame along the soft clouds and tasted the wine gratefully. "It's tiring being a God, isn't it? I'm quite exhausted."

Hera laughed. "Yes, you're probably right. If it hadn't been Hitler the House Painter, it might have been Grossman the Butcher, or Schlessman the Window Cleaner. The country was ready for such a leader, wasn't it? But, let's hope it doesn't happen again – after all, if it did, there might not be a man around called Churchill."

She settled herself comfortably and crossed her legs. "I have only one criticism to make of you, my darling God – why did you not use the Pool of Mist to see what was happening at that time and then go back not only five years, but to sometime before it all began and remove Hitler – or Grossman or Schlessman – from the volatile Germany that was?"

"I don't know the answer to that – except why didn't you do it yourself?" Zeus felt vindicated. "And who is this man Churchill you've just mentioned for the first time?"

Competition between the Gods was very much still alive. Zeus could see an interesting discussion ahead, possibly about someone called 'Churchill'.

The Grey Lady

She'd been spoiled from the moment she opened her baby blue eyes and screamed at the top of her lungs. Her given name was Amanda and she grew up in a beautiful home with adoring parents, who worshipped the ground she walked on from the very moment she began to use her chubby little legs. Two years after her birth, she was presented with a baby brother, for whom she didn't care much. He was pretty useless as far as she was concerned and she continued to think of him that way all her life. He was named James after his father and grew up in the shadow of his wonderful sister.

Amanda was to be 18, the following week and great plans were afoot for her birthday celebrations. The parlour was being decorated in glorious colours and lovely flowers and half the people in the surrounding area were invited to the party. Her mother and father had appointed a portrait painter to create a picture of their beloved daughter which would hang in the dining room, above the fireplace. She was a pretty girl and had already some admirers, only from the best families, of course. Amanda hadn't singled anyone out as a beau, but liked to keep them all on a string at her beck and call.

The day before the party, an unfortunate incident happened. The servants were all agog with excitement and several of them had been sent down to the bottom of the steep cliff at the front of the house, but there was little they could do; the worst had already happened. A ship had gone down in the storm of the previous night and many of the sailors were dead and lying around the beach. Much contraband had been washed up as well and the local villagers were seeking treasures from the ship, before the Excisemen arrived to clear everything away and to take charge of the contraband. There shouldn't have been contraband, of course – well, nothing not known to the officials already – but there usually was and everyone knew that.

Amanda was, of course, disinterested in what was going on, but James, her brother had gone down to the shore to see if he could help. He made his way across the sands right out to where the treacherous rocks began. The broken masts of the ship could be clearly seen in the deep waters of the sea and there were many things still floating around, bumping against the rocks. James moved in to the water where he thought he'd seen someone moving and sure enough, there was a man stuck in the crevice between two gigantic rocks. He was bleeding badly and using all the strength he could muster, James pulled at his one free arm. He couldn't budge the man though, who was obviously delirious and mumbling nonsenses.

James reassured him that he'd be back and ran along the shore to where the Excisemen had arrived. Somehow, they managed to free the sailor and dragged him onto the dryer sand. They were going to leave him there as there was nothing more they could do, but James ordered two of the servants from the big house to carry the wounded man up to the cliff top and then ask the butler where they should put him.

Everyone in the house was getting ready for the next day's party and chaos reigned in all the rooms. Amanda was pampering herself as only she could and took no interest in the ship wreck below.

"I hope they're not going to bring any of the dirty sailors to this house. There's no room for them here." She gestured to the maid to brush her long, golden curls. At that point, James rushed into her bedroom and told the maid she was needed below stairs to help with some poor souls who seemed to have survived the storm.

"Go away, James – you have no right in here. I need my maid and you don't." She shooed her brother into the hall. "Go and bother someone else."

Meanwhile, the workers were working flat out to clear the beach as best they could, before the high tide came back into shore. The weather promised was still not good and they were concerned about just how much more the sea would claim. The wounded sailor had been put in one of the servant's rooms and he seemed to be pretty peaceful at the moment. James had gone to see him and reassure him they would help him get back onto his feet. The master and mistress were too busy preparing for the next day's party, to bother with drowning sailors. It was easy to see from where Amanda had inherited her selfish personality. She'd never wished people well, she just wanted what they could give her. She'd been born with a mean streak that her lovely face concealed from lots of people.

The day of the party dawned and Amanda's maid was working furiously to ensure her mistress shone throughout the day. Her dress was a beautiful blue colour, in fact, the same colour as she'd worn to sit for her portrait, and her hair was dressed in pink and white roses, as was a sash she wore around her waist. She really did look amazing, she thought. As the day passed, the guests filled the main parlour and spilled over onto the patio beyond the French windows. The wine was flowing freely and an enormous birthday cake held centre place on the table. A small orchestra was placed in a corner of the room and couples were dancing in a myriad of glorious coloured gowns. Everyone was happy and after the cake was cut, James disappeared downstairs with a stolen slice for the wounded sailor, whose name was Philip, he'd discovered, and it turned out that he was the captain of the sunken vessel. It may have seemed silly to take him cake but he thought it was the most human thing to do. Amanda would not have liked it.

She was dancing with one partner after the other and her blue dress swirled in circles around the room. Two young men were singled out as her favourites – Billy Gordon and Terence Roberts – they both obviously adored her and she knew it. She kept them dangling on a string and danced with many other partners as well. At one point, she allowed herself to be danced out onto the patio by Billy

Gordon, closely observed by Terence, and she lingered there in the shrubs and trees. She flirted abominably with him and of course, he kissed her gently on the cheek. Amanda smiled encouragingly and fluttered her fan across her rosy cheeks. In the moonlight, she was the most beautiful girl he'd ever seen.

She danced away from him and ran towards the centre of the lawn. The night was dark and she was disappearing in the gloom. Terence came out onto the patio to see where the couple had gone and was just in time to see her run towards the outside of the garden, with Billy in hot pursuit. He hadn't quite caught up with her when she seemed to stumble and go down onto her knees. She twisted to the side and rolled a little towards the cliff edge. Billy made to grab her but she moved from his clutch and moved even further away from him. He managed to reach her hand as the rest of her body fell over the edge. She clutched at the turf edges with her free hand but they just slipped from her grasp. Billy had hold of her by one hand only and he looked into her face. "Take my hand Amanda – it's all I can reach of you – take my hand." He was desperate. She looked up at him, her blue dress billowing around her and screamed, "Pull me up, you moron – pull me up – or I'm done for." Even with her last breath, she still manged to hurt him and he realised she really was a bitch. Her fingers slipped from his hand and he knew he was losing her.

She fell from his grasp and went tumbling through the air towards the jagged rocks below. He lay there still, his arm outstretched towards the sea. Terence came up behind him at that moment and screamed, "Where is she, Billy? Where is she?" But he knew exactly where she was and he fell to his knees. "Why couldn't you pull her up – why did you let go of her?"

Billy managed to say, "I couldn't save her – she was too far over the edge. What should we do now?"

"Back to the house quickly – she might be lying down there wounded and waiting for someone to help. Come on, get to your feet and follow me." Terence was already turning towards the house. Billy got up and followed him.

They searched the coast line and quite far into the sea itself for three days but could find no trace of her body. There were some scraps of blue material stuck to the rocks – but that was all. Several fishermen took their boats out and searched around; in fact, everyone tried to do their best, but Amanda was gone. That pretty, vivacious girl was no more and she was just 18 years old. Her whole life had been in front of her. Even the wounded captain poured over local maps to try to work out where the body might have gone. He and James were becoming friends, they seemed to think alike.

One week later, the body was washed up in a sheltered bay a few miles away. Amanda was carried home on a wooden cart and her mother and father wept again for the loss of their perfect daughter. She was laid to rest in the family vault in the local cemetery and many mourners came from around the county to pay their respects. After the funeral, the family were gathered in the house's dining room when James suddenly noticed something odd.

"Look Father, Mother – the paint on Amanda's picture is changing colour. Not a lot, but quite noticeable." Both his mother and father told him not to be silly – the painting was perfect, as the sitter had been in life. "By the way, James, mother and I are going abroad for a few months – we're going to do Italy and Greece – in particular, the Greek Islands. We've always wanted to do it – and now with Amanda gone – there's nothing to stop us. It'll do us good too, don't you think?"

All his life, James had been used to being second to his sister and didn't find it strange that they should consider leaving him behind, but he knew they wouldn't have done it to his sister. He said, "If you're going away for that long, I'd like Philip to stay here with me. We've become good friends and he tells me things I never dreamt of – the countries he's visited and the things he's seen. Will that be acceptable to you, after all it's not so very long ago since he had the accident?"

"Of course, my boy – that's absolutely fine," Father went on reading his book. Mother, as usual said nothing – if it didn't involve Amanda, she wasn't interested. George, the butler, knocked the door and came into the room. "Master, there's been a dreadful accident on the High Road. The post chaise has overturned and other than the driver, everyone on the coach has been killed. The driver has been mumbling something about a woman in grey running in front of the coach and causing the horses to shy and claw at the air. She came to a stop right in front of them and caused the coach to turn onto its side, spilling all the passengers onto the road. As there were no survivors – no-one could corroborate or deny his story." George was agitated, "The driver is resting in our kitchen, Master – there was no one else to help him."

The master stood up. "My God, man, we're becoming a veritable hospital for the sick, aren't we? Still, there's nothing else you could have done, was there? Just carry on with whatever's needed," and he went back to his book again.

At first, no one believed the driver's story about the woman in grey. They said he was probably drunk but, two further incidents occurred over the next few weeks where people were either killed or injured. Now the people began to believe his story and the crossroad took on a new name locally. They called it 'The Grey Lady's Crossing'. For some reason, the news made James look up at the painting of his sister and sure enough, the colour of her dress had changed again. It was becoming darker and the blue was turning grey in colour. There was no point mentioning it to his parents, as they'd just disagree.

He did mention it, however, to his friend Philip who said he'd heard such stories before and had no trouble believing it. He'd heard that when someone departed this world and left a life size painting or image behind, that person's spirit was able to come back to earth for short times, and in some cases, do much good, but in some cases, much bad, depending on the spirit…

"Oh Philip, you can't really believe that," James scoffed but still felt the hair on the back of his neck stand bolt upright.

"Why has the colour of your sister's dress changed then – just at the time, the coach overturned. Tell me that. I have visited some of the Caribbean countries in my travels and seen and heard things you wouldn't believe."

Two nights later, something happened that was beyond belief. Beyond belief, except that it really did happen. The Grey Lady stood by the great rock down by the shore. There was no doubt that it was Amanda's spirit, except that her dress was dark in colour. The turbulent waves started to cover her feet. The tide was on the turn but she wasn't afraid of the sea claiming her. It already had and she knew it wouldn't come for her again. The moon was low in the sky and shed only a little light over the bay but there was a myriad of stars twinkling in the vast darkness. Not much could be seen but Amanda could see very well. The power of the sea and the wind whipping up the waves gave the night the strength to bring ships faltering to a watery grave. She'd stood here before, waiting for a stormy night such as this one. She was surrounded by bracken which she would set alight in due course. The welcoming light would lure ships in danger from the stormy sea onto the rocky shoreline. The desperate sailors would believe the shining light was telling them to come to a safe harbour; a harbour void of rocks. But this particular harbour was not void of rocks. It had some of the biggest, most jagged rocks around. Well hidden beneath the full tide, they lay there, waiting for the unsuspecting sailors to steer their ship in the wrong direction.

She lit the bracken bushes. The wind was gathering speed and she saw the expected ship rounding the bay. It was heaving and rolling. The fire was great now and lit up the corner of the shore and then as expected, the ship turned towards the bay. After much struggling and battering, it slowly went down as it passed over the jagged rocks, well hidden beneath the sea. Once the ship had foundered, men would emerge from the caves and run down to the bit of shore that was still visible in the light. They would wait patiently for the half-drowned sailors to stumble from the sea and fall at their feet. Swiftly, the men used their heavy clubs to finish off the sailors so there would be no witnesses. The men worked hard through the night, but making sure they'd be gone before day break, they pushed and carried their small carts of contraband and valuables. It was a rewarding way to live, as long as you had no conscience about luring so many innocent souls to their death, and these men had no conscience about that.

Near the end, when she saw the damage she'd done, she flew back up to the great house on the cliff and into the safety of her painting. The house was, of course, in uproar as they'd seen the ship go down but could do nothing to help until the morning. James and Philip went down to the shore but saw only devastation there and were ashamed of their fellow-men who were stealing many barrels of brandy amongst other things. They went back to the house.

James went straight to the dining room and stared at his late sister's portrait. Her dress was now almost black. "We're going to stop you, Amanda – Philip and I are going to find a way to stop you – we know you're involved with all the disasters happening since your death. Just give us time and we'll stop you." As he left the room, he could have sworn he heard shrill laughter echo along the corridor and a sudden breeze caused the heavy curtains to flutter.

There were two further ship wrecks in the rocky bay over the next month. Two sailors had survived one wreck and told how they'd seen a woman in grey standing half way up the cliff, beside a huge fire she continuously fed with dry bracken. She disappeared as they struggled towards her and disappeared into the darkness of the wild night. Now there was no doubt in James's mind that his sister was responsible for the recent disasters – for both the ship wrecks and for the coaches tipping over at The Grey Lady's Crossing. He was glad his parents weren't at home as they'd only have hindered what he had to do.

He and Philip travelled into Truro and spoke with many ship owners there. James may have been young but he was of a serious disposition and everyone had time for him. As a sea captain, Philip was accepted immediately by the ship owners. They'd studied maps of the area and knew exactly where the danger lay in the bay below the great house. Only a couple of miles up the coast, it was reasonably safe for ships to come through a safer sea, away from the stormy, turbulent waves caused by the huge rocks. They wanted to get a message to all the ship owners and captains to steer clear of the small bay, although, it seemed to be welcoming them into a safe haven, it was not. A burning fire there, really meant great danger.

They all banded together and one owner, in particular, arranged for eye-catching pamphlets and posters to be distributed to every sea-going man in the Cornish coast. An investigation was started by local citizens as to what was available to try and safeguard sailors and ships on stormy nights. Lighthouses were not yet in use but some areas built wooden towers with oil lamps to shine in the darkness. They weren't too reliable as they crumbled under the power of the waves and the wind direction created chaos, but there were many famous people working on a suitable invention. The day would come.

In the meantime, Philip had been searching the coastline for interesting shapes in wood and stone, things he could turn into beautiful ornamental shapes or useful objects. His days as a ship's captain were over. He'd always been interested in art and craftmanship and he thought he could make a living at this. He'd never quite got over the ship wreck and being stuck on the rocks. He'd discovered one of the great rocks was very life-like and resembled a woman in a flowing dress. He brought his working tools to the shore and began to chip away at the hard surface. Facial features were unclear but long, flowing curls were easy to create. She held one arm aloft and, in that hand, he carved and chiselled until a bowl was formed. The figure was scary and dominating.

James had to help him at this point. "How do I make a fire burn blue, James? I know there is a way – I can remember being told about it in the Caribbean."

"If you get hold of copper chloride and make sure there's no salt near – you can burn sodden material into a bright blue flame." James had been a keen scholar when he'd had a private tutor. "We'll also need thick glass to encase the flame so that the wind doesn't blow it out. But where do you plan to put it?"

They went down to the shore, to the rock that Philip had been working on and James was amazed. "My God, it actually looks like Amanda. Let's go into Truro and buy copper chloride. Can you contact the ship owners and their captains and tell them they must warn their ships not to go near the bay where there is a blue light shining? Tell them to say it'll only happen on stormy nights but we'll make sure the blue light burns when it's needed. I can send a servant down and he can reset the flame."

Philip said: "It's a plan, James – at least, we have a plan," and he slapped James on the shoulder.

Back in the big house, the two men were having a well-deserved brandy in the dining room.

"Shall we tell her now James?" Philip asked. "Yes, let's." James was enjoying himself.

They both looked at the portrait and James walked towards the fireplace.

"Well Amanda, your last day has come. We thought our incredible blue light would have been enough – but something also has to be done to stop you from jumping in front of coaches. You've got to be banished completely to stop your wicked ways. You were always a spoiled child who wished no one any good – but I never thought you were evil. I was wrong. Come on, Philip – it's a big painting – I can't do it by myself." James looked grim. The two men struggled to get the painting off the wall and slowly managed to get it upstairs into the attic.

"Over here, I think," and they placed it – face to the wall – in the darkest corner of the room. "Let's go – it's what she deserves." Her dress was almost black – which was a reminder of what she was capable. They went back downstairs and had a second brandy.

After a few days, everything seemed quiet. The blue light was working well, the pamphlets had been distributed and, as far as they knew, they'd stopped Amanda from wandering around outside the house. Only time would tell how successful they'd been.

"Let's go for a holiday, Philip. My parents are due back soon and I'd rather not be here when they arrive and find Amanda's painting gone." The excellent idea was acted upon and a day later, they caught the coach into Truro – and from there, they didn't really care where they went. They could be gone for a while.

Everything seemed quiet and serene, until one week later, when the master and mistress arrived home from their own holiday. Their shock at finding the painting gone from the dining room was enormous and the butler and footman were immediately sent to find it and return it to its proper place.

They sat back in the armchairs by the fire and stared up at the wall. There she was, as pretty as a picture. Her dress wasn't black but it seemed a much darker blue than they remembered. "And George – tell the servant he doesn't have to go down to the shore – as he's been doing – another mad idea of James's, I'm sure."

"Very well, Madame," and he bowed his way out of the room, closing the door behind him.

"There now, everything's as it should be, my dear – all's right with the world," and he fetched a new book from the case.

"That painting looks almost real, doesn't it? I want her happy spirit to be back around us again. We'll soon be able to feel her presence – as she goes about her everyday business. I can almost see her now – do you see her too?"

"I certainly do, my dear. The only thing is, now that we have no living daughter – I don't believe we'll ever have any grandchildren." He paused and looked meaningfully over the rim of his spectacles. "You do understand what I'm saying, don't you?"

She looked at him with a sad expression, then said, "Unfortunately, I do, my dear! James seems very content with his captain!

Pretty, Witty Nell

She climbed the gentle slope to where she could see the entire wood covered in bluebells. The bright blueness was amazing, from almost white flowers to deepest blue spread everywhere like a thick carpet covering the ground. The trees were coming into bloom and the greenness of the leaves was in contrast to the colour of the flowers. Birds and bees were high in the air and it was as if the whole countryside was coming alive. It was the end of spring and as the season moved into summer, it spread great beauty all around and even she could feel the blood rising in her body. She was a bonny, healthy young girl of 15 years, almost sixteen, and she felt excited as she thought of her entire life still to come.

A bombshell was recently dropped; however, her mother had told her that morning that their pub was to be sold and they would move into the centre of London. It wasn't that far to the city centre from the pub but the scenery would be like chalk and cheese. Unfortunately, the pub was not a great money spinner and the owner had decided to get rid of it – and that would leave the Gwynns with no place to live. Nell's mother had found a cheap set of rooms for them in Coal Yard Alley in the city and in a week's time, they'd all be settled there. Nell sighed loudly and looked again at the beauty of the bluebells all around, but she was also excited to be going to London and knew the world was her oyster, if she chose to make it so.

The silence was suddenly broken with a shrill voice calling out, "Nell, get your lazy, good-for-nothing backside in this pub and get behind the bar. Customs beginning to pick up." Her mother was a slave driver, of that, there was no doubt and she liked to use her two daughters work to their full capacity. They cleaned and brushed and cooked, enough to fill their waking hours. Nell's sister was called Rose and she was two years older. She was a real country girl, unlike Nell who'd always had a yearning for the city. She'd loved her life in the country for her first few years but now she was growing up, she'd like to experience the bustle and glamour of the city. She believed she could make something of herself amongst all those people and she was determined to try one day soon. She realised however, she'd have to move fast as when her mother took her to Coal Yard Alley, she'd work her to death and ruin all her chances to better herself.

"Comin' Ma," she shouted. "Do you want any bluebells for the bar?"

"No, I bloomin' don't – they die too quickly," was the reply from the woman who couldn't see beauty in anything she looked at. This miserable personality was the main reason she had to get away. Nell feared it was infectious and she never wanted to be like her mother, that was for sure.

Nell worked hard that night. With the weather picking up, there were a few thirsty men around. She knew her bottom would be black and blue by the next day, strange how men couldn't let her pass without reaching for her bottom. She was carrying a heavy tray to a table where several young men were sitting. They were not local, she could tell, and they were laughing and joking and generally having a good time. One of them wrapped an arm around her waist and she almost dropped the tray.

"Leave her alone, Mick – can't you see how heavy that tray is," one young man told his friend. He was good looking, with brown hair and eyes and had a gorgeous smile.

"Thank'ee sir, you're the kind one." She put the tray on the table, smiled at him which caused her dimpled cheeks to shine even more and bobbed a low curtsey.

"And you're the pretty one." He smiled at her again. Two tankards of ale later, the group were even louder but their laughter was happy and good natured. They were from London, and were performing their act locally in the nearest town. They were jugglers, acrobats and dancers with one singer who'd already given the pub two or three bawdy songs. It was easy to tell what kind of performers they were and as the pub closed for the night, three of them climbed the stairs to the one bed they shared. It was the cheapest pub they could find in the area. Nell hung around and brought her new friend, John, another tankard of ale for which she didn't charge.

"Can I talk to you when everyone's gone? I know you're tired but I won't keep you long." She used her most winning smile as she finished tidying the bar. She came straight to the point when her mother finally went to bed. "I want to go to London, right into the city centre. I've always wanted to go there and I'm getting older all the time. I'll be 16 next birthday and I'll soon be past my first flush of youth. The only thing is I have to go soon – as my family are to move there next week and my mother will work me like a horse – when what I want to do is to become an actress."

"I don't doubt that Nell but you've a few good youthful years in you still to come. But I'm afraid I travel on my own. The others wouldn't want you to tag along with us, I can tell you that much." He finished his ale and stood up to leave.

"Please John take me with you and I'll do anything you want." And she realised she meant it. She would do anything to get to London as soon as possible.

She sensed he was a pushover and wasn't surprised when he said, "Be outside at five o'clock – that's when we're leaving – but pretend you're surprised to see us – and that as you were going to the city anyhow, you may as well walk with us. I think they'll believe that." And then he really did leave and go upstairs.

Nell was so excited, she couldn't sleep, so she packed her bundle and took what little money she had. She wore her stoutest boots and took along her one other dress and a couple of shawls. She'd soon be earning money, she told herself, as she planned to get a job right away and she'd make sure she'd earn more money than her skinflint of a mother would give her in Coal Yard Alley.

Not that Rose would get much more and the Alley would probably suit her very well but then she was much more easy to please than her sister. The younger one had always been the more forceful of the girls – whereas Rose just went along with whatever came her way.

Needless to say, Nell got no sleep that night and when the sun came up, she was ready and waiting outside the pub. The four men came tumbling out of the door, unclean and unshaven as before. John, however, was different; he was clean and had combed his hair. She pretended to be surprised to see them and asked them innocently where they were going.

"We're off home to London – too much fresh air around here for the likes of us," and they linked arms and marched off up the road. Nell followed them and only when asked, did she tell them, she too was going to the city.

"What will you do when you get there?" one of them asked.

"I'll find a job and someplace to live." She knew it sounded too simple but she thought the truth was the best plan.

"You'll be lucky!" They laughed and walked on with her trailing behind.

After about two hours, they all stopped for a rest. Nell had brought some bread and cheese in her bundle and a flagon of water, which she was happy to share with them. They seemed to accept her more after that and even suggested she might try the market for a job. The fruit market at Covent Garden was always looking for workers, but it was hard work and not for the faint hearted.

"I'm not afraid of hard work," she bit back. "I'll do a fair day's work for a fair day's pay. That seems right, doesn't it?"

Soon they had gathered their things together and were on the road again. No passing cart stopped to give them a ride and it was getting dark when they finally reached the middle of London. She didn't like the smell, it didn't smell clean.

John said, "You'll soon get used to it. After a while, you won't even smell it," and he laughed at her turned-up nose. Her boots were pinching her toes and she knew she'd have to stop for a rest soon – but John added, "We're nearly there, Nell – keep going."

He had a room over a shop, it wasn't very pretty and smelt really bad, probably due to the raw effluence that was regularly thrown out of windows and which ran down the streets. She soon learned to avoid the places where the words 'Gardez-La' were shouted loudly from the windows.

However, she realised that John was being kind to her to let her stay for a few nights. She knew she'd have to pay him in kind as she had very little money but that didn't bother her, she'd always thought her body would be useful one day. She was a very buxom girl with a voluptuous figure for someone so young and she knew men liked her and thought her comely. She had realised some time ago that it was something she could use to get what she wanted and she fully intended to do just that. A country girl one day and a worldly, wise young woman the next.

Her real name was Eleanor Gwynn but she'd always been called Nell and she saw no reason to change it; anyhow, she felt more like a Nell than an Eleanor. So Nell Gwynne's new life in London began with her sharing a bed with a young actor who planned to use her and then discard her. She knew the life would be hard but she had every confidence in her ability to always come out on top. Life seemed good so far.

Next day, John came rushing up the stairs. "Nell, get yourself over to Convent Garden Market in the Strand – they're taking on workers as we speak." She grabbed her shawl and ran past him into the street. He sat on the only chair in the room and gratefully ate the bread and cheese she'd prepared for him. At least, he hoped it was for him but he ate it either way.

She reached Covent Garden at three o'clock that afternoon. The busiest time at the market was over, fresh fruit, flowers and vegetables were almost all sold out by that time but there was still a chance to buy some left over bits and pieces. She sauntered over to one of the larger stalls and asked the man there if he was looking for any more helpers. "I can come as early as you like – and I'm very strong – I can move anything you like. Look how strong I am!" And she flexed her arms to make her muscles stand out – but also her breasts in the low-cut dress. It all helped and if there was one thing Nell understood, it was a man.

"Yeah, I could do with another pair of hands – but you've got to be here at six in the morning to help unload the carts – and then serve at the stall until the afternoon. Do you think you're up to that?" A tall man with absolutely no hair answered her without even looking up. *Wasted effort,* Nell thought and put her muscles away.

"See you at six then. Can I take some of this bashed fruit that's on the ground," and with her arms full of spoiled fruit, she made her way home feeling very positive.

She worked there for a couple of months before she ventured to ask how much he'd accept from her if she were to buy a dozen good oranges each day. She was told he'd let her have them for threepence each, and that was a bargain. She'd been speaking to a woman who was called Orange Moll, who already sold fruit in the streets at a pretty good profit and who'd told her threepence was a fair price for oranges. She accepted his offer and from that day on, she bought twelve good oranges from the stall holder, and at first, wandered the streets trying to sell them to passers-by for sixpence each. Her profits soon mounted and she began to think of having a permanent place to sell the fruit, and John, with whom she still shared a room, suggested the theatre in Drury Lane. It was a royal theatre and people sold things to the audience in the evenings and he knew it to be a good spot for selling. He'd seen it often on the nights he worked there.

"Sometimes the king even comes there himself," he told her. "You might even be able to sell him an orange if you're lucky." She laughed at this and tried to picture herself talking to a king.

The comely girl was soon recognised as one of the orange sellers at the pit in the theatre, and it wasn't only the audience who bought them but so did the thirsty actors. She always had a smile and a ready wit to deal with their cheeky comments – just as she was used to the pinching of her bottom and the brushing against her breasts well remembered from her days in her mother's pub. She'd got the job selling oranges and other sweet bites from the lady in charge there, who turned out to be her friend from the market, Orange Moll. Moll taught her the value of a ready tongue and polished wit. "The men love it," she told her, "but don't try to outsmart them as they don't like that – they like to believe themselves to be cleverer than any woman." And she laughed at their obvious stupidity.

"Come buy my lovely oranges – they're juicy and ripe." She'd sit on a box in the pit and cheekily cross her legs until her knees were showing. "Come, quench your thirst in the pit and have a squeeze of my… tasty fruit." Her amusing taunts actually sold many more of her oranges than normal and she rarely had even one left when the theatre closed for the night. Her funny jokes and brazen manner were attractive, not only to the audience but to the actors themselves. Being such a bonny, buxom young woman, some of them watched her with interest, sometimes she could claim the audience's attention more than they did themselves. She followed Orange Moll's advice to the letter and found that it always worked. One man in particular watched her closely. His name was Charles Hart and he was one of the main actors at Drury Lane, being known as a 'king's player'. He was a smart man, however, and he didn't rush things; he watched and listened and laughed frequently at her sayings. He especially liked:

"My name is Eleanor but you can call me Nell
They say I'm beautiful and should be called 'Belle'
If you need a cuddle, kiss or even just a smile
Come buy my fruit – it's only ripe for a while."

And they flocked down into the pit to force their sixpences on her – and get their kiss or cuddle for which she never charged, Charles Hart thought she'd be good on stage – in comedy parts, of course – nothing too serious. She'd need quite a bit of training, he realised but he'd be willing to do that, after all she was a comely wench and very free with her favours. He could arrange for other actors to teach her singing and dancing and the good timing of flirtatious talk on stage. She would be well trained in the end. Women's' parts on stage were usually taken by boys – but she might help change that.

He'd watched her closely for some time before speaking to her. He'd bought many oranges by this time and he asked, "Have you ever trod the boards, Nell? Or ever helped behind the scenes, perhaps?"

"No, this is the closest I've ever been to the stage – standing in front of it. I would love to perform for the audience – I believe I'm quite talented and I can sing and dance," Nell volunteered.

"Are you able to read – you know, like books or journals?" he went on.

"'Course I can read and write for that matter – do you want me to show you?" She was quite indignant.

"No need my dear, I believe you. I'm only asking to see if you'd be able to read scripts and the like. Would you be able to learn speeches and stand on the stage and say the words loudly? Your voice sounds quite good but you'd have to make sure it could travel to the very back of the theatre. Do you think you could do that?" Charles was becoming quite besotted with her and offered some immediate training if she came to the theatre before the evening performances began – something she readily agreed to.

And so began Nell's first experience of the stage – something that would take her to heights she could never expect. Her orange selling went on however, it was a good money-spinning job and she enjoyed the quick repartee she had to cultivate to hold the interest of the audience. Charles didn't find it easy at first to coach her as she was an independent and strong-willed woman who felt sometimes, that she knew more than he did. But he decided she was refreshing and would be good at amusing the audience, and she'd be ready with banter if she ever fluffed her lines and had to make up something on the spot.

That day, she agreed to meet Charles at three o'clock and she arrived on the dot. She was beginning to dress better than before and wore a green dress with a feather boa around her shoulders. Her long hair was piled on top of her head and held there with a silver coloured clasp, and her shoes were the same shade of green as her dress. They peeped out from her hemline, but still making sure her pretty ankles were showing to perfection. She was almost, but not quite, a real lady. Charles had found a small part for her to play, it was only a few lines but they were good lines that would have the audience in fits of laughter. It was about a man who sold chickens and cockerels in the market place, sometimes they escaped and Nell was employed to chase after them and catch them. Many funny lines supported this fiasco and Nell's 'double-entendres' were given with excellent timing and deliberate suggestive glances at certain members of the audience – some of whom were already primed to come back at her with cheeky rejoinders. Charles had realised very early on that her character would appeal to today's vocal audiences who loved to play a part in the performance.

She proved to be a success in the comedy plays and easily learned her lines very quickly. One day, Charles waylaid her as she was heading for home and asked her where she lived – and would she find it easier to live closer to the theatre. He had some rooms in the Strand and she would be welcome to move in with him until she could find some for herself. Nell jumped at the chance – she was no fool and this would be moving up the status ladder. She told John it was to make her stage performances easier as she wouldn't be so tired – and he swallowed that. In fact, he didn't really mind as there was little more, she could give him and he'd have his room all to himself again.

So Nell now lived in the Strand – quite near to Covent Garden – and she was now and again employed at the Royal Drury Lane Theatre as one of the king's players. She knew she'd soon have to stop selling oranges but went on as long as she could as it was a good money maker. She wasn't paid much for her stage work at the theatre – not yet, anyway – but she'd soon change that. She was proving to be popular with the audiences who came, not only to see her perform, but to buy one of her oranges and get a kiss or cuddle as well. Charles encouraged her in this as it brought in good business for the theatre and Nell was happy to comply.

A famous writer called Samuel Pepys spotted Nell very early in her career and recognised her as a rising star. He wrote about her on more than one occasion and so helped with her popularity. She was the first woman actress to perform on stage and for this reason alone, she'd become quite famous. King Charles even knew of her as he'd only recently returned to England from France, where it was quite common for women to tread the boards. So, he positively encouraged it. More parts were being introduced for women but nearly all of those were for boys so that the women had to wear breeches. This showed off their shapely limbs and made them even more popular and Nell was always willing to take these parts. Unfortunately, this enhanced her reputation as a prostitute – something the first actresses all had to deal with – but then as this was exactly what they were, it wasn't such a big thing.

The next night when Nell was on stage, she played the part of a drunken youth. She wore bright green breeches which the crowd loved. She was fooling around like a drunk man, bending back and forth to show off her lovely legs and arguing with the audience about whether she was a man or a woman, when she noticed a very still figure sitting at the side of the wooden seats. It was her sister Rose and Nell waved her hand and smiled – but the figure didn't move a muscle, but sat there with a very solemn expression on her face. Nell planned to catch up with her when the play was over – but by that time, the figure had disappeared. Rose had looked thinner and paler than when she'd lived in the country – but then, that wasn't surprising. So she made up her mind to visit Coal Yard Alley to see her mother and sister. It was time she did it, she knew – but they'd never bothered to come looking for her.

In the meantime, King Charles was becoming very popular with his people – particularly after the harsh years of Cromwellian thinking – austerity, seriousness and perpetual negativity. The king was used to the French ways and wanted England to be just like Paris, so he encouraged the theatre, the actresses and even the prostitutes. Nell soon became one of his mistresses and left Charles Hart's home to live on her own, so that the king could have a special passageway built to visit her secretly – and apparently to play cards. Nell's life was undergoing great changes and although King Charles had many mistresses, it was said that she was his favourite. She wanted no political advantages nor more money than she earned at the theatre – so there was rarely any argument between them.

Two days later, Nell looked for Coal Yard Alley and after asking several people, she found it.

"God, this is bad," she said to herself. "This is worse than any place I've lived." Eventually, she found the right house – or hovel, which was a more accurate a description. Rose was nowhere to be seen and nor was her mother. She knocked on the next door and a scruffy woman appeared shouting, "What the bleedin' 'ell do you want? There's no one lives in that 'ouse no more – they're both dead," and she went back inside and slammed the door shut. Nell thought she was going to faint as she'd only seen Rose a few days before. She started to cry, knowing she should have come to see them before now. She went to the door on the other side and a child appeared. Behind her stood a young woman, who grabbed the girl by the shoulders and pulled her inside.

Nell shouted through the door, "I only wanted to ask what happened to the two women who lived here." The woman opened the door a crack and looked outside. "They're both dead Chuck – the mother a while ago – they do say she drowned hersel' and the daughter just a few days ago." She gave no sympathy nor asked how Nell knew them – she just went back inside and closed the door. A heavy guilt fell about her shoulders – she should have looked them up long before – they were obviously in need of her. She could have found a job for Rose – and given her mother some money. Then again, they'd never come looking for her.

Nell wandered back to the theatre but before going inside, she slumped down on the ground and cried bitterly. She felt very guilty about what had happened. She suddenly realised that the Rose she'd seen a few days ago must have been an apparition – that was why she looked so ill. She struggled to her feet and strangely enough, made her way back to John's rooms as he was the only person who had known her relatives and for some reason, she felt this was important. John made her a drink and tried to cheer her up. "Come on, Nell – look what a grand lady you've become. They could have come looking for you, you know – so you're no worse than they were." She definitely felt better when she left there and said she'd come back to see him later, knowing full well she wouldn't.

In the middle of her next performance when she was again playing a youth, she spotted Rose again, sitting on the same seat as before. She looked exactly the same – still unfriendly and severe as though she was trying to tell her sister something. This time, Nell ignored her but found it difficult and kept looking back at the solemn girl. When the performance was over, she looked again for her – but alas she'd gone.

That night, she was entertaining the king, who'd crept along the secret passage from the building next door. Not very kingly perhaps, but it was part of the excitement of seeing his mistress. Nell was rather sad this time and on being told what was wrong with her, he told her there was no such thing as ghosts and she must try to clear her head of such thoughts. This man had seen many things and knew so much more than she did, that she took seriously what he said and set about tantalising him as only she could. This was something she was good at – and helped ease her mind.

"I do love you, Nell. You're one of my special friends whom I feel I can trust – you want nothing from me and never ask for any favours. Some others use me for who I am and what I can give them – but not you." He sat her on his knee and stroked her hair. "Why Nell, I do believe you're putting on a little weight. Have you been at the sweet table too much?"

"No, I haven't my Lord, this swollen stomach is your doing as well as mine," she retorted.

"Why Nell, are you trying to tell me you're carrying my child? You clever girl. Several other women have done this but I value your child much more than theirs." Charles was obviously pleased with the news.

"I'll make sure neither you nor he suffer – don't you worry – I'll make him a Duke and give him a title. Just wait and see." Obviously, it would be a boy – as the king decreed!

Nell carried the child well and went on performing on stage as long as she could – but even she had to stop in the end. Rose had visited her frequently – but never saying anything and every time Nell tried to approach her, she just disappeared without trace. Until the day Nell knew the baby would be coming – and soon – she was laid up in her bedroom and the king had sent a nurse from the palace who would care for her – and even better, become her wet nurse after the birth. Labour had started some time ago and Nell was lying in bed and writhing in agony – the wet nurse was hovering around her, not helping much at all, when Rose suddenly appeared standing by the door.

"Oh Rosie, Rosie – you've come to me at last. Push that woman out of the way and come, hold my hand." Rose slowly came across the room and leaned over her sister. "You left us Eleanor – you left Ma and me with nothing and no one. Why did you do that?"

Nell was too involved with giving birth to deal with a disgruntled sister and told her so. "I had nothing either and had to look out for myself. There were two of you and you could have done the same." She stopped reprimanding Rose to scream out loud – the pain was bad. The nurse pushed through the ghost and pushed up Nell's knees. "It's coming, ma'am – I can see the head now. Nothing to worry about – all's as it should be." And then the pain suddenly ceased and her son was born. The king would be pleased as he'd wanted a boy. He and his legal wife had never managed to produce an heir between them and every time one of his mistresses produced an illegitimate son, he was able to look the world in the face and say, "I can do it – there's nothing wrong with me," and he could gloat to all the courtiers and to his people.

He was as good as his word and bestowed the title of Duke of Beauclerc, First Duke of Albany on his new born son – and Nell was delighted. A year later, she gave the king a second son, whom he called James after his brother and he always made sure the boys were well cared for. Rose appeared from time to time and always managed to surprise her sister. In her eyes, Nell had deserted her mother and herself and said she'd come back again and again until Nell admitted she'd done wrong. She could have found her sister a job selling oranges at the theatre – but she hadn't even bothered to do that. The king told her to forget about the ghost – she just had a guilty conscience about leaving her family when she did – and the ghostly appearance of Rose was because of this. Nell did wonder if this was what it was. Charles was a very wise man after all.

The successful actress, mistress of a king and mother of a Duke just shrugged her shoulders and said, "So be it. I'll see you next time," and went on performing at the Drury Lane Theatre. Since it was public knowledge that she and the king were sweethearts, her fame on stage had become even greater – and her success knew no bounds. Samuel Pepys, the great diarist, wrote about her, calling her 'Pretty, witty Nell' and she soon became known as this. The famous play writer Dryden, had even written some woman's parts for her and she didn't always have

156

to wear breeches so often after that. But the raucous audience still liked to see her in her breeches – she was no less comely since the birth of her sons.

Time passed and King Charles and Nell remained close friends. It did seem that they actually loved each other – not just king and mistress but loving husband and wife. The two sons they had were healthy and happy and who wouldn't have been with a mother like Nell. She really was the epitome of the Restoration period in England at the time – as was Charles himself, after the austerity of Oliver Cromwell's country and the execution of his own father. The pair were jolly, happy and wealthy – an ideal arrangement.

But the king was ill. The news spread like wildfire and his subjects were truly worried and sad. He had made such a difference to the country that they didn't want to lose him. Nell was frantic and sent a messenger to Whitehall Palace every day seeking news of the king. The stories of his illness were soon on everyone's lips. He'd been shaving on the Monday morning when he suddenly shouted out in pain and fell to the floor, having one fit after another. Six physicians were immediately with him and they bled him profusely, they made him vomit and gave him an enema, they cut his hair off and used suction cups to cause blisters to form on his scalp. They used pigeon droppings as a healing poultice and they force-fed him with a drink made of human skull that had come from a violent criminal. The treatment seemed barbaric but it was accepted at the time and they worked hard to come up with new macabre cures.

Each day, they did all of this and repeatedly bled him until he was so weak, he couldn't move. Of course, Nell was unaware of what they were doing to him although she wouldn't have been any wiser as to whether this was good or bad. For five days, the king continued to suffer in this way. On the Saturday, his brother James – his heir – came to sit with him, and ask if there was anything he wanted. Charles managed to croak the words, "Let not poor Nelly starve," which became a phrase repeated for many years to come. James promised and kept his word to look after Nell the mistress – he even gave her a good pension from the Treasury.

"You're on your own now, Sister – no king to protect you." Nell awoke to find Rose standing at the foot of her bed. "The word is that he killed himself by messing about with chemicals in the Royal Laboratory where there was no ventilation – and that was what caused him to breathe his last – mercury poisoning. What do you think, Sister – or did he just want to get away from you?" Rose's ghost was still very bitter.

Nell's face was ravaged with tears and she covered it with a lace handkerchief. "Go away, you wicked ghost – you can't say anything more to upset me. I've lost the one person I loved beyond all others. I am alone now and don't know what will happen to me (she didn't yet know about the pension). Leave me alone, Rosie – I am ready now to say I didn't do right by you and Ma. I no longer care about my pride and I am ready to admit I could have been kinder to you." At those words, the ghostly figure disappeared like a willow-the-wisp and Nell was alone. At last, she'd got rid of that awful apparition.

A courtier from Whitehall Palace came to Nell's home. He asked if there was anything, he could do for her – but she said there was nothing. He told her of the pension and about King Charles' last words: 'Let not poor Nelly starve.' He explained that the new king couldn't have anything to do with her and Nell nodded her head in understanding. She felt that her life was over and she had little left to live for. But with the passage of time, her grief would ease and perhaps she could start living again. *I might even go back to the theatre,* she thought quietly, *only not yet.*

When Charles died, he was only 54 years old and two years later, a sad Nell joined him. She was only 37 – no age at all. But she was happy on her death bed because he came to fetch her himself. She opened her still lovely eyes and saw him there – a younger Charles than when she'd last seen him – he was in his prime again. He leaned over the bed and kissed her forehead. "Come now my true wife – I've missed you."

"And I love you, sir – take my hand please – I never want to lose you again. We've both had a short life, I know – but hasn't it been full and happy?"

"Full and happy, Wife, as you say but it's not over yet. We're going to a better land where we'll always be together." Her limp hand fell from his and she got up from the bed – a frail but still beautiful ghost. They both walked off together, first looking back at the body on the bed.

Pretty, witty Nell was no more.

The Arrogant Pitiful Man

He was tall, blond, broad shouldered and handsome. He was only 20 years of age and he was the king of England. His name was Henry and there was a definite air of arrogance about him. He looked as though he owned all around him and indeed, he did. His older brother Arthur, had recently died and left the throne in the very capable hands of his younger brother, Henry, who was going to make sure that his reign was very different from that of their father, Henry the seventh. His father had been a mean man who didn't spend one penny if he could avoid it – and because of this, he left the royal coffers very full indeed. His son was now king in his place and intended to spare no expense in making the country and his subjects happy and full of life.

Henry the eighth had his brother's crown, his throne and now he wanted his wife, Catherine. She was five years older than Henry but he'd always admired her, ever since she'd come from Aragon to marry Arthur – he still admired Catherine and By George, he would have her for his own. Henry would always get what he wanted – he just wouldn't take no for an answer. She had suffered a lot since the death of her young husband – she was banished from Court, given very little funds to live on and her clothes were shabby and even torn Once Henry became king however, Katherine was brought back to Court and they married within a few months and very soon later, she was pregnant with his child. Henry was proud beyond measure of both her and of himself.

He held one pageant after another and she was always the star of the ceremony, after himself of course. He was a born show-off and needed always to be the winner of everything that even resembled a challenge. His jousting was second to none and he sat a horse very well; his song writing was clever and inspired; his writing and ability to discuss subjects in several languages was better than anyone else around; he was loved and respected by his noblemen and subjects alike – and when he sat in Council, his word was law and he always got his way. The man really was a king in all aspects.

One day, in the middle of a pageant, a servant came rushing up to him and cried, "Sire, your lady wife has gone into labour and your child is shortly to be born." Henry rushed to Catherine's apartments and was met there by her ladies in waiting, who were clustered around the Queen's bed.

"Come, come my Lords and witness the birth of my son." He waved his arms in welcome and pushed his way through the Queen's ladies. He'd brought his courtiers with him – something he shouldn't have done as a birthing was not something they usually witnessed – but then, this was Henry and it was what he wanted. She had lost her first baby – a girl – and this one just had to be a boy or the king would be most displeased. Blood was everywhere and the Queen was in a state of great distress. Henry looked perplexed and held out his hands to the ladies as if pleading with them to help. They did – and within minutes, a lady nurse held the baby upside down by the feet and smacked his bottom, to make him cry and draw his first breath. The men in the room stood very still – it all looked so barbaric – but of course, it wasn't. Catherine had fainted back onto the pillows, pale and shaking – but she managed to hold out her frail hand to the king and smiled. Henry fell onto his knees and clasped his wife's hand. It was a boy and he was delighted.

The men began to leave the chamber one by one – some looking rather sheepish and some rather green. Henry joined them and left the ladies to clean their mistress and tidy the room. The baby was also cleaned and put into a magnificent cradle which had been placed there for this moment. The nobles called for the servants to bring wine and food.

"Giving birth is a tiring thing," they joked and Henry joined in. He had an heir at last. His father had been wrong in not wanting him to marry his brother's widow – she had done well and there would be more to come. Despite his father's anger at his choosing Catherine, the moment he died, his son went completely against his wishes and brought her from her isolated dwelling and poverty-stricken ways – and showered her with valuables and possessions. She was a good Queen and would most likely, be a great one. He finished his drink and reached for another one.

"Fetch me my lute," he told a servant, "I feel like composing a new song for my son." He began strumming the instrument and humming a tune. He was very talented in most music and could play anything he chose. This song emerged as 'Drink to me Only with Thine Eyes' and was sung for many years to come – it is a song of love, as all his songs were. He was to spend his whole life looking for love, but more importantly, looking for a son to inherit his crown – and in his own eyes, to prove him not only a king, but also a man.

The little boy was called Henry and delighted both his father and his mother. He lived for just under two months and died quietly of what, no one knows. A bereft king at first blamed his wife for this – but as the child was looked after by some of the most important people in the land, he couldn't justify this belief for long. Catherine went on to have a further two miscarriages – both sons – but in between their births, she had a daughter, Mary, who survived and in time, became Mary First of England. Perhaps better known as Bloody Mary – but that was still to come.

Meanwhile, King Henry's eyes were wandering over the ladies at Court – and one in particular caught his attention. Her name was Ann Boleyn and she was regarded as a beautiful woman and also a very witty one. She had spent many years at the French Court and then a further number of years at a French Priory and Noble House. She was a most sophisticated woman. She knew how to catch Henry's attention and her witty remarks pleased him and he began to ask questions about her. His noble friends were always eager to please him and were quite willing to help arrange his courting quietly and secretly.

"Well, what have you found about her today, Sir Henry Compton? I hope you're not going to waste my time by telling me what I already know." Henry's mood was not good that day. He was over the excitement of his son's birth and death and needed more to keep him motivated. He wasn't really proud of how he was thinking of his wife these days but couldn't help feeling increasingly disappointed in her.

"Majesty, of course I will not waste your time – that is too precious a commodity for that." The two men spoke about her charms and Henry enquired as to her likelihood to meet with his advances. He must be sure about her before he showed his hand.

"Nothing is impossible where Your Majesty is concerned." Henry muttered beneath his beard and hoped the king would believe the flattery. He usually did. "Shall I arrange for you to meet with her in the rose garden, perhaps, nothing could be more innocent than that."

"Pray do, Henry – as you say nothing could be more innocent. The Lady's manners and style are very French and I find this most attractive." The king fetched a book from his shelves and began to peruse it. He was an avid reader and was always learning more and more. "Keep an eye on Wolsey, Henry – he is attempting to enquire of the Pope in Rome if my marriage to Catherine is moral and legal. She was my brother's wife of course and there are some who believe my marriage to her was wrong. It may even be the reason she fails to give me a healthy, living son." He was deliberately starting the rumour about his marriage to Catherine being a great mistake – and he'd appointed Cardinal Wolsey, his Chief Minister, to speak tentatively with Rome on his behalf – he'd been married to her for a long time now and he was growing tired of her. When Henry had married his brother's widow, he had to get a Papal Bull from the Pope himself, to allow the marriage to go ahead – and because of this, only the Pope could annul or end the marriage. This was something the present Pope was not willing to do.

Sir Henry Compton went off to do his bidding and Queen Catherine knew nothing of her husband's planned deception. She had the baby Mary, to keep her occupied and knew of nothing adverse that was happening. The king's interest in Anne grew more each day – but she was a wily, intelligent lady who knew how to keep him interested in her – and that was to keep him at arm's length for as long as she could. He had more than one illegitimate child – but no child was born and lived within the confines of marriage, who could be his heir.

Meanwhile, despite many attempts, Cardinal Wolsey was meeting with no success with the Pope in Rome and yet again, had to come back to the king with no hope of a divorce from Catherine. She knew now what Henry was trying to do and beseeched him not to treat her in this way – but to no avail, he was mesmerised with Anne Boleyn and wanted her for his wife. To do that, Catherine must go. And go, she did. She even faced a trial before many Lords, swearing her loyalty and love for the king. She failed and was banished from the Court.

She lived in solitude for years and in the end, died of a cancer – her daughter Mary was not even allowed to visit her.

Cardinal Wolsey had completely fallen out of favour with the king and in an attempt to placate him, the Cardinal gave the new, magnificent Hampton Court Palace to the monarch – as a gift. Henry had initiated the gift and took it with no quibble, then had the Cardinal arrested for treason because of his failure to do what was needed. A divorce was the absolute minimum he wanted and he would get it. Henry VIII always got what he wanted and if things went subsequently wrong, there was always someone else to blame. The chief minister to the king became very ill – probably brought on by fear as to what was going to happen – and died in prison before he could be tried for the crime of dishonouring the king. It mattered little to Henry – and just saved him a job – and he now had two of Wolsey's palaces, Whitehall and Hampton Court. He always got what he wanted – except a healthy male heir.

The years were passing and the king had put a new man on the case. That man was Thomas Cranmer, who was the Archbishop of Canterbury and who convened together a Council of high clergy and state ministers and together, they pronounced the marriage between Henry VIII of England and Catherine of Aragon as being null and void – indeed, it should never have taken place at all. Cranmer, therefore, was very high in the king's esteem, after all the 'Great Matter' which Henry preferred his divorce to be known as, had lasted for six whole years. Henry declared himself – not only the king, but the head of the Church of England – and the Roman Catholic Church had no say in the matter. There now was no need for a Papal Bull from Rome. Henry was a Protestant and so therefore, was England.

"Thomas, you have done well and I am now married to my beloved Queen Anne who is pregnant with my son. We had a private marriage in the king's Private Chapel in Whitehall Palace and all because of your cleverness, Anne is already with child and assures me it will be a boy, Thomas – a boy, do you hear?" The king was visiting Thomas Cranmer's family home at Lambeth and was in a very good mood. He ate well of the feast that Cranmer's wife had provided and repeatedly patted the Archbishop on the shoulder.

"Nothing bothers me, Your Majesty – and I shall pray for the safe delivery of the next Tudor king." Cranmer knew how valuable it was to please Henry and he could only hope that he always would.

She lost the child, however, and had more than one miscarriage afterwards. She did give birth, however, to a girl, whom Henry was not interested in – and with the passing of just one thousand days of marriage, Henry had her executed on Tower Hill on charges of: 'Incest: Witchcraft: Adultery: and Conspiracy against the king.' Of what she was really guilty, no one would ever know – but of course, she denied everything. Unfortunately, with her fall from favour, she also took with her several young men to their deaths – they'd been put in prison, tortured and executed – probably because they had been too friendly with her – and one of them was her brother. Henry didn't mourn her. She hadn't lived up to her promises and he needed a new wife.

"Come," he called to his noble companions, "follow me and we'll visit the Lady Seymour – Jane's the one for me." And the men laughed and followed him on horseback. Jane Seymour was at her country house and the king rode up to her, swung her up onto his horse and rode away, the nobles following. "You'll marry me Jane, won't you? You can deny me nothing, can you?"

They were married two weeks later – in all just 12 days after Anne's execution. Henry seemed to have no conscience at all in his quest to have a legitimate son and heir. Jane was a sweet, young woman – the complete opposite of Anne Boleyn. It had been said of her that she wasn't very intelligent – but she was clever enough to keep Henry on a string until he proposed marriage to her. Not so low in intelligence after all. She may not have been witty and fiery as her predecessor had been but rather gentle and comfortable to be with – just what he needed. Life was good again and he intended to enjoy it. He was king of one of the greatest countries in the world and he had a young, nubile lady for his wife. Next a legitimate son!

The couple lived most of their time at Hampton Court Palace and Jane made it her business to change the fashions and manners of the Court – to bring them back to a level of modesty and simplicity, after Anne Boleyn's wild frenchified ways. Almost a year into the marriage, Jane's pregnancy was celebrated and Henry knew this time he'd have a son.

"You are clever my Queen and as soon as I settle this uprising in the North of the country, you will be crowned, with all the ceremonial pageantry possible. Do you hear me Jane, your status of queen will be established for ever. I am pleased to see that as your personal badges, you have chosen the Phoenix and the Falcon – both favourites of my own – and the choice of Phoenix is true to yourself and to how you have worked at returning the Court to a more moral and acceptable place. In effect, raising it from the ashes." And on this approving note, he went off drinking with his noblemen and following the Hunt – both things which he loved.

Jane gave birth to her son, Edward in 1537. The girl who had been Lady-in-waiting to both Catherine of Aragon and to Anne Boleyn, had given the king something they could not. It was a long labour and she suffered much in its course. She could not rise from her bed due to complications following the birth – but was encouraged by Henry to get up from her sick bed and attend the boy's Christening in the Royal Chapel.

"My Lord, I'm afraid I am far from well – and seem to have no strength at all." She was pale and was weeping, but Henry said, "Come now, Wife, you cannot miss this occasion. Once over, you can return to bed and rest." So she struggled and went with the other royals to the Christening. As Henry led the way, he thought he saw someone he knew standing beside the wall tapestry. It was a big man dressed in a bright red gown, cape and cap, – he knew it to be Cardinal Wolsey, who'd been dead now for some years – but of course, had lived in and once owned Hampton Court Palace. He was frowning at the king who had drawn his sword and stabbed at the tapestry, shouting at the apparition. "Get thee gone Thomas Wolsey – I know you're not a real person – you come to scare me on the day of my son's Christening. Do you hear me, Wolsey – my son, I say." And the Cardinal's ghost disappeared.

Jane died shortly after this incident, having contracted Child Bed Fever, something she had no strength to fight. It was only 12 days after the birth. The baby thrived and of course, that pleased Henry. However, losing Jane in such circumstances, broke his heart. He believed he had loved her more than his first two wives and he continued to mourn her for two whole years, before his small eyes turned to look at other potential queens. He must have regarded her highly, however, as he had her buried in his own tomb at Windsor, built for himself, an honour none of his other wives had been given.

There were, and still are, many sightings of Jane wandering up and down the passageway to Silver Stick Stairs – just outside the bedchamber at Hampton Court where she had given birth to her son. She is said to be very pale and ghostly frail in stature. She is apparently looking for something and it is believed she looks for her baby.

However, Henry's blood was on the rise again and he looked around the globe for a suitable consort. He must have more children to keep the crown secure, and he wasn't as strong as he had once been, since he'd fallen from his horse in a Jousting Match and injured his leg and side badly. There were also problems growing in Europe and he needed power and money to support his place in the world, so he turned to Germany, specifically to achieving an alliance with Cleve – a rich and important principality. In order to do this however, Henry instructed his Lord Chancellor, Thomas Cromwell, to go to Cleve and negotiate a marriage between himself and the daughter of the royal House. With Hans Holbein, the artist, he carried out his master's wishes and brought back to the king a miniature portrait of the lady. The king seemed satisfied.

King Henry and his courtiers were in disguise. They wore cloaks and hoods, even masks. They arrived at Rochester where Anne of Cleves' party had stopped to rest on their way to Dover to meet the king of England. As was the custom, the disguised king had come in advance of this meeting to see his new Queen, for himself. The rowdy party broke into the room where Anne was sitting and Henry kissed her boldly on the cheek.

"What are you doing, sir – do you know who I am?" Anne was indignant and angry. She even pushed him away and told the courtiers to "get you gone". This was all said in German of course.

"Anne, do you not recognise your future king and husband?" He was willing to be patient with her. He reached out his hand again towards her.

She pushed him away and entreated her ladies to help her. Henry removed his disguise and shouted, "Madame, look at me now. You must know who I am." Now he was dressed in deep purple velvet with jewel encrusted chains around his neck. He looked every inch a king, but Anne still did not understand it was a game and ran out of the room, leaving him alone there. From that moment, Henry did not like his betrothed. He accused Cranmer and Holbein of duplicity and told them, "I like her not, gentlemen – she is plain and unsophisticated and not the stuff of which queens are made. She also has a strange body odour which I find disgusting – like an animal." Lord Chancellor Cranmer was instructed to return to Germany and get him "out of this marriage". Henry was 48 years old and Anne only 24. A young girl in a foreign country where people spoke a different language and had a completely different culture. It must have been hard for her.

However, this was impossible as the alliance between the two states depended on the marriage going ahead and King Henry of England and Anne of Cleves were married in June 1549 at Greenwich. According to Henry, he had attempted to consummate the marriage several times, but failed nonetheless, as he found his new wife ugly in the extreme. He thought her plain, badly educated, lacking culture and not to his liking at all. She was however, a clever woman and agreed to an annulment and six months after the wedding, she was no longer queen, but she was the recipient of £4000 a year and several houses and castles. She and Henry actually became good friends and he referred to her as his 'Beloved Sister'. She was included in all royal functions and even grew fond of Mary, his eldest daughter and of Elizabeth, the younger.

As she left Hampton Court, she told the king, "Let us remain friends." And they did. In fact, she out-lived his other five wives and was the only one of the queens to be honoured and buried at Westminster Abbey, with a bold epitaph that defined her as 'The Queen of England'. The plain, uneducated woman was the most successful one of all it seemed, and she had retained her head and life.

His eyes moved onto a very young lady-in-waiting – one Catherine Howard, who was possibly as young as 16 or 17 years of age. "Come Mistress Catherine and kiss your Lord and Master." She did as she was told and easily won the heart of the aging man, whose health was becoming worse by the day.

He was no longer the tall, athletic man he'd once been. He was losing his hair and teeth and the wounds he'd sustained from his riding accident, would not heal. He walked with a pronounced limp – always in pain it seemed but still eager to prove he was still virile enough to produce another son and heir – all he needed was the right Queen!

"Kate, you are a tease and know well how to please me." Henry loved to have the young girl near him and also took her to Hampton Court Palace where he actually was callous enough to give her the suite of rooms previously occupied by Jane Seymour, the mother of his son.

"Sire, now that I am your Lady Queen, may I ask a boon?" Catherine Howard knew exactly how to get him to do her bidding. "May I have a different suite of rooms than the ones by the Candle Stick Staircase? I don't feel comfortable there." She stroked his face as she asked him.

"Why my Duckie – what makes you uncomfortable there?" He was reading a fascinating book about the Chinese Empire – he read and spoke four different languages and found this book very interesting. He was slightly annoyed by Catherine's request.

"There is a lady there, who frightens me. She is very pale in colour and frail in build – sometimes, she even has the impertinence to lie on my bed – or stand in the corner and watch me sleeping. I don't like it, Henry – she even scares my ladies-in-waiting and has been seen to fly at them in a rush of ghostly temper."

He could see the tears in her eyes and knew he'd have to do something. "Very well, my precious one, have the servants move your belongings to the rooms closer to mine own." He returned to the book and sent her out of the room. She was still a child, he must remember that. She was only about 17 he believed and she'd had a difficult childhood with an unloving mother and a debt-ridden father. At ten years of age, she'd been sent to live with her Aunt, the Dowager Duchess of Norfolk, whose home was always in disarray and full of transient visitors – the moral code there was rather loose and Catherine was left much to her own devices. With that sort of upbringing, Cathcrine was a happy-go-lucky child who grew into the same kind of woman.

As Henry thought of this, he made his mind up that he'd never visit the room at Candlestick Stairs. He was a very superstitious man and he knew exactly who the pale, frail lady was and although he'd loved her dearly, he preferred her when she was alive.

The first few weeks of the marriage were happy enough, although it was more like an uncle and niece relationship, rather than husband and wife. One evening, after dinner, they were both lying by a lovely, warm fire and sipping red wine. Henry suddenly asked her, "Kate, why do I see you in the rose garden, talking with that young man, Thomas Culpeper. You seem to meet him there regularly – and always as if by chance – did you know him before you came to Court?" She thought for a few moments and said, "Why, yes, I suppose I did know him in Norfolk where he was the Duchess's secretary. A nice young man but very immature. He was very friendly with Dereham who was a Music Teacher there. I knew both of them."

From the mouths of babes and sucklings, the truth will be out. Henry made a note of the names and told the Archbishop of Canterbury, to find out what life had been like at Norfolk. The Archbishop believed that, if you dig deep enough, you'll come up with something, and so Cranmer left a secret letter with his findings for the king. He left it in the king's pew in the Royal Chapel. He obviously couldn't bring himself to say the things it contained to the king's face. He was known for being wise. Rumours stated quite clearly that, Catherine whilst very young, had been intimate with a Music Teacher and then another gentleman of the House.

The king was furious and his attitude towards his young wife changed after reading the letter. He had his ministers look into Catherine's life to date and they discovered that what she'd done was done when she was still very young – almost a child. Henry thought this made no indifference to her questionable background. And although she'd become friendly and loving to Henry's two daughters, Mary and Elizabeth, Henry still regarded her behaviour as unacceptable.

"Thomas, the Queen is here at Hampton Court Palace just now – send my personal guards to arrest her and bring her to the Tower in London. The whole matter needs investigating."

"At once, your Majesty and if I may say so, she has behaved abominably. She has blackened you honour and has been treasonous in her actions. Her great sin, was what she'd done before marrying but she should have spoken up and confessed her wrong doings." Cranmer knew how wise it was to always agree with everything the king said.

He also arranged for the two male offenders to be arrested and tortured, until they confessed to their closeness with Catherine. They were tried and found guilty, subsequently executed, one hanged, drawn and quartered and one beheaded, with both their heads being placed on pikes on London Bridge.

Henry pretended, even to himself, that his heart was broken over Catherine, but who will ever know? Did he realise he'd married a child and found her uninteresting and boring?

Only the king knew the answer to that, and it was far simpler for him to accuse her of treason and get rid of her that way, by An Act of Attainder, an old Law of the time. She was not tried but found guilty by the Act which proved useful in cases such as this. A trial would have made the king's washing being done in public again. This Act allowed him to get rid of a wife with no Judge and Jury to hinder him. His arrogance had not diminished, even a little.

Catherine was dallying with her ladies at the palace when there was a commotion outside her door. Loud noises and shouting could be heard and then the door burst open and armed guards came inside. The Captain told Catherine he'd come to arrest her on grounds of treason and she was to come with him immediately. She was to be taken to the Tower of London. The ladies screamed and surrounded their mistress which allowed Catherine to escape the room and run away from the guards. She ran down the Long Gallery, screaming and calling for the king, who was at Prayers in his chapel. She never did reach him as the guards caught up with her. She'd run up and down the corridor, demented and not knowing what she had done to so displease her husband. She stopped running when she spotted the same very pale and frail woman all dressed in white, watching her from one end of the corridor. She knew who it was this time, she even held out her hand as though beseeching help, but the figure just turned away and disappeared.

The very young Catherine was beheaded at the Tower in 1452, along with one of her ladies, Lady Jane Rochford, who had helped her to meet with Thomas Culpeper in secret – even after she had actually married the king. She had never really had much of a life although she'd ended up as Queen. Her actual guilt was never proved as she was never trialled but where Henry was concerned, this was a small matter and he knew he'd made an error in marrying her.

His eyes were already moving onwards to the other Court ladies and he had noticed one Katherine Parr, more gentle and sombre in personality and he desperately needed a nurse to care for him at the present time, as well as a loving companion. He was in permanent pain and suffered greatly, which didn't help his already bad temper. His legs were ulcerated and oozed puss and blood, he couldn't walk unaided and needed servants to support him all the time. His wounds smelt badly and needed regular cleansing and changing.

Nonetheless, he was still amorous and would have given much to father another son. Although he'd never have spoken of it, he was disappointed by his earlier wives, whom he believed had let him down. He saw himself as a virile, active man who had chosen the wrong women to share his life.

"My Lady Katherine, how are you today?" The king came upon the lady as she sat sewing with the other ladies of the court. "Why do you not take your work into the garden – the sun is bright and warm today and would bring roses to your cheeks." Henry was being supported by two of the burliest servants but still managed to sit close to Katherine.

"I will move into the garden, Sire, if you think it would be good for me." Katherine was careful in how she spoke with him.

"Come madam, take my arm and I shall escort you there." He stood up and an odd group of people made their way into the garden – Henry, Katherine and two servants on either side of the king. Henry had always been a big man but he was a huge man in his later years and the servants had to work hard to keep him upright.

"Pray Sire, shall we sit on this bench? I can see that your leg gives you trouble. What are the physicians doing to help? If you wouldn't consider me being forward, may I suggest a cream that I have, which will help soothe the pain. I have used it myself from time to time – and so did my second husband, Lord Latimer." Katherine knew exactly what to say.

That was it, Henry was hooked. A woman who cared. He scrutinised her carefully, about thirty, he thought, and well dressed in fashionable clothes and impressive jewellery. She was a comely woman and had been married twice before so she was aware of her role as a wife. and in this case, as a nurse. She looked like a passionate woman and was an intelligent one, which was something he discovered in the continued conversation they had. She told him she had already written several pamphlets, mostly around Biblical themes and theoretical matters.

"I should very much like to see your writings, lady Latimer – or may I call you Katherine?" He was on his best behaviour but suddenly turned on one of the servants and struck out at him with his stick. "Be careful man – you jolted my bad leg." Katherine was left in no doubt about his short temper.

Following a short courtship, the two married at Hampton Court Palace in 1543 and Katherine quickly fitted in with her wifely duties. She was still in love with Thomas Seymour and had been secretly engaged to him, but he chose to encourage her to marry the king and that way, he would probably raise his status in Court circles. "Anyway, dear Katherine – the king's health is so bad that he won't last for much longer." Thomas was wise enough to see the opportunities being closer to Henry would bring, although he soon learned that Henry's first decision after his marriage, was to send him abroad on repeated political and military duties which kept him well away from Katherine.

The months turned into years and the King and Queen worked well together. Katherine was a very religious woman but veered towards the new, emerging religion of the Reformation. In fact, she played a large part in bringing about the Protestant Religion of the future but always kept her actions away from the King's ears, as she knew it would displease him. One thing that did please him though, was the fact that she became close to his children, Mary, Elizabeth and Edward. She helped them in many ways, the main one being to bring them all under the one roof at Hampton Court and she helped them with their interests and hobbies. They too grew fond of her and she, of them. In effect, she brought the children back into the royal family.

To some of his Ministers, Henry was too trusting of his wife and they raised questions about her religious beliefs. They were afraid of how much influence she had over the king. Henry would not have liked to hear of her involvement with The Reformation and with her apparent fascination with Martin Luther and they arranged for a well-known heretic to be arrested and tortured, trying to make her say that the Queen was one of the supporters. Their torture failed, however, and Katherine went directly to the king, threw herself down on her knees and asked for mercy.

"I have had no involvement with this Reformation, Sire – I respect your position as Head of the Church of England and all that entails." She cried real tears as she knew how tenuous her position was, remembering the sad ends of many of his earlier wives. He blamed the Ministers instead and turned on them.

Three-and-a-half years after marrying his sixth wife, Henry lay in his bedchamber, propped high on pillows to help him breathe. He was sweating and seemed beyond the pain in his leg. He was not long for this world and one of his Ministers approached him and said, "Sire, would you like to speak with Archbishop Cranmer or some other learned gentleman?"

Henry mumbled with some asperity, "Should I have any learned gentlemen that is – it may as well be Cranmer. Do not fetch him yet however, as I will have a little sleep and when I awake and feel more like myself, I shall see him then." His eyes travelled around the bedchamber and he saw Cardinal Wolsey standing beside the door and there were his wives whom he'd either executed or sent away in disgrace, there were several young men too, some of whom he recognised, but all of whom he'd had executed. All were staring at him with accusing eyes.

The king did not awaken from his sleep but sunk deeper into a delirium, first sending for Cranmer, who arrived just after midnight. It was the month of January and for the first time ever, the two high status men were just a priest and a sinner. Cranmer asked the king, "Sire, please will you put your trust in Christ." Not able to speak, King Henry reached for Cranmer's hand and squeezed it as hard as he could – a clear indication that he did just that. No masses or prayers were said for Henry – but his attitude to religion had clearly changed since the Dissolution of the monasteries. He obviously never regretted his break from Rome, Catholicism and from the Pope. After all, he was the Head of the Church of England, and had he lived long enough, to ensure the Church underwent a huge change. Having said that, did he die a Catholic after all?

Henry VIII was dead at 55 years of age. The news was suppressed for a further ten before bell ringing was heard all over the country, the world was told that the great king had died. It took two full days for the Funeral Procession to reach Windsor and the carriage that carried Henry was seven layers high with an effigy on top. The effigy was dressed in crimson velvet with miniver lining and wore velvet shoes. It was dressed too with a black cap encrusted with precious stones and topped with a magnificent crown, his gloved hands wore rings on each finger.

It took 16 men to carry the coffin and lower it into the grave, alongside his third wife, Jane Seymour, the mother of his son. Ironically, Henry had taken the tomb from Cardinal Wolsey many years before – a tomb Wolsey had created for himself – so Hampton Court Palace as well as his tomb had been confiscated by Henry from his once chief minister. It was covered by a slab of black marble and inscribed with gold letters.

Queen Katherine Parr watched the proceedings from her private chapel. Henry had valued her throughout their marriage and left her a great fortune in gratitude. The whole thing was over and she was free to marry the man she loved, Thomas Seymour, with whom she had one child. That was in 1548 and it was her fourth marriage. She was only about 34 years of age at the time.

How does one end this saga? What kind of man was Henry? It is alleged that he was responsible for the deaths of 'over 70,000 people', although this seems hard to believe. Having said that, however, when someone did something to displease him, his solution was often 'Off with his/her head' or 'Execution by the Sword'. If he wanted anything, he just took it. Such was the nature of both man and king.

Was he the most arrogant man on earth or was he the most pitiful? He desperately wanted sons, but this proved very difficult. He felt he was seen to fail at what even the most ordinary man in the street could achieve, a continued family line. He wanted to be seen as a normal, virile man but he was embarrassed and believed that his subjects thought he was weak and unable to keep his wives in order.

Well, was he arrogant or was he pitiful? You must judge for yourself. Why not take a stroll around Hampton Court Palace yourself? You may come across a pale, frail white lady or a screaming teenager, or even a crimson dressed Cardinal. Indeed, you may even come across the great King Henry VIII himself, after all, it was one of his most favourite homes where he took all of his six wives. (One at a time of course.)

The Holy Man of Russia

Grigori pulled the heavy sledge through the village streets. He had been gathering wood and was bringing it home to heat his family. The snow was falling heavily, in fact, he'd never seen such large snowflakes. On the ground, it was about a foot deep and he was grateful for the stout, heavy boots he'd inherited from his father. The village was called Pokrobskpe and it was in Western Siberia and both he and his wife, Praskovya, had been born there in 1897.

He stopped to rest and blew into his gloved hands before pulling the sledge from the deep rut into which it had sunk. He had been married when he was 18 and he now was the father of two children, a boy and a girl, and another on the way. They all lived in a small house which was really only two rooms, one on top of the other; the house was attached to a larger one next door, which belonged to Grigori's mother and father. He had been educated in a fashion as his father was a headmaster and a farmer and was respected in the village. On his farm, his son and wife helped. Grigori must have worked mainly on the farm however as he remained illiterate until adulthood. His mother was of Mongolian origin and her culture was always to work hard and help others, and she was very fond of her children of whom there were originally seven but almost all of them died in childhood.

He saw his house just a few yards ahead and it had a candle burning in the window to help bring him home. The door flew open and his wife stood there, her belly swollen with the child. "Come Grigori, you have been a long time." She disappeared inside and waited for him to bring several logs indoors. He did this and saw the old village fortune teller ensconced in the armchair by the low burning fire. She too was waiting for the extra wood for the fire and for the hot cup of tea which she knew would follow. She was a very old woman whose name was Madam Ivanov and she had been telling people's fortunes for many years. She'd come to see Praskovya to see which sex her next baby would be, she always got this right; also, she could tell if someone was going to die soon, or have some unforeseen and horrible accident. She was a useful woman to have around.

"Have you been far, Grigori? How far were you able to go through the snow?" she cackled rather than spoke and gave her usual little laugh which meant nothing.

"Not too far, Madam Ivanov – it was very bad underfoot and the tree branches were hidden beneath the snow – a real blanket covered everything." He smiled at her and said, "The hot water will be ready in a jiffy." Praskovya placed the bowls on the table and served some small biscuits she'd baked that morning. The children were asleep upstairs.

The group sat there together, around the fire and soon the logs began to smoulder in the old ashes. A fire was never allowed to go out all the way before fresh wood was found. They didn't have to wait too long before the wood was burning well and the pot of water was almost boiling. Half an hour later, they'd all been warmed by the tea and biscuits and Praskovya gave the drained bowl to the fortune teller. Swirling it around, Madam Ivanov turned the bowl upside down on a plate and stared long and hard at the tea leaves sticking to the sides. "A boy this time – no doubt at all. A fine, big healthy boy just like his father." She cackled.

Grigori preened himself, stood up and planted a kiss on his wife's cheek but she was staring at the fortune teller who had fallen into a trance. She was mumbling something and then she spoke quite clearly, "You – Grigori Yefimovich Rasputin will go on to great things – I see it in your bowl – you will leave this place and wander for a few years, just like Moses in the wilderness. I know you wanted to be a monk but the Orthodox Church wouldn't allow it – well, one day you'll become the nearest thing you can. A veritable Holy Man." Her head fell forwards onto her chest and she breathed loudly.

"Vodka," she muttered, "get me some vodka." And they obliged as quickly as they could.

Grigori looked at his wife and laughed. "What a woman, eh, Wife – me, a kind of holy man, I ask you!" He placed another log on the fire. "Mind you, I have seen the Virgin Mary out in the fields – so maybe that's a sign." Grigori would always justify the things he wanted to believe.

Well, the third baby was a boy – she had been right in that at least, and after another four pregnancies, Grigori left his native village and his family for ever. He had lived all his life so far in a village at the very furthest point in Russia and he was a peasant – but not in the usual sense. He'd visited a local monastery and found he had healing hands and hypnotic powers; he now regarded himself as a holy man – in fact, he often referred to himself as 'Christ in Miniature'. He did return home just once after this visit but found he couldn't stay as he believed he had a message for 'the people' and had to get on with the work of spreading it.

He wandered from village to village, making himself well known wherever he went. He was a womaniser and seduced many of the women in every walk of life. His sexual exploits were legendary and he fathered many illegitimate children, never staying long enough to be blamed for it. He hypnotised the women with his piercing blue eyes and seldom failed to attract any and all he met. His appearance was not particularly attractive but his magical powers worked miracles with everyone he met. He was a tall man with long, black greasy hair which he never washed. He smelt badly and had no time for hygiene. His eating habits were atrocious and he always used his hands to tear the food apart and his beard always had pieces of bread hanging from it, some becoming mouldy with the passage of time. If anyone with whom he was eating, asked for a spoon to sup their food, he would grab the spoon before they got it and lick it all over before handing it to them. His manners were disgusting, and yet he was welcomed everywhere he went, perhaps not through admiration but rather more through fear. He didn't have to try to look evil, it came naturally to him, and yet the women still flocked to welcome him in all senses of the word.

"Come my Sweet – come dance with Grigori – you will be greatly revered by all your friends once you have been with me." And he grabbed a young blond waitress who was working in the public house. Of course, she did exactly as she was told. In fact, he went after two women at a time and apparently pleased them both.

He was working his way towards St Petersburg, healing people as he went and preaching morals which was amusing as he had none of his own. His reputation grew as did the number of people who followed him and came to hear him speak. He had no money, but he needed none, as he was treated to food and drink and a roof over his head by all he met.

One day, as he got nearer to St Petersburg where the Tsar and Tsarina had their family home at the Winter Palace, he came across a peasant woman who was a comely wench. "Come my pretty and make Grigori welcome," and he reached for her and put his hands on her breasts. She whipped a knife from under her shawl and ferociously stabbed him full in the stomach. He was shocked but pushed her aside and clamped his hand over the heavily bleeding wound. He staggered along the street when he spotted a royal coach approaching with the Tsarina sitting by the window.

"Hold, driver – we must help that man." And being told who the man was, she was even more eager to help him. The wounded man was helped into her carriage and taken to the Winter Palace. A doctor was immediately called and he was operated on the Tsar's dining table and of course, he survived and got back on his feet very quickly. He was of course, taken to a small bedroom where he was put into a sumptuous bed and tended by a nurse. He slept the clock around and didn't wake up until 12 o'clock the next day. The Tsarina herself came to visit him and brought two of her daughters with her – to see the famous 'Holy Man' whose reputation was well known to them.

"How can I thank you my Tsarina – you have treated me better than anyone I've ever met. I am your servant now and will always obey your orders." Suddenly, he sat up in bed and said, "How is your son, Lady – something tells me that all is not well with him." She was shocked beyond words as it had always been kept a secret that Alekskei had a disabling condition known as haemophilia.

"What do you know of my son Holy Father?" She called him this name although the Russian Orthodox Church had always denied his holy status. But then, she was the Tsarina and held herself above even the Church.

"I know he is not good just now and is bleeding profusely. Get the servants to fetch a wheelchair and take me to him." He didn't ask her but ordered her to do this. She did.

Grigori was taken to the child's bedroom where Alekskei was lying on his bed with blood-soaked towels around him. He had only knocked his knee but it was enough to make him bleed and it was already turning dark blue. Grigori went to him and took his hand. He stared into the boy's eyes with his own piercing blue eyes that were full of promise and mystery. He didn't blink, he just stared. The boy was bordering on losing consciousness, but the Holy Man moved him gently and carried him to the window. He made the sign of the cross on his forehead and then kissed his brow. One of the doctors made to go forward and take the child to his bed again, but the Tsarina held up her hand. "Leave him be, Doctor – he is actually gaining some colour in his cheeks." And the doctor stepped back. He was angry and worried but the Tsarina had spoken.

Grigori asked the doctor, "What medicine are you giving him?" And being told that Aspirin was one of the medicines, he shouted, "Stop giving him that immediately – that will make the bleed worse and allow the blood to leave his body very quickly."

He took Alekskei back to bed and already, the child looked better than before. The bleeding was slowing down and had almost stopped completely. The boy's mother was crying and fell to her knees before Grigori. "Thank you, Holy Father – you have saved my son."

Shortly after this, she gave instructions to her secretary to find a suite of rooms in the capital, where the Holy Man could live when he left the palace. A lovely suite was found for him in a city tenement building, it was the middle floor and he was left there in the lap of luxury. When he looked around, he smiled and immediately drank two bottles of vodka.

Soon, word of his arrival spread throughout the aristocratic families and people arrived daily to look at him and worship. He was happy to let this happen as they always brought him gifts which he was quite willing to accept. The ladies in particular formed a circle of spectators in the street below his apartment and when he spotted those he thought attractive, he would beckon them indoors; they were more than happy to oblige. There were days, however, when he couldn't look after his 'Little Ladies' as he called them, because he'd been summoned by the Tsarina to the Winter Palace. Alekskei sometimes had a bad day and she needed the reassurance of the Holy Man. A royal carriage would arrive and wait for him as he slowly made his way downstairs. The 'Little Ladies' would part to let him through when they saw the royal carriage, he was suddenly a very important man. The Tsarina had instructed her security guards, the Okhraha, to watch over him and to keep him safe but they also decided to build up a picture of where he went and what he did. They were still suspicious of the Tsarina's new friend.

He was always able to calm the boy and reassure him he was feeling fine. One afternoon, when he arrived at the palace, he was introduced to the Tsar himself, who was not as enthusiastic about him as his wife was. The piercing blue eyes did little to impress Nicholas II of Russia.

"Seat yourself down, Rasputin, I wish to talk with you. Tell me what you think of the state of Russia?" It seemed a very big question with which to open the conversation but the Tsar's mind was greatly troubled at the time. Obviously, the Holy Man was taken aback by the importance of the question. "I am having great trouble on the Front and losing my army at an alarming rate." The Tsarina sat quietly by his side, whilst she worked on her embroidery.

Rasputin was quick to sit down, with no invitation to do so and spoke up readily, "Papa. I think your men at the Front need their Tsar and you should travel there to be with them. Mama here – can look after the running of the country in your absence – and I can always come to her side when she calls for me. Does that answer your question, Papa?"

The Tsar thought for a few moments and then sat down opposite the Holy Man. "Are you really a Holy Man – or does it mean nothing?" The Tsarina rose from her chair and said to her husband, "We already know the answer to that question – hasn't he healed our Alekskei more than once – more successfully than any of the doctors have managed to do?" She was angry.

"Mama, Mama calm yourself. Papa is just trying to get to know me and to learn if he can trust me." He looked towards the Tsar. "You know you can trust me, don't you Papa?" The Tsar nodded his head and poured a glass of wine for his guest to have.

From then on, Rasputin was a frequent visitor to the palace and became used to offering advice on State matters. He was not a violent man and didn't like the thought of war and killing but he knew war was inevitable and like the Tsar, he must be for it.

The Tsar went to the front and stayed there for a long time. The Tsarina ran the country, and Rasputin ran her, much to the annoyance of many aristocrats and members of the royal family. The people of Russia were starving and thought their country was being run badly – very badly – so it was inevitable that a Peoples' Movement formed in St Petersburg and grew quickly in number. They became known as the Bolshevik Party and Vladimir Lenin was their leader. The Russian government was called 'The Duma' and worked with and advised the Tsarina in the Tsar's absence, alongside Rasputin, that is.

Time passed and Rasputin became even closer to the Tsarina. Rumours were rife about her 'carrying-on' with him but there was no actual proof that anything ever happened between them. Even her daughters became fond of him but again, there were no rumours involving them, and he even advised them on school matters and on their studies in general. However, he still had his harems at home and his exploits were incredibly wild. He'd become a rich man as well, people would make him generous gifts of money as well as trinkets, and he loved the life. He continued to help those who were ill or just hypochondriac, using his healing powers, most likely for a price. There was little doubt that he was successful in this.

The Tsar came home from the Front. His ability to run his army was not impressive and his campaign was a complete failure. The St Petersburg he came back to was a completely different place from that he'd left. There was unrest in the streets and even his own guards questioned his authority. Rasputin came to the palace one day and was confronted with peasants living around on the lower floors, the guards just allowed them to come and go as they pleased. He knew it was time to tell the Tsar of his prophesy for the future and he had written it down in a letter as he couldn't bring himself to say the words. The letter said:

'Tsar of the land of Russia – if you hear the sound of the bells, it will tell you that Grigori has been killed. You must know this: if it was your relatives who have wrought my death then, no one in your family, that is to say, none of your children or relations will remain alive for more than two years. They will be killed by the Russian people… I shall be killed. I am no longer among the living. Pray, Pray, but think of your beloved family.'

In the private rooms of the Yusupova Palace in St Petersburg, several aristocrats had gathered to discuss something rather serious. They still drank and smoked heavily but they were deadly serious in their opinions of what must be done to rid Russia of Rasputin, the Holy Man.

"He is destroying our country by leading our Tsar and Tsarina astray. We have as good as lost the war at the Front and now, the people have risen up because they are starving and frightened." Prince Felix Yusupova was adamant that his half-drunk comrades too, must take the matter seriously. He was a young, handsome man who dearly loved Russia and was proud of the Romanov name.

"Well then, let's remove him. We have no option," one of the noblemen slurred his speech. "Let's invite him here one evening, ply him with drink – apparently, he can drink most people under the table – so we must have plenty of vodka and wine – and just kill him. If we all have a hand in it, then no particular one can be blamed." There were cheers of agreement and the host smashed his glass against the fire and said, "Let's do just that, my friends – someone has to put an end to him – he is changing our magnificent country all by himself – except for the help he's getting from our royal family."

And it was agreed. The Holy Man would be invited to the Yusupova Palace as an honoured guest. After all, he was big-headed enough to believe it possible. The party was arranged for 29 December 1916 and Rasputin accepted the invitation to the palace.

It was a long night. There were five men, other than Rasputin. Lying on several sofas arranged around a roaring fire, they were raucous and loud, not to mention vulgar and argumentative with each other. The Holy Man fitted in very easily with the party mood and drank copious flagons of vodka. He shouted at one of the servants who were rushing around, "Boy, get me more vodka – I am still thirsty – or reap the consequences of being slow." The boy looked at him in puzzlement. "Have you never heard of the boy in the barrel – it's played at my parties over and over again. Of course, we have to send out for fresh boys from time to time." He laughed and held the boy by the arm. Felix Yusupova disentangled the boy and pushed him away, telling him to move more quickly and fetch what the guest wanted. He did as he was told.

One of the men brought out a tray of chocolates and one of sweet cakes. "Help yourself, Rasputin – or may I call you Ras?"

Rasputin bridled and spat out. "No, you may not. Use my full born name – or don't talk to me at all." He grabbed a handful of chocolates and the men sneaked knowing glances at each other. These were the chocolates laced with cyanide and should deal with him very quickly. All he did, was burp loudly and spit on the fire. "Have some more Rasputin and have some of the sweet wine prepared specially for you." He poured the liquid to the brim of a large glass and the Holy Man scoffed the lot. The wine also contained cyanide but to no avail. He just became wilder and louder and the men in the room began to fear what he would do next. He actually fell off the sofa onto the floor and Felix used the commotion to fetch a pistol from a secret drawer in a bureau.

Rasputin reached up and grabbed another handful of poisoned chocolates and crammed them into his mouth, he washed them down with more of the 'special' wine. A shot rang out in the room and then a second shot, two bullets entered his body but still he laughed, even when he was looking down at his blood. The men overpowered him and started to beat and kick him, they were panicking now as the man just wouldn't die. He was bleeding however and for a few moments, seemed to get weaker, then he jumped up from the floor and made to charge at the men, growling like an animal.

Felix took out another pistol and aimed it carefully at Rasputin. He fired and the bullet entered the middle of the man's forehead. There was blood and brains everywhere. He fell to the ground, as before, but again staggered to his feet. All the men gathered around him and started beating him again before taking him outside the palace and rushing him towards the bridge, overlooking the frozen river. It was just a few feet away. They picked him up and threw him into the river's freezing cold water – he went under the surface, coming back up twice before completely disappearing from view. They had killed him at last but it had not been an easy task. The man was incredible and had amazing resistance to the poison, the beating, the shooting that would have floored a normal man. But then, Rasputin had never claimed to be normal.

The swore each other to secrecy and went their separate ways. His body was not found for several days, but when it finally did wash up further down the river, a forensic examination showed that even when he was thrown into the icy water, he must have been still alive – even after everything – because his lungs contained water which they wouldn't have done had he been dead when he entered the river. He was missed, of course, by the people who knew him. In fact, just before his death, he was becoming known as 'The Tsar of the Tsars', so influential was he over the royal family.

The Imperial Romanov family were imprisoned at the Winter Palace where Nicholas II abdicated his throne as Tsar; this followed the actual Revolution and was in the year 1917. The Japanese/Russian war decimated the Russian troops and then, the war with Germany added to the overall losses. After almost a year, the family and their servants were moved from the Winter Palace and then moved once more, before ending at a place called Yekaterinburg, which really was at the back of beyond in Siberia. The windows of the house were painted solidly with white paint so 'watching the world go by' was not an option for the prisoners. Their diet was sparse and the guards followed them everywhere they went in the house, even to the toilet. It really was a miserable existence. In 1918, Civil War had well and truly broken out in the country and the Bolsheviks and the White Russian Army were at each other's throats. There was a rumour which the Romanovs certainly didn't hear, that the White Russians were heading for the town, intent in rescuing the Tsar's family and because of this rumour, an order was given to make sure no one gets close to the Romanovs. Something had to be done. The local authorities were instructed to deal with the problem and a death penalty was passed on the whole family.

"Can we really kill such an important family as the Romanovs? If we do, what will happen to us if the White Russians are successful and arrive here before the Bolsheviks." The chairman of the authority was wisely hesitant in carrying out the order but the other members of the committee over ruled him.

"If the White Russians arrive here first, we can always plead we were just carrying out orders – orders we couldn't disobey. If the Bolsheviks arrive here first and we haven't done as they ordered they will kill every last one of us."

They seemed to have no option and 12 men were chosen to do the deed. Not one of them liked the job, especially killing children, but it was either the lives of the Romanovs or their own lives.

On 16 July, late at night, Nicholas, Alexandra, their five children, the doctor and servants were told to dress quickly and they were taken down to the cellar. "What are they going to do?" Alexandra asked her husband.

"I have absolutely no idea," he replied, scooping his son into his arms and carrying him to the cellar. The girls were frightened and shaking. It had been cold in their rooms but it was freezing in the cellar. There were chairs in the middle of the room and they were told to sit on them. The leader told them they were going to have their photographs taken to show the Russian people that they were safe. It seemed an odd time to do it, but at least it was an explanation. They all settled down on the chairs, forming two rows with the servants standing at the back. Anastasia whispered to her sister Maria, "I don't like this, Sister – they are not to be trusted."

The whole family spotted him at the same time. They knew he was dead but it was definitely Grigori Rasputin, the Holy Man of Russia. He stood at the back of the room and raised his right arm to make the sign of the Cross. He was smiling at them, an almost saintly smile, completely unlike the leer he usually wore on his face. He said, "Be brave Mama and you, Papa – and all you young people – soon you'll be with your God and there will be no pain from then on."

He disappeared as the door burst open and 12, armed men came rushing into the room. They immediately formed a line with the rifles pointing at each of the seated family. A hail of gunfire was shattering to the ears and the victims began to shake, at least some of them did, but the bullets were true and hit their targets. There was blood everywhere and the girls were screaming and trying to get away, but fresh shots were fired and one by one, they fell to the floor. Maria tried to take Alekskei's hand but his father was lying on top of the child. Alexandra had fallen where she sat, dying immediately, her body hanging off the chair. The gunmen searched through the bodies and any that were still moving, were viciously bayoneted to death. It only took about five minutes but it seemed to take a lot longer; the gunmen stood around, unsure of what to do next, but the one in charge told them, "Pull yourselves together. You've done what needed to be done and you should feel proud." But they didn't feel proud and a couple of them were actually crying. Their clothes were blood spattered and bits of brains were sticking to their bayonets.

First thing in the morning, at day break, they carried the bodies to a waiting lorry and took them to a forest outside Yekaterinburg. A deep pit had been prepared before and the bodies were thrown unceremoniously into it and covered with an acid solution to try to destroy their identity. For some reason, one daughter and Alekskei were taken further on, perhaps, the pit hadn't been dug deep enough and buried on their own, but together.

The Tsar, Tsarina, the Grand Duchesses and the Tsarevich were disposed of like animals. It was believed by many that Grigori Rasputin had played a part in what happened, not in the actual killings but because of his influence on the Royal Family since arriving in St Petersburg. It could be argued that his relationship with the Romanovs did help bring about the Revolution, the need for the Tsar's abdication, and the cruel assassination of the family; Royals, whose line went back 300 years and who had been the end of a true Dynasty.

However, Rasputin was a Mystic and Holy Man, whose prediction in his letter to the Tsar a long time before, was very true. '*Rasputin himself was dead and all the Tsar's relatives were dead within two years. His prophecy really was quite incredibly accurate.*'

Call Me a Witch – At Your Peril

Five people, three women and two men had been cast into the town cells. They were accused of witchcraft and were to stand trial the following week. The women were in one cell and the men in another. All five were scared out of their wits, because they knew what would happen to them if they were found guilty of witchcraft. They would be bound together and burnt alive on the town green, they would feel the fiery tongues creeping up their legs and blistering their skin. They would choke on the acrid smoke and their eyes would bulge out of their heads. No one of right mind would choose this way to die, but they had no option.

It had begun only a few weeks before when a young girl, called Christine had told her father, who just happened to be the local Laird with a lot of power, that the people lying in the cells had put the evil eye on her and since then, she'd felt sick and weak and subject to fits; something she'd never experienced before. She'd seen one of the women steal a cup of milk and she reported the theft to her mother. The thief's name was Catherine and she worked as a servant in the Laird's kitchen. The other servants defended her, saying she had been in sore need of a drink but both the Laird and his wife wouldn't listen. Catherine sought out the girl and cursed her with the most vicious words she could find. She told her the curse would ensure she was chased by the Devil through all the fires of Hell and it would be soon. "You're nothin' but a little snitch – I've probably lost my job now and it's because you grudged me a drink."

The other women were soon included in the charge of witchcraft, they too were accused of being in league with the Devil and one of them even had a large wart on the side of her nose for all to see. This was called a witch's teat and was claimed to be the actual mark of the Devil, which he put on all his servants. Two men were also accused of the charge, one was the stable boy and one a general servant who happened to be married to the woman with the wart. It was claimed they were part of the team of witches and were also accused of forming a coven when they all met together and put curses on their chosen victims. Young Christine claimed she was one of the victims and so, was taken by her parents to visit a Glasgow doctor who was famous for his exceptional skills in medicine. Dr Bolton was his name. He thoroughly examined the young girl and tested her in every way possible. However, he could find nothing wrong with her and concluded, as had her parents, that she was suffering from a witch's curse.

The whole matter was enjoyed by the townspeople. Pointing the finger at each other and accusing neighbours of being witches was becoming a regular occurrence. The reasons for pointing the finger were usually trivial, in fact sometimes, it was just because they weren't popular or they were very old, or even because they were kind and tried to help folk who were ill. Christine's own accusation was feeble in the extreme but she was having fits so someone had to be blamed.

"Papa. I'm so scared of Catherine and her witch friends. What will happen to me?" Young Christine looked so pitiful and she seemed to be developing sores all down her arms. "Look, Papa – my arms are so sore and it's all Catherine's fault." Her tears were real as she was in quite a lot of pain.

"Stop scratching your arms, Christine – you're only making those sores worse," her father chastised her. She was seen again by the eminent doctor but he could still find nothing physically wrong with her and in the end, he repeated there was no other answer but to say she was under some kind of witch's spell. By this time, Christine's afflictions were getting worse. She was now pulling hair balls from her mouth and claiming they'd been put there by the accused witches. More trash and odd bits and pieces came from her mouth and she was having increased fits and sometimes, remaining motionless for hours on end.

Her father was afraid for her life and pleaded with the authorities to arrest the ones who had been identified by Christine as her tormentors. And that is how the five people ended up in the town cells and were judged by those in authority, including a clergyman, of possessing an innocent young girl. There was no question of their guilt and as sentence was pronounced, one of the women in the dock cursed everyone who was in the courtroom and said she'd make sure the devil would haul all of them and their relatives, through the burning fires of hell.

"See!" shouted the Parson into the crowds. "From her own mouth comes an admission that she's one of the Devil's followers." Everyone shouted their agreement and the five pathetic figures were led back to their cells. The jailers were not afraid to use instruments of torture on the victims. Finger nails were pulled out by the roots and victims were chained to the cell wall and deprived of sleep; the 'Witch's Bridle' was commonly used to try to get confessions. The bridle was fixed to the head and had iron prongs that stuck both into the roof of the mouth and under the tongue. It would be horrifically painful and yet many people still refused to confess to being witches.

The young stable boy asked the others, "Are they really going to burn us? For what? We've done nothing. How can we get out of here? I'm only 15 and I've done nothing – is my life over?" And he wiped away the tears that fell from his eyes.

"Aye lad, it looks like that. Try to be brave – we're all in it together, aren't we?" The other man actually tried to comfort him although he was as frightened as everyone else.

The boy didn't last the night – he was too scared. He tied the string that held up his breeches around his neck and tied the other end to the high bars on the window. He kicked away the stool in the cell and dangled freely in the air. He showed such courage, it was amazing, but to him, it seemed preferable to burning.

And the three women and the one remaining man were tied to the stake and with a jeering crowd all around, they suffered the incredible, cruel pain of the ferocious flames. The pain must have been unbearable but they had no option but to bear it. The Hearing had found them guilty of murder and of tormenting many people and yet, it had all started with Catherine stealing a cup of milk. This was not mentioned in the Trial. The Preacher even gave a sermon at the Trial, as was common practice at such a time, and advocated finding the prisoners guilty to be the right judgement. Before the young Christine stopped having fits and strange sleeps, she implicated a further 35 people and accused them of being in league with the Devil: many investigations were held and the number found guilty of the accusation was never established.

It was over and the carcasses were removed from the fire embers and everyone went home but always watching their neighbours, in case of more accusations.

Remembering all the people who died and suffered because of the young Christine's accusations, please see **Author's Notes – paras 3 and 4.**

A few days later in the same area, a very old woman who lived on the edge of the next village became a figure of interest. She'd lived there all her life and when she was younger, she'd been the local birthing helper to the women of the surrounding villages. She was too old now to travel any distances and she'd turned her attention to healing hurt and frightened animals and birds. She was very knowledgeable about herbs, flowers, seeds and grasses and had even devised cures for many of the ailments of which people complained. She'd started with a rabbit with a broken leg and a cat, who'd lost an eye in a fight with a bigger cat. Now, there were wooden slatted cages all around her old cottage and many different creatures were being kept there until they healed or died. The cottage was falling down but it was sheltered by many trees and there was a sweet tasting stream running by the edge of the small patch of garden. A perfect 'hospital' for all who were in need of help.

Her name was Betsy and she'd always lived on her own, never marrying or even courting. She was well thought of by the locals and was always willing to help anyone in pain or discomfort. But not everyone liked her, as was proven one day when two Goodies (Married women) reported the old woman as a witch. They claimed they'd seen her talking to the animals and actually heard the animals answering back. She held long conversations with them and spent a lot of time putting fresh bandages on various limbs. The women told the court officials that Betsy often gave some villagers small tubs of cream, wrapped in large tree leaves. She then told them to rub the cream well into their wounds and to drink the potions she emptied into the small vials they'd brought with them. Most of that was harmless water from the little stream.

That night, she was sitting in her chair by the fire, well wrapped in her shawl, when there was a loud bang on her door and two village officials stood there. They told her why they were there and that she had to come with them.

"Will I be away long?" she asked them. "I have to look after my wounded animals."

"Never mind about your wounded creatures – you've got far bigger problems facing you." And they hustled her out of the cottage and into the cold night air. They took her straightaway to the village cells and put heavy chains around her thin ankles and wrists.

"What have I done?" she asked and hobbled over to the one stool that was in the room. "May I have a drink of water?" But she was refused this and offered no bread to eat.

Soon, three other Goodies joined the first two informers and told how they'd all suffered after swallowing her potions. They lost control and couldn't stop screaming and they pinched each other's' arms and legs. They even said they'd seen the Devil's mark on the old woman's thigh. Oh yes, she was in league with the Devil all right. Then they remembered names of those who'd died after taking her medicine, and of babies who died after totally normal births. "She's probably got records of their names in a book somewhere – we're sure we've seen it." The women were getting more excited as they thought about it. Sure enough a piece of paper was found in the cottage with a list of babies' recorded births.

"I always kept lists of those babies," she explained. "I was proud of helping them into the world. Yes, some may have died later but that had nothing to do with me. I have always meant well and tried to do the right thing." Betsy cried at the interrogators.

One morning very early, a little girl came to the barred window in the cell and called out to Betsy. "Are you thirsty, Betsy – and are you hungry?" The child was only about eight years old and was the only child of one of the jailers. She'd known the old woman for a long time – Betsy had helped heal her dog when he'd got into a fight with a fox – and she'd loved her since that time. She passed through the bars, some bread and a cup of water which Betsy took gratefully.

"Now get away from the window, child – or they'll catch you and put you in here with me." And she gobbled down the bread and shooed the girl away.

The jailers tried to make the old witch talk, and confess she was a witch. They called her 'witch' now, although nothing had yet been proven. Her chains were strung up on the walls now and she was fitted with a witch's bridle. Its sharp prongs cut into her mouth and she couldn't speak. She'd been there a week and was dirty and bedraggled with blood running all down her front and forming scabs even on top of her clothes.

"I am not a witch," she tried to say but they believed she was just talking gobbledegook. The women accusers had made statements by now, nothing new to what they spoke of before, except to show the bruises they now had on their bodies, put there by Betsy, the old witch. The young girl brought more bread but Betsy couldn't reach it from where she was chained to the wall, so the child stopped coming to see her.

"You're in Court tomorrow, Betsy – and then maybe you'll be put out of your misery." The jailer knew he wasn't comforting her – but he didn't care. She knew that burning was something she'd have to endure. They dragged her from the cell and removed the witch's bridle from her head. She bled profusely but the jailers didn't care. The Goodies (women) all testified against her and despite one woman speaking in her defence, she was pronounced guilty and told she was to be burnt at the stake the next day. She saw the little girl in the Court and managed to smile at her – although it was more of a bloody grimace – but the child knew what it was.

The Judge at the Trial declared the old woman was to be hanged first and then burnt. It was a mercy because of her age and she knew that – so she thanked him. Next day she was taken to the village green and lifted onto the high platform there – the executioner put a rope around her neck and placed great lumps of peat around her feet. Peat would always burn well. To pay for the rope and peat, they would search through her cottage to get something of value. It was common practice that the condemned paid for whatever it took to complete their sentence. She stood there and looked around at the crowd who were straining to see everything – people who'd been her friends before, but not now.

"I swear to you all, I am not a witch – but just one of your neighbours and friends." Her speech was mumbled and the blood covering her face, added to the grotesque look she now had. But the little girl – Grace – heard her and held up a hand, holding a flower and offered it to Betsy, who of course, couldn't take it. But she did smile at the child, even as the rope was placed around her neck and the box on which she stood was kicked away from under her feet. Her tongue protruded from her mouth and her eyes slid shut. It took a few moments before she was gone. They lit the peat and the flames slowly reached up her body and engulfed her. She was a brave woman, of that there was no doubt.

Before she walked away, Grace placed the flower beside the flames. It was the saddest moment of her young life and she cried bitter tears. Her mother put her to bed that night and told her to remember the old witch was at peace now. If she hadn't been a witch, God would look after her.

"She wasn't a witch, Mama – she was just a poor, old woman who helped people all her life. She was clever and very kind and those women who said such terrible things about her, should be ashamed of themselves." Grace barely slept that night. But what she did do, was to work hard for the rest of her life – to grow up and become the birthing nurse for the village and for all the other surrounding villages and to become known as 'The Lady Who Helps Others'. It reminded her of Betsy.

The old lady was never forgotten and Grace often told her own children the story. In fact, Grace's Great, Great Granddaughter ended up working with the Sisters of Charity in France. They were an organisation who trained each other and looked after sick people in their own homes as at that time, there was no such thing as hospitals – and leading on from this, they emerged as the type of nurses who worked alongside Florence Nightingale herself and one of Grace's descendants actually worked alongside the nurses at the time of the Crimean War. Grace would have been proud – just as Betsy would have been.

***

There are of course too many such incidents to mention them all, but let's look at other judgements served on accused witches – and how they were treated by the system at the time. The Church played a big part in looking for witches, helping to prove a case against them. In one town in Wales, there was a Pastor who held his post there for more than nine years and from his first day, he was determined to find all the evil doers and make them suffer. 15 inhabitants were initially found guilty of brewing ale on the Sabbath Day which in the eyes of the church, was a very great wrong doing indeed. The worst they could be charged with was ignoring an ecclesiastical rule – but for this they were all fined 40 shillings each which was a hefty sum in the seventeenth century. Following their trials and their fines, records at the time showed that – of the 15 original men and women accused of the blasphemous act – eight of them were actually burnt at the stake as witches. Their accusations of each other – and claims that each other was a witch – served to give the Pastor and his clergy the reason they needed to make the sentences into executions. They were burnt together – and as was the practice, and one of the woman's husbands was instructed to pay for the cost of the burning just because he had a few shillings.

One of the eight had (allegedly) put the evil eye on an old beggar woman and made her curse a ship where her hated brother-in-law was captain – and to make it sink to the bottom of the sea. The unfortunate ship did just that and the two women – both old and young – who told on each other, were burnt at the stake based on an unprovable charge. The night the ship went down was horrific – with great storms and no moon to light their way – a night when the ship could have sunk without the witch's hex – but it suited those in authority to use what evidence they could to justify their judgement. It didn't really matter that there was no real evidence at all.

One of the last burnings in the town was of an elderly woman who was showing signs of senility and for how she treated her daughter, who had deformed hands and feet. Some neighbours even gave evidence that they'd seen the old woman use her daughter as a pony and whip her around the garden. Needless to say, this was sufficient proof that they were both witches and in league with the Devil, who had made sure his mark showed on both of them i.e. both had a similar mole on their arms. They were stripped, their bodies smeared with tar and were paraded through the town and then burnt alive.

Many men set themselves up as official witch finders and travelled about the country looking for evidence from the locals, who were only too keen to identify those they disliked, for whatever reason.

Although Europe began its witch hunts as long ago as the 14th century, similar incidents happened all over the Britain. In Scotland, witchcraft was rife in the 17th century – as it was in America.

One such incident took place in Salem, Massachusetts:

"Please Abigail, don't say that about me – if you do, you know what they'll call me," Betty Parris begged, wanting her cousin to stop tormenting her, and when she found she couldn't stop her, she immediately returned the compliment and said, "You are much more of a witch than I am Abigail Williams. Tituba told me last night that you are much more qualified to be a witch than I am – cause you're nastier."

Betty was crying. She was very afraid as she had recently become aware of a great interest in witches in her village of Salem, Massachusetts. Although Tituba was a slave, she had become more of a companion to the two girls – and she was a great story teller who knew all about voodoo and magic that she'd brought with her from the country of her birth.

Betty was nine years old and Abigail eleven. Both girls (one of whom was the daughter of a clergyman) started throwing things about within a couple of days, uttering peculiar sounds and contorting themselves into strange positions. More girls began to experience such things and under great duress from Magistrates, they told of three people whom they believed had done this to them. One was Tituba of Caribbean extract, one a homeless beggar and one an elderly impoverished woman. Needless to say, they were all found guilty. In her confessions, Tituba told of black dogs, red cats, yellow birds and of a black man who made her sign his book – which she did. Tituba was obviously pleased about the predicament in which she found herself. It made her feel important.

On the day the girls first began to act strangely, Tituba appeared in the room as if by magic and told the girls to stop talking about such things. "You mustn't tell tales about your cousin or the Witchfinder General, Matthew Hopkins will come and get you." She tut-tutted at the girls, whereupon Betty fell onto the floor and started kicking her legs in the air. She screamed at the top of her lungs and saliva began to dribble from her mouth.

"Let's just leave her there, Abigail, she can't hurt herself. Come on, let's get ourselves something to drink." The slave spoke like the mistress – she felt powerful, especially over the girls. They left the fitting Betty in the room and went into the kitchen, where Cook asked where Betty was. Little did Tituba know her days were numbered.

"We don't know, I'm sure," Tituba spoke up. Cook was also of the Caribbean race and was also a slave in the household. She left the kitchen to fetch some vegetables and found Betty still fitting on the floor. She screamed and ran out into the yard calling for help. "There's witches here – I just know it. Come, help me," and she covered her face with her apron and crouched on the floor.

Tituba was the first of the Salem accused to be called witch and she just laughed and shrugged her shoulders. However, she was arrested and taken to jail. A few days later, Betty and her cousin, Abigail had accused two other women of being witches – and they were taken into custody alongside Tituba to stand trial in the town courtroom. Suddenly, the whole town was buzzing with excitement and people were closely watching their neighbours. Finding a witch was an enjoyable occupation, as long as you accused first and saved yourself.

The Native American war had started close by – only 70 miles from Salem and the local people must have seen some atrocities committed by the natives and the puritanical villagers saw close-up the burnings and killings of the war. This type of excitement seemed to rub off onto Salem and a mass hysteria broke out with everyone accusing everyone else of witchcraft. These thoughts, however, did nothing to help Tituba and the other two women – who were all imprisoned and awaiting trial but it may have added to the hysteria building up all around them. The court that would try them was called Oyer and Terminer and meant in English Hear and Decide. In 1692, Governor William Phipps created this special court and the first accused to come to court was an older woman called Bridget Bishop, who was well known for her gossipy ways and promiscuity. On being asked if she was a witch, she replied, "I am as innocent as the child unborn," but it failed to convince the Court as two days later she became the first witch to be hanged on Gallows Hill. This hill became the burial place of all executed witches, who were always put in unmarked graves.

Women were the target – especially young and very old women. Children also figured in the accusations – they were not exempt because of their youth. Theories emerged also that the extreme cold weather at the time could have had an influence on creating the atmosphere in Salem. It badly affected the crops. Very cold weather is excellent for the production of Ergot on the grain, as it cools down – a fungus that grows on spoiled grain and is obviously eaten when all food products have to be eaten because of overall shortages. This fungus is closely aligned to the drug LSD and can cause hallucinations especially in women and children. This is suspected to be the basis for the hallucinations experienced by some of the witches.

Tituba didn't even wait for her judgement but volunteered her confession of being a witch. The other two women were also found guilty but records of their punishment were not recorded and so it is not known if they lived or died at that time – but it is most likely that they died.

With the movement of time passing, many relatives of the executed victims tried many times to seek compensation for the wrongful deaths of the accused witches. It took several years (1710) before any monies were offered. £578 British Pounds were paid to all the claimants but with such an unfair distribution of the monies that justice wasn't served at all, e.g., John and Elizabeth received £150 pounds whereas Elizabeth Howe's relatives received £12 pounds. Hardly fair.

The minister who replaced Parris as Salem's preacher, helped to secure a redress of excommunications which was dealt out to all those found guilty. However, the accused and executed still lay in unconsecrated ground, something that was never redressed.

See Notes 5 and 6 for more information on the Salem conclusion.

A final and unexplained tale of witches:
Although those accused of being witches suffered all over the world throughout the 14th, 15th and 16th centuries – even into the early 17th, This tale cannot come to an end without mentioning Maggie Wall, a very famous 'witch' and known to any and all who visit Perthshire in Scotland. Near Dunning, in the old parklands of the former Duncrub Castle Estate, stands a monumental cross

and cairn which is almost 20 feet in height and reads simply, 'Maggie Wall burnt here 1657 as a witch.' Strangely, however, no Parish records that go back hundreds of years have any mention of Maggie Wall herself – nor is there any mention of her execution as a witch. Witch Trials were overseen by the Church and State and therefore, excellent records were mandatory – yet strangely not for Maggie.

It is the only monument in Scotland that has been erected to a witch – no other exists. So, why this one? There are beliefs that it may have been intended for all of the 4,000 'witches' executed in Scotland over the years and also that the name is really Muggie's Walls, named after ancient woods that lay close by. But the mystery of who places flowers and an annual wreathe on the 'grave' remains a secret. And who is it who repaints the inscription on the stones – whose hand is so steady as he or she paints the words exactly as they'd been painted many times before. No one has ever been seen doing these things – but they are done regularly nonetheless. Some of the stones show evidence of gunpowder shot and therefore, it is believed the monument was built in the very late 18th century – perhaps, by descendants of those witches accused, but not executed in the previous century. In fact, around the date inscribed on Maggie's monument – 1657, there are records that show six women were executed as witches in Dunning – and in a village of just 200 people, this was a very large number.

Some people believe, therefore, that Maggie Wall never really existed but is a representative of all the poor souls executed for something they didn't do, for the torture they had to endure – both mental and physical – and for the dreadful pain they suffered in their execution. And not to forget, the money their relatives had to pay to offset the costs of burning them. The clerks at the time even recorded the amount of peat used for the actual burnings – not to mention the ropes used. It all had to be paid for somehow!

Maggie Wall's monument is eerie and sad. Standing there, one can feel a heavy depression and a great sorrow for all the scared and probably completely innocent women – and men – who had to endure some of the worst torture ever imagined. If you're ever in Perthshire – near Dunning in particular – do take some flowers to place on the monument for Maggie – and for all the other 'witches'.

Author's Notes:

1.
At this time in Scotland especially, fear of witchcraft was rife and people began to suspect anyone they didn't care for – or even know for that matter. In Glasgow, near to the castle itself, there is an iron plaque still on the wall that speaks of the 300 people who were burnt on that spot and all for being witches. Between the late 15th, all of the 16th and the very early days of the 17th centuries, there were 4000 to 6000 people – men as well as women – accused of being witches and a very great number of them were found guilty and executed. However, these estimates apply to Europe as a whole – but it does emphasise

how witchcraft was feared – particularly in France and Switzerland. Sometimes the witches found guilty were burnt at the stake, sometimes hanged first and then burnt, sometimes tied to a ducking stool and sunk into murky waters – until they managed to release themselves and float to the surface or never re-appear again. If they died of drowning it proved they were innocent, (or they'd have saved themselves) – if they managed to free themselves, it proved they were guilty and were executed anyway. (Because only the Devil could have saved them). It seemed they lost either way.

Witches were so feared at this time because it was a common belief that witch covens were set up to destroy Christianity – they would meet up with other covens and in the end, take over the whole world. It was easy to understand why the Church itself was so afraid and just wanted them all burnt. It wasn't a good solution but was what they'd reasoned would work.

It is quite obvious, with the hind sight of history, that the horrific incidents of accusing completely innocent parties of being witches was because the environment was a male dominated one. The men were all powerful and although, some men were also accused of being witches, the vast majority of victims were women, old and young.

2.

Incredibly, sometimes an accused witch had done nothing more than look at a potential victim and that was enough to put the evil eye on them – and they could then be accused of being in league with the Devil. Neighbour was afraid of neighbour and spied on each other so as to make the first accusation before the finger was pointed at themselves. Sometimes, the 'witch' just had to be old and that was enough for them to be suspected and condemned to death.

3.

The young Christine (the accuser) in the first tale, grew up and married twice, becoming a very successful and wealthy woman as she did so. Much later in time, when some builders were working on her father's house, a strange hole was found in a bedroom wall. It was thought the hole may have been the means by which an accomplice could have passed through the odd objects which Christine was supposed to bring from her mouth. You must be the judge.

4.

Many years later in Edinburgh, by the castle, a memorial was erected on the spot where the witches were executed. The inscription read:

Pain Inflicted. Suffering Endured. Injustice Done

The very last witch in Scotland to be burnt at the stake was Janet Horne in 1722.

5.

In 1692, a well-respected minister wrote to the special court and implored it to stop accepting 'spectral evidence' i.e. evidence of dreams and visions. The request was ignored and within the next few weeks, a further 18 people were found guilty and hanged in Salem. The President of Harvard University publicly declared his abhorrence of the use of spectral evidence. His words were:

'It were better that ten suspected witches should escape than one innocent person be condemned.'

Notice was taken of this as the Governor's own wife was accused of witchcraft. He dissolved the Special Court and set up a superior one where spectral evidence was not allowed. By 1693, he had also pardoned all the imprisoned 'witches' – but the damage had been done already in what was actually a short time. 19 'witches' had been executed on Gallows Hill, a 71-year-old man had been 'pressed' to death by having heavy boulders heaped on top of him and an unknown number of people had died in prison whilst awaiting trial. By 1693, the Governor had pardoned all those still held in prison for charges of witchcraft.

6.

Although those accused of witchcraft – and of the 20 subsequently executed, as well as those who died whilst lying in prison – were actually pardoned, none of the judges showed any remorse at what had been done. They claimed the Devil had bewitched the whole village and everyone had been duped. It was a weak defence made by all of the officials and on 14 January 1697, the Massachusetts Legislature declared it to be a day of fasting to commemorate the victims of the trials. On the day, 12 trial jurors signed a petition, admitting that they had convicted people to death on the basis of insufficient information. The document actually stated:

'We do, therefore, signify to all in general (and to the surviving sufferers in especial)… that we were sadly deluded and mistaken for which we are much disquieted and distressed in our minds and do therefore, humbly beg for forgiveness. We do heartily ask for forgiveness from you all, whom we have justly offended and do declare to our present minds, we would not do such things again on such grounds for the whole world, praying you to accept this in satisfaction for our offence, and that you would bless the inheritance of the Lord that he may be entreated for the land. (From Hill, Frances. A Delusion of Satan.)'

One of the main Magistrates went a step further. He said he accepted the blame and shame of it and asked God to forgive his part in the Trials. His declaration was read aloud in the Old South Church in Boston and he asked God to spare the rest of the community and place the blame on him instead. The Magistrate's name was Sewell and he swore for the rest of his life, he would hold a day of fasting each year in atonement for his sins.

Parris left the village of Salem where he was pastor and took with him, his daughter Betty, who was one of the initial instigators of the whole Salem witchcraft story. He didn't actually leave Salem until 1697 when he tried to keep the Deeds to his property and lands – but this was denied him and he left the village with nothing. He was, however, awarded £150 British Pounds a few years later as compensation for his sufferings! No records ever showed what happened to his daughter Betty Parris – nor indeed to Abigail Williams – the two instigators of the whole thing in Salem.

Blackbeard – The Pirate and the Man

"There is little doubt but that we should call him Edward, after all you're an Edward and so was your father. Yes, he's an Edward, my dear – and he'll grow up to be a great and good man just like you – Captain Edward Thatch, the once-mariner." Elizabeth Thatch was adamant about her newly born boy's name – he would be Edward after his father, as her daughter was Elizabeth, after herself. The Thatch family were well-to-do aristocrats and they lived in Redcliffe, a good area right in the centre of Bristol, which was a very prosperous city. Captain Thatch dealt in importing goods from the Caribbean Islands and the West Indies in general. He also imported goods from the East Coast of the UK colonies of North Carolina in America. He was always busy though and keen to do even better. Married now and with two children, he sought out other ventures in order to make more money to care for his family. Several hundreds of years later, his family home still stands, as a reminder of the money that Bristol could generate at that time.

Little Elizabeth was standing by the bedroom door. "Come in, Elizabeth and see your baby brother." The girl crossed the room and tentatively reached out for the baby. "What's his name, Mama?" On being told it was Edward, she immediately said, "Why, that's the same name as yours, Papa." They all laughed and Rose, the maid appeared with fresh tea and cake for them to enjoy.

The family stayed in that house for some years and the children grew up there but when they were both still quite young, their father made the decision to move them all to Jamaica, where he'd bought a large plantation. He farmed the land and owned many slaves, who worked on the land for him, so Edward Jnr grew up knowing both Britain and the world of the West Indies. Both children were educated and schooled as best as was possible and when he was a young teenager, Edward knew he'd have to decide what path to follow as an adult.

"Father, I want to leave home and go to sea." He knew the direct approach would be best. Throughout his childhood, they had walked together around the wharf and harbour and Captain Edward would tell him of the faraway lands the ships would visit and the wonderful things they would bring back.

"Father, are you listening to me – I want to go to sea." Young Edward was persistent. He enjoyed the thought of the independence it would give him and welcomed the opportunity of becoming a Privateer – and all under the protection of Queen Anne's Flag. He would be able to confiscate, not only the vessel itself, but also the valuables and cargo it carried. And of course, as a Privateer, working for the Crown, he could keep a great number of valuables for himself.

"Well my Boy, I see nothing wrong with that. Although I had always thought you would work alongside of me and run the business. But I suppose privateering would teach you much and might even make you a rich man." Captain Thatch was really quite pleased by what his son was saying. He'd been a Royal Navy Man himself and knew the strong pull of the sea to some people.

Edward soon settled down to the life of a Privateer and loved being able to 'take' what he wanted and yet be protected by the Royal Navy. His ship operated in the Atlantic and raided many parts of Britain's North American colonies and of course the Caribbean itself. The West Indies was a most attractive destination and a great number of other Privateers went there, as there was so much bounty to be had. Doing as he wanted, he did it well and was soon well-respected by colleagues and at a young age. Still in his early 20s, the captain under whom he was serving, one Benjamin Hornigold gave him command of an ex-slave ship. Blackbeard – as he was then known – sailed that ship with great success on behalf of Queen Anne's War during the years 1701 to 1714. He was becoming a rich man in his own right and then he captured a much larger ship from the French which he renamed as 'Queen Anne's Revenge'. It carried 40 gun carriages.

On board Hornigold's ship one day, he and Edward were discussing issues in general, when Hornigold suddenly blurted out that Britain was considering abandoning the whole concept of Privateering. "What?" said Edward. "That cannot be. How will we be able to live then? I am happy with this life I've carved out for myself." And he banged his tankard of ale on the captain's table.

Hornigold looked thoughtful and wondered if he could truly trust this man. He hesitated and then said, "If we are not to be Privateers, then why not be pirates? That way, we'll never have to share any spoils of war with the Government. Everything would belong to us – and so we just keep on doing what we do best."

This excellent idea soon became the choice of profession for many privateers, including Edward Thatch himself, who was now even more well known as 'Blackbeard', the fiercest and most terrifying pirate of them all. He had learned early on that he had to look the part and worked hard on his image. His dark hair and beard were long and greasy and he always wore black clothes. His sword and cutlass were of enormous size and he took to tying brightly coloured ribbons in his hair, to which he fixed gunpowder caps and plaited smoking hemp in his hair, which served to terrify his opponents. The fiery caps went off regularly, giving him the look of a mad, wild devil, who would stop at nothing to get what he wanted. He sailed around the Atlantic Ocean and his fame spread around the Seaways. In fact, he looked so scary that many of his enemies gave themselves up voluntarily, rather than fight the mad man – the prize for this was that he let them go without even drawing his sword but woe betide those who chose to stay and fight. And in either case, he took possession of the ship and cargo, sometimes pushing the crew overboard for some other ship to rescue.

Between late 1700s and early 1800s, it really was the Golden Age of Piracy and Blackbeard took full advantage of it. "Avast Ye, Scum o' the Earth" was his common cry and his men followed suit, dressing in similar terrifying pirate clothes but only he, ever used the gunpowder caps. His head must have looked as if it was on fire with mini explosions going off at random times and scaring all around him. "We surrender" was the common cry from his opponents. Sometimes he won the battle without even firing a shot. In fact, over a period of three weeks, he captured fifteen vessels that had been sailing between New York and Philadelphia. He was a successful pirate. Suddenly, and at the peak of his success in piracy, he made his mind up about his current life and sought out a new way forward. He banged on the big front door of the mansion house belonging to the Governor of North Carolina, Charles Eden. Word spread quickly throughout the mansion that the pirate Blackbeard was at the door. After much discussion, one servant was eventually pushed forward to open the door. "Yes sir," he said through quivering lips.

"I demand to see Governor Eden – and be quick about it, Man." Blackbeard was nervous but would never want to show it, so he stuck his hand in his leather waistband that held his pistol. The gesture was intended to menace and indeed it did.

"Come in sir and I'll see if the Governor is available." He showed the big, wild pirate into a sumptuous and elegant drawing room, not the kind usually frequented by Blackbeard. He threw himself down on one of the armchairs and spread his legs before him. He may not have been at ease but he certainly looked as if he was. The servant soon reappeared and invited him to follow, the Governor would see him.

"Now what can a Governor do for a pirate, may I ask?" He was a small, rotund man, dressed impeccably in cream breeches, an embroidered brocade jacket and a long lacy cravat. He had a florid complexion caused probably by the gifts of wine and brandy given him from many toadies, who received 'little favours' in return. Whilst not strictly dishonest, he often sailed pretty close to the wind.

"I've made up my mind to stop being a pirate and become a solid citizen. I want to be respectable and respected by others – not feared." Blackbeard stood up to his full height. He was a scary sight and he knew it.

"Well, that seems a very good decision to me – what has made you think this way." Charles Eden couldn't help smiling as it seemed as though this fierce pirate was actually asking his permission to become honest.

"I am to be wed," Blackbeard explained. "Her name is Mary Ormond, but she won't consent to marry me until I give up piracy. So, I have little option but to stop being a pirate and work alongside my father on his plantation in Jamaica – which he has recently bought. To do this, I must have an official pardon from someone like you. Will you give me that pardon, Mr Eden?"

The Governor sat at his desk; his feet stretched before him. He clasped his hands across his waistcoat, his thumbs touching each other and he seemed to be turning it over in his mind. "I only do favours for people who do favours for me – when I need them. I don't need anything from you just now – but may need something in the future. Do you think I can trust you to do what I ask in the months to come?"

194

Blackbeard bristled and replied, "You most certainly can. I may be a pirate but I am a trustworthy fellow." On being asked if he could come back the next day for an answer, he agreed and also accepted an invitation to stay for dinner afterwards.

Reflecting on this, Blackbeard thought dinner was a good omen for a decision on the pardon and so he accepted. He and Mary Ormond were married by the Governor and both settled down to a normal, married life in Bath, North Carolina. Two newlyweds, whose pasts no one knew anything about. But that would change.

"Oh, you have become a dull fellow since giving up piracy." Mary complained as she sat in the drawing room, working on her embroidery. "You used to be full of fun but now, there is nothing interesting about you. In fact, I can't even refer to you as Blackbeard any more – you're definitely an 'Edward'." He was getting fed up as well, with little to do but help his father on the plantation. "Well, what do you want me to do, Wife? I've done as you asked and now, I am a solid, respectable citizen."

"You're certainly a solid citizen – in fact, you're getting fat and I like you not this way." She was being deliberately provocative and put down her embroidery with a heavy sigh. He left the room and half an hour later, he returned flinging the door open with a loud bang.

There he stood in all his glory, all in black with sword and cutlass hanging from his belt buckle. He wore a big, black tricorn hat and his hair hung down in strands around his face; his beard too was dressed in many different coloured ribbons with smoking hemp that he'd lit up just before coming into the room.

"Is that better, wife – it's the only other thing I know how to do?" With that, he bounced onto the street and scared the passers-by out of their wits. They'd only been out for a leisurely afternoon walk and were suddenly confronted by a wild, and seemingly mad, pirate. The neighbourhood was obviously going downhill, they thought.

Blackbeard left his house that afternoon, knowing full well that he'd not be back again. Mary had been the reason he'd stopped being a pirate and now she was the reason he'd started again. Rather unfairly, she then decided to leave him as the only reason she'd married him was that he'd turned his back on piracy, now she couldn't live with him, a very boring and fat gentleman. She returned to her old home and never saw him gain. He didn't care. He eventually went down the street, swinging his sword and shouting, "Avast Ye Landlubbers – I'm back – Blackbeard's back."

And so he was. But before returning to his ship, anchored down by the harbour, he went to see his father on his plantation. Blackbeard had lost his mother three years before and his father had since married again to a lady called Lucretia who'd given him two children in those years, so now the notorious pirate had a very young half brother and sister. His father welcomed him, even dressed again as a pirate and the boy and girl were mesmerised by him. His own sister, Elizabeth still lived at the family home and she was delighted to see him again. They'd always been fond of each other.

"I need to speak with you, Father before I go back to sea." They were both seated in the library, completely surrounded by shelves of books. His father was a great reader. He even showed his son a book he'd bought about Blackbeard himself. "A load of tommy-rot," Blackbeard exclaimed. "No one knows anything about me."

"You'd be surprised – you are one very notorious fellow." His father laughed. He was looking older than Blackbeard remembered and was glad he'd come to see him. "Now what did you want to see me about, Son?"

"Father, I'll come straight to the point – have you yet written your will – and does that will refer to me at all?" He was obviously ill at ease. "As you can see, I'm returning to piracy – I can't go on living as an upstanding gentleman – God knows, I've tried but I just can't do it. She'll leave me now and I really don't care. I'm a pirate, Father, and have to be true to my calling." Slowly, he raised his head and clearly saw his mother, Elizabeth, standing behind his father's chair. "Pa – Mother is in the room. Turn around and you'll see her there."

"I don't have to turn around – she visits me regularly – and always in the study, where we were at our most happiest. Just enquire of her what she wants and she'll tell you – your dear mama." And a great tear ran down his cheek. "Well Elizabeth, tell your son what he wants to hear."

"I came to tell you that you have my blessing to become a pirate again. You were always happy whilst at sea, so you must continue Edward." She'd never looked lovelier and she blew him a kiss across the room. "I'm going now to let you talk to your father – about which I also approve, although the two youngest children were not mine – just you and Elizabeth were mine own." And she was gone, just as quickly as she'd come and with no fuss.

"I feel more confident now, Father – I want to know if I am the beneficiary in your Will. I have a reason for asking which I'll explain. I am going back to sea and I'll be a rich man – I'm a good pirate and men fear me greatly. Hence, the costume." And he swept his hand over his front and stood up and bowed. I have no wish to be your beneficiary and want you to make Elizabeth and the two youngest beneficiaries in my place.

A long discussion ensued and ended with Blackbeard kissing his father on the cheek and sweeping out of the study with a flamboyant gesture of goodbye. They parted as friends, something they'd always been and always would be.

He was in control of the 'Queen Anne's Revenge' again and he never felt happier. He renewed his relationship with the Governor of North Carolina and between them they had several good deals. Both men became very rich from the spoils of Blackbeard's exploits. Blackbeard went on to even greater things and now added more frightening things to his appearance. His beard covered almost half his face and he would wave even more hemp into the hair which smouldered for a long time and made him look like the devil he seemed to want to be. He already was a giant of a man but now he wore a bright scarlet greatcoat which made him look bigger; his tricorn hat had many quivering feathers that dangled in the smoky mist of the lit hemp. Across his chest, he had several bandoleers

196

full of pistols and knives and hanging from his belt were two great swords, one at either side.

This then was the way he managed to capture 45 ships, and all their cargoes and valuables, and this with killing very few people. He scared the other ships and crews so much that many of them 'just gave up' and abandoned the ship. In fact, he killed very few people in his whole career, preferring to scare them half to death instead. He did however, blockade Charlestown Harbour in North Carolina at one point and looted the town itself of everything of value and also 'took' five ships that were anchored there, an enormous prize. What was particularly cunning and devious was that, immediately after gathering all these valuables, he 'laid off' half his crew and abandoned them on the land there, so that he was able to take more of the spoils of war for himself. He was an obvious strategist as well as a notorious pirate.

On leaving Charleston, he took his ship to an inlet called Ocrucoke where he and his crew spent the night drinking together. He'd allowed half his crew to take shore leave and so the 'Revenge' was quite quiet. "Well, Me Hearties – we've done a good job at Charlestown, haven't we and doubled our spoils by getting rid of those useless crew members!" he shouted.

"Aaar." They all cried and banged their tankards together. One of them, braver than the others, asked, "How rich are you Cap'n? You've not been a pirate all that long – yet you've been successful. How rich are you?"

"That's for me to know and you to find out. Keep your nose out of my business." And he banged the table for more brandy – which soon came.

"Why are those naval ships not coming to face us? We know they're over there, don't we? Shouldn't we be goin' over there and attackin'?" Two of the crew shouted their agreement, but Blackbeard held up his hand. "We'll face them sooner than you think – but not until the time's right. We'll wait till mornin' before we make our move, okay?"

"Aye, aye Cap'n – whatever you say." And the men fell asleep one by one, not even bothering to find their hammocks. Blackbeard was still awake when he felt a hand on his shoulder. He looked up and there stood his mother. "Ma, what are you doing here?" He thought at first, he was dreaming but he wasn't – there she stood, dressed in one of the old-fashioned outfits she wore when he was a child.

"I said I would always look after you when you had a big decision to make. And here I am. You're planning to fight the two naval ships I can see from here, aren't you?" She had concern written across her face.

"Not till the morning, Ma. You mustn't worry though; I'm used to such things." He stood up and made to walk towards her but she held up her hands. "Don't come close to me, Edward – my spirit is weakening and I can't stay long. I've come to say, think twice before you make any rash decisions about those naval ships. I have a bad feeling about them." He couldn't help but move more towards her – and her form seemed to shiver and then disappear completely.

"Ma – where have you gone?" Before waiting for an answer, he stumbled towards his chair and fell asleep with his head on the table. "Must have been dreaming," he muttered as his eyes closed.

Dawn broke on the day and everyone woke up very early. One by one, they dipped their sleepy, drunken heads in buckets of sea water and dressed as ferociously as they could. Using his telescope, Blackbeard stared across at the naval ships sent by the Governor of Virginia. "Well men, there aren't many on board her – maybe this is our opportunity to take her quickly as a prize." He made sure his sword, knives, cutlasses were all in place and he set fire to the hemp in his hair. He chose ten of the remaining crewmen to accompany him and they quietly slid over the side of the 'Queen Anne's Revenge' and stealthily stole across the waters in a small boat – across to the navy ship that was waiting for them. There appeared to be only four sailors on board and Blackbeard felt confident that he'd soon have the ship as his own. He and his men boarded the 'Jane' which had been especially sent to capture Blackbeard himself. He was dressed in his very best, and scariest clothes, a sight to behold.

The other naval ship, the Ranger was still some distance away, she'd run aground and temporarily couldn't move, so there would be no danger from her. Blackbeard felt he'd won the day already but, as always, pride comes before a fall and suddenly the deck of the 'Jane' was full of many Royal Marines who came from below deck and from every possible corner of the ship. There were too many of them not to overpower Blackbeard and his men, who fought long and hard, with blood flowing all over the deck and causing the men to slip and slide. Blackbeard fought as hard as he'd ever done before and eventually ended in hand-to-hand combat with one Lt Robert Maynard RN, the captain of the 'Jane'. Blackbeard was covered in cuts and stab wounds and at one point, it looked as if he was going to kill Maynard, when a British sailor intervened and came to his captain's rescue. He held his sword as high as he could and thrust it into Blackbeard's neck, which in a lesser man, would have been a fatal blow; but this was Blackbeard and he fought on regardless. Maynard slashed out at the big pirate and knew if he didn't end this, then it would end him. He thrust his sword as hard as he could – again into the pirate's neck – and almost decapitated him. Blackbeard fell to the deck in a pool of his own blood and just before expiring, he raised his eyes and saw his mother standing there. "I promised I would come for you, my son – and I have." She reached down and took his bloody hand in her own and Blackbeard was no more.

Maynard finished off hacking at the pirate's head and soon held the famous man's head in his hands. The battle soon ended, once the 'Revenge's' crew saw their captain had fallen. What a sight the deck of the 'Jane' was, with dead and bleeding bodies lying everywhere and right in the middle, was a headless giant of a man, dressed all in black and red – and with smoking tendrils still smouldering in his hair and beard. He had fought a good fight – of that there was little doubt – in fact, before throwing his body into the sea, the ship's surgeon confirmed the body had 20 stab wounds and five pistol shots – and yet he'd remained standing till the end. The date was 22 November 1718 and he was only 38 years old – but how he'd lived in those 38 years.

They did, however, throw his body overboard and many witnesses watched as it swam at least three times around the hull of the ship, as though still trying to get away. He was one brave and strong man but the Royal Marines had done for him. They took his head back to the 'Revenge', his own ship, and hung it from the tallest mast. It was taken back to the Governor of Virginia, who had promised a great fortune to the hero who finally brought Blackbeard down. In the end, the fortune was not so great, in fact, it was one hundred pounds, which Maynard shared with his crew; not a great fortune after all, for a very great and notorious man.

The Royal Marines then went ashore and gathered up the rest of the 'Revenge's' crew, who'd been on leave on that fatal night – or else the battle may have gone in a different direction. They were all hanged at Ocrucoke, North Carolina – all 13 of them together.

A tremendous life, not a very long life, but a pretty eventful one. Those who met him would never forget him, that's for sure.

Mackie Castle

The castle stood at the top of the winding lane and watched over the village, as it had done for many hundreds of years. It was a small castle, built just ten miles from the huge Bothwell Castle near Glasgow. It was called Mackie Castle but didn't belong to the Mackie Clan as the Mackies had never claimed any kinsman ship with any of the larger clans, and it hadn't been particularly important throughout history. However, still it stood there in all its glory, part of the landscape. The village of Mackie had grown up along the edge of the shore and a line of small cottages aligned themselves along one side of the road. They too were very old and some still housed descendants of the same families throughout repeated generations.

Today, old Bill Hopkins was perched on the stone wall outside his house, facing a turbulent sea. The waves were quite wild but nothing like when it was really stormy and the waters crossed the road and encroached on the cottage's front gardens, and sometimes, even their back gardens. It was actually a river, rather than a sea and it was called the River Clyde, 109 miles long, certainly the longest river in Scotland and possibly the United Kingdom itself.

Bill was a very tall, thin man with a bald head; he must have been about eighty years old, but didn't act like it. Everyone in the village knew Bill and there were many Hopkins spread along the coast, many of them descendants of his and many from: 'Who knew where?'

"Mornin' Bill, what you up to?" A young boy came along the road on his bike and did a couple of 'wheelies' to impress the pensioner.

"Mindin' my own business, Charlie Watts, like you should be doin'. Shouldn't you be at school, young man?" Bill was whittling a piece of driftwood with a very sharp knife.

"No, Bill – it's half term when I'm allowed to roam free. I've got an art project to finish and I'm on my way up to the castle to do that. Wouldn't you like to come with me?" He smiled at the old man, knowing full well that he wouldn't budge off his wall for anything, anyway not until he'd finished the boat in his hand.

"Come an' show me your drawin' when you come back then, won't you?" Bill reached down behind the wall and picked up a thermos flask filled with coffee.

"Give us some coffee, Bill – I'm pretty thirsty."

"Get on your way, you cheeky young thing." Charlie Watts laughed and pedalled off, sketch pad under his arm.

Two hours later, the boy appeared again but Bill had long since gone. He did appear however at the cottage window and beckoned Charlie over. "Show us then," he said and Charlie opened his pad and held it out to the old man, who'd put on his thick glasses to see the art work better.

"Eh by God Boy – that's good. You've got the castle to a 'T'," and he reached out for the sketch to hold it closer. "Only thing is, why have you put that extra window on the top floor? I've looked at that castle more times in my life than I've had hot dinners but I can't ever remember seeing a window where you've put one."

"What do you mean, man – that sketch is accurate and that window is definitely there." He came over to Bill and held out his hand for the drawing. "Yep, that window is definitely there – I wouldn't have drawn it otherwise." Charlie was indignant, but Bill went on, "And who is that figure standin' in the window – looks like a woman to me."

"I never drew a figure in my work – you're imaginin' it." But Charlie could see what Bill thought was a figure – it must have been a smudge, he thought, but it did look a bit like a lady with long hair piled on top of her head. Now, he was being daft – just like Old Bill.

"I'm goin' to check before I go home, just to shut you up." And Charlie cycled off at great speed towards Castle Lane. Laying his bike down, he looked up at the top of the castle – and there it was, clear as crystal, the middle one of three windows in a row. He peered at what he'd thought was a smudge, but it wasn't a smudge at all. It was the same lady as he'd seen there before, with long hair piled on top of her head and he could see she was wearing a plum coloured dress or robe – styled in a much earlier fashion. He waved to her but she didn't seem to see him – maybe, he was too far away to attract her attention.

"I'm goin' back to see Old Bill and see what he thinks." And then he remembered the camera he had put in his haversack and he grabbed it quickly before she moved away from the window. Click – click – he took two photos before jumping back on his bike and cycling down the hill towards the shoreline. He shot past Bill's cottage towards the chemist shop in the village. "It won't be developed for three days, Charlie – but if you come back then, I'll have it for you." He had no option but to go home, but not before he'd visited Bill again to tell him what had happened.

"Okay, Charlie – come back in three days and show me your photograph. In the meantime, I'll wander up to the castle for a look – although I already know what I've seen all my life." He went on whittling a new boat.

In the intervening time, Charlie went to visit the County Records Office in the nearby town and found a very interesting clerk there who was quite willing to help the young schoolboy. He asked for details of what the boy was looking for and immediately identified with Mackie Castle, a few miles from the castle at Bothwell along the River Clyde, but not nearly as important as Bothwell, which could be the reason it was still standing intact. He was going to enjoy this, there was nothing he enjoyed more than to acquaint people with local history.

"The Mackie Family," he began and gestured to Charlie to take a seat, "have lived at the castle for over 200 years. Outside it's crumbling and falling down but inside, it's only in need of some love and attention, I should think. It was built several hundreds of years ago, around about the same time as Bothwell Castle itself, but it was never regarded as a very important building, it wasn't a fortress and throughout the centuries, different Mackies owned and lived in it, and were until recently the last who stayed there."

He broke off from his delivery and asked if Charlie would like a drink. The boy shook his head, he wanted to hear more. "Isabel Mackie was the last owner of the castle and as she died childless, there was no one to inherit." He paused for a moment. "That's not strictly true – but I'll come to that later." He went on, "The story of the last of the Mackies is rather a sad one, I'm afraid. Although they lived in a castle of sorts, they had no money and the castle itself was in a pretty poor state. There was John Mackie, Isabel's husband and their one son Philip living there – but with no money, they could see no future for themselves."

Suddenly, Charlie was in a stone-walled room in the castle, with little furniture and what there was, in a tatty state. The clerk told the story well. John Mackie was speaking to his wife, "It's the only solution, Isabel and one I've got to take. I have a good feeling about it – I just know it'll work." Isabel looked very sad and held a small handkerchief to her eyes. "I don't know what I'll do without you and Philip. John, you're my rock, you know that. And Philip is only 15 years old."

He crossed the room and put his arms around her. "And you're mine, my dear. But I have to do something to help our situation – for all of her sakes, but maybe for Philip's most of all. After all, what'll he do when we're no longer here?" He knelt down in front of her and clasped her hands. "America is the place for us – I'll make our fortune there – and as soon as Philip and I have found a place to live, I'll either send for you or come back and get you. We'll let the future take care of that decision." He cupped her chin in his hands and kissed her gently on the mouth.

"Well, that's probably the way their conversation went," the records' clerk went on. "It was common knowledge that she didn't want him to go ahead of her to America – but we must do what we have to.

"On 7 April 1912, John and his son set out for Southampton to meet the ship that was on its maiden voyage to America. Apparently, she stood at the top most window in the castle, waving goodbye and watching until they disappeared from view. In fact, it was an odd thing, but people saw her at that window every day, watching for John and Philip – who couldn't possibly have been coming back that soon as they'd only just left – but the mind is an odd thing, isn't it?" he asked Charlie rhetorically.

The clerk crossed to another desk and came back with a big book titled 'The Disaster of the Titanic'. "I know I don't have to tell you what happened to that ship but I should confirm that the Mackie men were aboard her as she left Southampton. The ship called in at Cherbourg in France and Cobh in Northern Ireland before heading for America. She was a magnificent ship, in fact, the most magnificent ever built – although she did have a sister ship called the Olympia, an exact replica of her. The Titanic was actually built in Belfast. Of course, they had to travel steerage as they had so little money. They were given two bunk beds in a cabin at the bottom of the ship and they had to share with two other men. It was narrow and had absolutely no comforts, unlike the First Class which had nothing but comforts. It was however the cheapest way they could have travelled to New York on board the Titanic."

He opened the book and slid it across the table to Charlie. "See for yourself – four gigantic funnels and higher sides than you can imagine. In fact, as you stood on the pier at its side, you couldn't see the sky – the ship was so tall."

"Put your bag on that bunk and I'll take the lower one." John pointed to the small beds and Philip did as he was told. The two men with whom they were sharing were talking in a different language – Irish Gaelic – but no one understood them. "Let's go on deck and have a look around. We'll have to stay in our own deck, however – we're not allowed to go higher." First, they found their way to the canteen, they just followed the smell of roasting meat and found their mouths to be salivating.

"Come on lad, sit yourself down and let your Pa push into the queue and fetch your dinner. You may be steerage but at least the food's good – not as good as first class of course, but still passable." A friendly sailor spoke to them and showed John where to go. Next day, they were told there was to be a Lifeboat Drill. The ship was travelling at her maximum speed and the passengers were disgruntled with the imposition of a Drill, so the captain – E J Smith of the White Star Line – abandoned the plan. That seemed rather foolish just because a lot of rich people didn't like the thought – a drill would be good and certainly do no harm, in fact, the familiarity it would have brought to the passengers could have saved many lives. Still, it wasn't done.

Young Philip was talking to a very young crew member, called Fred Fleet who was getting ready to go up to the highest turret of the ship, it used to be called the Crow's Nest, but on the modern Titanic, it would be 'The Lookout'. Fred told Philip, "I'm really quite worried as I can't get access to the binoculars I'm supposed to use. One of the officers has locked them in a cupboard and gone off with the key. I really need them, we seem to be in the middle of an ice field so I'll need all the help I can get." He never did get his binoculars however and Philip saw him going off to make his way to the top of the ship – to the Lookout.

"Bye Fred – take care now," but Fred didn't even turn his head, so intent was he to get on with his job.

The night was getting darker but there were a lot of stars around and Fred had no sooner reached the Lookout than he spotted an enormous iceberg just ahead. He alerted the Captain and other officers but the ship couldn't be turned around or veered away enough to avoid the iceberg. The Captain actually seemed unaware of the danger, although he'd been warned about the ice field. A loud bang was heard by many people although some passengers heard nothing. Great chunks of ice began to fall onto the ship's deck and the steerage passengers started to play football with them. The collision happened at 11.40 pm, but at first no one was unduly concerned.

Philip grabbed his father's hand. "What was that father?"

"I don't know, son – but remember we're quite safe – this ship can't sink." But John Mackie was worried. Suddenly, there was a huge explosion which came from the bowels of the ship and panic began to build. There was still lovely music playing on the first-class deck and the musicians refused to leave their duty. Some men's bravery can be quite amazing – and so the musicians played on whilst the ship sank.

Within a short time, the officers were telling passengers that they had to abandon ship, along with the crewmen; the crewmen only after the passengers were safe, of course. Everyone was telling each other not to worry – even if the ship was sinking – an impossible thought – there was a wireless telegraph on board and help would come very quickly, if it was needed at all.

Everything developed into pandemonium on board and people were bumping into each other, with none of the usual very British apologies being offered by anyone. The lifeboats were being slowly lowered over the side of the ship, some of them still only half full. John and Philip had on their life jackets and they were crouching in a corner of the deck. John was trying to get an officer's attention to ask for his help in getting Philip in one of the smaller boats, but the officer was too distracted to deal with him. Standing beside them were two men, obviously foreign and wearing a sort of khaki uniform. Their English was quite good and John asked them, "Which country are you from?" He knew it was an odd question, but it was such an unreal situation, that nothing made sense.

"We come from Egypt, sir and we're here to escort an ancient Egyptian Princess to New York. She is in the cargo hold of the ship," one of the men answered.

"You've kept a woman in the hold?" John asked incredulously.

"Not just any woman – it is the mummified Princess Ahmen-Ra. She has been dead for one and a half thousand years B.C. and she brings a curse on whoever owns her. That is why there's no hope for this ship. A rich American has bought her mummy and she will most certainly have cursed the ship which is taking her from her native land." The other man interrupted his friend's conversation, "And she has been owned by several people before this American and each owner has died in some horrific way. I myself am quite calm as I know there is no hope for all these people." And he waved his hand across the turbulent crowd. "The ship is supposed to have watertight compartments so that no water can get in, but you saw what it was like below deck, sea water everywhere. Princess Ahmen-Ra is more powerful than anything else. When the authorities heard she was to travel on this ship, they increased the ship's insurance only six days before the maiden voyage."

The Egyptian men seemed to feel better for sharing this information. It was as though no blame for the collision could be laid at their door. They both stepped away from John and Philip, said something in a foreign tongue and leapt over the side of the ship, hands clasped in front of them – down, down into the freezing depths of the sea.

"Oh Father, is what they said, true – is there no hope for us?" Philip was crying and blowing on his cold fingers. "Will Mama be told what's happened to us if we don't make it – she told us not to come, didn't she?"

There was a loud crack and everyone fell to one end of the ship, rolling uncontrollably over the railings and spilling into the freezing water. One of the four funnels broke in half and fell onto the deck, then into the sea. John and Philip were swept along with the throng, they saw babies and toddlers tumbling into the sea, but there was no one to save them. First Class passengers were mixing with steerage, there was no class system in such turmoil but many more First-Class passengers were packed into life boats than were ones from Steerage. John and Philip saw each other no more. Son and father, as with so many other family members, sunk below the waves and floated away from each other. They died with the shock of the water's temperature even before their lungs had filled with sea water.

The Records clerk brought Charlie back to the present time and both felt an incredible sadness at what the clerk had read from the open book. He finished with, "Exactly 2 hours and 20 minutes later, the Titanic sunk under the sea – 375 miles off Newfoundland – and 1,500 people drowned with her. She lies at the bottom of the Atlantic Ocean at a depth of 12,500 feet although her actual location wasn't found until a further 14 years had passed."

He went on, looking at Charlie in a mysterious way. "Well, Young Man – was it simply the slash along her sides caused by the iceberg: was it the watertight compartments and the double floor failing to so what was promised: was it the lack of lifeboats and the cancelled Drill: was it the curse of the Egyptian Princess: was it the Captain's disinterest in the ship's closeness to the iceberg: was it the incredibly fast speed at which the ship was travelling – it was her maiden voyage after all: was it the lost binoculars that stopped Fred Fleet seeing the iceberg in time: or even more strange, was the explosion people heard in the bowels of the ship after the collision, actually a torpedo fired by a German U-Boat. So many possibilities and so many contributing factors – but who could ever tell?" The clerk was breathless after that list.

"I really didn't expect such a clear picture of the sinking of the Titanic. Thank you so much for giving me so much of your time. I really appreciate it." Charlie felt quite mesmerised by the whole story and had almost forgotten that he'd really come about the owners of Mackie Castle. That mystery was still to be resolved.

"About the Mackie family – do you know anything about them? What happened to Isabel Mackie when her husband and son failed to come back to her?"

"Well," said the clerk, "that's a story all by itself – although more of a local one. Isabel Mackie stood at the top most window in the castle and she stood there every day. People saw her as they passed by – some waved, but most didn't – and the one maid servant who looked after her, confirmed to those she knew in the village, that the mistress had a habit of going to the window every day, in the hope that she'd see John or Philip. Of course, she never did but that didn't stop her. They had said they'd either come back for her or at least send for her, but for things beyond their control, that never happened.

"She became a recluse, with the maid being the only one who ever went down into the village to order food and necessities. She had had two letters from the White Star Shipping Company, but she took no notice of them; John and Philip hadn't been lost when their ship sank in the Atlantic Ocean. She disregarded the letters and, in the end, they stopped writing to her. She knew she just had to be patient and her patience would be rewarded one day soon. She told herself this frequently and just went on waiting. She did this for 50 years and then one day, she didn't go to her window and the new maid went looking for her. She did find her, dead in her bed. She must have been sleeping when the Grim Reaper came to fetch her. She was 85 years old; it seemed he'd taken a long time to come and find her. The new maid was very upset as Isabel had been a kind, if rather mad, mistress. The castle was boarded up and put on the market for sale; it had been badly neglected for many years and its condition was not good.

"Two weeks later, some people were walking up the lane towards the castle, when they spotted something at the top most window of the building. The woman, who had the sharpest eyes, said, 'That's not a thing, that's a woman – in fact, I recognise her – that's Isabel Mackie.'

"Her friend said, 'Don't be ridiculous, you went to her funeral a week ago don't you remember?' But her friend insisted that it was Isabel Mackie. 'I've seen her many times before standing there, waiting for her family to come home.' And so the story spread all around the village and out into the wider countryside. Isabel Mackie's ghost had come back to haunt Castle Mackie. Every day, people and more people came up the lane to see the ghost, who never looked down at them or made any gesture at all. Soon, some of the wilder village boys broke into the castle and climbed the stairs to find the room where Isabel stood, but they never did find it. Instead, they damaged a lot of things and ransacked the castle.

"Within a short time, the building became a dangerous place and of course, a broken-down castle with a daily visit from a ghost, encouraged lots of visitors and spectators. The authorities soon got involved and agreed that something had to be done to make the place safer. They decided to brick up the window where she stood every day and they made a good job of it, in 1966, there was no longer a place for Isabel to watch for John and Philip. However, on the same day, the vicar was invited to the castle where he held an exorcism service. He invited the ghost to leave that place, which wasn't the right place for her to be. He said, 'Go and find your husband and son where they rest today – and then you will be happy.'

"Of course, as with the other 1500 victims who drowned when the Titanic sunk in the icy waters of the Atlantic, Isabel, whether she was dead or alive, could not do this. They lay in the ruined hulk of the most famous ship ever built.

"As the window had been bricked up, people soon stopped coming and peace broke out around Castle Mackie. There was the odd whisper that someone, a couple of young boys, had seen the ghost standing at the window, but as the window no longer existed, this was obviously a trick of the light.

"The story goes," the clerk continued, "that any male youth could see the window with the ghost standing there – but only the boys – it seemed that Isabel was obviously still looking for her son." He paused for breath and closed the large book. It was time to close up the office and go home.

"But that explains why I see the window in the castle wall, but Old Bill can't. Can't you see that?" Charlie felt he'd solved the mystery at last. He gathered up his things and left the Records Office. Before going home, he walked up the twisted lane – the sun was just setting and everything looked so peaceful. He threw down his satchel and stared at the castle wall. Sure enough, the window was there – back in place where it had always been – but on closer inspection, Charlie could see the smudge on the glass was even bigger than on previous occasions. Isabel Mackie stood there still, but behind her, was a tall man with long hair and whiskers. It must have been John Mackie, her husband. In front of her and with her hands on his shoulders, a young fair-haired boy stood. The family were reunited at last.

Very slowly, the apparitions raised their hands and waved solemnly to Charlie. "Goodbye," Isabel mouthed clearly – and John and Philip smiled a little. "Goodbye," Charlie shouted and waved furiously, sure that they could see him. The window faded into the castle wall and soon there was nothing to be seen, not even a slight smudge.

Next day, Charlie went to Old Bill's cottage and insisted he come with him up to the castle. After grumbling, Bill did as he was asked but couldn't resist ridiculing Charlie's photos he'd got back from the shop. "No window, as I told you, Young Charlie – I knew I was right all along."

They reached the castle and stood for a moment until Bill got his breath back. Charlie was tempted to tell him the story of the window that could be seen only by certain people, but couldn't be bothered. Bill would only accuse him of making it up anyway.

"Look, there's someone standing by the door and he seems to have a very large key in his hand. He's trying to put it in the lock. Excuse me, but what do you think you're doing? You have no right to be going in there – it's dangerous."

The man turned around and Charlie was amazed to see who it was. The clerk from the Records Office had come to visit Mackie castle. "What are you doing here?" Charlie asked.

"Before I answer that, can you tell me if you can see the top middle window in the wall – or is it blocked up with bricks." Charlie looked closely and told the clerk, "There is no window now and I don't think there'll ever be one again. I saw Isabel Mackie at the window yesterday and with her, was a man and a young boy – her husband and son. They're gone now – they waved goodbye to me – so again, I ask you what you're doing here?"

The clerk smiled and said, "I'm the new owner. I plan to have the castle worked on and put to rights again – but I wanted to be sure there were no ghosts there now – I'll be living in it from now on, but I didn't want to have to share it with my great aunt and her family."

He moved forward his hand outstretched, "Let me introduce myself – I'm John Mackie."

Where Do We Go from Here?

"Not corned beef hash again Marge." Old Tom had eaten corned beef hash three times already this week and he would have welcomed a plate of tripe and onions or a bowl of pigs' trotters. Something other than corned beef hash.

Marge completely ignored him and plopped the dish on the table. "Stop moaning, Tom – you're lucky to have that. There's a war on or have you forgotten that?" She called for Christine to bring the child for her supper – and she left the big jar of malt with a spoon on top. "Don't forget her malt, dear – you know it's good for her." It was amazing how many things were supposed to be good for you since the war began. It was just a trick to make people eat the only food that was readily available, rather than what they'd really like. Christine sat little Molly at the table and started to spoon feed her – Molly licked her lips. She didn't mind corned beef hash again – she liked it.

Christine asked, "Do you think they'll come over again tonight? I think they will 'cause they've not been for a couple of days now." She shared her meal with her daughter who was still hungry, it seemed. Marge gave her a piece of buttered bread, sprinkled with sugar – not generously sprinkled, of course – but just enough to please the child. Sugar was very much still on the ration.

"Finish quickly, all of you – I think I can hear the first drones of the engines – and it's not ours. We'll have to get under the stairs and table – there's not enough time to get down to the air raid shelter now." Marge began to feel flustered and grabbed the flask to make some tea.

"Okay, Ma – I'll just get Molly's coat and pixie hood. It's going to be cold tonight. The Gerries will love that bright moon." Christine left the table and went upstairs. Molly got off her chair and started to play beside the fireplace. She could play with anything, that child could.

Tom and Marge got their coats and, after clearing away the dishes, crept under the heavy wooden table. People didn't really believe a table would save them if a bomb fell in a direct hit, but it was better than nothing.

The bombs began to fall – yes, they were aiming in this direction tonight. They pulled Molly under the table and told her not to worry, it would be all right. Christine's legs appeared and she crouched down beside them.

It was a big bomb that fell on their house. Christine's legs buckled and they saw her fall to the floor. They saw nothing else, not even dust and debris. It was as though the trio under the table, and the table itself, had been blown to smithereens. Then there was silence. No struggling people trying to get to safety, just an eerie silence. It was cold and the moon was brighter as it was shining directly onto the demolished house. The sound of the dropping bombs was still all around but now it seemed they were falling further up the street.

The Foster family was no more. One minute, all alive and talking to each other, then just part of the miscellaneous rubble that had been home. There was no little Molly but one of her slippers was lying by the hearth, beside both of her mummy's shoes. Funny that how peoples' footwear seemed always to fly off their feet. As the rubble began to cool down, some strange shapes began to emerge from the broken furniture. The odd photograph fluttered about as well and familiar faces stared at an earlier camera, some photos showed the people when younger, and some from more recent times. It was the Foster family as they'd been and would be no more. Scraps of paper stuck out of drawers and represented lives that had been lived and recorded for posterity, but no one would be interested in what the papers said, their whole story had been wiped out by some stranger they didn't know from Adam, who had flown over their home. There was nothing sadder than a bombed-out house and especially, if some family members still lay strewn around the home, in bits and pieces.

The cooling of the rubble produced a heavy smoke that cast a shroud over everything. Very slowly, some of the rubble seemed to move, but it was just the collapse of curtains, bed linen and fragments of the lighter furniture which were just ash shapes that once were solid fixtures. Some men would arrive probably the next day to begin clearing and trying to make the house safe, but not before the bodies of those who'd been inside were carefully taken to the several mortuaries that had sprung up from nowhere at the start of the war. It would be an absolutely terrible job and yet, to coin a phrase, someone had to do it.

At the spot where the old wooden table had stood, Marge's head leaned against one of the broken legs but the rest of her was scattered all over the place. Christine and Old Tom had faired the same as each other, sad and broken limbs with pieces of clothing still hanging off them lay between the rubble and broken furniture. One piece of wall was still standing and the outline of the fireplace was imprinted on it, with two broken china dogs that had come from the mantlepiece. It was all remnants of family life, the sadness and horror of it too much to bear, and yet those workers would come tomorrow and look upon atrocities that no one should have to see.

Suddenly, Old Tom stood up and slowly looked around the bombed house. He felt shaky on his legs and he tried to call out for Marge, but his voice wouldn't work. Probably full of dust, he told himself. Then little Molly appeared at his side. She looked exactly the same as she had before the bomb and she said to Old Tom, "Where is Mummy. I want Mummy." He lifted her up and cradled her in his arms. "She's coming Luv – in fact, she's around here somewhere." And he cuddled the child into his chest.

Christine crossed through the rubble to get to them. "Here you are," she said. "What on earth has happened?" The answer to this was obvious but like all people who've gone through it, there was just a little bit of hope that they were wrong.

"We're dead, aren't we, Dad?" she said to Tom.

"Aye Lass, I'm afraid we are. But where's Marge – where's your mother?" He started to look around the heaps of debris and then spotted her, standing by the broken sideboard, a couple of old photographs in her hand.

"Here I am, Tom," she called out. She was trying to avoid looking at her own severed head but realised there was little point. Where was the rest of her body?

The family joined up together, heads bowed and arms clasped around each other's shoulders. They had little problem in accepting they were ghosts of their former selves, but the odd thing was, they still felt their existence was real. Although not a physical feeling, there was a recognition of who they were and how much they meant to each other. They were still very much a family.

Dawn was coming up and the Fosters looked up and down the street, a couple of other houses had been hit and there were figures, similar to themselves, standing around in piles of rubble, looking lost and bewildered. Little Mrs MacGillacuddy's house was completely flattened and she was sitting on her doorstep which was about all that was left of the building. They went down the street and spoke to her gently.

"Why Mrs MacGillacuddy – you're just like us. We'll have to look after each other till we learn what's to become of us." Marge put her arms around the little woman and bending down, she kissed her ghostly cheek. "Everything's gone for us as well – so you're not alone."

"I've got my memories but nothing tangible to hold onto." The tears were running down her face and she rubbed them with a ghostly arm. The sooty marks came away on her hand and Marge was astounded to see that happen.

"We've not got much strength but it looks as if we can do some things that we used to. Look Christine, try to lift up that plant pot." She pointed to a pot full of Tulips. After a couple of attempts, Christine managed it and held the flowers above her head for all to see. Even Mrs MacGillacuddy smiled at the gesture and Little Molly tried to pick one of the Tulips but couldn't quite manage it. "You'll do it in time, Sweetheart – just keep trying." Christine encouraged her. She felt odd, giving advice in such circumstances.

Looking down the street further, they saw the Milligans, also looking lost and confused. There were three of them, one boy and a mum and dad – Sam and Brenda and their son, Peter. They crossed the street with Mrs MacGillacuddy in tow. Old Tom greeted them and said with a wry smile, "We're all in the same boat, I fear," and he shook Sam's hand. Two ghostly hands touching each other but feeling nothing. Although there was a spark there, they were two human beings who had just changed their status.

They all agreed to wait in the street to see what would happen next and as the grey light of dawn emerged, they saw a couple of fire lorries trundling down the road, carrying several men with picks and shovels. Behind the lorries, was one ambulance – just a glorified van with a big red cross painted on the side. They could hear the men talking.

"Don't think there'll be much for the ambulance here – three direct hits and no one left alive." They jumped off the fire lorries and began to move around the rubble, looking for anyone left alive. There was, of course, no one but one of the men spotted Marge's head by the fireplace and gently lifted it and put it in a small sack. He did it with great reverence and care. What a job it must have been but they carried it out with as much dignity as they could.

The next couple of days passed with the workmen clearing the bombed houses and the ambulance collecting as many limbs as they could find. The street was looking much barer than before and Marge and Christine spotted a Royal Navy Officer walking along the pavement.

"Mum, it's Jim. He must have heard what happened – and they've given him leave to see what he could do. He wasn't stationed very far away – he must have still been at Portsmouth." He looked very handsome in his smart uniform and Christine found tears welling up in her eyes. Jim was her husband and Molly's dad, except that he had no one now. He was carrying a bunch of carnations, pink and white, and he stopped at where the gate used to be. He walked up the garden path to the stone doorstep which was still left in place. He bent down and laid the flowers on the ground, wiping unmanly tears away as he did so.

"I've come to say goodbye – goodbye to all of you – my lovely Christine and darling Molly – and Tom and Marge, who looked after everyone so well." He looked around surreptitiously in case any of the workmen were watching him – but they made sure they weren't. "A man should be able to cry for losses like this, shouldn't he?" The men nodded in agreement with each other.

Jim turned and went back down the path when something odd happened. One of the white carnations lifted from the ground and floated towards the naval man. Little Molly had managed to move something at last and she chose to give her daddy a present before he left. He bent down and picked up the flower, smelt its perfume and nodded into the wind. He felt their presence and knew what the flower meant but they were all gone from his life and there was nothing he could do about that. Slowly, he walked back down the street, looking backwards a couple of times. The Foster family watched him go and shed ghostly tears in goodbye.

Sam and Brenda had been wandering a bit further afield than the bombed street and they'd come across an old cinema that didn't have any bomb damage – but it looked quite dilapidated – and had been so for a long time. It had showed films until the start of the war but had been closed for safety reasons and although not having been bombed, it had suffered quite a bit from flying debris. They all went together, the Fosters, the Milligans and Mrs MacGillacuddy to look at the cinema. It was dark inside but the men pulled down some shutters that had been fixed when it closed, and it was amazing to see all the seats that looked perfectly usable and probably quite comfortable.

It smelt a bit of damp and had a few mice running all over the place but none of that bothered the bombed-out ghosts. There was a heavy, dark curtain still hanging in front of the screen. It was a bit torn but not too badly and there was a band pit in front of it, still with its drum standing there alone. They all wandered around the place and even went up to the projectionist's room, from where an old projector still stood in front of a window, it looked through into the open auditorium. It was as though people had just walk on the day it closed and never looked back. Under an old sack there were old reels of films, still in the original cans and although the equipment looked dusty and dirty, it was all recognisable as what it had once been.

"Amazing," said Sam and rubbed his ghostly hands together in excitement. "What's to do next – we have to do something, don't we? That's until we learn what's to happen to us next."

Brenda looked round in disbelief and added. "Wouldn't it be good if we could tidy it all up and make it work again?"

Optimism had always been her middle name and Sam put his arm around her shoulders and kissed her cheek. "Quite a big wish, Brenda – but not impossible, let's hope." Meanwhile, Christine was looking through the film cans and marvelling at some of the titles. A lot of them were new films and known quite well to some of the people. "Look everyone," she shouted, "here's the Wizard of Oz – Gone with the Wind – Bringing up Baby – Scrooge – and a few others." She looked as if she'd found gold.

"Oh," Marge said, "I've seen all of those." Christine couldn't help but laugh. "That won't stop you from seeing them again, will it?" Marge could be funny sometimes without meaning to. Sam and Brenda had already started tiding up. It was amazing how quickly they all had learned to focus on an object and imagine it moving – to make it actually happen. People really were resilient. Little Molly came wandering down the passageway. "Mummy, there's two men in the little shop next door – and one of them gave me threepence to make me go away."

"And what did you do?" Christine asked.

"I took the money and went away." Molly's innocence made them all laugh, but Old Tom went out of the cinema to see who was in the shop next door. It had obviously been a sweet shop in its earlier life but now there were no sweets around. Tom could just manage to squeeze through the crack down the side of the window and he saw two young men crouching against the far wall. They seemed to be messing about with some kind of black box and getting quite frustrated in the process. He didn't speak but went back to join the others.

"Well, they're not ghosts like us – they're very much still alive – and they're English. I could hear them talking, but they didn't see me." Tom seemed very curious about what they were doing.

The time had come to attempt to run the projector and the film they'd all chosen as the first one was, 'The Wizard of Oz'. Sam took responsibility for this as he knew a little bit about it and after much chopping and changing, the old screen lit up and the familiar music filled the theatre. The big tear across the screen didn't detract from the film's magic, it was exciting and cheered everyone up at a time they hadn't thought possible, especially just after that bomb had dropped a few weeks before.

Little Molly had gone outside and met some young children who were playing in the street. She asked them if they'd like to come into the cinema and see what was going on. Of course, they followed her inside but they had to prise open a window to get in. It was odd how she manged to make herself understood but she did. Perhaps, the innocence of children was magic too. The street kids

213

thought it was wonderful the way she could just walk through the walls and she became their heroine immediately. They all sat down and stared at the screen in wonderment. Marge, Tom and Christine were sitting in the front row and Brenda was helping Sam with the projector. Mrs MacGillacuddy had fallen asleep despite the sounds of the film. The children were as good as gold and agreed to leave the place when Dorothy floated away in the balloon on her way home to Kansas.

Molly waved them all off shouting, "I–It," as the children left. "What are you saying, Molly – you're not making any sense. What does 'I–It' mean?" Christine quizzed the child.

"Don't know, Mummy – but it sounds good, doesn't it?" Christine decided to leave her alone in her own little world.

The next day, the few children who'd seen the film came with many of their friends in tow. For such few children, they managed to make quite a noise – and the two young men from the shop next door, came to see what was happening – and stayed to watch the film. They were suspicious of the ghosts who seemed in control but said nothing as everyone accepted them for what they were. And as one of them said, "There's many a strange thing on earth, as in heaven." It may have been a misquote but it still made perfect sense.

And so the cinema shows became an established occurrence. It was actually quite far down a narrow street and not many people passed by – so no authorities ever discovered anything unusual. The two young lads only came in one more time – as what they were doing in the little shop, seemed to keep them quite busy. "I–It," Molly shouted to them as they left but they completely ignored her. But Tom was still keeping an eye on them – he couldn't work out why he was so suspicious of them – but he was.

He called Molly over and asked her, "Why do you keep saying 'I–It' darlin' – have you heard someone saying it?"

"Oh yes, Grandpa – my two friends next door keep saying it to their black box." She still held the doll she'd managed to salvage from the bombed-out house and she said to the doll, "We know another of their special words, don't we, dolly? The kind of words they speak into the black box." She looked at Tom slyly and said, "Do you want to know that word?"

"Yes, please darlin'. What's the word?" Tom was getting even more curious.

"Wasika, that's the word Grandpa. Good word, isn't it?" She was very proud of knowing something that no one else did. Tom looked thoughtful and kept repeating, 'Wasika' to himself. It took a couple of days before his thoughts became clear.

He went looking for Sam and shared his thinking with him. "Say 'I–It' and 'Wasika' quickly several times – and then let the words run together. I don't want to actually say them – I might be talking rubbish – but what do you think, Sam?"

"I think we should go in next door next time the blokes are there. They may be quite young – but they're not children – and could be up to anything."

The very next time they heard the lads moving things about next door, they crept in through the crack in the window. There they were as usual, crouching in the corner with their black box. One of them was wearing something like ear muffs and the other one was holding a pencil and piece of paper. The one with the ear muffs was speaking out loud and the other one was very quiet – listening intently. The word they were saying was clearly 'Heil Hitler' – but in Molly's quaint childish way, she heard it as 'I–It'.

"My God, Tom – they're speaking in German, I bet. Did you pick up the other word too – it's not 'Wasika' – it's 'Swastika'. That must be some sort of radio that lets them communicate with Germany. What are we going to do about it? We can't just ignore it."

Sam was really excited.

Tom was calmer and said, "Let's go back into the cinema and think about it. Of course, we can't let it go on – but we're ghosts, remember – and our powers are very limited." Tom's advanced years of wisdom stood him in good stead. The very next day, they heard the two lads in the sweet shop and very quickly they left the cinema and went next door. There were many children in the cinema, watching a film called 'Duck Soup' with Groucho Marx and laughing so hard, it sounded like pandemonium. Little Molly was running around what had been the entrance hall to the cinema and banging a tambourine and shouting 'I–It', 'I–It' over and over again. She soon fell asleep – as all ghosts have to do after a while – and the grown-ups shooed all the live children from the cinema – for their own safety – and the men told the women what had happened that afternoon.

Mrs MacGillacuddy was the first to speak. "Well, we've got to tell the Police or the Home Guard, haven't we? And we've got to tell them soon. Those lads could be sending information that might kill or maim our people and even help the Gerries win the war." She folded her arms and stood up – to all of her four feet. "Have you heard any of the rumours about the Jewish people and what's being done to them all over Europe? Not only are they murdered in their beds and stripped of all they possess – but they're being loaded onto trains and taken to big camps – men, women and children. They're being worked to death, not fed and when they're too tired to even walk, they're being put in chambers and killed by poisonous gases." She had tears running down her withered cheeks. "We've got to stop Germany from coming here or they'll do the same to us." She stretched to four feet one inch and said, "I am a Jew, you know. I married a Scotsman who wasn't – but my maiden name was Judith Samuels – and I came from a proud family of Jews." She was almost preaching from a pulpit but all the others understood. Although they couldn't bring themselves to believe, anyone could commit such atrocities in the way she described, they still felt very vulnerable and knew the Germans had to be stopped.

Marge was furious at what she heard and was ready to believe some of what the old woman said. "Of course, we have to tell someone, but how are we going to do it? We can't just walk into the Police Station and tell them. They wouldn't be able to see us." Marge looked thoughtful. "But we can lift a pencil and somehow make it write. Find some paper, Sam – there'll be something up in the office we can use." Everyone agreed – Marge had always been the clever one.

And so the deed was done. It took quite some time to write the note, but they all took a turn, even Mrs MacGillacuddy, who felt it was her duty. She signed the note, 'A Well Wisher'. Two days later, they heard the young men next door in the sweet shop and almost immediately, a police car drew up and stopped. Several policemen rushed from the car and into the shop and moments later, they came back holding the two young men between them. Two policemen were actually carrying the black box and many wires and bits and pieces. One of the German lads, for German they both were, turned on the policemen and all the children who were still standing around the street and shouted, "Du bist tot (You are dead) – Deutschland wird den Krieg gewinnen (Germany is going to win the War) – Du bist alle tot (You are all dead)" and he was bundled into the car with one of the policemen helping him along, by pushing him in the small of the back and shouting back, "Nein meine Manner – Deutschland wird den Krieg verlieren (No chaps, Germany is going to lose the War)."

No one had any problem with the translation, all the children started shouting 'I–It' over and over again and blowing raspberries, thumbs to noses and laughing about 'Wasika – Wasika'.

Ghosts or not, they had succeeded in stopping the spies from doing their dirty work. It had been an exciting time and one that made them feel very proud. "Still doing our little bit," they told each other. But now it was over and they'd have to get on with tidying more of the cinema. They'd become quite expert at moving things around now and didn't let much stop them.

There were more and more ghosts joining them, the bombing of Britain was not yet over and conversations between them all made it clear that, until the world war was over, the ghosts of those bombed and killed would have to remain in limbo until their souls were taken up to Heaven. Everyone accepted this, after all, it was just a part of the war and they were proud to take part. Although there were many ghosts wandering the streets now, they sheltered sometimes in places like the cinema or any large (and empty) buildings that were available. It was someplace for them to go.

Then a large bomb dropped on the cinema itself and about quarter of the building disappeared over night. Strangely enough, it didn't destroy any of the film cans and the torn screen itself, which was holding up very well. Many, many live people, as well as ghosts, were still coming to watch films – over and over again – and the cinema was more often than not, crammed to the gills with audiences. Then one day, a crowd of singing and dancing people came to the cinema. They were laughing and singing and even kissing each other.

"VE Day," they shouted, "thank God for VE Day." All the ghosts tried to learn what had happened and were delighted to learn that the war was over. It was May 1945 and Hitler had committed suicide and killed his wife, Eva Braun. One week after his death, the Allies accepted Germany's surrender. The western world went mad – Death and Destruction were a thing of the past and Winston Churchill was the super hero of the day. Japan was still at war, however, and it wasn't until a few months later that America dropped a Hydrogen Bomb on two Japanese cities where thousands of people were killed. Japan surrendered and the war was almost at an end. Korea still had to be dealt with.

"Marge, Marge – have you heard?" Tom kissed his wife's cheek and swung Molly around in circles until she laughed so much, she cried and wet her pants at the same time.

The next day there was a big street party outside the cinema – ghosts and live people all mixed together – one side couldn't see the other and the other side, didn't care anyway. Everyone was so relieved and happy. They heard the Royal Family had come out on the balcony of Buckingham Palace and that the two young princesses were allowed to wander the streets and go amongst the cheering crowds.

The euphoria was almost worth the terrible war just to feel this exhilaration, but not quite, of course. Tom and Sam were whispering to each other and they beckoned to the women to join them. "Listen – can you not hear it? We're getting a message intended for all the dead people who died in the streets or in their homes. We've to return to the exact spot where we were killed and wait there. It looks as if Heaven is at last opening up to us – at least I hope it's Heaven," and he laughed nervously. Very slowly, the shadowy figures began to leave the partying crowds and turn towards their individual streets – it was a sombre, but very large, group of people. The Foster family and their friends took one last look at the cinema and at all the happy folk in the street. Strangely enough, they didn't really want to leave what they'd achieved at the cinema – but truth to tell, they were suddenly feeling very tired and slow. Tom was carrying Little Molly, who really didn't want to leave all the friends she'd made but – as Christine explained – it was time to go home.

The walking parties began to split up, each finding the street where they'd been bombed and died. Mrs MacGillacuddy went on further than the Fosters to where her house had once stood and sat on the doorstep, the remaining bit of rubble still there. Sam and his family crossed the road. "Bye Tom, Marge and your two lovely girls – you never know, perhaps we'll meet again."

"Let's hope so," Tom responded. "Who is that standing on our path? It' a man in a dark suit. Maybe he's got the wrong house. Easily done, I suppose." The family walked on towards their old house. And there stood a tall, young man in a Naval Officer's uniform.

"It's Jim," Christine shouted and started to run. This time he could see her and he took her in his arms. She was crying and laughing at the same time. "Molly, Molly – come and see your daddy." She looked at him and realised he was a ghost now, just as she was. "What happened, dearest – how did it happen?" Marge and Tom were crowding around him too, shaking his hand and kissing his cheek.

"Welcome back, son," Tom said in a gruff voice. "Well, how did you get yours?"

"I was on a destroyer and although, we got the Gerries too, they hit us enough to disable us – and we all went down with the ship. I don't think anyone survived." He smiled despite what he was saying and lifted Molly high in the air and swung her around. She squealed with delight.

The sky had turned an odd colour, sort of orange and yellow with pink streaks pointing upwards towards the sky. It was like a moving staircase with the last bit disappearing right up into the yellow clouds. Tom gathered his family and so did Jim, they all started to walk up what looked like a yellow brick road and as they did so, many others joined them and soon, all the poor souls who'd been held on earth until the war was over, came together in a mass exodus. Someone began to sing 'Follow the Yellow Brick Road' softly at first but then stronger, as the crowds swelled and disappeared into the clouds and to their places in Heaven. Tom's strong voice could still be heard, saying, "I hope it's not corned beef hash for supper. That's all I have to say."

It was over. The bombing had stopped completely and the fighting men had stopped fighting. Peace had come at last and nothing like this could ever happen again. At least, everyone hoped not.

Now everyone's main concern was to rebuild the world they'd once known, from those in charge, to the ordinary people who'd lost everyone fighting a war that could have been avoided, had there never been a man named Hitler. Just off the street where the Fosters had lived, was the old cinema that had protected ghosts and live people alike. It had been damaged when the bomb fell on it, but could be rebuilt everyone thought, and not be completely demolished.

It became a sort of memorial to the people who had struggled through the past six years and the workmen were soon deployed to make it good again. They did better than that and made it great, rather than good. It became a lush cinema that could house many people and they arranged for a complete set of new films to be delivered. A proper projectionist was employed who looked after the cinema as though he owned it. Granted, it could only house live people, or could it? Who would know the difference?

The day its name went above the entrance door in large gold letters was celebrated and everyone was allowed inside free of charge. It was quite luxurious and with beautiful lights all over the ceiling and red plush seats to sit on. The name it was given was 'SAFE HAVEN' as that was what it had been for many people.

The first film they chose to show was called 'Mrs Minever' which became a classic of its time. A story about some ordinary British people, who never gave up fighting the Germans, who believed in the greatness of their own little world and who joined together to bring their 'boys' back from Dunkirk – an amazing time which produced many heroes. Hitler was already dead, of course – by his own hand – so they couldn't say to his face. "Don't mess with this country Hitler, or you'll get what you deserve." And he would have, wouldn't he? In fact, he did.